Winta's Day
Seekers: Book Three

Josie Jaffrey

CONTENT WARNINGS & SERIES RECAPS

There is a full list of content warnings at the back of this book, and also available at Josie's website at the link on the left below.

Recaps of the Silverse books are available on Josie's website at the link on the right below.

CONTENT WARNINGS

SERIES RECAPS

www.josiejaffrey.com/content-warnings   www.josiejaffrey.com/series-recaps

By Josie Jaffrey

Stories from the Silverse: the World of the Silver

The Seekers Series
Killian's Dead (short story prequel, free to Josie's
subscribers)
May Day
Judgement Day
Winta's Day
Valentine's Day
Dark Days
End of Days

The QuickSilver Trilogy
Kill Me Quick
A Quick Study
Quick and the Dead
QuickSilver Omnibus Edition

The Solis Invicti Series
A Bargain in Silver
The Price of Silver
Bound in Silver
The Silver Bullet

The Sovereign Trilogy
The Gilded King
The Silver Queen
The Blood Prince

Silverse Serialised Stories
Dead Box
Dead Road

Silverse Short Stories
Encounters: Silverse Short Stories

Other Fiction

The Deluge Series
The Wolf and the Water

Short Stories
Broken Wings (collection)
Ring The Bell

For Bex Wilkinson, whose book this is.

1

CHRISTMAS IN OXFORD is… Well, it's not Christmas in Vienna. Let's just leave it at that, shall we?

But if you want specifics, then here's my main objection: it's cold and it's wet and it's miserable. When it does snow, which happens rarely because the city is a river-filled sinkhole, the flakes quickly turn to grey slush on the grimy streets, then refreeze into a sheet of unnavigable ice. One false step, and you go fully arse over tit. Funny to watch, less funny when it happens to you, which it will sooner or later. Even with vampire agility, black ice is a bastard.

On top of all that, the Christmas lights are crap, the shopping is shit and for some reason the tourists refuse to bugger off back home to celebrate with their own families and instead prefer to stand around in crowds of gawping idiots, taking selfies in front of every church, college and tower, and generally making a nuisance of themselves.

And the Christmas market. Ugh, the Christmas market.

If you're so inclined, for ten full days in December you can browse booth after booth of twee rubbish, from scented candles to alpaca mittens, all served up with a side of migraine-inducing mulled wine and more raclette than can safely flow through the average artery – on chips, of course, because this is England.

'Did you want grated truffle on those?' the stall-holder asks.

'No,' I say, at the same time as Cam says, 'Oh, go on then.'

He gives me a look that says I'm being a party pooper.

I sigh and force a smile. 'All right, then.'

'Yay!'

Yes, he just said *yay*.

We take our cheesy, smelly chips and wander off into the market of inanities. Fairy lights are fighting the street lamps to chase away the evening's darkness, and losing. Everything is bathed in orange. Oh, Christ. There's even a fucking clown.

You might be wondering why I've bothered coming at all if I'm going to be such a Scrooge about it, but here's the thing: Cam loves this place. He bloody *loves* it. He loves the lights, he loves the atmosphere, he loves the overpriced crap they sell as artisanal goods for hopeless Christmas shoppers, and I love watching him revel in it all. While all I can see is stall after stall filled with worthless junk, his eyes sparkle as though we really are in snowy, magical Vienna, not stuck here on Broad Street surrounded by muddy potholes, choking on bus fumes from nearby St Giles.

I might be a miserable cow most of the time, but Cam's joy is enough to make even me smile, so I keep my mouth shut and eat my weird chips.

'Balloons!' he yells, rushing over to the vendor without waiting for me to follow, then rushing back with one helium-filled monstrosity for each of us, plus three more for us to take back to the college for Boyd, Naia and Ed. For some reason, mine is a misshapen cartoon fish.

'I love balloons!' He grins.

I grin back, kissing him on the cheek as I accept my bulbous trout. It's impossible to be unhappy in the company of such a hyperactive puppy of a man, and we all need a little happiness right now. The past few months have been tough. With the captain leaving the Seekers and formerly-deputy Boyd taking over, everything is in flux. At the same time, we've lost the trust of the Solis Invicti and every single one of our contacts has dried up. We have no police access, no mortuary service access, and the only Silver scientist who'll still give us the time of day is Ed. Suddenly, solving scab crimes – crimes committed by Silver that risk revealing our existence to humanity – has got a whole lot harder.

In the circumstances, Cam's Labradorish charm is welcome enough that I let him talk me into going on the kids' merry-go-round. Twice.

'Right,' I say after he's been around the market several more times, which doesn't take long because the whole thing is only half the size of a football pitch. 'Are you ready to go home?'

'Nearly.'

He shoves the balloons at me then rushes off once more. When he returns ten minutes later, he's wearing a new winter cardigan, carrying fresh churros in one hand and a steaming bratwurst in the other. It couldn't get much more phallic, but I forbear to comment.

'Churro?' he offers.

'I'll pass.'

'Suit yourself. So, are you thinking of streaming something or do we raid Naia's DVD library?'

'I've had enough Vin Diesel to last me a century, thanks.'

'Streaming it is, then.'

We walk to the end of Broad Street, past the Sheldonian Theatre and onto Catte Street. We're just turning onto New College Lane, an ancient winding road that wiggles around the back of the colleges, when a crash draws our attention upwards. The buildings on either side of the lane both belong to Hertford College and they're connected by a skyway that arcs over the road. We call it the Bridge of Sighs after the one in Venice, even though they look nothing alike.

The crash originates from the tall central window in the bridge above us. It shatters, raining down pieces of glass and lead into the lane below, followed by something else.

I don't recognise it immediately because it's so dark – more than one of the street lamps is out – but the weight of the object as it falls, then jerks back on the rope, is unmistakable.

It's a person. A hanged man. And judging by the kicking of his feet, he's still alive.

There's a flash of white from eyes opened too wide, fearful, fixed on mine. Eyes I recognise as those of Matthew Felton, Silver pharmaceutical creator and sampler extraordinaire. From the panic swirling in them, I know he recognises me too.

His gaze flicks down to his chest, where a piece of paper is pinned.

I start forward to grab him, my balloon's ribbon sliding up and out of my grip, but I only have enough time to read the words before the whole thing goes up in flames, along with Felton, the rope and all, leaving behind nothing but ash.

All Cam and I can do is watch.

'No trace on the bridge,' Cam says to Boyd.

We're just around the corner from Solomon College, so Boyd and Naia arrived on the scene seconds after our call. That's just as well, because with the police no longer our allies, we need every moment we can get. Unfortunately, this murder was extremely public. We've had to call in another Seekers team – Ellie, Quentin, Rolf and Cheryl – to hold back the crowds while we work. Even more unfortunately, there's an ex-police officer amongst the rabble, and she's not buying our story. I'm trying to concentrate on the scene, but all I can hear is her kicking up a stink in the background.

'You're sure it was a scab murder?' Boyd asks, looking down at the sad pile of ash and glass at our feet. It's all that remains of Matthew Felton, the Thrice-Burned-Alive. I'm pretty sure he's not going to be able to resurrect himself from this.

'Sure,' I say. 'I got close enough to smell the violence mark on him before he went…' I flick my fingers out from my fists, demonstrating the *poof* of the flames.

Violence marks are a bit like an anonymous calling card. Whenever a Silver commits a violent act against someone – say, by throwing them out of a window and setting them on fire – they leave a scent behind on their victim. If that scent were unique to the Silver who left it, then our job would be a hell of a lot easier, but sadly that's not how it works; all violence marks smell the same, so the only thing we know for sure is that whoever killed Felton was Silver. If we'd been lucky, maybe Cam would have picked up a personal scent on the bridge itself, but we rarely catch a break like that.

'So we have nothing,' I summarise. 'No scent, no blood, no fibres—'

'No eyebrows,' says Naia, laughing at my scorched face.

I swear back, tentatively feeling my brow. The skin is already healing, but unfortunately it'll take a couple of weeks for the hairs to grow back. Until then, I'm either going to have to pencil them in or go around looking like a half-painted drag queen.

'And you're sure it was Matthew Felton?' Boyd asks.

'One hundred percent,' I say. 'I'd know that bastard anywhere.'

But Boyd looks troubled. In fact, all of the team does, and I can guess why.

'He's not coming back from this, is he?' I say.

The Silver have incredible powers of regeneration, but Felton isn't old for a vampire, and I've never heard of one so young resurrecting from a pile of ash so completely burned. If it was going to happen, there should probably have been some movement by now, but the only thing stirring the dust is the wind.

'You mentioned there was a note pinned to his chest...?' Boyd asks, avoiding the question.

'Yes,' I reply.

'What did it say?'

I keep my mouth shut, so Boyd turns to Cam.

'I didn't get close enough to read it,' he says.

Boyd looks back to me. I know exactly what it said, but I really, really don't want to tell him.

'It happened so fast,' I say. 'I'm not totally sure what I saw. I saw him fall, then his eyes opened and he looked down, and there was this paper on his chest, and then...' I make the *poof* gesture again.

Boyd gives me a chastening look. 'Unless you've forgotten, I'm your captain now.' As if he'd ever let us forget it. 'I can tell when you're holding out on me, Jacqueline.'

I know for a fact that he can't, because I do it all the damn time and he doesn't bat an eyelid, but I'm clearly making a bad job of it tonight. It seems wiser to give up now than to start digging myself into a deeper hole.

I sigh, resigned. 'It said: *For Jack, with love.*'

'*With love*?' Cam asks.

'Yup. Love.' I can feel the heat in my cheeks.

'Like, a love letter?' Naia asks.

'I don't know,' says Cam. 'This whole thing feels more like it's a threat to Jack. They set the man on fire.'

'So did I,' I point out, recalling that time Naia and I beat Felton unconscious and let his still-lit cigarette do its worst. And that time I'd let myself into his house and burned it to the ground, with him still inside. In my defence, the guy was scum, and I served out my probation like a good little Seeker.

'So you think they're saying that you're, what, kindred spirits?' says Naia. 'Soulmates? Jesus, you sure can pick them.'

'Shut up.'

'I'm just saying, between the one-night-stand who turned you Silver, the doctor who spied on you for the Invicti, and the baron who ditched you for a movie star—'

I groan.

'—I just don't think the serial monogamy thing is working out for you. Maybe it's time to try something new.'

'Naia, I am not moving in with you and your sexy housemates.'

Naia's moving out of Solomon College in a couple of weeks' time and she still has a room left to fill in her new house. She's on a serious recruitment drive and as far as she's concerned we're all fair game, even Boring Boyd, who's been off the market for months now.

'Aha!' she says. 'So you admit that you think Rajni is sexy.'

'No! I mean, yes, but look, I never said she wasn't. I just don't think living in a polyamorous collective is the solution to my shitty love life.'

'Maybe your problem is that you keep picking people up at work,' Cam suggests. 'Office romances never last.'

'Because you're the authority on romance,' Naia says.

Cam stifles a snicker, poorly.

'Look,' I say to her, 'I just don't do sharing. I've got nothing against polyamory, but it's not for me.'

'You said you wanted to move out.'

'Yes, because I want to get *away* from you, not share a bathroom with you.'

'All right,' she says, letting the subject drop. 'Your loss.'

But I know this won't be the last I hear of it.

'If we could focus on the case, please, rather than our personal lives,' Boyd says, in a tone that makes it clear this is an order.

'It does look like Jack's might actually be relevant to the case, sir,' says Cam. 'Given the note.'

Boyd sighs and runs a hand back through his tightly-curled hair. He's been letting it grow out a little recently, for the first time in the twenty years I've known him. I wonder if that's the doing of his girlfriend.

'All right, then,' he says. 'Jacqueline, I suggest you make a list of all the Silver who might have done this, either as a threat to you or as a sign of affection. Everyone who loves or hates you.'

'That's going to be a long list,' Naia says. For a moment, I think she might actually be giving me a compliment, then she adds, 'I can't think of many Silver who *don't* hate her.'

'Fuck off.'

The others ignore us. They're used to the bickering and there's no heat in it. Much as she might fight it, Naia's on the *loves me* list. I know this, because despite her teasing, she's taken off her favourite red beanie hat and is now pulling it onto my head to cover my missing eyebrows. With Naia, you're better off watching her actions than listening to her words.

'Sirens,' Cam says, calling us back to the urgency of the moment. A second after he says it, I can hear them too.

'Then let's scoop and go.' Naia takes two plastic bags out of her pocket, using one as a glove as she unceremoniously shovels Felton's remains into the other. Meanwhile, I gather the bits of broken window and lead together into bags of their own.

'Is that everything?' Boyd asks, taking a last glance at the scene.

We all nod, but I can't stop looking at the bag of ash. For what was once a person, even a person as weaselly and insignificant as Matthew Felton, it doesn't seem like much at all.

We meet back at the lab, leaving the police to puzzle things out for themselves. The onlookers all saw us – there was no avoiding it – but I'm willing to bet that won't be a problem. Even if they're no longer working with us, there are Silver planted in the highest levels of the police who won't want to expose themselves by exposing us. They'll find a way to cover it up, then come after us later.

Hopefully much later, because there aren't many of us left.

'Did any other Silver see the body?' Ed asks.

'No,' Cam says. 'No one except us and the killer. I didn't pick up on anyone else.'

'Me neither,' I say.

'So this is just with us for now?' says Ed.

'Until the police catch up with us,' Cam says.

'Then we'd better work fast.'

Ed is standing behind his lab bench with my team on the other side, as though he's taking a class. I know he's unsettled because he's not wearing his glasses. He doesn't need them – the Silver have 20/20 vision, so they're pure affectation – but I've never seen him abandon them before. He's also cleared away all of the fancy old-school equipment from the main lab – the retorts, distillation columns, Bunsen burners and flasks – in favour of the bleeping machinery he usually prefers to keep in the back room. If I hadn't known it already from the events of the past six months, then those two things alone would be enough to tell me that the Seekers are in serious shit.

'How long did the body burn for?' Ed asks.

'Ten seconds?' I guess.

'Longer than that,' Cam says. 'Twenty.'

'That's not possible,' Ed says. 'Even in a minute, an hour, a day, the fire shouldn't have burned everything away. It couldn't have got hot enough.'

'I give you Exhibit A,' I say, gesturing to the zip-locked bag of dirt that's now sitting on Ed's lab bench. 'He's dead, right?'

'Oh, yes. Very definitely dead. But there should still be flesh, bone, metal from his clothes. Something. Fire alone shouldn't have killed him. Are you sure it was really him and not some kind of paper mannequin?'

'Positive,' I say. 'I recognised his scent.'

'And there was a Silver violence mark,' Cam adds. 'Those only attach to people, not things. Right?'

'Right,' Ed confirms.

'Plus,' I say, 'he was conscious.'

The memory turns my stomach. I have little sympathy for the rat – obviously, since I was the one who set him on fire the last couple of times – but it was a gruesome way to go. Every time I let my mind wander, it takes me back to the pleading look in his eyes the second before he went up in smoke. At least when I burned him, he was asleep. At least he didn't see it coming. At least he was able to heal up afterwards, to come back from it.

But those excuses won't fly. What I did to Felton was just as ruthless, even if he deserved what he got – and he did. He deserved every moment of it. Nonetheless, it's sobering to be confronted with my own brutality.

'Well, if it really was his body, then I can't explain it,' Ed says. 'He shouldn't have burned like that. It doesn't make sense.'

Which leaves us royally fucked. If Ed can't explain it, then we have no one else to consult. Dead end.

'You know what else doesn't make sense?' I say. 'The last time we saw Matthew Felton, he was in the custody of the Solis Invicti, then he disappeared off the face of the Earth. So here's what I want to know: where has he been hiding for the past few months, who brought him back to Oxford, and what did the Invicti have to do with it?'

'Maybe nothing,' says Cam, ever the Invicti-fan, but for once the others agree with me.

'There's definitely something to investigate here,' Boyd says.

'But how?' I say, exasperated. 'The Invicti won't talk to us now, and even if they did, I can't imagine they'd be thrilled if we accused them of going scab.'

Worse, I'm not sure they'd care. Who's going to pull them back in line? The Seekers don't have the power, and from what I saw of the Primus earlier this year, he doesn't have the inclination. If I'm honest, I'm starting to lose faith in the Seekers altogether. What's the point of doing this job if the people who make the rules won't follow them? We're sworn to protect the Silver by keeping their existence secret from humans – mostly by bringing the Silver who kill humans to justice – but the majority of the Silver don't even want to uphold the secrecy pact anymore. I know this because when they took a ballot on the issue earlier this year, the Primus had to rig the vote to maintain the status quo.

I saw him do it. And he knows I saw.

I have no idea what to do with that information, so I'm just keeping it to myself while I carry on with my pointless job and try to work it out. Nothing's really changed – we were always powerless – except now I know just how powerless we are, and that *sucks*.

'Can you do anything with that?' Naia asks, nodding at the bag of ash.

'Maybe,' Ed says. 'I'll try.'

'There's this, too,' I say, handing over the bags of glass. 'Maybe you can pull a fingerprint?'

'I doubt it, but I'll take a look after I've tested the ashes. I've got to warn you, though: all this is going to take a while now I'm operating solo. In the meantime, you might want to call in some favours to keep the police off my back and find out what the hell the Invicti are up to.'

Cam and I exchange a glance and I can't hold back my grimace. We both know what this means: I'm going up to Summertown.

'You don't think he did it, do you?' Cam asks as he walks me back through the college.

'Drake?' I laugh bitterly. 'You think he's sending me love letters? I'd say he's made it perfectly clear that he doesn't give a single solitary shit about me.'

Cam sighs. 'I'm sorry, Jack.'

'It's not even a thing.' I brush it off. 'Don't worry about it.'

'You know who would be a good suspect?' Cam says, changing the subject with his usual tact. 'Sir Percival Windsor.'

Sir Percival Windsor – or Sir Percival Wanker, as I have unaffectionately renamed him – is a local Silver big shot who was once an ally of Felton's. Until, that is, Felton killed Windsor's girlfriend and sent the old boy into a downward spiral of solitary drinking. Windsor was a big proponent of abolishing the secrecy pact before the grief derailed him. I bet he'd love to light Matthew Felton on fire and watch him burn.

He would be a great suspect, except…

'I don't think he'd have written me that note. Do you?' I say. The thought of it makes me a little queasy.

'Probably not,' Cam agrees. 'Plus, the last time we saw him he didn't look like he was in any state to plan his revenge. Is he even still in Oxfordshire?'

'With any luck he's crawled into a hole somewhere and died. It's worth checking what he's up to, but I think we'll probably find our murderer a little closer to home.'

'You're not thinking it was Tabitha?'

You'd think that after all she did to me – the spying, the lying, the betrayal – I'd be immune to the formerly-delectable Dr Tabitha Ross, my ex-girlfriend and biggest mistake of my life. I wish I could say that the sound of her name doesn't move me at all, but the truth is that the complicated clusterfuck of emotions I still carry for her makes me shiver every time I bring her to mind.

'I don't know,' I say. 'She was close to Felton. She worked with him on the formulae the Invicti used in the autumn.'

'She wouldn't.'

'Wouldn't she? I didn't think she'd go through my phone or sell me out to the Invicti or try to poison the Primus and out the Silver. The truth is, we don't know what she'd do. But I'm not convinced that she'd care enough to kill Felton for me either. In fact, I can't think of anyone who'd give me a twisted gift like that.'

'Not even your nemesis, the baron?' he teases.

'Not even him.'

But as I walk out of the college towards North Oxford, I can't get those words out of my head, promising something I want more than I will ever admit.

With love.

2

KILLIAN DRAKE'S SUMMERTOWN mansion is a monument to inhumanity. It's pretty enough on the outside and plush enough on the inside, but it's built on the bones of Silver prisoners. Within its foundation, behind hundreds of carefully-marked doors, the criminals of our kind wait out their sentences, drained and strengthless, suspended in a state of agony between life and death for however many years, decades or centuries the baron has decreed.

Our current baron is not known for his leniency.

I stomp my way across the drive, taking my aggression out on the gravel. It's so thick that I'm sinking in it.

'Bad day?' the goon at the door asks me. I recognise her, but I don't know her name.

'No worse than normal. Can I go up?'

The goon talks into her collar for a moment, then opens the door wide to admit me. 'You know the way.'

I could walk to Drake's office in my sleep. That doesn't bother me so much as the knowledge that, even though I've only been there once, I could say the same of his bedroom. The place is unforgettable, even though months have passed since I ran out of his bed, never to return. For the first few days, the memories burned. I couldn't stop thinking about the touch of his hands, the taste of his lips, the silver in his eyes broadcasting the impossible truth: Killian Drake is in love.

But now, with everything that happened afterwards, remembering that night just turns my stomach.

I don't bother knocking before barging into his office.

'I've got news,' I say, collapsing into one of the leather chairs. 'Bad news.'

'Oh?' The woman behind the desk stands from her chair the moment I walk in, still not entirely comfortable to be occupying someone else's space, but reclaims it quickly. 'What happened to your eyebrows?'

'That's part of the news.'

'Then ditch the preamble and spill it.'

I tell Kulika about Felton's death, the note, the bizarre way he burned. She takes it seriously, giving me her full attention. She was once Drake's right-hand woman, but his continuing absence has required her to step up in ways neither of us ever anticipated. We work together well, and I respect her, but I know she resents her new role. She always seems to be watching the door, waiting for Drake to come back to her.

Unlike Kulika, I gave up on him months ago.

'And you want me to talk to the Invicti about this?' she asks when I finish speaking. She looks terrified at the prospect.

'And the police, to make sure there won't be a fuss. You're the acting baron, Kulika. You've got the authority.'

She nods, but I get the feeling that she's reassuring herself rather than answering me.

'We need to know what the Invicti did with Matthew Felton,' I say. 'We need to know where they've been holding him and how he got out.'

'Okay,' she says. 'I'll make the call. You want to be in on the meeting?'

'Ideally, I'd like it to be Seekers only. We can be civil.'

She gives me a sceptical look, but says, 'I'll see what I can do.'

We sit together for a moment in companionable silence, neither of us relishing the tasks ahead of us. They're tasks that aren't even properly ours; Drake should be handling them. He should be handling everything, like he always did, but instead he's abandoned the city to fend for itself.

Those first few weeks after he left were carnage. The Silver were in uproar after the followers of the Secundus and the Tertius were denied the revelation they'd campaigned for. Lots of fingers were pointed, because they couldn't understand how the vote could have come out against them without the help of dissenters amongst their alleged allies. If they suspected the vote had been rigged, none of them went so far as to make the accusation. Perhaps, even after such a betrayal, none of them dared to go directly against the Primus.

That's probably why, when the shit hit the fan, it happened here in Oxford, where the vote was held. No one had the balls to challenge Solomon directly, so instead they brought their acts of petty insurrection to Solomon College, the base of the Seekers. With our old captain gone and the baron off pissing about on the continent with his girlfriend, we were already destabilised. With a carefully-placed firebomb here, and a poisoning there, it didn't take much to convince most of our numbers to quit. Even in an eternity of Silver years, life's too short for that.

Now running at a fraction of our usual numbers, we can't cover all the scab crimes that are happening across the country. No one can. That's spurred a lot of people, like Kulika, into a punishing work ethic. Others, like me, have simply ceased to give a shit. Humans are murdered in impossible ways. Silver scabs are responsible. In those circumstances, it's inevitable that, sooner or later, we'll be dragged out of the shadows, which is exactly what the majority of the Silver voted for.

It seems futile to swim against the current.

'This didn't end the way I thought it would, you know,' Kulika says, looking at me with sympathy in her eyes. I'd really rather she didn't. 'You and the baron—'

'It doesn't matter.'

'I didn't think it would be her.'

'It really doesn't matter,' I insist. 'It was a one-night thing. That's all.'

And I mean it. I was very clear, and so was Drake. I can't fault him on that. Right from the start, we were explicit: one night and one night only, no strings. That's why I freaked out so much when I saw that he'd silvered, that the silver in his eyes had bled into his irises. It happens sometimes to the Silver, rarely and irreversibly, but only when we're in love. It would be impossible to see most of the time, because we hide the silver in our eyes constantly so humans won't notice that we're not like them, but when we let our guard down – during sex, for example – it's hard to maintain the concealment. It had been a long while since I'd seen Drake's eyes unmasked, and when I saw how they'd changed, I thought he'd silvered for me right there and then. That was *way* more than I'd signed up for. I didn't hang around long enough to let him to explain, and by the time I'd screwed up the courage to go back and ask, he'd already left to go traipsing across Europe after Carlotta Arden.

Because, of course, he'd silvered long before we ever fell into bed together, but not for me. No, he silvered for the world's most desirable Silver actress. She's the one he loves. It seems so obvious now that I can't believe I ever thought that it might be me. How arrogant, how presumptuous, how fucking *humiliating*.

The shame of it burns.

And that's not even the worst of it. What makes the whole situation so indescribably awful is that everyone knows about it. Not about the silvering – no one else knows Drake silvered, except presumably Carlotta Arden by now – but they know he slept with me then ditched me hours later to go after her. To be fair, that was kind of my fault. I was the one who went running out of his mansion first thing in the morning with my shirt on inside-out, wearing his scent mark, broadcasting serious walk-of-shame vibes. But since everyone knows that I was the one who ran from him, why does everyone seem to think *he* ditched *me*? Why am I being made into a laughing stock? No one's laughing at him. No one thinks less of him for it, quite the opposite in fact, because he's just a handsome rascal who charmed my pants off like the loveable rogue he is, whereas I'm to be pitied for allowing him bed me for one night and one night only. It doesn't matter that it was what we both wanted at the time; the world still thinks I've done something wrong for letting him leave without commitment, the height of impropriety, like we're stuck in some regressive Regency-era bullshit where it's *my* fault that he's an unscrupulous bastard.

Feminism, my arse.

'I just don't know what happened between the two of you,' Kulika says with a sigh.

And, I vow, she never will.

I shrug. 'It's no big deal.'

'You seem to feel that way about most things these days.'

'What do you mean?'

'Like this murder. You're just going through the motions.'

'I'm investigating. It's my job.'

'But you don't care about it anymore. You're not invested

at all, which I might be able to understand in normal circumstances, but this isn't just any other case. The victim is *Matthew Felton*, the man you hated enough to burn alive. Not only that, but whoever killed him put a note on him addressed to you. Worse, they waited for you to walk down that road so you could *watch* him burn. You know all this, so you know you're being stalked by a scab murderer, but you don't seem to care. You don't seem to care about any of it. Where's your drive gone?'

She's right: I really don't care, and I don't want to have this conversation.

'Matthew Felton deserved what he got,' I say.

'Maybe, but whoever killed him still broke the secrecy pact. You're a Seeker. It's your job to find them and bring them to justice.'

'Because everyone cares so much about the secrecy pact these days.'

'I do,' she says, looking me right in the eyes. 'I do, Jack. If you think things are bad at the moment, then imagine what would happen if we really did reveal ourselves to humans. The confusion, the fear, the lives we'd put in danger. For however long I can, I'm going to work to stop that from happening, even if I'm in the minority. So we need to solve this case, to show that there's still Silver justice in this city, even without the baron. All right?'

'I don't know what you want me to say.'

'I want a theory,' she says, exasperated. 'I want you to give a shit about who might have done this.'

'I'm making a list,' I say. And then, because I can't resist, I add, 'I'm checking it twice.'

She doesn't even smile.

'But I do know one thing,' I say. 'It wasn't Drake.'

'I almost wish it had been.' I can see the sadness in her eyes. 'At least that way I'd know he was coming back.'

'He isn't, Kulika,' I say. 'He never will. Just give up on him.'

'I can't do that.'

'Why not? He's given up on us.'

She doesn't reply, so I leave her alone to meditate on my words. She'll see soon enough that they're true.

I sleep in the next morning, because it was a late night and also because, really, why bother? When I finally get to work at lunchtime, none of the others seems particularly motivated either. They're all lounging around in the common room watching a show about antiquing or, in Naia's case, reading one of those spy thrillers that she pretends she enjoys for the action, but she actually reads for the sex scenes.

'Nothing new?' I say, lingering in the doorway.

'Waiting for Ed,' Cam calls back. His eyes are glued to the screen where contestants are assessing pottery of questionable provenance. 'Are you off to speak to the Invicti?'

'Kulika's making an appointment. I haven't heard back yet. Where's Boyd?'

'Captain's office.'

'So we're just… doing nothing?'

'Yup.'

'Roger that.'

It's fine by me, because I have some work of my own to do. Naia had one thing right: after twenty years in this dump, it's time I moved out of my mouldy, damp little college suite. The moment I can find an affordable flat on my paltry Seeker's salary, I'll be ready to hand my keys to the college porter and never look back. The fact that this place has become a target recently is just one more reason to get out – this morning there was yet another pipe bomb left in the lodge – but the truth is it's far from the only reason I have.

There's the lack of space, the lack of autonomy, and the lack of privacy. It's about time I struck out on my own. I went almost straight from my parents' house to living in college accommodation after I turned Silver. I've never had the chance to control my own space and, particularly in the current circumstances, I'm feeling trapped. Suffice it to say that I have plenty of incentive to move.

Case in point: someone's been in my room. The moment I walk through the door, I know she's been here again. The sweet, buttery scent of her skin is everywhere.

Winta.

My first love, the woman who made me what I am today. I haven't seen her since she went on the run twenty years ago, but I remember her scent like it was yesterday.

I don't know how she does it, but she's been breaking into the college – specifically my bedroom – on a sporadic basis for the past few months. The first time was just after the Drake debacle, just after we boxed Yolande Leclercq. Leclercq warned me it would happen.

She's coming back for you, Jack. It won't be long.

And it wasn't.

What confuses me most is that she hasn't actually *done* anything. Nothing's ever out of place – which is to say that all my belongings are still on the floor where I usually keep them – and she never leaves anything behind except her scent. There's something threatening about that, because it makes me feel as though the other shoe is constantly about to drop, but I'd be lying if I said I couldn't feel the promise in it as well. She plants her scent in my bedroom like a slow seduction: a touch on the door, on the sheets, on my pillow. I've been missing her for two decades, and now she's in my space, unseen but not unremarked. She's yet another reason I'm moving out: I need a home that's more secure, and safe from the confusing feelings she stirs in me.

Safe from the memories that haunt this place, too, because Winta's not the only woman I've loved who's been here. Once upon a time, not so long ago, there was Tabitha.

Tabby. My ex. The only real ex I've ever had because, aside from my two disastrous one-night stands, I've never had a relationship with anyone except Dr Tabitha Ross, the great deceiver. It was a beautiful few months, months rolling around in my college bed together, months that convinced me I might be happy with her for the rest of our eternal lives, until I found out the whole thing had been fake. She was only with me to get access to the inner workings of the Seekers so she could feed enough information back to the Solis Invicti to destroy us. And of course she succeeded, because she succeeds at everything she sets out to do. Including making me fall in love with her.

I still find reminders of her everywhere. There are the water stains on the ceiling that we used to stare at after sex, pretending we could see shapes in them as though we were looking up at clouds in the sky and not the evidence of a negligent maintenance regime. There's the faint scent of her blood by the door from the night everything changed, the night that still comes back to me in my nightmares. And then there are the very real traces of her scattered amongst the detritus on the floor: a stereotypical tartan skirt, a cardigan, a lab coat, a hairbrush that glints with strands of her auburn hair, and a mug holding an assortment of her makeshift hair ornaments. Perhaps I should have cleared her stuff away when we first broke up, but it was too painful at the time, and quickly her remnants just became part of the tapestry of mess that is my current home. It seemed pointless to extract the little pieces she'd left behind in my rooms when it was impossible to extract those pieces from my memory. She's part of me, now and always, but if I'm moving on then I don't have to take her with me when I go.

It's time to tackle the clutter.

It takes a few hours and a lot of angry, shouty music, but soon enough my own possessions are tidied away – all the easier to pack when it's time to move – and Tabitha's are collected into a single box. It doesn't hurt quite so much to look at her things now, though I still get a twisting feeling in my stomach every time I catch a glimpse of the glass rods and chopsticks poking out of the top of the box. The sooner I can get rid of it, the better.

There's a knock on the door. I open it a crack to reveal Cam on the other side.

'I had a thought,' he says.

'Oh?'

'Can I come in?'

No. If he sees that I've tidied up my rooms then he'll know something's up, and I don't want him to guess that I'm planning a move, not until it's already a fait accompli. I can't deal with the puppy-dog eyes that I'm sure are inevitable once he discovers that both Naia and I are leaving him behind.

'I was coming back to the common room anyway,' I say, then slip out to join him in the corridor, locking my rooms firmly behind me. 'What was the thought?'

He gives me a funny look, but if he thinks I'm being weird then it doesn't bother him for long.

'Felton,' he says. 'We should check out his place.'

'The house on Iffley Road? But he hasn't been there for months. By the time we caught Leclercq hiding out there, Felton was already with the Invicti. The place was practically empty anyway.'

'Maybe we missed something.'

'Like what?'

'Come on, Jack. It's not like we have any other leads to follow.'

'So what you're saying is that you're bored.'

'Of course I'm bored! I've been watching bloody Bargain Hunt!'

'Fine,' I sigh. 'But I'm driving.'

I pretend not to notice his grimace.

3

THE BUILDERS WERE halfway through renovating Felton's house when the Invicti grabbed him, and it doesn't look like they've done a thing to it since then. The roof is still more tarpaulin than tile, and it looks about a week away from total collapse. Not that I care. After all, I'm the one who set it on fire.

We come in through the front door – Felton's keys were still in our evidence store – and start at the top. It's clear that no one has been in the main house. Everything inside is exactly as we left it on the day we apprehended Leclercq, right down to the blood on the walls from the explosive she rigged, along with the ripped shreds of my old leather jacket. God, I miss that thing.

'Memories,' I say.

'Yeah, none of them good.'

'I don't know about that.' I'm thinking about the rush of vindication I felt as I tossed the match onto Matthew Felton's petrol-soaked body. He deserved it, that time and the last, for what he did to the girls he kidnapped. Apparently Cam doesn't agree though, because he's looking at me as though I've lost my mind. Time for a little white lie. 'I meant when we caught Leclercq hiding out here. You know, the thrill of the chase? That's a pretty good memory.'

'Sure,' Cam says, but he doesn't sound convinced.

'Nothing here,' I say, doing a final sweep of Felton's old bedroom. The dust is thick and undisturbed on the floor.

'That just leaves the cellar, then.'

'After you.'

'Ladies first,' Cam says.

'Age before beauty.'

He gives me an exasperated look, but leads the way through the door in the kitchen and down the steps into the basement. The wooden staircase turns to Victorian brick halfway down, where a pull cord for the lights dangles from the beams. When Cam tugs it, a bare bulb illuminates the charred bones of what was once Felton's laboratory.

'Ugh,' Cam says, covering his face with his sleeve. He's got a sensitive nose. 'I guess the builders never made it this far.'

'Guess not.'

It's damp. When we reach the bottom of the stairs, my shoes sink into the layer of soggy ash that covers the floor. It looks like the cellar was left to collect the runoff from the fire hoses. There must have been some subsidence down here too, because the bricks in the floor have all come out of alignment. A few have broken away from the mortar entirely and are poking out of the black slop like icebergs, waiting to trip us up. It's a filthy mess, except in one small area that's tucked away around the corner of a supporting wall. That little nook has been cleared and swept, and furnished with a shiny new computer table. A bunch of cables dangles down from the ceiling before plugging into the back of a shiny new computer.

'Weird place to keep an office,' Cam says.

'Super weird. This damp can't be good for the computer.

And it looks like it's hard-wired into the internet. No wireless.'

'Maybe someone was paranoid.'

'About what? Someone piggy-backing on their wireless?'

'Isn't it easier to hack into someone's computer if they're connected to the internet wirelessly? I mean, if you hack into the network then…'

Cam raises his eyebrows at me, encouraging me to finish his sentence, but whatever conclusion he's reached, it's beyond my grasp. I know nothing about hacking.

'Then what?' I ask.

'Um, I don't know. I was kind of hoping you would.'

As it turns out, neither of us knows anything about hacking.

'Why would I know?'

'You're the millennial. You grew up with this stuff.'

'Yeah, using it, not studying it. I don't know the first thing about coding.'

We look at each other for a long moment, pondering our ignorance.

'You know what we need?' Cam says. 'We need to recruit a Zoomer. But in the meantime, we can just ask Frank the… Oh.'

'Yeah. Oh.'

Until recently, Frank the Hacker was our resident computer expert. Sadly, no longer. A month ago he packed up his things and left Solomon College for good, just like all the others. He was one of the last to go, making me hope that maybe, just maybe, we might manage to hold onto him. No such luck. Cam and I are going to have to puzzle this out on our own.

'I guess we'll have to do some Googling,' I say, then start opening drawers. There are four in the computer table, two on either side, plus one of those shaky roll-out keyboard trays straddling the middle. When I pull it out, the screen flashes on, casting blue light onto the walls of the cellar.

'It's unlocked,' Cam says.

He's right. The screen has opened on the desktop, bright icons beckoning invitingly. I grab the mouse, heading straight for the folder marked "Formulae" while Cam watches over my shoulder.

It's empty.

'Fuck.'

I check through the emails, the trash and every other part of the computer I know how to search. Maybe Frank would have been able to dig something up from the hard drive, but I'm coming up empty.

'You think he cleaned it out?' Cam asks.

'No, I think whoever set up this computer did. Felton was locked away with the Invicti for months. I seriously doubt they gave him the opportunity to come back here, but someone's been using this place.'

'Yeah,' Cam says, kicking around in the soot, 'as a lab. They've picked up where Felton left off. There was a bench here: you can see the dents left behind by the feet. And look.' He's using the toe of his boot to point to bits of detritus that have sunk into the dirt: coloured powders and broken glass. He sniffs. 'These are new. Not more than a couple of days old.'

Cam's sense of smell is prodigious. There's more than one reason I think of him as an overgrown puppy.

'And there's something else,' he says. He follows his nose, sniffing his way back to the computer. 'It was lost in the wet, burned scent before but… Jack. She's been here. Recently.'

My stomach plummets. 'Who?'

'Tabitha. Your…'

'Yeah. Okay. I know who Tabitha is.' I should have picked

up on the scent too, but my nose isn't as good as Cam's, and all the soot is overpowering her fresh, nectarine perfume. 'What would she be doing here, though? She's got her own lab. Why would she need to use this shithole?'

Cam shrugs.

'Maybe she wanted somewhere more private,' I suggest. 'Or maybe there was a particular reason she needed to be in Felton's space.'

'There's an easy way to find out, you know.'

'No.'

No no no no.

I know I'll have to see Tabitha eventually. Having spent the afternoon neatly packing up her things, I can't pretend that I meant to throw them away. And they do say you should face your demons, right? So I will go and see her. Sometime soon. I really will.

Maybe.

'We should go over there this evening,' Cam says.

'All the way to Nash Lee? Now?'

'It can't be a coincidence that she was here.'

'I'm sure it's not. She's working with the Invicti. Of course she would have searched through Felton's place once they had him in custody. She'd want to work out what concoctions he's been brewing up here.'

'But she's been here recently enough to leave her scent. We need to talk to her.'

'She won't be at home,' I say. It sounds like an excuse, because it is.

'Are you avoiding her?'

'Um, yes. Obviously. She betrayed me to the Invicti and broke my heart, so yeah, I'm not super keen to see her right now.'

'Jack...'

'I know, I know. I'll do it, because it's my job. She'll

probably be with the Invicti, though, and I'm sure they won't let us talk to her until they're good and ready. We'll have to set up another bloody appointment.'

Cam sighs. 'You might be right.'

'Look,' I say, not wanting to infect him with my apathy, 'I'll call Kulika – I need to chase her up about the first appointment anyway – and we'll track down Dr Ross as soon as we get the go ahead from her. Okay?'

'Okay.'

That buys me some time. Don't get me wrong, everything I said was true: I'll do whatever I have to in order to see this case through, despite my waning enthusiasm, but I can't say I'm not relieved that protocol is slowing things down a bit.

Besides, I'm planning an early night, for reasons I don't want to explain to Cam. I have to be up early tomorrow. After some time spent on the phone earlier today, I'm ready to go house-hunting.

Estate agents are like maggots: they always make the most fuss over the least appealing carcasses. The guy accompanying me right now is no exception. As I gape, open-mouthed, at the stained furniture and tiny proportions of the filthy cesspit I'm touring, my over-aftershaved and hair-gelled guide is waxing rhapsodic about the excellent transport links provided by its unique location. What he means is that the train tracks run literally metres from the back door, which explains why the entire miniscule flat is caked in a kind of oily, sticky grime that's turned the wallpaper yellow.

I didn't think it was possible to find worse accommodation than my leaky college rooms, but I was incredibly, tragically wrong.

'And it's only a fraction over your budget,' the haircut says.

'*Over* budget?' I'm sure that I must have misheard him. 'You're telling me I can't even afford to rent a vermin-infested shithole like this?'

'Well, as you know, the property market in Oxford is incredibly competitive. Between the two universities and the fantastic business growth we've seen in the past…'

I zone out and let him talk to himself for a while as I ponder my options, of which there are none. He's shown me five places over the course of the afternoon, and this is the best of the bunch. My meetings with other estate agents over the course of the day have been no less disastrous. There was the attic flat near Donnington Bridge with no bathroom, which was described as being "convenient for wild bathing", the boarding house room that was only within my budget because it came with twenty-five cats and all their unique odours – "adorable housemates included" – and the place off the Abingdon Road that turned out to be a wooden shed – "eco-friendly living". The harsh reality is that there is not a single solitary dwelling in Oxford that I can afford to rent. That leaves me with two options: move into a shared house, or stay where I am. The problem is that I can hardly share a house with a bunch of humans, because that's a recipe for disaster, and the only Silver house I know with a spare room is Naia's sex nest.

I'm so desperate that I actually contemplate it for a moment, but that moment is blissfully brief.

At least for the foreseeable future, I'm stuck where I am.

The estate agent is just starting the sales pitch for a great little canal boat that would only need a few months' work to make it almost habitable, when my phone rings.

'Jack,' the caller says.

'Kulika.'

I had no intention of chasing her up today, but now she's calling me before I've had the chance to procrastinate properly. I'd be disappointed if I weren't so desperate to get away from this shiny-haired snake-oil salesman.

'You've got it,' she says.

'Huh?'

'Your meeting with the Invicti. One hour this evening at the house in Henley. You have to go to them.'

'Surprise surprise.'

'Well what did you expect? I'm not a fucking miracle-worker.'

'I know, I know. Thank you, Kulika.'

'That's more like it.'

I don't want to bring up the subject of requesting a second meeting with Tabitha, but I know I must. I promised Cam.

'While I have you on the phone…' I begin.

'No.'

'You don't even know what I want.'

'Whatever it is, just no.'

'I need you to ask permission from the Invicti—'

'Ask them yourself. Your appointment's at seven. Good luck. You'll need it.'

She hangs up before I can say anything else, so I follow her lead and bid farewell to the estate agent while he's mid-pitch. We've wasted enough of each other's time for one day.

4

I CATCH UP with Cam in the common room later that day.

'Rolf and Ellie checked up on Sir Percival Windsor,' he tells me.

'Oh?'

'Apparently he's still wandering around his mansion in his dressing gown, swigging from a bottle of blood and scotch. I doubt he could have planned something as intricate as Felton's murder, since he's not even sober enough to find the cord that holds his dressing gown closed.'

I grimace at the mental image. 'Did they get the full frontal?'

'Yup.'

'Rather them than us.'

After our last case involving Sir Percival Wanker, which included some seriously graphic photos and a lot of poor post-sex housekeeping on the part of his girlfriend, I have seen enough of him to last several lifetimes.

'Have you made your list yet?' Cam asks as I slump onto the sofa next to him.

'What list?'

'You know, your lovers and haters list. Like Boyd said.'

'Wait, you actually expected me to do that?'

'Um… yes? Captain's orders?'

'You're such a goody-goody.'

'And you're so lazy.' He prods me in the arm. 'Come on, Jack. Where's your drive gone?'

'Up in flames with Felton, or off gallivanting around Europe with Drake. Take your pick. I find myself entirely at my leisure now that I've vanquished both of my nemesises. Nemesi? Nemeses? What's the plural of nemesis?'

'I think the fact that you don't know is probably a good indication that having more than one is a bad idea.'

'Then isn't it lucky that one of mine is dead?' I grin. Cam does not grin back.

'Someone killed him for you, Jack. So no, I don't think it's very lucky at all. I think it's a tiny bit scary.'

He has a point. I've been trying not to dwell on the weird love letter that was Matthew Felton's immolated body, but Cam's right: I need to put some serious thought into working out who was behind it. The problem is that the suspect list is about a mile long. I take pride in making enemies wherever I roam, enough that I can reel them off endlessly: Benedict – Tertius and member of the Solis Invicti – and all his allies, Sir Percival Wanker Windsor and everyone in his boys' club… Hell, probably the Primus himself wouldn't be sad to see me gone. After all, I'm one of the few people who knows that he rigged the vote. Maybe Felton's murder was a threat to encourage me to keep my mouth shut, or maybe it was a gift for my silence.

That thought really is a bit scary.

Best to start with listing the lovers, I decide, because that won't take long.

It couldn't be Drake – he's off on his Grand Tour with Carlotta Arden, and besides, he's with *Carlotta Arden*, sexiest Silver woman alive. Whatever might once have fizzed between me and Killian Drake has now thoroughly fizzled out.

Then there's Winta. I know she's around, and I know from Yolande Leclercq's final words that she has something in store for me. That should make me shiver with horror rather than anticipation – particularly since I suspect she's the one who tried to shoot me with tranquilliser darts not just once, but *twice* this year – but what can I say? Distance makes the heart grow fonder, and twenty years is a whole lot of distance. It feels even longer when there are so many questions still unanswered about our brief past together, and apart.

And, finally, there's Tabitha. Tabitha, whose scent is in Felton's basement, and who's been working with the Invicti on various chemical substances, including the tranquilliser in those darts. If anyone has the wherewithal to come up with an accelerant hot enough to burn away one of the Silver, leaving no chance of revival, then it's Tabitha. The evidence is piling up against her in my head. And who last had Felton in their custody? Her buddies, the Invicti.

I'm puzzling all of this through when our latest recruit joins us in the common room. Raul is a soft teddy bear of a man with curling brown hair and a round, friendly face. He got caught up in all of the drama at Crimson – Oxford's short-lived open blood bar – earlier this year, and Drake ended up boxing him for a while. As it turned out, Felton had been poisoning the patrons' drinks to make them attack humans, so Raul was pardoned and decided he wanted to join the squad.

God knows why. He hardly saw the best side of the Silver justice system while he was trapped inside it. Perhaps I should be optimistic about his positive influence on the Seekers, but the truth is that every time I have to explain to him why we do what we do, I feel more disillusioned with the whole institution. It's hard to justify your purpose when you feel like little more than a clean-up crew for the misdemeanours of the rich and powerful, and a hammer they use to beat down anyone who isn't in their exclusive club. Now that a vote has proved that most of the Silver don't even want us to fulfil our mandate – to keep the Silver hidden from humanity – I'm struggling to see the point of us at all.

Raul, new to the job and starry-eyed, is not so jaded.

'Hey squad!' He smiles and takes a seat in the armchair opposite us. 'What's happening? Any bad guys for us to chase down this evening? Any leads on the bridge-fire-hanging thing? Anything I can do?' He's so keen to please that it makes me almost sad.

'We're waiting on the lab results,' Cam says, smiling back. It turns out that the Labrador puppy and the teddy bear play well together. 'We're waiting on an interview with the Invicti to follow up a couple of other leads.'

'Oh, shit,' I say.

Two sets of puppy-dog brown eyes turn to me.

'I forgot to say. I got a call from Kulika. We're on for seven tonight, in Henley.'

'Jack!' Cam jumps out of his seat. 'It's already half past five!'

'Really?' I must have been lost in thought for longer than I realised. This is the problem with English winters: it's pitch black by this time of day, so the afternoon drops straight into nighttime without leaving you any indication of where the evening is. 'Well, calm down, we've got plenty of time to get over there. I'll drive.'

'We're not in *that* much of a rush,' he says. He grabs a set of keys from the rack on the wall, then leans in close to whisper, 'We should take Raul.'

I wince. 'Do we have to?'

In the armchair at the other side of the room, Raul is sitting to attention with an eager look on his face.

'It'll be good for him,' Cam says. 'He needs the experience.'

'I guess so, but…'

I don't have to say what I'm thinking, because Cam knows very well. I love Raul, he's a great guy, but he doesn't make the best first impression. The Invicti will hate him. Even when he's stone cold sober, he acts like he's smoked a whole boatload of weed. He isn't the kind of Silver that we'd normally recruit, particularly given his questionable drug activities, but with the Seekers depleted and Boyd moving up to the captaincy, we needed another member to fill out our team. I'd like to say that Raul stood out amongst the other applicants, that there was something that made him shine, but the truth is that there were no other applicants. Since the vote, the rest of the Silver have decided that the Seekers are toxic. Raul was the only person willing to wade into the slurry with us.

He's not much of an investigator, not yet, but I'm glad he's here. If nothing else, he gives excellent hugs.

'All right,' I relent. Raul bounds up to us before I've even finished my sentence, so I hold up a finger to halt him. 'But I'm riding shotgun, and you have to help me pencil in my eyebrows before we leave.'

The fact that I have to see the Invicti at all is bad enough, but I am certainly not prepared to do it with wonky eyebrows.

I'm not sure what I was expecting from the Henley base of the Solis Invicti, but it certainly wasn't a well-appointed riverside home with its own boathouse. Henley is an affluent town on the River Thames, filled with antique shops and tea rooms. It's not the kind of place the Invicti would normally set themselves up, but they've maintained a small base here ever since a Silver called Charles Legrange killed a bunch of humans at high-profile public events earlier this year, including one at the Oxford and Cambridge boat race. There was some concern that there might be a repeat performance at Henley's annual regatta, so here the Invicti are. Why they've decided to stay here, months after Legrange has been caught and boxed, is anyone's guess.

We pull up onto a driveway lined with patterned brick and edged with borders filled with shrubs. I'm sure they're pretty in the spring when whatever flowers they have start to bloom, but right now they look sad and grey.

A woman I don't recognise meets us at the door and leads us through the house to a tastefully-decorated sitting room that looks out down a long lawn to the river. In the light of the solar-powered torches that line the back garden, I can just make out a jetty at the end.

We wait.

The woman brings us drinks.

We wait some more.

This is doing nothing for my nerves. I'm not sure who we're meeting tonight, but I'm not overly keen to see any of the Invicti. I only know a few by name: the big cheeses are Andrew – the Secundus and leader of the Solis Invicti – and Benedict – third in command of all Silver in the U.K. – and then there's Thomas Meyer, who we've worked with before, and a couple of new recruits called Alistair and Adewale. Our last few encounters haven't left a good impression. There was that time when Thomas and Benedict stole Felton from our custody, and the time when Benedict and Andrew took sides against the Primus in the recent vote. Given that the Solis Invicti are supposed to be the Primus's elite bodyguard, that was tantamount to treason. Not to mention the fact that Benedict authorised the murder of a bunch of people, possibly with the Secundus's approval, in order to secure funding for their failed coup. And he got my girlfriend to spy on me for him. I dread to think what intimate details he learned during the process.

I'll admit that the Solis Invicti aren't my favourite people at the best of times, but recent events have left their affairs in such disarray that I have no idea who's on whose side anymore. It's a mess that I have no desire to be caught in the middle of, and yet here we are again, all because that rat Matthew Felton didn't have the good manners to die quietly in a ditch like he deserved.

'Mr Sawyer, Ms Valentine,' the Secundus greets us as finally he strides into the room. He looks at Raul. 'And this is…?'

'New recruit,' Cam says, looking as surprised by the Secundus's presence as I am. It seems like overkill for him to be the one meeting us. I thought we wouldn't get any information at all from the Invicti, but I'm starting to think I might have been wrong.

'Raul Ortiz,' says Raul, extending his hand to shake, but the Secundus has already breezed past him to take a seat opposite us. A moment later, he's joined by a red-headed woman who must be one of his colleagues; she's dressed in black cargos and she looks lethal. The Secundus doesn't introduce her.

'I was sorry to hear about you and Baron Drake,' the Secundus says.

I have to restrain myself from reaching across the coffee table to throttle him. If I have to hear any more condolences for missing out on the great Killian Drake then I think I might follow Felton's lead and self-combust.

'It's fine,' I say. 'It was nothing, really.'

He gives me a sympathetic look. Sensing my mood, Cam puts his hand on my thigh to hold me in my seat.

'We wanted to ask about Matthew Felton,' he says.

'Yes,' says the Secundus, 'I heard that he died.'

'He did,' I say. 'Right in front of us. We're wondering what you might know about that.'

The Secundus exchanges a glance with the woman sitting next to him. 'Why would you think we'd know anything about it?'

'Because Matthew Felton was in your custody.'

'Yes,' the Secundus agrees, 'until last month.'

'He escaped?' Cam asks, with appropriate scepticism. If the Solis Invicti want you in custody then, one way or another, you stay in custody.

'No. He was released.'

'*What?*' This explosion comes from Raul, who's now on his feet and almost vibrating with rage. It might seem like an overreaction, but Matthew Felton's poison is the reason Raul ended up in a box in Drake's basement, and also the reason he ended up attacking and killing a human friend of his. Given his history, his outrage is more than justified.

Cam encourages Raul back into his seat while I continue the conversation.

'You let him go?'

The Secundus shrugs. 'He was very cooperative.'

'He murdered one human, and was responsible for the murder of another. A third was seriously injured because of him. And you just… let him go?'

The Secundus fixes me with a level gaze. 'I don't need to explain myself to you, Ms Valentine. You'd do well to remember that I'm your superior.'

I'm about to snap back with something profane and undiplomatic, but Cam cuts in to save me from myself.

'He made a deal with you, then? His expertise in return for amnesty?'

'I'm not at liberty to discuss the details.'

Which is a very definite *yes*.

'Did he go back to his place in Oxford?' I ask. I'm thinking that he could be the one behind the recent use of his basement laboratory, but it seems odd that he would use that space and not even enter his bedroom.

'I've told you all I can,' the Secundus says, effectively closing the subject. 'If there's nothing else?'

'Actually, there is,' I say. 'We need to speak to Tabitha. I'm guessing we'll have to go through you to do that?'

'I can't help you there. Dr Ross is no longer in our employ.'

I look at Cam and see the same look of bewilderment on his face that I'm sure is on mine.

'What do you mean?' I ask.

'I mean she left, at the same time Mr Felton was released.'

'But… why?'

'She didn't say. Actually, I got the impression that it had something to do with you.'

'With me?'

That makes no sense. The last time I saw Tabitha was after the vote, when she left Crimson in the company of the Solis Invicti. She made it very clear that night, and in her silence since, whose side she was on. She voted to dissolve the secrecy pact, which would render the Seekers – and, by extension, me – redundant. Worse, she did it all whilst hacking my phone and violating my privacy in the most invasive ways possible. Why would she do all of that, destroying the relationship we had built together, only to turn her back on the very people she'd betrayed me for?

I can't make it add up.

'Whatever her reasons,' the Secundus says, 'Dr Ross has been out of contact with us since last month. We've tried to get in touch, but she's not taking our calls. Under the circumstances, we decided to give her some space.'

'But if she's not working for you,' Cam says, 'then what *is* she doing?'

'You'll have to ask her yourselves when you find her. If you'll come with me, Mr Sawyer, I'll get you a list of her addresses.'

'Addresses, plural?' I ask.

'Dr Ross has been working very hard for a very long time, Ms Valentine. She has the means to support several properties. As for the circumstances in which she left, Viv can fill you in,' the Secundus says, nodding towards the redhead. He rises from his chair, then he's ushering Cam out of the room ahead of him.

Raul and I are left alone with the woman he called Viv.

'What was that about, then?' I ask her.

She sighs. 'It was all a bit of a drama, I'm afraid. She was your girlfriend, right?'

I nod before I can stop myself. I don't want to open up to this stranger, a stranger who is most definitely on the side of people I dislike, but she has the kind of face that wills you to trust her: bright eyes, round cheeks, freckles *and* dimples. I'm sure that her body is a deadly weapon, but the vibe she exudes is soft and open.

'Things were tense after the vote,' she says, 'as I'm sure you can imagine.'

'You were there?'

'I was. And I remember you.'

'You do?' I don't remember her at all, which seems odd because she's striking enough that she'd be hard to miss. 'I didn't see you voting.'

'I didn't qualify, but I was there doing the same thing you were: protecting the integrity of the vote. You aren't the only one who knows what really happened that night.'

Is she saying what I think she's saying? Does she know that the Primus rigged the vote? Did she help him? I'm not sure, but I *am* sure that Raul has no idea what we're talking about. He's looking between the two of us, confused, but I don't want to explain. I've kept this secret for months and I'm not about to spill it now, not before I understand what any of this means.

Pointedly, I say to Viv, 'You mean that someone spiked the Primus's drink?'

'Yes,' she agrees, but her tone of voice and the significant look on her face make it clear that this was not what she meant at all, which seals it for me. She *does* know. 'We won't forget that you're the one who saved him from drinking it.'

I could take that comment as either gratitude or a threat, and Viv's face is giving me nothing. The concoction in the Primus's drink would have revealed the silver in his eyes, making it impossible for him to hide his supernatural nature. I was the one who smacked the glass out of his hand, thwarting the rebels' plan to force their agenda.

The question is: is Viv pro-reveal, or anti-reveal? Pro-Primus, or pro-Secundus? It's impossible to tell, though her presence at Andrew's side is a pretty big clue.

'Did you ever work out where the chemical came from?' I ask.

I'm treading on dangerous ground here, and we both know it. I asked the question not so much to hear the answer – I already suspect that Tabitha developed it for the Solis Invicti – but because I want to draw Viv out. Unfortunately, she's smart enough to know that I'm playing her.

She smiles. 'Let's just say that there are a few amongst our number who couldn't wait for change. I understand that the pro-reveal lobby was desperate, but it was a stupid thing to do. If they'd been patient, then we could have called another vote soon and maybe got a different result. But they came out swinging, and that turned the tide. There were a lot of moderates who were wavering, but after that night they turned right back around to uphold the status quo.'

'They don't like change,' I say.

'Not when it's out of their control. They certainly didn't enjoy the threat of having their silver revealed against their will. They want to come out of the closet when they want, on their terms, instead of being forced out along with everyone else.'

'And is that the way you feel?'

She shrugs. After a few seconds pass without any further response, I guess that's all I'm going to get.

'And Tabitha?' I prompt.

'She didn't want to hang around for the fall out. You understand.'

I do. If the pro-reveal Silver were upset with the few who arranged for the concoction to be put in the Primus's drink, then they weren't going to be happy with the scientist who created it. If I were her, I'd be lying low too.

The three of us sit in silence for a few minutes, contemplating what we've discussed. At least, I think that's what Viv and I are doing, but who knows what's going on behind Raul's eyes? He's smiling to himself slightly, as though he's watching something pleasant that neither of us can see. It looks like there's music playing in his head. The quick switch in his moods from rage to contentment is a little disconcerting.

After a few more minutes pass, I start to get antsy. It's getting late, I'm tired and it's clear that Viv has told me all she's willing to tell. I'm ready to head home, but Cam still hasn't reappeared.

How long does it take to find a few addresses? I'm worrying about how many properties we'll have to search to track Tabitha down when Cam finally returns. He has a piece of paper in his hand and a worried look on his face, but the two don't seem related because he spares the paper no attention. Instead, he keeps glancing over at the Secundus as we take our leave, and though he musters up some polite goodbyes, he sounds deflated and confused.

'Are you okay?' I whisper to him. He nods back, but he's not very convincing.

By the time we get into the car, he has sunk into silence. He starts the ignition, but he doesn't take off the handbrake. Instead, he just sits there with his hands on the wheel, with the car still stationary, staring straight ahead into the darkness.

'Cam?'

He turns to look at me, blinking, as though I've roused him from some deep reverie. 'Huh?'

'Did you want me to drive?'

'No, it's fine.' He puts both himself and the car into gear and pulls out of the driveway. Still, there's a wrinkle between his eyebrows that doesn't go away. It worries me. This isn't the happy-go-lucky Labrador that I know and love. Something is seriously wrong.

'Do you want to talk about it?' I ask.

'About what?'

'Come on, Cam, don't try to play the idiot with me. I'm talking about whatever it was the Secundus said to you in there that has you so distracted.'

'It was nothing.'

'I don't believe you. Is it something to do with the case?'

'No, nothing like that. I've just got a lot on my mind, that's all. Trying to piece it all together.'

He forces a smile, then his gaze flicks up to the rearview mirror for a second and I realise what the problem is: whatever the Secundus said, he doesn't want to talk about it in front of Raul.

'Okay,' I say, willing to play along for the moment. 'Then

let's get back to the college. We can order in.'

'Pizza?' Cam asks.

Raul leans forward from the back seat, putting his head between our shoulders like a badly-behaved St Bernard. 'Pizza? I love pizza.'

'Then pizza it is.'

After a carb-heavy dinner and a couple of drinks, Raul will be out for the count and I can find out what's really wrong with Cam.

That's the plan, anyway. As usual, it goes horribly awry.

5

NAIA INTERCEPTS US the moment we get back to the college, and the rest of our evening promptly goes off the rails.

'Boyd's on some sort of power trip,' she says, grabbing my arm. 'He must be stopped.' I can tell she's angry, because her fingers are digging into my elbow and her jaw is clenched so hard that the tendons in her neck are popping out.

'What's he done now?' I ask.

'You'll see. This way.'

All three of us follow her through the college quad and into the wing of the main building where we have our offices. Correction: where we *used* to have our offices. What was once a corridor with an array of unique little two-person offices lining either side is now an open space filled with desks that echoes with each footstep, despite the carpet tiles. It's only half the size it should be. The rest of what was our area is now walled off into the domain of the history faculty.

'What the fuck is this?' I say. 'What happened to our offices?'

'Our great captain declared than open-plan working would

make us "more efficient and collaborative", and got the whole place gutted and refinished while we were out today. But you'll notice that *he* still has an office to himself.'

I can see him, the weasel, through the glass panel on his door at the far side of the room. Despite the late hour, he's pretending to be absorbed in something on his computer, but every so often I catch him peeking above the monitor. Coward.

'Boyd!' I yell. 'Get your arse out here right now!'

He picks up the handset of his desk phone and puts it to his ear, pretending he's just received a call.

'He's locked himself in there,' Naia says.

'We could break down the door,' I suggest.

'That would be poetic justice.'

Cam and Raul have said nothing since we walked in. When I turn to gauge their reaction to my and Naia's plan to engage in a little creative property damage, the look on Cam's face stops me dead.

Cam is a gentle creature, but he's resilient. Throughout our time working together, he's treated everyone with compassion and tenderness, despite the awful things we've seen. All the while, he's never been too tender to get to the truth, and never lost the soft-heartedness that makes everyone love him. He is always in perfect, careful balance, even when he's hurting. But right now, he's hurting too much to hide it.

'Cam?'

A tear slips down his cheek. He wipes it away quickly, but we've already seen.

'Sorry,' he says. 'It's just, all the years. All the memories. That room…'

I pull him into my arms and hold him close. A second later, Raul joins in, wrapping us both in one of his best hugs. Naia prefers to take direct action, so while we're consoling

Cam, she walks over to Boyd's office and smashes open the door. The first we know of it is when we hear the glass tinkling to the ground. By the time we've turned to look, Naia has already wrenched the door off its hinges and is starting on the wall.

'What are you doing?' Boyd yells, finally coming out from behind his desk.

'If the rest of us have to go open plan, then so do you,' says Naia.

'But I'm the captain!'

'So you admit that getting rid of our offices and not yours is just as cynical and elitist as it looks?'

'I have to have important, private conversations! I can't sit out there with the rest of you.'

'Well, tough.' With one last kick, Naia topples the wall between the main room and Boyd's sanctuary, turning his desk into a battered mess of bricks and plaster. 'Now you have no choice.'

I'm not going to criticise Naia for her principles or her gumption, particularly not after Boyd upset Cam, but it has to be said that her understanding of architectural engineering leaves something to be desired. This becomes evident almost immediately when, before Boyd even has a chance to step out of his former office, dust-covered and furious, the entirety of the ceiling comes crashing down on his head. Unfortunately, this includes the shower cubicle, bed and belongings of whoever has the rooms directly above us. Stuff tumbles down from the edges of the ceiling for a little while, but it settles soon enough. All we can hear now is a steady stream of water pouring from the broken pipes in the floor above.

'Oops,' says Naia.

'I think that was a load-bearing wall,' Cam says.

'Oh no.' Raul rushes towards the rubble and starts pulling

things away from the spot where Boyd was standing. 'Do you think he's okay?'

'He'll be fine.' Naia waves a hand dismissively. 'It'll probably knock him out for a day or so, but he deserves it, so I'm struggling to care.'

Raul has reached Boyd now and starts dragging him out from under the masonry. We gather around to look him over, but aside from a cut on his head, there's surprisingly little by way of external injuries. He's probably broken some bones and ruptured some internal organs, but that's nothing that the Silver can't repair with a good dose of intravenous blood and some rest.

'I'll call sick bay,' says Naia, with a sigh. Now that her anger's spent, she's probably feeling a tiny bit guilty, though she'd never admit to that. She's just pulling out her phone when she does a double take at something on the floor. 'Hey, Jack, isn't that your shitty sofa?'

I follow her gaze to a stained piece of once-beige furniture that's half-buried beneath a load of broken planks and wiring. Now that she mentions it, the ink stain on the arm does look a little familiar. In fact, as I look around the floor of what used to be the captain's office, I'm seeing more and more familiar items: a shampoo bottle, some bedding, and all the clothing I just neatly tidied away.

'For fuck's sake.'

It's the contents of my bloody rooms.

I spend the night in a tiny college guest suite with borrowed toiletries and a bundle of clothes I liberated from the lost property box. Perhaps inevitably, the only items that survived their descent through the ceiling unscathed were all Tabitha's, because they'd been securely boxed. Everything of mine is either smashed, ripped, stained or soaking wet.

My mood is not much improved the next morning when I

realise that none of the clothes I've scavenged from lost property for my daywear actually fit. The jeans are a size too big, which is not the end of the world since I can cinch them with the belt I've also appropriated, but the T-shirt is a size too small. Not only are my tits being squished uncomfortably flat, but the arm holes are too small, so it looks like one flex of my not-particularly-impressive biceps would shred the top to pieces. In the end, I give up and pull on the plaster-caked clothes I was wearing yesterday when I waded through the rubble in a futile attempt to find something worth saving. The top doesn't bend much and the jeans are still damp.

All of this goes some way to explaining why, when Naia joins me for breakfast in the canteen, I am less than polite.

'I fucking hate you,' I murmur through my Coco Pops.

'Good morning to you, too, sunshine,' she says. 'Boyd's up.'

'Well, whoop-de-doo for him.'

'The offer's still open if you want to move in with us. Now that your rooms are trashed, what do you have to lose?'

I don't even waste a moment contemplating it before saying, 'No.'

'You can have the room at the top of the house,' she says, attempting to make it sound enticing.

'So I have to run the gauntlet past all of your rooms every time I want to escape? No, thank you.'

'Then you can have the room closest to the door.'

'Not if you paid me a million, billion pounds.'

'Rajni told me she fancies you.'

I finally look up from my cereal.

'She does?'

Naia winces. 'Probably not right now, with the burned-off eyebrows. Did you know you have plaster dust up your nose?'

I return my attention to my food and say, 'Go away, Naia.'

She ignores me and tucks into her bacon sandwich. At this point, keeping my eyes on my own food becomes a necessity rather than a statement; Naia's eating habits are frankly repugnant. It's a bit rich of her to criticise my grooming when, after who knows how many years on this earth, she still hasn't learned to close her mouth when she chews.

Cam and Raul's arrival grants a short reprieve from the revolting noises filtering across the table.

'Hey, squad!' Raul says, all cheer again this morning. Cam, by contrast, is clearly still upset about what happened last night, though he's trying to put a brave face on it.

'I got a call from Ed,' he says as he takes a seat next to me. 'He's found a fingerprint on the glass we collected beneath the bridge.'

'Really?' Raul says. 'That's awesome!'

'Can he match it?' I ask. My enthusiasm is more muted, because I can read Cam's face like a book and it doesn't look like this is good news.

'No,' says Cam. 'He can't.'

That takes the wind out of Raul's sails. 'What does that mean?'

'It means that whoever's prints they are, we don't have them on record,' I explain. We may as well use this as a learning opportunity for Raul. 'We have the prints of every Silver who's resident in an area of the country that's controlled by one of the barons. One of the reasons that newcomers need to check in with the baron on arrival is so their prints can be checked. Since the print isn't in the system, the best-case scenario is that it was left by a visiting Silver, or someone who somehow slipped through the net.'

'And the worst-case scenario?' Raul asks.

'The print has nothing to do with the case at all, it was just left behind on the glass by some student. There's no way to tell how long it's been there.'

'Given how careful our scab was about everything else, probably more likely a student than our killer,' Naia says through what is, thankfully, her final mouthful.

'Probably,' Cam agrees, 'but we should check the police database anyway.'

Naia groans. 'What's the point? We won't find anything.'

We never do. The problem with the U.K. fingerprint database is that it's a little sparse. It only contains offender fingerprints, and then only for certain prescribed amounts of time, so the likelihood of finding the fingerprint of a random university student in those records is pretty damn low.

'Captain's orders,' Cam says.

All our heads swivel towards him.

'You've seen Boyd?' I ask.

'Yes.'

'This morning?' Naia asks.

'Yes.'

We all wait for him to elaborate, but he doesn't oblige.

'*Well?*' I say.

'He's fine. Still in sick bay, but he asked me to go and see him. He wanted to talk about the new deputy.'

Boyd was the captain's deputy until recently, but since he's moved up his old position has been vacant. Speculation has been rife about who will be chosen to replace him, particularly since there are so few of us left. My vote's for Cam, and I think Naia and Raul agree, but who knows what Boyd's thinking these days. He seems to have gone mad with power.

Cam's expression confirms my worst fears.

'It's not you?' I say.

'No. It's Quentin.'

'*Quentin?*' Naia and I yell at the same time.

Over the other side of the canteen, Quentin pops up from

his seat.

'Yeah?' Quentin says. 'Oh, hey, guys. What's up?'

His hair is lime green today and slicked into spikes. I'm not one to judge on appearances, but Boyd definitely is, so I don't understand his decision at all. This is who he wants as his deputy? Not Cam, or someone from his former team, but Quentin? Quentin, who's so feckless that earlier this year he misplaced vital blood evidence in a scab case?

It feels like a personal slight.

'It's nothing, Quent,' I say, waving him back down to his seat. 'We'll catch up with you later.'

'Not if I see you first!' He yells back, then laughs as though this is the most hilarious quip in the world. The guy means well, I know, but he is more than a little weird. And that's coming from *me*.

'So we need to search the fingerprint database,' Cam says, pulling us forcefully back to the point. It's clear that he's not willing to discuss the deputy position any further.

'Well, bagsy not it,' says Naia.

'You are very much it,' Cam replies.

'Cam...'

'Jack and I have another lead to follow up today.'

'We do?' I say, unaware that we had any plans.

'Yes. We'll help you get the searches started,' he says to Naia, 'but then you're on your own.'

Naia sighs dramatically, but she doesn't argue. You don't with Cam, not on the rare occasions that he puts his foot down. It's exactly why he would have made a perfect deputy.

What the hell is Boyd thinking, choosing Quentin over him?

After breakfast, all four of us traipse along to what used to be the IT suite, the erstwhile domain of Frank the Hacker, to see formerly-DCI Faizan Malik.

He works for us now. When the police cut ties with the Seekers, they wanted a clean break. Faiz was a complication. To be honest, it was a relief when he was made redundant, because then he was free to cross over to our side. He's a great investigator, and with Seekers dropping like flies, we need all the help we can get.

'Oh, look,' he says as we walk in, 'it's the demolition experts. You do know that you destroyed thousands of pounds' worth of computer equipment with the stunt you pulled in the captain's office?' For some reason, he's looking at me, not Naia.

'It wasn't me!' I say. 'Why would I want to destroy my own rooms?'

'You're always destroying something, Jack.'

'He's right,' Naia chimes in. 'It was a fair assumption.'

'But… but…' I'm so outraged that I'm struggling to get the words out. 'You're the one who kicked the wall down!'

'And did you stop me?' Naia crosses her arms over her chest. 'No, I don't think so. Case closed.'

'Case *not* closed!'

'What happened to your eyebrows?' Faiz asks, wrinkling his nose at me.

'That's why we're here,' Cam says.

'For Jack's eyebrows?'

'Sort of. You heard about the body on the Bridge of Sighs?'

'Oh, right. The flaming one. Hence the…?' Faiz gestures at my face in a way that invites everyone to appreciate the extent of the disaster.

'All right, all right!' I say. 'So I haven't looked in the mirror yet this morning. Give it a rest.'

'As it turns out,' Cam continues, unperturbed, 'there was a fingerprint found at the scene, and it's not in our system. We were hoping you could help us access the police database.'

'Databases,' Faiz corrects him. 'And sure. Have you got the print?'

Cam fiddles with his phone to forward the details to Faiz, then all of us take a separate desk and get the searches running. Once that's done, Naia starts teaching Raul how to compare the various whorls and loops to one another to find a match.

'Right,' Cam says, 'come on, Jack. Let us know if you find anything,' he says to Naia.

She gives him a distracted wave, then we're off.

I'm just not sure where we're going.

'Cam?' I say once we're a fair distance down the corridor. 'What's with all the cloak and dagger stuff? Where are we going?'

'Did I ever tell you why I joined the Seekers?' he asks.

'Boyd recruited you, right?'

'Sort of. The baron was seeing a woman named Elise—'

I groan. 'I don't want to hear this.'

'—and she went scab.'

'What?' This is a story I have not heard before.

'I sort of fell into the case. I saw Elise attacking someone, but it wasn't until later that I realised who she was, and she realised who I was. I helped Boyd get the proof we needed to put her away, but the baron had no clue what she was doing.'

I scoff. 'Yeah, right.'

'You didn't see his face when he found out. Whatever else he's done, he wouldn't condone that. But that's not the point I'm trying to make. What I'm saying is that if there's any reason to suspect that Tabitha's gone scab – and I think we both know there is – then you should be the one to look into it. I know we're all feeling… Well, with everything that's happened over the past few months, I guess we're looking for reasons to keep doing what we do.'

I stop walking. A step later, Cam does the same.

'I had no idea you were feeling that way,' I say.

He gives me a wry look. 'You're not the only one who can feel the way the wind's blowing. I'm not a complete idiot. The vote was just the start. It doesn't matter that the Primus won. Now that everyone's started talking about the Silver coming out of the closet, it's only a matter of time until it happens. It'll be like a bad tooth people can't stop prodding at, however bad an idea it might sound, until it's too late. Then you, and me, and all the team will be out of a job.'

'And no one will be policing the scabs.'

'No one except the humans, and how far will they get without supernatural assistance?'

Not far at all. No wonder Cam's emotions have been so close to the surface recently; he's been as confused and anxious as I have.

'It just doesn't feel like we're doing much good anymore,' I say. 'Felton's death was a great thing for humanity. Why should we be chasing the perpetrator, when they did us a favour?'

'Because you think it was Tabitha.'

I didn't realise that I'd given the subject much thought until the words were out of his mouth, ringing with truth. He's right: I think she might have done this, but if she did then I don't want to know. That's why I'm avoiding this investigation. That's why I'm not pushing it forward.

It was bad enough that she spied on me, recorded our conversations, and handed the whole lot to the Invicti. I can lay the fault for that firmly at her feet. What I can't stand, the thought that eats me up inside, is that I might have infected her with my own brutality. The Tabby I loved would never have done what I suspect she may have done to Felton. If she did, then it feels like it's my fault.

'Maybe,' I concede.

'Why?'

'Because of the look on her face when she left Crimson that evening, like she had something to prove to me. Because the last thing she said was that she still loves me.'

And, I don't have to add, because she's the only person who has ever said those words to me and meant them the way she did.

'Then shouldn't you be investigating this case with more energy than normal, not less?' Cam says, his tone softer now. 'She was your girlfriend, so it's personal. Maybe we won't be able to stay motivated forever, and maybe we won't always be able to find a reason to keep going, but we can for this case. Because it's Tabitha, and because for all that happened between the two of you, you loved her once. Right?'

'Right,' I sigh. It still hurts to admit it, but there's no pretending with Cam. He knows exactly how I felt, and exactly how to press my buttons to get me to care. The sneaky bastard.

'I saw the look on Baron Drake's face that day,' he says. 'I don't want you to be left feeling like that, like you were kept in the dark. This is your case, Jack. You need to own it.'

'It's really tedious how often you're right, you know?' I kiss him on the cheek and say, 'What would I do without you?'

For a moment, I think I see a shadow crossing his face, but it's gone just as quickly, leaving me to wonder whether I imagined it.

'Come on, then.' He pulls the list of Tabitha's properties from his pocket and flourishes it with a smile. 'Let's go find your ex.'

6

I STOP BY my temporary rooms to wash the plaster out of my nose, redraw my eyebrows and collect the box of Tabitha's things. If I really have to track her down, then I might as well kill two birds with one stone. No point in dragging things out.

We arrange the list of properties in order, starting with those closest to Oxford and ending with those furthest away. I hope we find her somewhere near the top of the list, because it turns out she has property all over the place. I'd rather not have to fly halfway around the world just to take her a box of sad mementos that she's probably forgotten all about. And to question her about Felton's murder, obviously.

The first property is a flat in Oxford that I didn't even know existed. We break in through the balcony to find a sprawling open-plan apartment that looks like it's come straight out of the centre spread of a lifestyle magazine. On one side, floor-to-ceiling windows curve around a luxurious seating area, giving panoramic views of Oxford's dreaming spires. On the other, overflowing bookcases create a cosy reading nook around a wood-fired stove that definitely contravenes the city's clean air regulations. There's a shiny kitchen and, down a corridor at the back of the property, two master bedrooms, each with king-sized beds and ensuite bathrooms.

But no Tabitha.

'Bloody hell,' I say to Cam as we search the place for recent signs of habitation. 'Why didn't she tell me about this place? Why were we crammed into my shitty college single bed when we could have been here?'

'Dunno. It doesn't look like there's anything particularly secret going on here,' he says, rifling through the fridge. 'And it doesn't look like she's been here recently. No food, no blood, no nothing. Oh, wait.' He pulls a piece of paper off the front of the fridge. 'Um.'

'*Um* what?'

'Um, this is a letter from her conveyancer. The purchase for this place went through a couple of days after you broke up. I guess maybe it was supposed to be a surprise, and—'

'No!' I say, covering my ears with my hands, even though it's too late. 'I don't want to know!'

'Okay,' he shouts. 'It's just that with your rooms not having a floor and everything—'

'No, Cam! Just, no, okay?'

He tacks the letter back onto the fridge with a magnet and says, 'Okay. If you're sure. But—'

'I'm very sure, thank you. Where's next on the list?'

I need to keep moving or I think I might cry, or scream, or break something. She bought us a flat. She was hinting at it before we broke up, now that I think about it, making several none-too-subtle suggestions that maybe we could do with a bit more space, and that maybe she could do more work in Oxford, maybe hire a space she could work more locally, but then that night in my rooms—

No. Now is not the time for reminiscing.

I secure the flat on our way out, pocketing the keys, then

get back in the car with Cam and head out to Nash Lee.

This is the one I've been dreading. I'm more than happy to see all Tabitha's other properties – though the flat was a shock I could've done without – but Nash Lee is different. When Tabitha and I were dating, her witchy cottage in this sleepy village near Aylesbury was the only place I ever visited her. There's a lab in the back garden for when she wants to bring her work home, and the inside of the home itself is furnished with all the colourful softness that is characteristic of my ex-girlfriend. The only time I've spent here was when the two of us were together, or in the process of getting together, so the place is filled with painful memories. I know before we even pull up to the cottage that this is going to be hard, but when I see that the front door is open, I realise that I may have underestimated just how hard it will turn out to be.

'Shit,' I say, bracing myself as Cam parks on the kerb in front of the house.

'What?' He follows my line of sight to the open door. 'You think she's home?'

'Looks like it. Shit *shit*.'

'Isn't this a good thing? The whole point was that we wanted to find her.'

'Yes, but as it turns out, I might not be ready to find her *quite* yet. Can we maybe do another property first, then come back to this one?'

Cam gives me a level look. 'The next closest one is in Glasgow.'

'Is that a "no", then?'

'Just get out of the car, will you?'

I do as directed, taking some deep breaths to try to steady my nerves. My heart is thudding in my chest and there's a growing numbness in my fingers. I feel sick.

'I'll go first, shall I?' Cam offers.

I can only nod in reply as I follow him towards the front door.

He gives it a knock in a cheerful rhythm and calls out, 'Tabitha? Dr Ross? It's Cam Sawyer.'

We both listen for a few tense seconds, but there's no response and no sound of movement from within the house.

'Maybe she's in the lab out back,' I suggest, but I don't move from the front step.

Cam sighs. 'You want me to lead the way, don't you?'

'Yes, please.'

He makes his way along the path around the side of the house as I follow at his heels like a scared lapdog.

'I'm only doing this to give you some time to pull yourself together,' he says. 'She's your ex-girlfriend, not some kind of terrifying psychopath.'

'She could be both.'

Cam's snort of derision tells me he disagrees.

When we reach the small laboratory at the bottom of the garden, we find the door open here as well. Not just unlocked, but standing wide open.

'Dr Ross?' Cam calls.

'Cam,' I say. 'Look.'

There's ice on the tiles just inside the door, along with a handful of leaves and garden detritus that has blown in with the wind.

'That can't be a good sign,' he says.

At this point, my concern for Tabitha's safety overrules my anxiety at the prospect of seeing her again. I step into the lab and start riffling through the papers spread over her lab benches, taking a quick look at the various bits of machinery as I do so. I can decipher none of the paperwork, but several pieces of electronic equipment are still turned on. It's not like her to leave them running when she's not actively using them. Her laptop is open at her desk, but when I press the power key to try to bring it to life, the screen stays black.

'Out of battery,' I say.

'So it's been sitting there a while.'

'It looks like all of this has.'

I push past Cam and make my way back to the house, only to find that the back door is hanging open too. It leads into the kitchen, where I find a plate smashed on the countertop and a knife missing from the rack. There are muddy streaks on the floor, as though something – or someone – has been dragged through here. I follow the trail into the sitting room, where I find the knife in a dark patch on the carpet, stained with dried blood. Whatever happened in this house, it looks like it started out in the lab and ended here.

Cam crouches down to examine the blade.

'Are you picking up a scent?' I ask.

'Only the violence mark and Tabitha's own scent.'

Which means the blood is likely hers, and she was stabbed by a Silver.

I shouldn't care. Tabitha is the worst thing that ever happened to me, with the possible exception of Winta. And Killian Drake of course. My point is that Tabitha's betrayal was a definite low, even within the general bin fire that is my love life, so my reaction to this scene makes no sense. She means nothing to me, less than nothing, so why am I sweating and why is my mouth watering like I'm about to be sick?

'Nothing else?' I say, swallowing down my fear.

'Sorry. Whatever happened here, it happened a while ago. Maybe as much as a week. Maybe longer.'

Now that we're inside the house, other signs of a long absence that we missed from out front are becoming clear. There's a pile of post on her doormat, including several "sorry we missed you" cards from failed deliveries. A few boxes have just been chucked inside the open door, stopping it from opening the whole way.

The scene speaks for itself.

'She must have been working in her lab,' I say. 'Someone busted in and dragged her back through the house. There was a struggle in the kitchen and Tabitha or the attacker picked up the knife. They fought over it, until the attacker stabbed Tabitha here.'

'Probably to incapacitate her,' Cam adds. 'So they could snatch her.'

'It looks that way. Unless…'

'Unless what?'

'Unless,' I say, grasping for a comforting alternative, 'she just wants us to think that someone snatched her. It can't be a coincidence that Felton goes up in smoke right in front of us, then we find Tabitha's scent in Felton's cellar, which leads us right here to find this. Someone is leaving us breadcrumbs.'

'And you think Tabitha would do that?'

I shrug. 'I wouldn't put it past her. We know she's manipulative.'

'But to be *that* manipulative? Isn't it more reasonable to assume the likeliest explanation is true: that someone snatched her?'

'Okay, then if someone really did take her, where's her car?' I say, looking out the front window.

When we were together, Tabitha had a cute little turquoise Mini that she loved like it was her own child. The whole inside was customised in turquoise accents. I can't imagine her ever getting rid of it, but I also don't see it parked at the kerb.

Cam forces the front door open all the way, dislodging a drift of letters and parcels, and looks up and down the road outside.

'No sign of it,' he says.

I give him a look that invites him to draw the same conclusion that I have: if Tabitha was snatched, her car would be here.

'The kidnapper could have taken it with them,' he suggests.

'Then where's the car they came here in? We're out in the middle of nowhere. They would have had to bring their own vehicle, and Tabitha's car would have been here if she was.'

'Maybe there were two kidnappers, and they left in different cars.'

'That makes no sense, Cam. Why would they go to the extra effort of taking her car, when they could stay together in the vehicle they arrived in and have one to drive and one to make sure Tabitha stayed under control?'

He's quiet for a moment, then says, 'Maybe there were *three* kidnappers—'

'Let's just agree that it's weird her car is missing, and see if we can find anything else that'll help us work this out. Okay?'

'Okay,' he agrees, but I can tell he's not going to let his multiple-kidnappers theory go. He's desperate to see the best in Tabitha, even now, after all she's done. It's just who Cam is.

I trawl through the rest of the house to check Tabitha's bedroom and bathroom, but there's nothing out of place. Her clothes are all still here, and her suitcase is under her bed as usual. Everything is just as it should be, as though she were intending to return at any moment. Not even her toothbrush is missing.

This isn't like her. I want to think that she's staged this scene, because then I won't have to deal with the intense and conflicting emotions that I'm feeling, but I know that Tabitha wouldn't just up and leave without locking her lab securely. But then she *knows* I know that, so perhaps she's deliberately left things this way for us to find. The more I try to puzzle it out, the more I find myself thinking in circles.

And the blood… I don't want to think about the blood. When I get too close to it, the scent wafts over me with the violence mark and it drags me back to the night we broke up, the night I found out just how many lies she'd been telling. I bit her, and the blood…

I can't bear the scent of her blood.

While I search the house, Cam calls in the rest of the squad. They arrive within the hour, along with the clean-up team. The whole place will be swabbed and scrubbed in short order, but I'm too antsy to join in. When I try to help, my hands shake too much for the precision the job requires. In the end, they just wave me away and Naia gets down to the business of teaching Raul how to collect evidence on her own.

'I should be doing something,' I say to Cam.

'There's nothing you can do.' He squeezes my shoulder, trying to reassure me, but I'm too worked up to be soothed. 'Faiz is going to see what he can do to track the car. It's got built-in GPS, right?'

'Right.'

'Then maybe he'll be able to get a location for us. In the meantime, how about you and I head back to Oxford and take you shopping?'

'You want me to go shopping?' I ask, incredulous. 'Now?'

'I love you, Jack, but you're kind of a wreck.'

'He means you look like shit,' Naia yells over at us, 'and you smell worse.'

I sniff my armpit discreetly. It's true that I'm not at my most fragrant right now, but in my defence it's been a busy couple of days and I've been wearing this plaster-caked T-shirt the whole time.

'I don't think I should just leave,' I say.

'You know you've got a hole in those jeans, right?' says Cam.

'What? No. Where?'

He clears his throat and nods at my back. I look over my shoulder and swivel my hips from one side to the other, trying to see what he's talking about, then give up and feel for the tear with my hands. It is right in the middle – I mean *right* in the middle – of my left bum cheek. And I'm wearing rainbow knickers.

'You waited until now to tell me this?' I yell at him.

'I thought maybe it was a fashion statement,' he lies.

'Give me your jumper.'

'What?'

I hold out my hand. 'Your jumper. Now.'

'All right, all right.'

He shrugs out of it and hands it over so I can tie it around my waist to hide the damage. He's so tall and gangly that I'm practically wearing the thing as a skirt.

'Okay,' I say. 'I admit that it is possible that I need to go shopping.'

'I'll drive you back,' Cam offers.

It's sweet of him, but my head is buzzing and, with the scent of blood and the weirdness of being in this place without Tabitha, I'm starting to feel claustrophobic.

'Thanks,' I say, 'but I need some space. You can get a lift back with the others, right?'

He hands over the car keys then I'm off, trying to make it look as though I'm striding out of the house with purpose rather than running scared. The effect is spoiled a little because I have to go back inside to drop off the box of Tabitha's things – no way I'm hanging onto those any longer than necessary – but soon enough I'm speeding back to Oxford, music turned up loud enough to blare any unwelcome thoughts clean out of my head.

* * *

You'd think that after twenty-odd years of buying clothes for myself, I might have some clue how to go about it. You would be wrong.

The pair of ripped jeans I'm wearing right now were hand-me-downs from Naia, originally bought from a retail chain that has since closed down. The top was a birthday gift from Cam. I have no idea how to replace either of these things.

I've just decided to start with underwear first – multipacks from Marks and Spencer are all I know – when it begins to chuck it down. This isn't just rain, this is apocalyptic, soak-you-to-the-nipples rain. And it's *freezing*.

The streets empty out quickly as shoppers flood into restaurants and cafés to escape the downpour. Sheltering in an alley on the High Street, I hear the familiar fluttering behind me a millisecond too late: a soft buzzing sound, like the brushing of fabric against fabric, or the beating of a moth's wings. Something sharp lands in my neck. I know exactly what it is without looking, because this is now the third time that someone has tried to hit me with one of these. At last, they've succeeded. Finally, after months of searching, I've found the last Silver tranquilliser dart stolen from the Invicti by Yolande Leclercq.

Or, rather, it has found me.

7

WHEN I BLINK awake, my head is spinning, my throat is dry and my mouth tastes like arse. Cam instantly hoves into view, offering me a straw.

Cold water. Blissfully, gorgeously cold water.

'Fuck me,' I groan when I've drunk my fill. 'Everything hurts.'

I'm looking up at what turns out to be the sterile white ceiling of sick bay. There's a machine beeping at my side and a drip in the back of my hand feeding me blood.

'Was this really necessary?' I whisper, waving the hand that has the cannula.

Cam stops me gently and lays my hand carefully back by my side, his every touch as delicate as if I were made of fine china. He looks more concerned than seems warranted by the circumstances.

'You've been missing for seven days,' he says.

'A week?' I croak.

'We don't know where you've been or what's been done to you, so yeah, the drip is necessary. What do you remember?'

I think back to the last time I saw Cam.

'I drove back to the college, ditched the car and walked into town to go shopping, like you said. I ducked into an alley to get out of the rain, then I got hit with one of those tranquilliser darts.'

'The same ones that knocked out Baron Drake?'

'I didn't get a good look, but I think so. I guess I should feel lucky to be alive, huh?'

The Invicti designed the darts as a safe way to tranquillise Silver prisoners, but something went wrong in the formula that was in the pack Yolande Leclercq stole, giving a small percentage of Silver a violent and deadly reaction to it. When Drake got stuck with a dart, it nearly killed him. Since I've been Silver for so much less time, if I'd had that reaction then it really would have killed me. As it is, it looks like I've just been knocked out for a while.

'What happened next?' Cam asks.

I shrug, bewildered.

'You don't remember anything from the last week?'

'I've told you all I can. Why? What did I miss?'

He sits back in his chair, rubbing his hands over his face as he gathers his thoughts. He looks like he hasn't slept in days. I feel a pang of guilt as I wonder how much time he's spent looking for me, and how long he's been sitting by my bedside, waiting for me to wake up.

'It makes sense that she'd use the darts,' Cam says, talking more to himself than to me. 'She's the one who made the tranquilliser, after all. It would be easy enough for her to make more.'

'You mean Tabitha?' I ask. 'You think she's the one who shot me?'

'It's looking more and more likely. We finished processing the scene in Nash Lee then brought everything back here to Ed and Faiz. Ed was still working on the ashes from the Felton murder scene, but when none of us could get hold of you the next day and we realised you were missing, he switched his focus to the samples we'd taken from the cottage.'

'Wait,' I interrupt. 'What day is it today?'

'Tuesday. Tuesday the twenty-first. You've been gone since the fourteenth.'

'Huh.'

'You scared me, Jack.' He runs a hand back through his hair. 'You just disappeared. I had no idea where you were, but with all this stuff with Tabitha I thought maybe you'd gone off on your own to find her, or that you'd found her already and decided to run off with her, because when you didn't—'

'I wouldn't leave you behind to run away with Tabitha, Cam.' I reach out to take his hand, squeezing it tight in mine. 'I haven't forgotten what she did to me. To all of us.'

He exhales heavily, composing himself. The past week has obviously taken a bigger toll on him than I thought.

'Eventually, Ed got through all the samples and determined it was probably Tabitha's blood – the DNA mix fits with the blood bottles we found in her fridge – and we couldn't identify any prints in the house that didn't belong there. So I started thinking about your theory that maybe she'd staged the whole thing. Just because it was her blood on the knife and in the carpet, that doesn't mean anything actually happened to her. She could easily have cut a vein to make a convincing pool, then drunk a few bottles from the fridge to heal herself up. She could have made the mess in the kitchen. She could have left the doors open herself.'

'But why?' I ask.

'To throw us off her trail and make us go looking for someone else. Or to distract the rest of us so she could get to you. Maybe it's not a coincidence that you got shot just after you'd been to her cottage. She could have followed you and then just waited for her moment. But whatever her plan was, she must have snatched you from that alley and taken you somewhere for the past week, somewhere we couldn't find you. And we've been looking. Faiz has been doing everything he can to track down her car electronically, because we figured she'd be wherever it was, but it turns out that the GPS only switches on when the car is in use, and for days it's been going nowhere. For *days*. Until finally, last night, we got a ping and found the car parked outside Felton's house on Iffley Road. You were in the passenger seat, out for the count. When I first saw you, I thought…'

He's rubbing his eyes now, trying not to let me see the tears.

'Cam.' I wave him over for a hug and he falls into my arms. 'Oh, Cam. I'm so sorry. But everything's okay. I'm back.'

We stay like that for a while, until his shoulders stop shaking. I don't realise I've been crying too until he pulls away and I see my tears on his T-shirt.

'You still smell like her,' he says.

I pull a lock of my hair loose from my ponytail, bring it to my nose and sniff. He's right: I smell so much like Tabitha that I can barely make out my own scent.

'But you don't remember anything?' he asks. 'Nothing at all?'

I shake my head.

'Maybe you will. Maybe she's been using chemicals to erase your memory and you just need to wait for them to wear off. I don't know. But wherever you've been, you've been with her. And there's something else, too.'

'What?'

He licks his lips nervously. 'Your tattoo is gone.'

'Gone? What do you mean, "gone"? Tattoos don't just get up and wander off.'

While I speak, I push him off the bed then scrabble with the bedsheets until I can see the hip where I have a tabby cat tattoo. Or, rather, *had* a tabby cat tattoo, because there's no trace of it now.

'You didn't do it to yourself?' he asks.

'No. I didn't…' I should have, I realise. The moment Tabitha and I broke up, I should have had the damn thing lasered or cut out or whatever, but it felt the same as all the belongings she'd left behind at my place: too personal to get rid of. 'The idea hadn't even occurred to me.'

'Well, it occurred to someone.'

'You think Tabitha cut out my tattoo?' I ask. 'Why the hell would she do that?'

'I have no idea. I have no idea why she'd stage her own kidnapping, or kidnap you only to let you go a week later. None of it makes any sense. There's something going on here that we're not seeing.'

'As usual.'

'I do have some good news, though,' he says with a smile.

'What's that?'

'Your eyebrows are finally starting to grow back.'

'*Starting*?' I feel around on my brow line and encounter not much more than a couple of stubbly patches of fluff.

'Yeah,' he smiles. 'I wouldn't chuck out the eyebrow pencil just yet.'

The door opens behind Cam and Boyd walks in, without knocking, I notice. The captaincy has really gone to his head.

'Jacqueline,' he says. 'You're awake. Good.'

He stands in the doorway for a moment, looking awkward. I pity him a little, despite all the dickheadery he's been pulling recently, because it's clear that nothing about this new promotion is going how he planned. And he's been planning for a long, long time.

'What can you tell us about your captor?' Boyd asks.

'She doesn't remember anything,' Cam says, stepping in to shield me from his questions. 'I'm thinking maybe she was drugged. She needs to rest.' It's not normal for him to be this fierce with Boyd, but then the new captain has been rubbing us all up the wrong way recently.

'All right. I'll just…' He looks utterly lost for a second, then draws himself up to his full height and says, 'Let me know if there's any change,' before striding from the room.

Cam glares after him.

'Brr,' I say. 'Is it me, or did it just get a little chilly in here? Looks like maybe you need to fill me in about what's been happening over the past week.'

Cam's face clouds over in a way that is entirely uncharacteristic. He's not prone to fits of bad temper. He doesn't get grumpy and stay that way, but it's clear that whatever else Boyd's done, he's crossed a line with Cam.

'It all went downhill after he took away our offices,' he says darkly. 'First it was the open-plan policy, and then he introduced a rota. A *rota*.'

The Seekers have never bothered with that kind of thing before. We wait until a case comes in, whichever team is free picks it up, and then they work it until it's done. Days off happen when necessary, when specifically requested, or when there's nothing much going on. It might not be the most efficient system in the world, but it works, so why change it? When you're dealing with centuries-old people, I've learned that it's best not to introduce too much change too soon. Boyd clearly has not.

Still, annoying though it is, a rota alone shouldn't have sent Cam off the deep end.

'Then he sacked Faiz,' Cam says.

'He *what?*'

Since the Great Exodus, we can hardly afford to lose anyone else. Besides which, Faizan is a great guy and an excellent investigator. Again, I'm left wondering what the hell has come over Boyd.

'I know,' Cam mutters.

'But why?'

'He said it was because of "budgetary constraints", but you'd have to ask him for the real reason. I don't know. It feels like everything's falling apart.' He looks like he might start crying again, and then I'm not sure what I'd do. I already feel awful that I've caused him so much anxiety.

I take his hand in mine. 'We knew things would change after the vote,' I say. 'We knew the *world* was changing. You said it yourself when you convinced me to go find Tabitha.'

'I just didn't think it would happen so quickly, I suppose. And I was wrong about her. I know she did some awful things, but I didn't think she had it in her to do what she did to Felton.'

'She's been around a long time, Cam. I get the feeling that, back in the day, people used to do whatever they had to in order to survive. Or am I wrong?'

I can tell from the look on his face that I've hit the mark. Back before Solomon College had a regular blood supply, back before Cam was a Seeker, I bet he did a lot of things he'd rather not remember just to get the blood he needed to survive. Once you've done the unthinkable, it's hard to claw your way back from it, and harder still not to slide back into homicidal habits. With the older Silver – like Cam, like Tabitha – the wonder is not so much that they're all murderers of old, but that they no longer kill on a regular basis.

'We'll find Tabitha,' Cam promises me. 'We're doing everything we can to track her down.'

'Like what?'

'We're staking out her properties, and of course there's the car. Ed's processing every inch of it, looking for clues. We should be able to get historic GPS data off the computer too, so we can see where she's been, though that'll take five times longer now we don't have Faiz to help. Naia's working on it.'

'Okay, where do you want me?'

He gives me the kind of look you would give a child who's reaching for a toy that she's already been told five times she can't have.

'You're staying right there in that bed,' Cam says.

'Bollocks.' I fling back the covers and swivel my legs off the mattress. I'm wearing one of those extremely attractive, bum-revealing hospital gowns, but it's only Cam and he's seen me in much more compromising attire in the past, so I'm not embarrassed to get to my feet. Until, that is, I promptly fall right off them and onto my face.

'The doctor did say it might take a while for you to get all the feeling back in your limbs,' he says, helping me back into the bed. 'We've taken a sample of your blood so Ed can take a look and maybe see what she used to knock you out. It might give us a clue about where to start looking. In the meantime, you're staying here. When you're fully recovered, you can buddy up with Raul and finish off his training. There's no call for you to be running around the city chasing after Tabitha, especially since we're not sure she's finished chasing after you.'

'But Cam—'

'Nope.' He puts his fingers in his ears, which is usually my move. 'I'm not listening. You're going to stay here and be a good patient, aren't you?'

'I'm not going to just sit here and—'

'I can't hear you,' he yells. 'So just nod your head for *yes*.'

'But I—'

'Nod, Jack.'

I dutifully nod my head, but I give him the finger at the same time.

8

THE DAYS THAT follow are possibly the most tedious and mind-numbing of my life. Worse than revising for exams. Worse than travelling by rail replacement bus service. Worse than that time I had to file my tax return without Ed's help.

I'm not cut out to be a teacher. That's no surprise, I'm sure. I lack the patience and temperament to impart knowledge to other people. I can barely keep hold of the stuff I've learned myself, so why Cam thinks it's a good idea for me to be teaching the next generation of Seekers is totally beyond me.

Still, here we are. Day three, and I've shown Raul around the college, explained the new rota system to him – a bit of a lost cause, since I don't yet understand it myself – and talked him through how we work cases. Today, stumped for any other ideas, I've decided to take him to the IT suite and show him our files.

'We have two external storage drives,' I explain. 'Everything's on hardware with nothing in the cloud, for maximum confidentiality. The first one contains details of all our closed cases – we call that the Dead Box – and the second has profiles of all the suspects we've bumped up against over the years – the Creep Box. Which do you want to look at first?'

'Creeps,' Raul says, without hesitation. 'Definitely the creeps.'

We dive in. I show him how to search the records for particular characteristics, then he has a general browse, flicking through the profiles to get an idea of the kind of things we note down.

'You've got everyone in here,' he says as he scrolls. 'There's Matthew Felton... Oh, Jesus. Did he really do all that stuff?'

The profile lists Felton's more deviant proclivities. Along with the drug-making and -taking, he also enjoyed kidnapping humans, drugging them and hanging them from ribbons like marionettes in his attic so he could dress them up and pose them while he drank from them. When I said the guy deserved to burn, I wasn't exaggerating.

'Yeah,' I say. 'He was scum. Did you really expect the Creep Box to be cheerful reading?'

'No.' He flicks through a few more profiles. 'I guess I thought it might be more interesting, but less gruesome.'

'Well, that's the Silver for you. At our best, we're parasites. At our worst, we're a bunch of truly sick bastards.'

He moves onto the next profile, then freezes.

'Fuck,' he mutters. Raul's own picture is staring back at him from the computer screen. The real Raul looks at me with big, sad eyes. 'I'm one of the creeps?'

Well, this is awkward. I'd forgotten that he was in the Creep Box, but it feels like bad luck that it's come up. There are thousands of profiles in our records. What are the odds that he would stumble across his own during an idle browsing session?

'You're not a creep, mate,' I say, putting my hand on his shoulder. 'You know why you're in there. You were a suspect in a scab case, and you were a Starblood user.' Starblood is basically cocaine for vampires: it makes you hyper, manic and totally lethal to nearby humans. Raul is clean now, I think, but for a long time he was an addict, and Felton was his dealer. 'You're not a creep, though,' I say again, just to make sure he gets it. 'You're a Seeker now.'

The door opens and Cam wanders into the room. He's making it look casual, as though he's just killing time until lunch, but I know him well enough to know that he's here for a reason. After a few minutes spent idly picking bobbles off the jumper I've liberated from lost property for today's fashion statement, he gets to the point.

'Anything yet?' he asks me, hopefully.

He's been asking me at least three times a day since I woke up in sick bay, so I know what he wants without clarification: he's here to find out if my memory is returning.

'No,' I say. 'Nothing. Sorry.'

His face drops for a moment, but he turns it into a smile for me. 'I'm sure that'll change soon,' he says. 'Hang in there, Jack.'

He's so optimistic whenever he's around me, so cheerful, so careful not to let it show on his face that he's starting to lose hope that my memories will ever return. His constant concern is breaking my heart.

'You'll be the first to know when I have anything to tell you,' I promise. 'But for now, I really ought to…' I gesture towards the computer, where Raul is waiting patiently, his eyes blank and his mind clearly elsewhere. He seems to have a standby mode that he just switches on and off, one minute fully attentive – or as attentive as he ever gets, anyway – and the next off in a world of his own.

'Sure,' Cam says to me. 'Sure. We'll catch up at dinner. Right?'

We never get the chance though, because a few hours later

Ed calls us to the lab and turns the rest of the day on its head.

When we arrive, Ed is in the middle of one of his regular disasters. Before we even open the lab doors, we can see through the small windows that the place is filled with greenish smoke.

'What's he done now?' Cam groans. He pulls his T-shirt up over his nose then ducks inside, closing the doors firmly behind him. A minute later, he's coughing and spluttering as he drags an unconscious Ed out into the corridor.

We both stare down at Ed, expecting the fresh air to revive him, but no such luck. Whatever he's been brewing up in there, it must be pretty potent; it takes a lot to knock out one of the Silver.

'I opened the windows,' Cam says, 'and whatever was in his beakers seems to have stopped bubbling.'

'Do you think we should take him to sick bay?'

Between Ed, Boyd and me, that would be three knock-out visits in less than a fortnight. At this rate, the duty doctors are going to go on strike. Thankfully, we don't need to test their patience for our shenanigans because, at that moment, Ed opens his eyes and blinks up at us foggily. Even though they're useless, he gropes at his face for his glasses, but he must have lost them in the kerfuffle.

'What happened?' he says.

'We were going to ask you that,' I reply.

He sneezes into his elbow, leaving a gob of unattractive green slime on his lab coat.

'Oh,' he says. 'That's right. The antidote.'

'The antidote to what?' Cam asks.

Ed gets to his feet and peers through the little window in the door.

'Looks like it's cleared out now,' he says. 'You'd better come inside.'

We follow him into the lab, which has indeed cleared of smoke, but the gas has left behind a reek of rotten eggs and antiseptic that I find almost unbearable. With his sensitive nose, Cam must be in agony, though after centuries of tolerating Ed's concoctions he's probably accustomed to the discomfort.

'You had news?' Cam prompts him.

'Yes.' Ed retrieves his glasses from the floor. One lens has smashed. He pokes a finger through it mournfully, then puts the glasses on. I'm not sure why he's so sad; the missing lens might ruin the illusion, but he'll see better without it in the way. 'It's bad news. Very bad news. You remember Dr Jay?' he says to Cam.

Cam's face blanches. I'm not sure I've ever seen him so pale.

'I should have made the connection earlier,' Ed continues. 'But it was such a long time ago, and I thought his legacy was buried along with him.'

'You're telling me it's not?' Cam asks.

'I'm telling you I found traces of his formula in the remains of Matthew Felton.'

'Oh. Oh no.'

'Would someone like to fill me in?' I ask sweetly. I don't like being kept in the dark.

'Sorry, Jack,' Cam says. 'I forgot you weren't here when it happened. It was late in 1999, right?' he says to Ed.

'September,' he replies. 'There was a doctor who worked with me back then, Jahan Khalyed. Nice chap. Brilliant scientist. He had all sorts of ideas and we had a great time trying to bring them to fruition. But then there was an… accident in the lab.'

'You don't say,' I reply.

'They're not infrequent around here, I know. This one, though…' He takes off his glasses and goes to clean the missing lens, then sighs when he realises his mistake. He puts them back on his face, nervous habit unappeased. 'It would have been groundbreaking. We were trying to come up with a formula that would stop the Silver from needing to drink human blood.'

'Since we're all still drinking from bottles,' I say, 'I'm guessing you failed.'

'Sort of.'

'What do you mean, "sort of"?'

'I mean that we accomplished what we set out to do.'

'No.' Cam shifts uncomfortably beside me. 'I don't think you did, Ed.'

'I'm not trying to defend our errors,' Ed replies. 'We made mistakes. I know that. But, technically, we achieved our goal. We made a formula that obviated the need for the Silver to drink human blood.'

'By making them ravenous for Silver blood instead,' Cam adds.

'By making them *what*?' I say, incredulous.

Ed deflates a little, all his fight gone. 'Let's just say it wasn't a success.'

'Then what was it?' I ask impatiently. 'Come on, guys. Spill.'

'It was a disaster,' Cam says.

Ed doesn't disagree.

'We were trying to come up with a safe way to test the serum without going straight to testing it on the Silver,' he says. 'Dr Jay – that's what we all called Jahan back then – he was impatient. He always had been, but he was particularly impatient over this formula, knowing how important it might turn out to be. He wanted to free the Silver from the need to feed on humans, and to free humans from our predation, which had always bothered him, even when the humans were unaware. It didn't seem fair to him, and he was in a hurry to set things right. It was like he could see all the possibilities stretching in front of us, and he just couldn't wait to access them. He meant well, he really did.'

'He started testing on the Silver, then?' I ask.

'Not exactly,' Ed replies. 'He tested the serum on himself.'

'Oh.'

'With disastrous results,' Cam says.

'He was lucky, really,' says Ed. 'For ninety-nine percent of Silver, drinking that stuff would have been lethal, but there were some peculiarities in Dr Jay's physiology that allowed the serum to bond to him.'

'What was the problem, then?' I ask.

'He started biting people,' Ed says. 'Silver people. He couldn't stop himself. And when he bit them, they reacted to the serum in his saliva. The first person he bit – a friend of ours – became very sick. He survived, because the serum hadn't been refined at that point, but he never fully recovered. After that, Dr Jay modified the formula. The next person he bit died instantly. All that was left of his body was a pile of ash.'

'Like Matthew Felton.'

'Yes. Just like Matthew Felton.'

Shit. This is not good news.

'So are you saying that Dr Jay is back somehow?' I ask.

'No. No, Dr Jay has been in the ground for more than twenty years now.' Ed shakes himself out of his memories and drags his attention back to the present. 'And anyway, the formula in the ashes you recovered under the Bridge of Sighs isn't identical to the one I developed with Dr Jay. There are small differences. If I had to guess, I'd say that someone was trying to replicate the serum, and they fed the replica to Mr Felton. That would explain why he burned so fast and so hot.'

'But how could they do that?' Cam asks. 'You're the only

person still alive who worked on that project.'

Ed looks hurt by the insinuation. 'You know I wouldn't do this,' he says. 'Not even to someone like Matthew Felton, not if it meant resurrecting that formula. We all agreed it was too dangerous to be out in the world. If it got into the wrong hands…'

The thought gives me a small spike of anxiety.

'Maybe someone decided it was a risk worth taking in order to get Matthew Felton off the streets,' I suggest. 'He was a monster.'

Cam raises his eyebrows at me. 'If whoever killed Felton did it to try and impress you, it looks like they've succeeded.'

'I'm not saying I'm *impressed* exactly, just that I understand the impulse to burn the rat alive.'

'And you appreciate the fact that someone's now done it permanently.'

'Sort of.' I shrug.

'I don't understand how you can be so cold about it.' Cam shakes his head. 'Whoever sent you that love letter obviously knows you better than I do.'

'Don't say that.'

This is the problem with being honest with Cam. He's so desperate to think the best of the people he loves that he assumes they'd never cross the lines that he wouldn't cross himself. If he can't even see me clearly, someone with whom he spends half his waking hours, then how will he ever get a clear perspective on the Solis Invicti, or the Seekers for that matter? Even though our mission is to protect the Silver's secrecy, not to be moral heroes, he acts like we have an unspoken altruistic mandate. Sooner or later, he's going to realise how terribly wrong he is about that. I don't want to disappoint him, but I'm not going to lie and say I'm sad Felton's dead.

I know Cam's properly upset not just because of the look on his face, but because Ed steps in to mediate, which is not something he normally does.

'You're right, Jack,' he says gently. 'I think most people will rest easier now Felton's gone, but no monster is so bad that killing them is worth releasing that serum. When I say it's dangerous, I mean that if it ever got into the system of a Silver with similar physiology to Dr Jay, then that Silver would be killing another Silver every single night until they were stopped. We only managed to stop Dr Jay because he turned himself in. If someone were to take the serum intentionally, knowing what would happen when they did, then I dread to think what the consequences might be. Not to mention that the serum in its purest form would be simply lethal to any Silver *without* Dr Jay's physiology. They'd burn up like *that*.' He snaps his fingers.

'Like Matthew Felton.' I say.

'Exactly. Whoever killed him might have more of this serum, which means that they have the ability to murder any Silver at will, at any time, no matter how old or powerful or strong that Silver might be. Until we find the culprit, we're all in danger.'

'So that's what the green gas was about?' Cam asks.

'Yes.' Ed takes off his glasses again and wipes the single remaining lens on his lab coat. 'I was trying to make an antidote, to stop what happened to Matthew Felton from happening to anyone else. But it's not easy. We never managed to find a cure for the original serum, otherwise Dr Jay's story would have ended differently. I can't remember the ingredients perfectly anyway, and this new formula... I'm having to reverse engineer from what's left behind in Felton's remains. It's not going well.'

'I just don't understand how someone could have copied the formula,' Cam says, bringing us back to his original question. 'Didn't we burn all his notes?'

'I thought so,' says Ed. 'But then I remembered that Dr Jay gave copies to the duty doctor at the time, so she could try to treat his victims.'

They both turn to look at me.

'What?' I say.

'The duty doctor that day was Tabitha Ross,' says Cam.

For a second, my blood runs cold. I didn't know.

'Fuck,' I say.

'That would explain what she was doing in the lab in Felton's basement,' Cam says.

'All roads are leading to Dr Ross,' says Ed.

Cam looks troubled. 'But I just can't imagine it,' he says. 'We *knew* her. We spent time with her. We got so drunk with her that we had to carry each other home. She was Jack's girlfriend for months. If someone has that kind of darkness in them, I don't believe that they'd be able to hide it so well.'

Which is, of course, the root of Cam's problems.

'Not everyone is as open as you are,' says Ed.

'But don't you think *you* would have seen it, at least, Jack?'

'I think we're coming at this from different places,' I say. 'I don't think Tabitha's evil. Yes, she might have killed Felton, and yes, she might have spied on me and kidnapped me and done who knows what while I was unconscious, but I don't think she'd have done those things because she's a bad person. I don't know. Maybe she's trying to convince me to come back to her.'

Cam and Ed both go wide-eyed.

'I'm not saying she's doing a good job of it,' I add. 'But this feels like stalker behaviour, not serial killer behaviour. Something's knocked one of her screws loose, obviously, but I don't think she's about to start murdering random Silver. The only person she's physically hurt is Matthew Felton.'

'And you, Jack,' says Cam. 'I think knocking you out with that tranquilliser more than qualifies as assault.'

'Pffft.' I wave his concerns away. 'I'm fine. If she's going to hurt anyone, then I really don't think it'll be me.'

'Then who would she hurt? The baron?'

'I don't think so. Even if she did target him – and let me be clear that there would be *absolutely no reason* for her to do that because the whole thing between me and Drake is more than over – he's not here. I don't think she'd hurt any of my friends, and I've not been involved with anyone else since the two of us split up. I think she's done with the serum.'

We're all quiet for a moment, thinking through the mess that is my love life in a futile attempt to drag out some clues.

'We just need to work out what her next move is,' Cam says. 'What about Jack's blood?' he says to Ed. 'Do you have any answers for us?'

'Not yet. There's been a lot going on,' Ed says defensively. 'I'm all on my own here, you know.'

'I know. I know. I just…' Cam pushes his sandy hair back from his face, looking more worried than I've ever seen him. 'Please, Ed, it's important that you focus right now. I know you're worried about Dr Jay's formula, but we don't even know that it's a problem yet. If we're right about Tabitha being behind this, and Jack's right that she's out of targets, then she may never use the serum again. And anyway, it's so fast-acting that an antidote might not be much use. So for now, let's concentrate on the facts we do have rather than speculating about what might happen in the future. Okay?'

'Okay,' Ed says, jamming his glasses back onto his nose. 'I can do that.'

The lab doors swing open then and in walks Boyd. It is less than a second before his face crumples into disgust at the rotten smell still permeating the lab.

'What's been going on in here, Dr Castell?' he asks, holding a finger beneath his nose.

'Just a little miscalculation,' Ed replies. 'Nothing to worry about. It'll air out in no time.'

'It had better.'

I swear, Boyd didn't use to be like this. He's always been a bit of a dick about procedural bullshit that the rest of us ignore, but he's also had a geeky interest in architecture, a fervour for new gadgetry that borders on the fanatical, and – more recently – a fierce romance with a beautiful human librarian called Mildred Chen. Unfortunately, he got caught up with the drama at Crimson, drank one of Felton's poisoned blood concoctions and attacked Mildred. Thanks to some quick action on Tabitha's part, Mildred survived her wounds, but Boyd's not been the same since. The two of them are still a couple, as far as I know, but the experience seems to have drained out what little softness Boyd had. Personally, I think he's struggling with being the captain of the Seekers – whose mandate is to keep the Silver secret from humans – at the same time as he's dating a human who, because of the attack, knows all about us. It's the kind of hypocrisy that's bound to drive a man like Boyd insane.

'Jacqueline,' he says, turning to me. Behind his back, Ed looks like he's contemplating violence. 'Apparently I'm now your messenger.'

'Oh?'

'Acting Baron Yadav wants to speak with you.' Everyone else just calls her Kulika, but Boyd has always been a stickler for protocol.

'About what?'

'I don't know. Just don't keep her waiting.' With that, he turns around smartly and exits the lab the same way he came in.

'Has anyone considered that the captain might be behind

Felton's death?' Ed asks, with a face like thunder. 'After all, he had good reason to want Matthew Felton dead.'

'Wishful thinking,' I say, patting Ed on the shoulder. 'He didn't have access to the serum, he was with Naia at the time of the murder, and – most obviously – there's no way Boyd would be sending me love notes. We can rule him out.'

'If you insist,' Ed grumbles.

At this rate, Boyd's going to alienate the entire college by the New Year.

9

'HEY, KULIKA,' I say as I walk into her office. 'What's up?'

'What isn't up?' She groans. 'I hate this fucking job.'

It does look as though it's taking its toll on her. Before Drake left, I'd never seen Kulika looking anything but controlled and composed. She's one of those people who keeps perfect posture in all situations, not because she's got a stick up her arse like Boyd, but because her body is such a finely-tuned machine that it doesn't even know how to slouch. She's still sitting bolt upright now, but there are dark circles under her eyes and her muscular arms are draped over the desk as though they have no more strength left in them.

That desk. Much like it is for Kulika, that fucking desk is the root of all my misery. Every time I come into this room, the unbidden memories come rushing back of all the things that Drake and I have done to each other on that enormous desk.

Of course, Kulika's own associations with it are a little more tedious. I assume.

'You look like death,' I say cheerfully as I slump into one of Drake's leather armchairs. It's hard not to remember the things we've done in these, either. 'Why did you want to see me?'

She blinks. 'I wanted to see you?'

'I got a message from Boyd. Did you forget?'

'Oh god.' She groans and drops her head into her hands, ruining the spikes in her dark pixie cut. 'Not again. I'm not cut out for this, Jack. I swear. All I wanted was a good salary and decent hours so I'd have time to spend in the gym. I didn't mean to get into a position where I was the default option when the baron went on walkabout, and even after he began to involve me more in the management side of things, I never thought he'd actually ditch this place and leave me in charge. I just want things to go back to how they were. I want someone to tell me what to do for ten hours every day, then I want to piss off and do my own thing. I didn't ask for this.'

'Isn't there someone else who can take over?'

She lifts her head and looks at me in despair. 'He's counting on me. He's trusting me to look after things while he's gone. I can't let him down. I just can't.'

'Have you even spoken to him recently?' I ask.

Her silence speaks for itself.

'Then are you sure he deserves your loyalty?'

'He's earned it ten times over, more even,' she says. 'Trust me.'

I'm curious, but I don't pry. We don't, the Silver, as a rule. When you've lived several lifetimes, many of them in times more brutal and less moral than the modern world, the last thing you want is people poking around in your past. It's considered rude to ask.

'Have *you* heard from him?' she asks, sounding suspicious.

I laugh, meaning to be dismissive, but it just comes out sounding bitter. I've given up waiting for Drake to get in touch. I blocked his number on my phone earlier this year when he was getting a little clingy – all the fault of the haematopsychosis, as it turns out – and it wasn't until he ran off to Europe that I finally got around to unblocking it. Even then, he never called and never texted. After weeks of waiting, I finally accepted that he had left me behind for good. I thought I was over it, but apparently it still stings.

That pisses me right off.

'What did you want, anyway?' I ask Kulika, more brusquely than I intend.

She raises her eyebrows at my tone, then shuffles through the pile of papers on the desk, searching for something. Apparently she has not yet graduated to modern technology, so her filing system looks a lot like my laundry system.

'Here it is,' she says, brandishing a scrappy note. 'A guy called Adewale Ladipo wants to speak to you.'

'Adewale from the Invicti?' I ask. 'That Adewale?'

'Right. He said he'd come to you. Are you okay to talk to him?'

'About what?'

'He didn't say.'

'You mean you didn't ask.'

She fixes me with her narrow-eyed gaze. 'Despite what the Invicti might think, I am not your fucking secretary. I'm only passing on the message so the Solis Invicti can see that the Silver in Oxford are playing nice. Now are you willing to talk to him or not?'

'Okay,' I say, holding up my hands in surrender. 'Sure. If we're playing nice with the Invicti now then I guess I'd better play along.'

'For the moment at least. I'll get Ladipo to contact the college and arrange a time.'

She directs her attention back to her papers and starts shuffling again.

'Was that all?' I ask, more than a little irritated that she's dragged me up here for a meeting that could easily have been a phone call.

She puts the papers down again and fixes me with a stare.

'Drop the attitude, would you?' she says. 'I'm begging you, for both of our sakes. If it wasn't already obvious to you, I'm drowning here, and I'm doing my best, so maybe you could try not being a dick about it.'

'All right,' I say, holding my hands up in surrender. 'Don't mind me. I'll just scuttle back to the college like a good little Seeker.'

'What did I *just* say?'

'I'm being nice!'

Kulika drops her head into her hands and rubs at her eyes. She looks exhausted. It's late enough that it's dark outside, though that doesn't mean much at this time of year. If I had to guess, I would say her problem is more about sleepless nights than the late hour.

'What am I doing here?' she mutters.

'I know it's all going to shit, Kulika, but it's not your fault,' I say, adopting my most conciliatory tone of voice. 'With the vote and the infighting and Drake buggering off to Europe... Maybe he knew everything was going down the drain and decided to get out while he still could. There's nothing stopping you from doing the same. Don't you feel like we're fighting a losing battle here?'

She groans into her hands. 'I can't just give up.'

'You really can. It's easy. You just... give up. Done. Dusted. Walk away. It's what I'd do.'

'Maybe you would today,' she says, lifting her head, 'but what about tomorrow, when it's not Matthew Felton who's died, but someone else, some human we could have protected? You might be feeling disillusioned at the moment, Jack, but you know how important our work is.'

'I know how important it *was*,' I correct her. 'But things have changed, haven't they? No one's even pretending that our role is about protecting humans anymore. If the vote made anything clear, it's that most of the Silver couldn't care less about them. All we're arguing about now is what would make *our* lives easier. I'm starting to think a lot of people are only pro-revelation because it means better access to the walking human blood supply.'

Kulika looks vaguely horrified. 'I don't believe that. I don't think you believe that either.'

'Just think about it for a minute. No secrecy pact means no Seekers, which means no restrictions on the Silver openly attacking humans whenever they want. What are the police going to do about it? What's *anyone* going to do about it?'

'The Primus would make new laws. He wouldn't just hang the humans out to dry.'

'With the Secundus and the Tertius nipping at his heels, I think he'll be directing all his energy into keeping his position. If a few humans die, what does he care?'

'He's been the Primus for millennia, Jack. Thousands of years. That's not going to change.'

'Just because it never has before?' I snort. 'You sound as naïve as everyone seems to think I am.'

She's taken aback by that, enough that she has to give it a moment's thought before replying.

'But if there were no restrictions, it would mean all-out war. Silver against humans. Even if the Primus was no longer in power, people wouldn't be stupid enough to risk that.'

'Why not? We'd win. Easily.'

This is what I've come to realise recently: there is no way for the Silver to lose. We're so supernaturally strong and so hard to kill that we can make our own rules. A lot of the Silver behave like psychopaths – whether because it's always been their nature, or as a result of our physical superiority, or as a byproduct of the kind of apathy you pick up when you've seen it all over a long lifetime – and they don't care about humans at all. They don't care about maintaining the status quo, either. They'd burn it all up if it made life more interesting, or got them easier access to the things they want.

All they needed was a spark.

'The world would change,' I continue, 'but we'd still be on top. Apex predators, controlling humans just like we do now, only it wouldn't be a secret anymore. Maybe it would be a more honest way to live. Maybe Tabitha was right about that, if nothing else.'

When Tabitha talked to me about her pro-reveal stance on the night of the vote, that had been her defence: spending our lives in secrecy is a deception that crushes you a little more every day. It never bothered me. I like being in the shadows. I like knowing something that the rest of the world doesn't, though that probably doesn't reflect well on me. I have no problem with secrets, as long as they're not harming anyone, and I firmly believe that keeping the Silver in the dark is the best for everyone.

But I also believe that I'm now in the minority. Sooner or later, the scales are going to tip.

'Boyd told me,' Kulika says. 'About the abduction, I mean. The memory loss. I was going to ask if you were okay, but it sounds like you're really not.'

'It's got me thinking about things,' I say.

'I can see that. I don't think this is the time to be making big decisions, though. We don't know what you might have been drugged with.'

'I'm fine, Kulika. Ed's doing his tests, but I'm sure it was just the same tranquilliser the Invicti used on Drake. It's not like it's affecting my brain.'

She gives me a long, hard look. 'And you don't remember anything?'

'Nope. It's all a blank.'

'I hate this,' she says, kicking back in her chair. 'The vote, Felton's death, your abduction… It feels like everything's coming to a head, but I don't know why I feel that way and I can't see any of the pieces. And with Baron Drake away… Fuck, it's bad timing.'

'Boyd filled you in on the latest in the case?'

'He did. It doesn't look good for Dr Ross, does it?'

'No,' I agree. 'It doesn't. And with what she knows about weird chemicals that can fuck up the Silver, I think you're right to be worried. Until we track her down, I think we should *all* be worried.'

'Then I'll let you get back to work. I'll call next time, I promise.'

'Thanks,' I say. 'And if you ever need to talk…'

It's a bit weird for me to offer this, I know, and Kulika seems to notice that weirdness too. It feels like something Cam would say, not me. The thing is, we're both struggling with our own crises at the moment, so maybe we can help each other. I doubt she'll be calling me about anything not work-related, but I feel better for having left the door open for her.

Maybe, with a little encouragement, she might walk through.

We say our goodbyes. I'm just leaving the room when she says, 'Merry Christmas.'

'Huh?' I turn back.

'It's Christmas Eve, Jack. I know you've been out of it for a while, but surely you haven't forgotten about Christmas?'

'No,' I lie. 'Of course not. Yeah, Merry Christmas.'

'You forgot, didn't you?' she says.

'No. Maybe. Got to go.'

* * *

I check the time on my phone as I rush from Drake's office, out of the house and back towards town. It's already half five. If there weren't so many bastard people around then I could use Silver speed, but the streets are so busy that there's no way it would go unremarked. I settle for running at normal, human speed, which gets me to the Westgate within ten minutes.

And straight into the fourth circle of hell.

The place is rammed. I know, I know: what did I expect, going into the city's biggest shopping centre in the late afternoon on Christmas Eve? But holy shit, the place is *rammed*.

Here's the problem: as already noted, Cam loves Christmas. He doesn't just love it, he loves it like a five-year-old who's more excited by the wrapping paper than the actual presents, and will be bawling his eyes out by lunchtime because he's got himself all overexcited and peaked too soon, but still thinks it's brilliant because he believes in the magic and the wonder and the specialness of the whole day. That's how much Cam loves Christmas.

And I've forgotten to get him a present. Or a stocking. Or the customary pyjamas that we always exchange on the night of Christmas Eve. I am a *terrible* friend.

With Cam having such a shit time of things recently, and with the guilt I still feel for worrying him during the week that I was missing, there's no way I can let him down. So here I am, even though shopping on Christmas Eve feels like a suicide mission, desperately trawling through the shoddy remnants left behind by more organised shoppers as I try to cobble together some passable Christmas cheer for my best, possibly only, friend in the world.

When I finally struggle back to the college with a pathetic collection of gag gifts and a pair of cat-print polyester pyjamas, all beautifully wrapped in the bags from the shops where I purchased them, I find the whole squad waiting for me in the lodge.

'Hey,' I greet them.

Naia and Cam exchange glances. Their expressions are unreadable, but it's perfectly clear from the look on Raul's face that they weren't expecting me to walk in, and that they weren't, in fact, waiting for me at all.

'What's going on?' I ask, feeling the smile sliding off my face. 'Did something happen?'

All three of them look at each other this time, as though they're deciding whether or not they can trust me. That can't be good. Have they found something suspicious in my blood? Or has the GPS record from Tabitha's car thrown up something weird?

'What is it?' I say.

It's Cam who answers.

'Let's go over to the office,' he says. 'I think you should be sitting down for this.'

As we walk across the quad, my stomach is doing anxious flips. I don't know what they've found, but it can't be good. If Cam wants to discuss it with me alone, then either he thinks I've done something wrong, or it's so awful that it's going to devastate me. I can't decide which would be worse.

For a brief moment, I think about running.

It feels like an age has passed before we're sitting in one of the interview rooms together, just me and Cam, facing each other across the table that we usually reserve for interrogating suspects side by side. My shopping bags are piled haphazardly against the wall, all but forgotten as my brain rushes through the possibilities, desperately trying to understand why we're here before the hammer falls.

'What is it?' I ask, the moment we've sat down. 'Why all the secrecy?'

'Jack, it's…' He rubs his hand across his mouth, looking down at the table top as though he's searching for the right words. 'We need to talk about Tabitha.'

'Okay.'

This isn't a surprise. What with me being found in her car, and her scent on my skin when I woke up, not to mention her expertise in pharmaceuticals, we know she's mixed up in this. But I can tell from Cam's tone that they've found something new. Something worse.

'Ed got the results back from your blood tests,' he says.

'Okay…'

'The drug he found in the samples he took from you was the same formula as the drug from the tranquilliser vials that were stolen from the Invicti.'

'Okay…' I say again. I'm still waiting for the punchline, because none of this is news. It's exactly what we expected to find.

'The problem is that the single remaining dart out of that stolen pack would never have contained enough of the drug to keep you sedated for an entire week.'

'No, but Tabitha is the one who put that formula together. She knows how to make the drug herself. I thought we were assuming that she'd made more?'

'Which would make sense,' Cam says, 'if there were a build up of that drug's by-products in your bloodstream. But Ed can't find any evidence of that. In fact, he only found enough for half a dose, almost as though half of the tranquilliser in the last dart had been used to knock you out when you were taken, and the other half had been used to knock you out just before you were found.' I know things are about to go tits up for me at this point, because he's struggling to maintain eye contact. 'It looks a bit like someone abducted you, then kept you somewhere for the week, awake and fully conscious. That's what Ed says, anyway. So the question becomes: why can't you remember it?'

'I can't explain that,' I say, clutching at the edge of the table as my world spins off its axis. 'I don't know what to tell you, Cam.'

He chews at his lip before replying. 'There's more.'

My stomach drops, and keeps churning when he doesn't immediately continue. It looks as though he's searching for the right words.

'Just tell me,' I say.

'Ed found a memory stick in her car. She's planning to kill the Primus.'

'What? I know she voted against him, but why would she want him dead? And how is that even possible? Isn't he basically indestructible?'

'I'll let Ed explain the science,' Cam says, pulling out his phone. He dials the lab and puts the call on speaker when Ed picks up. 'I'm with Jack now. Can you tell us what you found on the memory stick?'

'Right.' Ed's voice sounds muffled for a moment before he turns his full attention to the phone. 'Well, there were a lot of formulae. A lot of notes, too. It looks like Dr Ross has been trying to recreate Dr Jay's serum. We suspected as much already, because it's what was used on Felton, but the copy she's made isn't as effective as the original. What the notes make clear is that she was trying to find a way to refine the version she made in order to make it as strong as the serum in Dr Jay's blood, but as far as I can make out, she didn't have any luck.'

He stops talking there, as though that's the end of the story.

'What's that got to do with killing the Primus?' I ask when he fails to elaborate.

'Ah. Right. Yes. As we know, Matthew Felton had only

been Silver for a few decades. That's why the version of the serum we found in his body proved lethal. When used on any Silver up to a couple of hundred years old, Dr Ross's notes indicate her copy serum would probably have the same effect. However, as we know, the Primus is several *millennia* old.'

'In fact,' Cam adds, 'he's the only living Silver who is that old.'

'Which is where Dr Ross's notes come in again,' Ed continues. 'She specifically references her plan to refine the serum so that it would be capable of killing a Silver several millennia old, and since there is only one…'

'You think she's planning to use the new serum to kill the Primus,' I finish.

'Or she *was* planning it,' Ed says. 'Because from everything I'm seeing, I don't think it would have been possible for her to make a serum as strong as Dr Jay's original from the formulae she has. Whatever Dr Jay did to make his own version so potent, he didn't make a note of it.'

'So we don't have to worry?' I ask. 'If she can't refine the serum so it's strong enough to kill the Primus, then what's the problem?'

'We're worried that she's planning it at all, Jack,' says Cam. 'You know better than anyone how resourceful she is. If this doesn't work, maybe she'll find another way. Which is why, if you remember anything about your missing week, or maybe something she said when you were still together, then we need to know.'

'You think I wouldn't tell you, Cam? If I knew anything about what she was thinking, I would tell you. I would already have told you. You know that.'

He looks at me for a long moment, searching my face for the truth of my words. I realise then that he doesn't believe me, not entirely, and I don't think I've ever felt so shitty in my life.

'You think I'd lie to you about this?' I ask, my voice cracking.

'No,' he says quickly, 'of course not.' But he doesn't look reassured.

'Why would I lie?'

'I'm not saying you're lying, Jack. But we don't know what that drug did to you. There's no way to know without reproducing it and testing it on a bunch of Silver—'

'Which is far too dangerous to contemplate,' Ed says. 'I'm not going to repeat Dr Jay's mistakes, Cam. I've told you that.'

'And with good reason, I know.' Cam sighs, then looks at me mournfully. 'It's just that we don't understand what happened to you, and that scares me.'

I lean across the table and take his hand in mine, squeezing it in an attempt to bring him back to me.

'I'll do anything you want,' I say. 'When we have the car GPS route, we can retrace Tabitha's steps to see if there's anything I recognise. Or we can go through her place again and see if anything sparks a memory. Whatever you want.'

After a moment's consideration, he says, 'Hypnosis? Would you try that?'

From the phone, Ed snorts derisively.

I hesitate, because I've seen enough true crime TV to know that firstly, hypnotism is junk science when it comes to retrieving lost memories, and secondly, you never know what you might do when under the suggestive influence of someone you've let inside your mind.

But in the end, I can't say no. I've already said I'll try anything.

To get Cam back on side, I agree.

10

UNDER THE CIRCUMSTANCES, Christmas at Solomon College is a very strange affair.

Cam and I go ahead with our usual Christmas Eve plans, in his rooms, of course, since mine are still scattered over the floor of Boyd's office. We curl up on his sofa to watch *Die Hard*, Cam wearing his awful last-minute cat pyjamas and me wearing the beautiful cotton set he's had bespoke printed for me with a cute cartoon vampire Jack.

Everything feels off. After he spent the early evening practically interrogating me, I knew it was going to be awkward, but I hoped we'd get through it somehow. It turns out that not even a vat of popcorn and a whole tub of ice cream can fully diffuse the tension between us. By the time I leave his rooms to go back to my own makeshift ones – which is weird in and of itself, because normally I'd be staying the night – I'm preparing for a decidedly blue Christmas.

When I wake up on Christmas Day, it's snowing. Fucking typical, isn't it, that it happens when Cam and I are on the outs? If it were any other year, Cam would be running breathless to my door in his pyjamas at sunrise, yelling with excitement to see actual snow falling on actual Christmas. He probably would have dragged me outside in my slippers for a snowball fight, too distracted even to look at his stocking before getting out in the gorgeous blank canvas the snow has created in the college quad.

And the view of the quad from my window really is gorgeous, particularly when seen in the dawn, enclosed on all four sides by warm yellow limestone and twinkling lights that the gardeners have draped in the trees. It doesn't mean much without Cam, though.

I wait for half an hour, then another, cursing the cruelty of my body clock in waking me this early when it's increasingly clear that Cam will not be joining me. I should have slept in. I should have slept through the whole damn day. Eventually, I give up and drag myself through the shower, into a bunch of ill-fitting clothes that I hate, then downstairs to the canteen. I should have done some shopping for myself yesterday too, but my patience and my wallet will only stretch so far.

I stop at Cam's on my way to breakfast to hang his stocking on his door handle. I consider knocking, but in the end I decide against it. Perhaps it's the wrong choice, but I don't think I can face more rejection from him right now, so instead of dealing with the issue I avoid it instead, and slink off to the canteen alone.

The place is a hive of activity. Christmas Day is a big deal here, because it's the only time we rope in everyone, Silver and human, to decorate and celebrate together. It's not the easiest of juggling acts, because the inclination to let loose when you're in the party mood is pretty strong, but we've yet to have a major incident that we couldn't explain away. Given how separate the Seekers often are from the students and faculty of the college – except the ones in the lab, of course – it's a good chance for the Silver members to mix with each other, as well as with the human members of staff who keep the place running for us. The old captain always said it was worth the risk of the odd minor indiscretion, for college morale. I'm a little surprised to find that, apparently, Boyd agrees.

In the kitchen, cooking for the main event is underway, so breakfast is piled on a help-yourself counter at the side of the room. Naia's sitting alone at a table in the centre of the canteen, and it looks as though she's loaded it with half the buffet already.

'Jack,' she yells through a mouthful of smoked salmon. 'Merry Christmas!'

I cringe. 'Thanks. How about, as a special Christmas present to me and everyone else, you mark the day by closing your mouth while you chew?'

'Someone woke up pissy,' she spits, pointedly failing to grant my request. 'You need to get laid.'

'That's your answer to everything.' I reach to take a croissant from her food mountain, but she slaps my hand away before I can make off with my prize.

'Get your own.'

'You can't seriously be planning to eat all of this yourself.'

'I can and I am,' she replies, chomping into the croissant in question. 'I have to line my stomach.' She toasts me with a glass of what I thought was orange juice, but I now realise must be Buck's Fizz.

'A bit early, isn't it?' Raul says as he joins us.

'Just trying to make Jack proud,' Naia says, then she downs the glass and goes to pour herself another. Raul and I follow her to the buffet to gather our own, more modest breakfasts. All the while, I have one eye on the door, waiting for Cam to join us. By the time Raul and I have finished our food and Naia's necked her fifth glass of fizz, I'm starting to despair.

'About your housing situation,' Naia says to me as she finally pushes away her empty plates.

'No,' I say. 'I'm *still* not moving in with you.'

'Well, I think you're being very stubborn.'

'And I think you're being suspiciously persistent.'

'Be realistic, Jack. You're living in a tiny college guest room and it'll be ages before your old place is ready for you to move back in. They have to rebuild the whole fucking floor.'

'And whose fault is that, exactly?' I ask. Naia pretends that she hasn't heard and breezes on with her sales pitch.

'What I'm saying is that you don't have a lot of other options. The rent's decent, the deposit's paid, and you can even have the first month free, on me. As your Christmas present.'

'I haven't really settled in to my rooms,' Raul interjects, 'so if you're looking for someone to—'

Naia cuts him off.

'You can move in this week,' she says to me. 'No hassle. I'll help carry your stuff.'

'Naia, for the millionth time, I am not moving in with you.' Then I realise that she's pushing too hard. *Way* too hard. I know she wants to fill the room, but I assumed it was just a money thing. Now she's offering to pay my first month's rent *and* my deposit? That's more than a little fishy. 'Wait a minute. What's really going on here? Why are you so desperate to get me – and me in particular – to move in with you?'

She looks down at the table top for a moment, fiddling with the crumbs she's left strewn across it. 'No reason.'

'No reason, my arse. Spill it.'

I'm not expecting a response, because this is Naia and she doesn't share. The fact that she isn't already yelling at me to fuck off and keep my nose out of her business is a good indication that there's something truly wrong here.

'It's… not going brilliantly,' she says. 'Everyone's getting stuck in their feelings, and I can't cope with it.'

As I've mentioned before, Naia does not do feelings. Raul, however, very much does. At the first hint of an emotional issue, he's leaning across the table towards Naia with a sympathetic expression fixed on his face.

'Do you want to talk about it?' he asks.

This is definitely the wrong tack with Naia. I expect her to tell Raul to fuck off this time, but she surprises me again. It makes me wonder whether I've been the one taking the wrong tack all these years.

'It's Rajni,' she says. 'She's not happy.'

'Okay,' says Raul. 'Why not?'

'It's complicated. She hasn't said as much, but I don't think she likes being the only pansexual in a house full of straight people. She feels isolated, I guess.'

'So, just to be clear,' I say. 'You don't want me to move in because you want to live with me, you want me to move in to be Rajni's mistress?'

'No! It's not like we're all having sex with each other. I just thought she might feel less alone if you were there too, and if you ended up hitting it off, would that really be such a bad thing for either of you?'

'Stop trying to matchmake, Naia. You're crap at it.'

'I just want everyone to stop fighting!' Naia leans back in her chair and groans. 'They're not even doing it properly. They won't shout at each other, so instead they just stop talking to each other and Rajni's threatening to pull out of the whole thing, but if she does then Chris won't move in, and if he doesn't then we lose Bonnie, which just leaves me and Jamie, and suddenly I'd be living on my own with one solitary guy like we're a real couple and that is *not* what I signed up for at all. I just wish everyone would chill the fuck out.'

'Relationships are tough,' Raul says sympathetically.

'Emotions are tough,' Naia corrects him. 'Where the hell is Cam when I need him?'

'I haven't seen him this morning,' I say.

'He's helping to decorate the common room,' Raul says.

'Right, then,' Naia says, rising from the ruins of her breakfast, 'that's where I'm going too.'

Cam and Naia spend the morning deep in conversation as they hang tinsel and put Naia's housing woes to rights. By the time lunch rolls around, Naia looks much happier, but Cam and I still haven't said a word to each other. When he does glance in my direction, he gives me a look that, on anyone other than Cam, I might characterise as unfriendly. But surely not on him, I tell myself. He wouldn't be unfriendly to one of his best friends just because of a slight cloud of suspicion hanging over her, would he? Not after all these years of loyalty and trust.

Right?

By mid-afternoon, I've had enough. I corner him in the corridor while he's going on a drinks run, determined not to let him leave until we're friends again.

'I'm not angry with you, Jack,' he says when I ask him why he is. 'I've just got a lot to think about. Things are changing too fast for me to keep up. And I'm worried about you.'

'Why would you be worried about me? I'm fine.'

He gives me a look, the one he always gives me when he knows I'm bullshitting him. I don't know how he always manages to spot it, but he does.

'Okay, I'm a little distracted,' I admit. 'But so are you.'

'You've been weird ever since we found you in Tabitha's

car,' he says. 'And I understand why. I know you're dealing with the aftermath, and that it must have been disorienting and scary and probably brought up all sorts of feelings you don't want to think about, but I just wish you'd talk to me about it. I can feel you holding back, but I have no idea what you're actually *feeling*. It worries me. It means I don't know how to act around you.'

'I'm fine, Cam.'

'No,' he says, getting pissed off now. 'You're not. You're on edge, like you're always looking over your shoulder for something, and I get it. I really do. But you're too stubborn to admit that this has affected you. And it's not just that Tabitha took you. It's like part of you wishes she'd never brought you back. Do you even want to track her down and bring her to justice, or would you rather be out there with her now, doing whatever it was you were doing in your lost week?'

'How can you even ask me that? Of course I want to find her. She belongs in a box.'

'Really? Why? You think Matthew Felton deserved what he got. You can't deny that, Jack, because you've already told me as much. If all Tabitha did was kill Felton, why would you want to punish her at all?'

'The formulae she's making. Ed said—'

'Yeah, Ed said, and he's right. So why do I still feel like you have one foot out of the door?'

'You said it yourself, Cam: things are changing. The Seekers are changing. But that doesn't mean things have to change between the two of us.'

'Doesn't it?'

His expression is so bleak, so pleading, that I want to pull him into my arms and hold him. At any other time, that's exactly what I would have done, but in this moment we are so far apart I'm not sure how to reach across the gulf between us. We both know there's something wrong and neither of us, not even Cam, knows how to fix it.

'You're my best friend,' I say to him. 'You always will be, whatever happens.'

'I don't know.' He looks away and the wrench in my chest is agony. 'Maybe we're just going in different directions.'

'What do you mean?'

'You remember when we went to see the Invicti in Henley?' His eyes are fixed on the floor as he speaks. 'The Secundus offered me the Fidelis.'

'What?'

'He offered me the Fidelis blade, Jack. He offered me a place in the Solis Invicti.'

It's a stupid old ritual that's more than a little phallic, if you ask me. When the Secundus wants to invite someone to join the Solis Invicti, he offers them the dagger he carries on his belt: the Fidelis blade. It's a fancy thing, all shiny with a ridiculously extravagant jewel set in the hilt, and far from practical for everyday use. If the candidate wants to accept, they cut themselves on the blade and there's some kind of blood exchange where they swear to be faithful to the Primus and all that bollocks, then they're bound for life to a corrupt organisation that immorally serves the most powerful Silver in history.

It's archaic, it's more than a little unhygienic, and it's been Cam's dream for as long as I've known him.

'You're joining the Invicti?' I ask in a voice that comes out too quiet.

'I said no.'

'What? But you've always wanted to be one of them.'

'I didn't want to leave you all, not like this. Not with things the way they are. You're my family, but now everything's falling apart and I... I don't know what to do anymore. Maybe I made a mistake.' He leans against the wall and tips his head back until it thunks against the plaster. 'Maybe I should have said yes.'

On the outside, I'm trying to keep my cool, but internally I am freaking the fuck out.

I can't lose Cam. I can't.

'But what about everything they've done?' I say desperately. 'The murders at Windsor's parties, the vote, the formulae Tabitha's been concocting—'

'They're just as eager to catch Tabitha as we are,' he says, 'and everything else... There are always bad apples. It doesn't mean the whole of the Solis Invicti is bad, any more than the existence of a few scab murderers means that all the Silver are bad. And I'm not going to pretend that the pro-reveal rebels don't have some good points. If that's the way we're going, and we both know it is, then I'm better off with the Invicti than I am here. We both would be.' He says these last words with a pointed look.

He can't be serious.

'You've lost your mind if you think I'd join up with them. After everything they did to me with Tabitha? Not a chance.'

'I guess I should have expected that.'

I've hardly been shy with my opinions about the Invicti, but he still seems disappointed.

'And let's be honest, Cam: they wouldn't take me anyway. I'm not the kind of obedient little soldier they like for their recruits.'

'But I am?' he says.

Uh-oh.

'I didn't mean—'

'No, you did. You think that just because I'm more cautious than you are, because I try to see things from every side before writing people off, that I'm some kind of biddable idiot with stars in his eyes. Did you ever think that after centuries of living among these people, I might understand them slightly better than you do?'

'I think I understand them well enough.'

'But that's the problem right there: you actually don't. You keep expecting them to be human. You keep holding us all to human standards, but we're not human. Our perspective on life isn't like yours. Nothing is black and white, good or bad, and you can't treat it as though it is, or it should be. That's not how the world works, however much you want it to. You'll see that eventually, like the rest of us do. We've seen and lived through more than you can possibly imagine, and maybe it's a tiny bit arrogant for you to assume you know better than we do after just two decades Silver, or to expect me to hate the Invicti just because you do.'

'Cam, I didn't—'

'I need to get back to Naia.'

He pushes off from the wall and disappears down the corridor without a backward glance.

Shit.

I royally fucked that up, but I'm not sure how I can fix it. The problem is that Cam has more reverence for tradition than I do. He respects the status quo because he thinks it's there for a reason, but to me that sort of complacency just feels like stagnation and resistance to change. In my book, having life experience doesn't make the older Silver right, it just makes them old. Whatever their age, after all they've done over the past year, I'm never going to be persuaded that the Solis Invicti aren't rotten to the core, and Cam's never going to be persuaded that they are.

He's going to choose them over me, and there's nothing I can do to stop him.

11

THE SOLOMON COLLEGE party is in full swing in the bar by nine o'clock, liberally lubricated by mulled wine and egg nog, but I'm not joining in.

Cam has spoken to me only briefly since our argument earlier today, to thank me politely for the shitty stocking gifts I left hanging from his door this morning. His forced courtesy made me feel even worse when I got back to my borrowed rooms to change for dinner and found what he'd left me: not a stocking, but a whole suitcase of new clothes in exactly the right sizes and styles. Because of him, I had something to wear this evening that didn't come from the college lost property box. His thoughtful generosity makes me feel so awful that I want to be sick.

Now, dolled up in a leather dress and red heels from Cam's gift box that are both totally me, I'm feeling awkward and alone. I want to go over and thank him, but every time I look over in his direction – he's standing at the bar helping to serve drinks – he looks away. He must know I'm here, because his nose is so sensitive that I'm sure he would have picked up my scent the moment I walked in the room, which means he's avoiding my gaze deliberately. If he's not ready to talk to me, it feels like a dick move to force myself on him, so here I am in the corner on my own with my boring human beverage, pretending that I'm enjoying the cheesy music.

Cam's right: it's all falling apart. I don't feel like I belong here anymore.

I'm looking around the room, trying to work out if I can make a break for the door without anyone noticing, when the rest of the Seekers walk in, and they're not alone. Naia has brought her new housemate, Rajni, and she's ushering her in my direction.

I cast around for someone to talk to, *anyone* to help me escape the awkwardness of this impending encounter, but everyone in my vicinity is deep in conversation with their neighbours, leaving me isolated as a prime target. I could just run, but I've wasted time looking for alternatives and now they're standing right in front of me, Naia smug in her usual workwear and Rajni radiant in her party gear.

'Jack!' Naia grins. 'You remember Rajni, right? Oh, look, there's someone I need to speak to.' And just like that, without even bothering to make a convincing excuse, she saunters off into the party crowd, leaving me and Rajni alone.

'Hi,' Rajni says, peeking up at me through her long eyelashes with a smile.

'Um, hi.'

There's no denying that she is beautiful. She's shorter than me by a good few inches, with long, black hair that curls over her shoulders in waves I want to gather up in my hands. Her skin is mid-brown with a golden shimmer that I guess she's achieved by applying lotion; there's an irresistible mango scent that wafts around her as she moves. It's making me thirsty. Between that and her teeny dress, which leaves her entire back and most of her thighs naked, I'm worried I might start drooling.

'Naia said you were looking for a place to stay,' she says.

Goddammit, Naia. This is the last thing I need right now.

I don't think I'm just imagining Rajni's seductive tone, but I can't work out whether she's using it because she wants to get me to move into her house, or into her bed. Given that she is the living embodiment of Venus while I am a mess who is still growing back her eyebrows, the latter seems unlikely.

'Yeah, I'm sorry,' I say, 'but I actually already have a new place.'

'Oh.' Rajni looks crestfallen enough that I think I have my answer, but then she looks up at me again with a twinkle in her eye and says, 'Want to dance anyway?'

Panic. Full-on panic.

'Um…' Then I spot Ed loitering by the bar doorway, looking about as comfortable as I do. I wave him over. 'Ed! You have to meet Rajni, one of Naia's housemates.'

He looks a little confused as to why this introduction is so urgent, but he smiles and says hello, then exchanges a little smalltalk about the weather: isn't the snow nice, but slippery, and a shame it goes grey so quickly, et cetera. Any lingering sizzle between me and Rajni is thoroughly quenched, just as I hoped it would be. By the time Ed starts struggling for more meteorological observations, Rajni is making her excuses and heading back to join Naia.

Disaster averted, for the moment at least, leaving me alone with Ed. This is convenient, because he has some information that I need to extract. The question is whether or not I'll be able to do that without raising suspicions.

'I've been thinking about what you said yesterday,' I say, coming at the subject obliquely. 'About Tabitha trying to refine the serum.'

'Oh?' Ed replies vaguely. He's looking around the room as

though he's wondering how long he has to stay. It makes me question where his girlfriend is, because usually she fills in where Ed's social skills are lacking, but I guess I should be grateful that he's on his own tonight. This would be harder with a witness.

I might as well go for it.

'Here's the thing: couldn't she just extract the old serum – the super potent one – straight from Dr Jay's body? If what you say about his toxic saliva is true, then wouldn't his blood be strong enough to kill the Primus?'

Ed smiles, relieved to be on familiar ground. 'In principle, sure. But Dr Jay's been buried for decades now.'

'Somewhere secret?' I push him. 'Somewhere Tabitha doesn't know about?'

Ed opens his mouth to answer, then freezes. His face has gone a sickly pale.

'Ed?' I shake him a little by the shoulder, but he just carries on staring into space for several long seconds.

Eventually, he whispers, 'Oh shit,' then promptly turns around and delves into the party crowd, searching for someone on the dance floor. I follow hot on his heels. Eventually, leaning up against the DJ booth, we find Cam.

'We've got to go,' Ed yells into his ear. 'Right now.'

'I'm not leaving the party,' Cam says to Ed. 'I'm having a good time.' He doesn't even look my way.

'It's important,' Ed insists.

'It's *Christmas*,' Cam replies, then he turns back to the booth and starts scrolling through songs.

But Ed's reached his limit. He grabs Cam by the wrist and drags him from the booth, across the dance floor and out of the bar. I trail behind them, adopting an expression of mild interest and concern. When we get out into the quad, it's dark and snowy. Cam rubs at his wrist and gives Ed an offended look.

'I'm sorry,' Ed says, 'but it really is important. Please. Just listen.'

A flicker of doubt crosses Cam's face. He glances at me before returning his attention to Ed.

'What is it?' he asks.

'Something Jack said about whether Tabitha would be able to extract the old serum from Dr Jay's body.'

'Would that work?' Cam asks.

'I think so.'

'It would be enough to kill the Primus?' Cam looks alarmed now, and it strikes me that he already has one foot out of the door, bent on his new purpose in the Invicti as the Primus's bodyguard. That hurts.

'I don't see why it wouldn't be,' Ed says. 'Which is why you need to tell me right now: where did the Invicti bury Dr Jay?'

Cam's brow crinkles in confusion. 'Why would the Invicti have him?'

'You mean they *don't*?' The first signs of relief appear on Ed's face, and I can tell he thinks that if the Invicti don't have Khalyed, there's no way Tabitha would have been able to find him.

'No. He's in Baron Drake's cellar. In a box.'

'*What?*' Ed yells.

After all this time, and after all the effort that went into burying Khalyed's lethal formula, keeping it out of the hands of people who might intend harm with it, Drake just buried it under his house with a bunch of psychopathic Silver murderers. What a joke.

'Does Tabitha know this?' I ask.

Cam gulps then whispers, 'Yes.'

With that, the party's over for all of us.

I am not exaggerating when I say that Drake's cellar is a

labyrinth. It's dim, it's dusty, and the tight, winding corridors seem to go on for miles in every direction. They all look the same, too: wall after wall lined with doors, each one locking away one of the Silver that the baron has decreed will serve their sentences here in the dark. The only things that differentiate one door from another are the names fixed to the plaques on each one or, if you're someone as dangerous as Khalyed, perhaps no name at all. If you don't know exactly where you're going, it's fiendishly easy to get lost. Since I've spent most of my time in the Seekers either avoiding the cellar or imprisoning people who are only being boxed for the short-term – those berths are all up front, easy to access – I have no idea where to start looking.

I hate it here. Always have, always will. I've never wanted to delve into the shallowest realms of this cellar, let alone the deepest, and yet here we are, rushing through the silent passages in the dead of Christmas Night. Down here, we are the only creatures stirring.

At least, I hope so.

'I don't know,' Kulika is muttering to herself as she reads door after door.

We're well past the corridors I've travelled before, into the depths of the store. I had no idea the place was spread over multiple levels, but we've gone down three staircases already and the ground beneath our feet is nothing but dirt. It's playing hell with my fancy red heels. There are no bulbs hanging from the ceilings, no torches to light our way, just cobweb-filled recesses in the walls where candles might once have burned.

'I don't recognise any of this,' Cam says, shining his torch on one door after another. 'I think it was back the other way.'

'Are you sure this is even the right floor?' Ed asks.

'Yes,' Cam says, but he doesn't sound sure at all.

'Were there really no records?' Ed asks Kulika.

'No.' She's starting to lose her rag. 'Think about it logically, Dr Castell. If you had the location of the most potent Silver poison in the world – a poison that's strong enough to kill the Primus, apparently – then would you write it down in a handy notebook and keep it in your desk drawer?'

'I suppose not,' Ed mumbles.

'Yeah, I wouldn't either. It would be pretty stupid, right? So what makes you think that Baron Drake is stupid enough to keep Dr Khalyed's resting place anywhere but in his head?'

'Shame he's not here,' Cam says.

'Oh, yeah,' I agree, going heavy on the sarcasm. 'Terrible shame.'

'You're not helping, Jack,' Kulika sighs.

'Wait, wait…' Cam has disappeared along the corridor, turning the corner so he's out of sight. 'This seems like… Maybe.'

We follow him. After all, no one else has any bright ideas, and Cam was the only one of us who was actually there when Dr Khalyed was boxed. When we join him, he's staring at one door in particular.

'It smells like it's around here,' Cam explains. 'But I can't pinpoint it.'

Ed pushes his glasses up on his head – still absent one lens, I notice – and squints at the name plate on the doors as though he is genuinely short sighted. I suppose he's been playing the part so long that it's sunk into his being.

'Something strange about this…' Ed says, more to himself than to us.

'What does it say?' Kulika asks.

'Nothing, in fact,' Ed replies. 'It's a symbol. Some kind of shorthand.'

I turn to Kulika, who's standing behind me, bringing up

the rear. 'Does Drake ever use shorthand?'

'Not that I know of. But maybe.'

'No, wait,' Ed says. He's moved on to the next door now and is examining its plaque just as closely as he did the first. 'They're all symbols, but they're not shorthand. It's more like… hieroglyphs?'

'Oh, come off it,' I say. 'This place hasn't been here that long.'

'No, but maybe the person running it has. How old is our baron, exactly?'

'Not that old,' I snort, but then I see that the others are exchanging odd looks. 'Is he?'

'They're pictographs,' Ed says, his focus still on the door plaques. 'See? Here's a little wave, and this one's a tree, and here's some sort of swirly thing—'

'Okay,' I interrupt, 'but what do they *mean*?'

I look at Ed. Ed looks at Cam. Cam looks at Kulika. Kulika shrugs.

'No one?' I ask. 'No ideas at all?'

'Wait…' Cam says, then he's off down the corridor again, disappearing into the darkness. Ed hurries after him, following the symbols and muttering. We let them go on ahead.

'Can't you just call Drake?' I ask Kulika.

'I've already left him a message, but I gather he's out of phone reception a lot.'

'In Europe?' I ask.

'In the mountains. Or on the Mediterranean. Carlotta has a yacht, so they're probably moving about.'

I'm sorry I asked.

'A-ha!' Ed's cry echoes down the bare passageway towards us.

We follow it to find him crouched in front of a particularly imposing-looking door, while Cam sniffs at the crack beneath it.

'Is this it?' Kulika asks.

It certainly looks like the kind of vault you'd choose to imprison someone whose blood is lethal. The frame is metal, of the lumpy, rusted kind you might expect to find in a medieval torture cell, and the door itself is made of wood so old that it looks and feels like stone. It's clearly been here much longer than the twenty-odd years of Dr Jay's incarceration. The biggest clue to its occupant, though, is the emblem on the bronze plaque nailed to its surface: a teardrop shape encircled with flame. If that isn't code for burning blood, then I'm not sure what is.

'It smells like him,' Cam says. 'Have you got the key?'

Kulika fumbles with several bundles of keys before finding the one with the largest, oldest specimens. They're made from the same kind of knobbly iron as the door frame. Each is marked with a symbol that matches the plaques on the doors, and the teardrop flame key opens the lock of Ed's chosen door first time. The moment the lock tumbles, it's evident that this door hasn't been opened for years and years. It swings open with an ominous creak and a puff of dust to reveal the motionless body of a Silver man, chained upright in the shallow recess beyond.

He's still wearing a lab coat and suit, but they're falling off his diminished figure. His dark hair hangs in a straggling mass from his skull and his cheeks are sunk into skin that's pallid not by nature, but because the darkness has bleached it of its normal tone. Worst of all are his eyes, glued shut with bloody tears.

'Christ,' Kulika says, turning away to cough and wipe her face. 'That's pungent.'

She's not wrong. It's never great when you open a box, because the Silver stuck in there will have been festering for at least a while, but this one is different. Usually, a Silver's blood is drained before they're boxed to make sure they're weak enough to be contained, which also means there's very little fluid in their body to rot or moulder. Instead, they just dry out into mummies over the course of their imprisonment, waiting for us to come along and pump them full of blood again when their sentences are complete. It's kind of like inflating a balloon, if the balloon is a murderous superhuman who wants you dead.

This time, with Khalyed, it's different. For whatever reason – probably because the stuff is so dangerous, and because he let himself be boxed voluntarily – the blood hasn't been drained from his body at all. Instead, the veins beneath his sticky skin are green with the stuff, as though it's stagnated during the decades of his tenancy here.

And it *reeks*.

'Jay?' Ed says, his voice barely more than a whisper. 'Jay, it's Ed. Can you hear me?'

He leans in towards the carcass of his former colleague, but Cam pulls him back. Just in time, because a microsecond later Khalyed's blood-rimmed eyes are ripped open and his teeth are snapping in the air where Ed's neck was just a moment before.

'He drinks Silver blood,' Cam reminds Ed sternly.

'I didn't think…' Ed splutters. 'I mean, it's Jay. He's… He wouldn't…'

'He's been in there for decades, Ed. I'm sorry, but he's not your friend anymore.'

Khalyed's eyes are open throughout this exchange, flicking between Ed and Cam as he follows their conversation, but the intelligence that lies beyond them is more animal than Silver. I'm inclined to agree with Cam that whatever mind Khalyed once had is long gone, until the doctor blinks three times in rapid succession. His focus wavers, clears, and comes to rest on Ed.

There's a noise, a rustling sound so quiet that even I can't work out quite what it is. When it comes again, I realise it's a breath. Khalyed is breathing, for the first time in god knows how many years.

'Jay,' Ed says. 'Can you hear me?'

Impossibly, the shell of the man nods.

Ed looks like he's about to cry, but he never loses sight of his purpose here. 'Has anyone been here to see you, to take your blood?' he asks. 'It's very important.'

The remnants of Khalyed give the tiniest shake of his head.

'You're sure?'

Nod.

And then, incredibly, the corpse's breath resolves itself into whispered words.

'Adinde,' he says. 'Cure?'

I don't understand what he's asking, but Ed must because he says, 'Not yet. I'm sorry. Adinde isn't… I'm looking into it.'

Khalyed sighs out one more breath, then lets his eyes close as he gives his strength back to the chains. A moment later, it's as though he never moved at all. Slowly, Ed closes the door on his friend and turns the key in the lock, shutting him away in the dark once more. He doesn't look as though he wants to talk about it, but I need to know.

'Adinde?' I ask. 'A cure for what?'

Ed doesn't answer. Instead, he hands the bundle of keys back to Kulika and makes his way to the staircase that leads out of this necropolis.

'Adinde was a Seeker,' Cam says quietly once he's gone. 'She was married to a friend of ours, the friend who got bitten by Dr Jay, the one who got sick. They were working together to find a cure for him, and maybe for Dr Jay too.'

'Oh,' I say. 'Is that possible?'

Cam shrugs.

'They didn't manage it, though,' I say.

'No,' Cam replies. 'They died.'

He walks away then, following Ed back to the world of the living. Kulika and I are left to trail along behind him.

I guess that means we're done here. On the way to the surface, I memorise the route carefully. After going to all this trouble to find him, I want to make damn sure that we don't lose the doctor again.

12

WE TAKE BOXING Day off, some of us because we overindulged at the Christmas party the night before, and some of us because we need to shower every hour to wash away the memory of Khalyed's decomposing body. Some of us a little of both.

When December twenty-seventh rolls around, Cam and I have achieved a fragile truce. It's nothing like our normal working relationship, but with any luck it'll be effective enough to help us track down Tabitha and close this shitty chapter of our lives once and for all.

We don't have much choice but to work together. You see, there's a good reason that it wasn't Boyd who grilled me about my lost time, or about Tabitha's plot to kill the Primus, and it's this: the captain doesn't know about it. Ed hasn't told him, and neither has Cam. At first I thought this was retaliation for Boyd firing Faiz, but that would be too petty and small-minded for Cam even to consider. It's the kind of thing I would do, but is completely outside of his repertoire.

So no, Cam didn't keep things hush-hush as revenge for Boyd's shitty management style. He did it to protect me. Cam, the one person in my life who can always be trusted to do the right thing and follow the rules, is lying to the captain in order to avoid throwing suspicion on me, which means he really does believe in me, and that makes me feel about fifty times shittier than I already did.

When he knocks at my tiny temporary rooms early that morning – much earlier than I would usually tolerate – I'm penitent enough to muster up a cheerful greeting. He's instantly suspicious.

'What did you do?' he asks.

'What? Nothing!'

'You're smiling at me before ten a.m. You've never smiled at me before ten a.m., not unless you were still drunk from the night before.'

'Forget it then,' I say grumpily.

Well, that was short-lived.

'That's better.' He smiles. 'I was starting to worry that you'd lost your personality along with your memory.'

I groan. 'Why are you poking the bear this early?'

'I've had a call from Ed. He and Naia are going to meet us in the lab. They've got news.'

'Both of them?'

'That's what he said.'

I look down at my vampire Valentine pyjamas and decide that, even by my loose definition, they're probably not appropriate work attire. Besides, they are my new favourite item of clothing and I don't want to lose them to one of Ed's frequent lab accidents.

'Give me five minutes,' I say. 'I'd invite you in, but…' I gesture around at the limited space. There's barely a foot clear on either side of the bed, and there's nowhere to sit that I haven't already covered with my meagre possessions.

'I'll just stand out here and watch the clock on my phone, then.'

Six minutes and forty-eight seconds later – I swear, Cam

is catching whatever's wrong with Boyd – we roll out towards the lab. I'm feeling pretty slick in my new jeans, jumper and Jordans combo. It's not my usual look, but Cam correctly predicted that it would suit me perfectly and be comfortable as fuck. I've topped the outfit with Naia's beanie hat to keep my ears and eyebrows warm. Altogether, I am as cute as a button.

'I did get you some grown-up clothes too, you know,' he says.

'What are you talking about? These clothes are by definition grown-up clothes, because I'm wearing them, and I am a grown up.'

'Says who?'

I thump him in the arm. He pushes me gently but irresistibly into the corridor wall. I tickle him until he lets me go, and by the time we barrel into the lab we're both breathless and laughing like kids playing tag.

Our equilibrium is, for the moment at least, restored.

'Children,' Naia says. She's waiting behind the lab bench with Ed, looking like a headmistress dropping in on a science class. 'Stop pissing about and pay attention.'

'Yes, ma'am,' Cam says, which doesn't help her mood.

'Seriously, guys,' Ed says. 'You're going to want to hear this.'

'Hear what?' I ask.

'We might have found where Dr Ross is hiding,' Naia says.

That shuts us up. The time for messing around is most definitely over.

There are hidden places in every city. You might think a city as overpriced and populous as Oxford would be different, but you'd be wrong. When the Westgate shopping centre got its makeover in 2017, it emptied the Oxford high street. Now more shopfronts stand vacant every month on Cornmarket, Queen's Street and the High, formerly the city's retail hub. If you're looking for somewhere to hide out, you could do worse than heading to the city centre.

Still, everyone is surprised when Tabitha's GPS records and the unique carpet threads Ed found in her car lead us to an abandoned unit on the High Street. It's so close to Solomon College that we walk there in three minutes, door to door.

'This is near where you were shot with the dart, isn't it?' Cam whispers as we approach the property.

'Near enough to spit,' I confirm.

It's a corner unit that used to be an upmarket clothing boutique, upmarket enough that it has bespoke multicolour carpeting in the front of the store. That, along with GPS routes that placed Tabitha's car in the alley behind the building, are enough to bring all four of us – me, Cam, Naia and Raul – to this dark, abandoned relic of retail.

'Is there a back door?' Cam asks.

'Yes,' Naia says. 'You and Jack can go that way.'

'We'll take the front,' I say. 'If you know where the back door is, it makes more sense for you to cover it.'

Which is why, when we bust into the place, it's Naia and Raul who do the takedown. Such as it is.

Naia shouts the all clear to us while Cam and I are still crossing the migraine-inducing bespoke carpet out front. We push our way through the box-filled space and behind a curtain to a staircase that leads down into a musty basement. It must once have been a stockroom, but now it looks more like a laboratory. There are benches against two of the walls, laden with various scientific ephemera. From the size and shape of the bench legs, it looks like they match the impression left behind in the floor of Felton's basement. The lighting is provided by fluorescent strip bulbs that flicker faintly in a random rhythm. There are no windows, just a door on the far side of the room leading to an outside staircase down which Naia and Raul must have entered. They're on the concrete floor in the middle of the room now, crouching beside a body.

It's Tabitha.

'She's alive, but she won't wake up. I'm calling sick bay,' Naia says with her phone to her ear.

The call's a short one, and I know it won't take long for help to arrive, even if it were coming at normal speed, but the wait still feels like an eternity. It allows me to see things I wish I couldn't.

I know she's not a tall person, but I've never seen Tabitha look small before. Now, half curled up on her side in this sad little room, she's tiny. She's got her lab coat on, as I would expect when she's working, but the clothes she's wearing underneath are absent her usual colourful palette: black trousers, black top, black shoes. It makes her skin look so very pale, though of course that might have something to do with her current condition, which is something like a coma. Raul is gently shaking her shoulder, as though that will help. The movement dislodges a tiny plastic lid, together with the glass vial it once sealed, which rolls out of Tabitha's hand and tinkles onto the concrete.

'Poison?' Naia suggests.

Raul goes to pick up the vial, which I notice is only mostly empty. I grab his arm just in time.

'Jesus, Raul,' I say. 'You don't know what's in there, or what it might do to you. Rule number one: use a fucking bag.'

'Sorry.'

'Don't apologise,' Naia says, 'just don't do it again.'

Ever-prepared, she pulls an evidence bag out of her pocket, uses it as a glove to pop the lid back onto the vial, then wraps the whole thing safely away.

'Don't touch anything,' she says to Raul, looking around at the equipment on the benches. There are retorts and Bunsen burners, beeping machines and test tubes full of what looks worryingly like blood. Cam sniffs it and confirms my suspicions.

'Some human,' he says, 'and some Silver.' I wouldn't be able to tell the difference, but Cam's sense of smell is off the charts, even for a Silver. 'I wonder what she was doing with it.'

'I'd guess she was trying to refine the vampire-on-fire serum,' I say, flicking through a notebook that's lying next to Tabitha on the floor. I can't make head nor tail of the contents, but it helps to be able to do something with my hands. If I don't keep them occupied, then I'm worried I might reach for Tabitha instead. Even after all her deception, after everything that's happened over the past couple of weeks, I'm still itching to pull her into my arms and try to make her better. The impulse is an unpleasant surprise.

Cam must notice that I'm struggling, because he crouches down next to me and puts his arm around my shoulders.

'I'm sorry, Jack,' he says.

'Why? It's not like she means anything to me.'

'You loved her.'

'Past tense.'

'Still.'

I tell myself the past doesn't matter, but I'm not fooling myself any more than I'm fooling Cam. Seeing her like this? It hurts, more than it should.

The doctors arrive and there's a flurry of Silver-speed activity – stretcher, monitors, transfusion – then they're gone as quickly as they came, taking Tabitha away with them, back to the college.

'Do you want to go with her?' Cam asks me.

I shake my head, because if I open my mouth then I might say yes. Instead, I get to work with the others, collecting all the detritus of Tabitha's experiments. There's a lot of it. By the time we're done, we've filled a van with the stuff to drive back to the college for Ed to analyse, but we keep the most important items with us: the notebook and the vial.

Cam flicks through the book as we survey the increasingly empty stockroom.

'It looks a lot like the notes Ed's already been through,' he says. 'But there's some extra stuff here that might be the formula for whatever was in the vial.'

Naia holds up the plastic bag to the light that's streaming through the open door, tipping the vial within so we can see the residue. It's a greyish sort of colour, with hints of blue and green that remind me of petrol.

'Is there enough in there for Ed to be able to test it?' I ask.

'Probably,' she says.

'It looks like Starblood,' says Raul.

'Really?' I say. I've never seen the drug myself, but since Raul was once something of an expert, I'll take his word for it. 'But Starblood's an upper rather than a downer, right? If she'd taken it, she'd be buzzing around the place like a hyperactive bee, not lazing around on the floor.'

'It could be an OD,' he says.

I panic a bit, then.

'I'm sure it's not, though,' Raul says quickly, panicking a little himself when he realises what he's said. 'I'm sure she'll be fine.'

'I think maybe I'd like to get back to the college now,' I say.

'Of course,' says Cam, handing the notebook off to Naia. 'I'll take you.'

'It's not that I'm worried about her.'

'Of course not.'

'I mean, I'm really not. After everything she did, it's not as though I care.'

'I know,' he says, but he's gentle with me as we walk back to the college and into sick bay.

Even though our relationship is still wobbly, he's there for me regardless. He sits with me for hours as I sit with Tabitha, hearing the monitors beat in time with my own heart.

I should feel nothing, but I just feel sick.

'Do you think she took the poison on purpose?' I ask Cam, though I already know the answer.

'I guess,' he replies. 'She had to know we were coming for her.'

'And she knew the punishment would be steep. Since she was planning to kill the Primus, wasn't she?'

He shrugs. 'That's what all her notes point to. It would make sense, given that she's pro-revelation and the Primus is the one standing in the way of the Silver coming out.'

'It all fits,' I say, hoping to put a bow on this once and for all. 'You're right. That must have been her motive.'

'Yes,' he agrees, but then he pauses for a moment. 'Unless it's you.'

That throws me. What exactly is he insinuating? Have I overplayed my hand?

Don't panic, Jack.

Clarify.

'What do you mean?' I ask, trying to keep my anxiety under control.

'I don't know,' he says. 'She killed Felton for you. That's all I was thinking.'

Okay.

'But there'd be no reason for her to kill him for me,' I say, following his train of thought. 'It's not like Felton. I don't have anything against the Primus, and he doesn't have anything against me.'

'Nothing you know of. She worked for the Invicti, so who knows what she heard? It's possible that she knows something you don't.' He says this lightly, as though he doesn't really believe it. Given his Invicti-loving nature, I doubt he's thought through what he just said, or that he means any of it. But it makes me think.

The last time I saw the Primus, he'd just won the vote that he'd rigged in his favour, and he was busy removing the evidence. He saw me watching him. He knows that I know what he did. Maybe the knowledge that I have is a liability. Maybe he'd rather wipe me out than gamble on my continuing silence.

'I don't know. But don't worry,' Cam goes on. 'We'll get her to talk. She'll tell us everything when she wakes up.'

The two of us sit together and wait for answers.

They never come.

13

THE DOCTORS TRY to revive her all night, but Tabitha won't wake up. In the morning, Boyd gathers us together in the open plan monstrosity and asks for our report. Our *written* report.

'Fuck off,' Naia says. 'Firstly, I'm not writing a report. And secondly… No, actually, that's it. I'm not writing a report.'

'We've been up all night, Captain,' says Cam. 'And Jack —'

'Jack is fine,' I say, even though the lack of sleep and my natural defensiveness has me twitching as though I've overdone the caffeine. Which is also true, but that shouldn't have any effect on me as a Silver.

'Then a verbal report,' Boyd says. 'For the time being,' he adds, making it clear that the tedious paperwork is merely delayed, not avoided.

They're still trying to resurrect Boyd's office – apparently the budget can't stretch to rush rates – and all of the furniture from the open plan space has been stacked against one wall to make room for the workmen. Instead of bothering to untangle it, we sit on the floor. Boyd, true to form, chooses to remain standing. I'm too tired to give a shit about his sense of superiority. So tired, in fact, that I choose to take this meeting lying down, literally.

'Run it down,' Boyd says.

It's Cam, ever-responsible Cam, who jumps in to take the lead. I'm reminded that he would have made an excellent deputy. If I were him, I'd be holding a grudge against Boyd for that slight, but apparently – and unsurprisingly – Cam is not only more responsible than me, but also more forgiving. When we lose him to the Invicti, Boyd's head is the first I'm coming for.

'Let's start at the beginning,' Cam says. 'Matthew Felton was thrown off the Bridge of Sighs before Christmas with a noose around his neck and a note to Jack pinned to his chest. Seconds later, he went up in flames. Ed's lab testing has revealed that the cause of the immolation—'

'Good word,' Raul says.

'—was a serum in Felton's blood, something a bit like the serum Dr Jahan Khalyed developed, but not as strong. Jack and I went to Felton's place to see if we could pick up anything, and it looked as though someone had been using the lab in his basement. We picked up Dr Ross's scent there, so we went to her place, only to find that she was missing and there was a pool of blood on the floor. We now believe that her kidnapping was staged.'

'But why?' says Raul, who looks as though he's struggling to keep up, despite having been through all this with us several times already. We really should put him through a drug test, just to make sure.

'To draw Jack to the house, so Tabitha could track her, then kidnap her, which is exactly what she did. Only something must have gone wrong, because a week later she left Jack in her car outside Felton's house, where we finally found and revived her.'

'And we still don't know what happened in that week?' Naia says, looking at me.

'No,' Cam says confidently. 'The drugs have wiped Jack's memory.'

'All right,' Naia says sceptically, but Cam stands firm. Whatever suspicions he has about my lost week, and whatever Ed told him about the inability of the drugs in my system to keep me knocked out for more than a few hours, he's still keeping it all to himself.

'I have a question,' says Raul, raising his hand.

'Yes?' says Boyd. I get the feeling he likes playing headmaster.

'We know it was Yolande Leclerq who stole the Solis Invicti's darts, right? Because they were found with her belongings, and she set Cam and Jack up to be shot at the Castle, and all the other stuff you've told me about that happened in September.'

'Right,' Naia confirms.

'Then how did Dr Ross get the last dart?'

This is a surprise. If anyone was going to pick holes in our theory, I didn't expect it to be Raul.

'Because there was a finite supply, right?' he continues.

'But Tabitha knows how to make the formula,' I say. 'She was the one who developed it for the Invicti in the first place.'

'So that means there's still one more dart out there,' says Naia.

I shrug. 'Maybe. But we're getting off track.'

'We do know one thing from Dr Ross's notes,' Cam says, taking my cue. 'She was trying to develop a more potent version of the substance that killed Matthew Felton.'

'*More* potent?' Boyd says.

'Potent enough to kill a Silver who's millennia old.' The words carry meaning that Boyd doesn't miss. He's been around long enough to know who Cam's talking about.

'Has anyone told the Invicti?' he asks.

'Yes,' Cam says, giving me a guilty look. 'I have.'

Of course he has. He didn't say anything about it to me, but of course he's reported back to his buddies.

'For fuck's sake,' I say. 'The last thing we need is them getting involved in this.'

'It's their job, Jack.'

'Maybe they can take her off our hands,' Boyd suggests.

'What are you talking about?' I say.

'What else are we going to do with her?' he asks.

'Keep her in sick bay until she wakes up,' Naia says, like Boyd's got a screw loose. 'Not least because we need to interrogate her. I've got things I want to ask her, and I'm sure I'm not the only one. She can't sleep forever.'

'Isn't that exactly what she's going to do?' asks Boyd, looking at Cam.

Naia, Raul and I look at Cam too. He looks at his feet, which is as good as confirmation.

'Why didn't you say anything?' Naia asks.

'I was hoping it wasn't true. The doctors say if she doesn't wake up now then she's not going to.'

'Keeping her in sick bay is using up college resources,' Boyd says, 'and we don't have any to spare. In any case, she's a scab. You can box her or transfer her to the Solis Invicti, your choice, but she can't stay here.'

'Jesus, Boyd,' Naia says, as shocked by his abrupt tone as the rest of us are.

'It's the way it is,' he says, his jaw set.

Cam puts his arm around me and squeezes. 'Your choice, Jack.'

'I'm not giving her to the Invicti,' I say. 'God knows what they'll do with her.'

'So you'd rather put her in a box?' Raul asks, horrified.

Having had some personal experience of what it's like to be a guest in Drake's cellar, I know why he feels the way he does, but he doesn't understand what's going on here.

'She heard us coming,' I say. 'She knew we were going to catch her, and she chose how she wanted to go into the box. Whatever was in that vial, she knew what she was doing when she drank it. At least if she's in a box then we know where she is, and she'll be safe when she recovers from whatever she's done to herself. If we give her to the Invicti, then I'm worried they might never let her wake up at all.'

'They wouldn't hurt her, Jack,' Cam says.

'Wouldn't they?' I ask.

'Drew wouldn't—'

'And Benedict?' I interrupt, irritated that Cam's bandying around the Secundus's nickname like they're friends. 'Do you think he wouldn't either?'

'I know you and Ben haven't got on well in the past, but —'

'*Ben*?' I yell. 'Since when are you all buddy-buddy with the Tertius?'

I'm losing him. I can feel Cam slipping away from me more every day and I can do absolutely nothing about it.

'The box, then,' he says, more to mollify me than because he agrees. 'We'll go this morning, just you and me. Okay?' He looks around at the others as he says this, making sure they agree.

No one argues. Between Cam's insistence and my dark mood, they wouldn't dare.

In the time it takes the doctors to load Tabitha into the van, Cam has clearly been reflecting on our conversation last night about her possible motives. He's putting the pieces together and finding that they don't quite fit. It's usually my job to pick holes in our theories of crime, but since I'm not stepping up, Cam is taking it upon himself to fill in the gaps. He starts airing his concerns the moment he puts the van in drive.

'There are things that still don't make sense to me,' he says. 'I understand why she would kill Felton for you, and why she would kidnap you, but I don't understand why she'd drive you to Felton's house and just leave you in the car outside.'

'Maybe she was taking me out of town. She could have stopped at Felton's place to pick something up,' I suggest.

'But she wasn't at the house when we found you.'

'Maybe she was inside, heard you coming and ran.'

'But we found no recent traces of her there. No scent in the house. Nothing outside the car.'

'Then maybe something happened to her before she could go inside. I don't know.'

He sighs. 'I just wish you could remember what happened in those seven days.'

'Maybe it's for the best that I don't. Either way, it's over now.'

'It's not going to eat at you?' he asks. 'I would have thought it would be driving you mad, not knowing where you were or what you missed.'

'This isn't a TV show, Cam. Sometimes you don't get all the answers. Who knows why she did it. Does it matter?'

'Yeah, it matters,' he insists. 'There was a threat to the Primus. We need answers, and since she's not going to give them to us, we'll have to get them some other way.'

'Like?'

'Well, there's always hypnosis, if you're still willing to try it.'

Oh, god. Not this again.

'I was willing to try it to find Tabitha,' I say, 'but we've done that already without needing to resort to stage magic.'

'Come on.'

'I don't want a stranger rootling around in my brain, thanks all the same.'

'Why not?'

Because there are things I'm keeping safe in there.

'Because it's all phony,' I say, 'but just in case it's not, I'd rather not involuntarily quack like a duck every time someone says *bread*.'

'And what if Tabitha wasn't working alone?' he says. 'What if she managed to synthesise a stronger version of Dr Jay's serum after all, and what if there's someone else out there who's planning to use it to kill the Primus? We can't stop investigating just because Tabitha's been neutralised.'

'If the Primus is in danger then that's the Solis Invicti's lookout, not ours.'

'We answer to the Invicti.'

'Do we, though?'

'We should,' he says.

'Who exactly do you work for, Cam?' I say, turning in my seat to face him. 'Because it sounds to me a lot as though you think you're one of them, not one of us.'

'We're on the same side, Jack.'

'No,' I insist. 'No, we're not. We don't kill humans – however repugnant the humans in question might be – to gather money for politicking. We don't recruit scientists to create chemical weaponry to use against people who piss us off. We're not preparing for war with our own.'

'Maybe we should be.'

I narrow my eyes at his cryptic comment. 'What did the Secundus tell you?' I ask.

'Nothing,' he says quickly, then he falls silent, which is how I know it's a lie. Cam's usually pretty good at deception, but not with me. I can see right through him.

We don't talk for the rest of the journey, but it's mercifully brief.

'One for the box,' I say to the latest door goon as Cam and I wrangle the still-unconscious Tabitha out of the back of the van. 'Could you call it up and buzz us through?'

I've just scooped Tabitha off the stretcher and into my arms when Cam's phone rings. He looks at the display and swears.

'What?' I ask.

'I've got to take this,' he replies with a cringe.

'*Now?*'

'Yes. I'm sorry. It's important.'

'Who is it?'

'Just a friend.'

'Who is it, Cam?'

He won't answer me.

'It's the Invicti, isn't it?' I say. 'I'm here with my comatose ex-girlfriend in my arms, about to box her for fuck knows how long, and instead of coming with me you're going to hang around out here and shoot the breeze with your new best mates. Is that about right?'

He mouths another *sorry* at me, but he answers the damn phone anyway. I hate being on the outs with Cam, I really do, but for fuck's sake, how am I supposed to make peace under these conditions?

I leave him by the van and carry Tabitha inside on my own. The door goon follows me, performing his door-goonish function by holding doors open and being solicitous in an awkward and unhelpful way. Unlike most of the goons I've met here, he's exactly what you'd expect: a big white guy with a shaved head and muscles so enormous that he has to enter rooms sideways. We make it into the basement eventually, but not without a lot more *you first, no I insist* than I would normally tolerate.

'Do you know where you're going?' he asks.

'Yeah, I've spent more time in this basement than I'd like.'

'Oh, then do you want me to do this while you go upstairs?'

'No, don't worry,' I say. 'This one's personal. I'll get her settled then report in at the office when I'm done.'

'You don't need a hand?'

'Thanks,' I say, putting on my nicest smile, 'but I've got it.'

'Okeydokey,' he says, smiling back, then he lumbers briskly up the stairs, doubtless keen to return to the exciting task of watching the front door. I wait until he's out of sight, then listen carefully until the moment I hear the front door shut behind him as he leaves.

Time to move.

Through the door to the closest boxes, carrying Tabitha in my arms. I pass along a couple of corridors, passing by the silent box of Gabriella de Palma, trying to remember my way, until I find the door I need. The box next to it is empty, so I stow Tabitha in there. Unlike the other residents of this crypt, she doesn't need to be drained of blood to keep her compliant. The formula in her blood will keep her sedated long enough for my purposes.

I should pause over this process, I suppose. I should take my time, buckling her in chain by chain as I reflect on our doomed love affair and berate myself for all the things I might have done differently. Perhaps I would do exactly that if I were a better person, but the truth is that I'm in a rush and I don't have time for tragedy. Instead of trailing a hand lovingly down her cheek for the last time, mourning the demise of our grand romance, I strap her in then lift up her cardigan and pull out the five bottles of blood I secreted there earlier in the day. I can only hope it'll be enough.

Next comes the tricky part: opening the box next door. I don't have the key, and I can't just bust the door open, because that's bound to alert at least Cam, and probably at least five other guards around the property as well. It occurs to me then that they might patrol these corridors from time to time; it would make sense, given how much of the property is underground. I'm already rushing, because Kulika will be waiting for me upstairs in the office, but that thought really lights a fire under my arse.

I have a plan. I just need to carry it out.

The thing about the doors of the boxes is that they're designed to keep Silver in, not to keep them out. That means the hinges are on the outside, where any sufficiently-determined idiot with a screwdriver – hello, there – can take the whole thing apart within about five minutes, or five seconds when they're moving at Silver speed. Once I'm done, I put the door to one side and deposit the bottles of blood into the arms of the captive Silver waiting inside.

'You took your time,' she whispers after she's finished the first bottle.

I don't bother to dignify her criticism with a response; she can look after herself from here on. Leaving her to regain her strength, I forge a path deeper into the cellar, down three more staircases to the place where the ground is dirt and the corridors are unlit.

I'm in and out in under a minute, with no one any the wiser.

14

'HEY, KULIKA,' I say as I barge into the office to make my report.

'Hello, Valentine.'

Oh, shit.

Kulika isn't the one sitting behind the desk. It's Killian fucking Drake.

'Long time, no see,' I say, trying to play it cool, while inside I'm scrambling for solid ground. The last time I saw him was in his bed, naked, and I've just unwittingly plunged myself back into the memory of that night. I can feel my heart thudding in my chest, and I know he can hear it because when he lifts his eyes from that fucking desk of his, they darken and narrow, like a hunter zeroing in on his prey.

'Not pleased to see me?' he asks, leaning back in his chair. Wherever he's been these past few months, it's somewhere with better weather than England; his skin is tanned to gold and his dark hair has the faintest tinge of red when the sun hits it.

'Surprised,' I say. 'I thought you were gone for good.'

'Wishful thinking?'

'I'll lodge a complaint with my fairy godmother.'

While my mouth spouts off, my mind is racing, trying to remember how I used to act when I was in his office. The problem is that the only memories I seem to be able to access right now are the ones that have me laid across his desk, or straddling him in one of the leather armchairs, or pinned up against the door with the full length of his body pressed against mine. My own brain is trying to sabotage me.

'Why don't you take a seat?' he says with a smirk that tells me he knows exactly what's going on in my head right now. He is gesturing, quite deliberately, to the very chair in which I straddled him. The absolute *bastard*.

Reluctantly, I perch on the other seat. The last thing I want is to be stuck here right now. This isn't how I planned things at all. The plan was to waltz in, chuck Tabitha in her box, do the sneaky bit, give Kulika a quick heads up before she left for the evening, then waltz right out again. Now that I'm faced with the return of Drake, I know everything is about to go to shit.

'What are you doing here?' I ask.

'In my office?'

'In *Kulika's* office.'

For a moment I think we're going to descend into our usual verbal ping-pong, then his expression changes to something I can't read and he says, 'She told me you were missing.'

I can only laugh at that, because the idea of Drake rushing back from his sexy sabbatical to rescue me is frankly absurd.

'Were you planning to charge in and play the hero? You've tried that one with me before, Drake, and it doesn't suit you. You're no hero.'

He looks down at the blotter on his desk and says, 'Yes, I'm well aware of that.'

Faced with a contrite Drake, I have no idea how to

behave. Trust him to grow a conscience and play the penitent now, when the clock is ticking.

'What's wrong with you?' I say. 'Don't you have something you need to shout at me about?'

'You worried me,' he says, raising his gaze to mine. 'Shall I shout at you about that?'

'Oh, fuck off.' I say dismissively. 'You're a week too late with your concern.'

'Well, obviously you turned up.'

'Like a bad penny,' I confirm.

'What happened to your eyebrows?' he asks.

I clap a hand to my forehead. Why did Drake have to come home before they grew all the way back? 'There was a fire.'

'Oh, yes. I heard about Matthew Felton,' he says. 'It wasn't you, was it?'

'No. Was it you?'

He puts his elbows on the edge of the desk and props his chin on his linked hands, gazing at me intently. His eyes are still as shark-black as always, but I know that's not all they are. Under the blackness, under the face he shows to the world, there's a network of shining silver threaded through the depths of his irises. I wonder if I'll be able to get out of here tonight without talking about it.

'Now, why would you think that I would kill Matthew Felton?' he asks.

I shrug. 'Who wouldn't? He was a rat.'

'But why would you suspect me in particular?'

'No reason.'

'Might it be because there was a note pinned to his chest before he self-combusted?' he says. 'A note that was, as I understand it, addressed to you?'

'Yes, all right,' I say quickly, 'forget it.'

I'm trying to spare myself some embarrassment, but

Drake carries on with his monologue as though I haven't spoken at all.

'Was is because the note said it was sent to you "with love"?' he says, his voice so low that it's practically a whisper.

In this moment, I hate him so very, very much. I want to reach across the desk and smash his smug face into the blotter. I'm not sure why he's come back from his wild European sexcapades, but right now it feels like his only reason for being in Oxford is to taunt me with the fanciful hopes I might once have harboured about our failed nearly-romance. Sure, I knew it was a one-night thing. Sure, that was all I wanted. And sure, the very idea that he might have deeper feelings for me had sent me running from his house in the most dramatic walk of shame of my life, but that didn't mean that some small, secret part of me hadn't been a tiny bit pleased at the prospect. I mean, an absolutely minuscule bit. Microscopic, even.

But still.

This is Drake, I remind myself, who targets every vulnerability with cruelty. The only possible defence is not to care at all.

'Actually,' I say, 'we know who killed Matthew Felton. I came here to box them up. Case closed. Done and dusted. Nothing more for you to do.'

'*Them*?' he says, emphasising the neutral pronoun. 'About whom, exactly, are we talking?'

I sigh. 'Do you really want the whole story? It's done.'

'I was under the impression that listening to the whole story before passing sentence was my job. When did the Seekers become judge, jury and executioner?'

'If you wanted to keep your job so badly then maybe you shouldn't have buggered off to Europe for months on end without leaving a forwarding address. We've had to adapt.

And, by the way, we've been doing totally fine without you. Frankly it makes me wonder what the point of you was in the first place.'

Perhaps that was a little harsh. I'm considering some attempt to row it back when he says, 'It seems that you're not the only one who thinks that way.' Then he sighs and makes his way over to the bar. Yes, he is exactly the kind of wanker who has a fully-stocked bar in the office where he is supposed to do his work. Archaic, isn't it?

While his back is turned, I take the opportunity to pull out my phone and send a text message. No chance of that being overheard.

We have a problem, I type quickly. *I'm all done, but Drake is home.*

Dancing dots appear on my screen almost immediately — the reply is on its way. Not fast enough, though.

'Am I boring you?' Drake asks.

'No,' I reply airily, 'but you are being a bit rude, actually. Were you not going to offer me a drink?'

He stops in the middle of pouring his whisky. 'Isn't it a little early for you?'

'Not if it isn't too early for you.'

'I'm still on French time.'

'They're only one hour ahead of us. Knock it off and pour me a gin.'

By the time he turns his back again, the answer has arrived.

Find a way to get him out of there.

Shit. Shit shit shit.

'On second thoughts,' I say, scrambling, 'how about we go out for a drink? You know, catch up on everything you've been doing for the past few months while you've been swanning around Europe with your girlfriend.' There's a bitter edge to my voice that isn't intentional.

'Jack, I didn't mean to——'

'Is she here?' I say.

'Funny you should ask, actually. She's at the new open blood bar in town.'

'Excuse me?' After the dramatic and calamitous demise of Crimson earlier this year, I hadn't heard about any plans for further blood bar ventures in Oxford. With the Seekers in disarray and the Solis Invicti barely on speaking terms with us, perhaps I shouldn't be surprised. 'There's a new one?'

'Yes.' Why does he suddenly look uncomfortable? 'Carlotta's running it.'

Ah. That explains why he's *really* come back to Oxford. It's pathetic, the way he's chasing this woman from country to country, but I suppose that's what happens when you silver for someone. I've never known anyone who's been afflicted before, so I'm not an authority on the matter, but I've heard stories about the way it bonds you to another person, life to life, so when the person you've silvered for dies, you die too. People say other disturbing things about that bond too, like you can use it to heal the person you've silvered for, or that you can track their location through some kind of mystical GPS. It sounds creepy and stalkerish to me, but if I've learned one thing in this job it's that some people's idea of romance is far from healthy. Mind you, since I've just locked my ex in a box in the cellar, I'm probably not entitled to the moral high ground here.

Either way, as far as the bonding thing goes, rather Drake than me.

'We should talk,' he says, handing me my gin.

'What did you think we were doing, exactly?'

'I mean really talk, Jack. About what happened that night.' As he says this, he takes his own drink and leans back against his desk.

The scene of the crime.

So much has changed over the past few months – the past few days, even – that I'm surprised to find this one thing is the same: I still feel his pull. Even if he is the devil incarnate, I can't deny that the sex was phenomenal. That's the only reason I'm struggling with these memories right now. If he hadn't been such an incredible lay, then the spectre of Killian Drake would have stopped haunting me the moment I walked out of his bedroom three months ago.

Thankfully, there's a whole list of reasons it will never happen again. He's not just off the market, he's irretrievably, permanently in love with someone else. Which is fine. It's good, really. So much better than him having any kind of feelings for me. It doesn't matter what his scent does to me, or what's happened between us in the past, or how mind-blowing it might have been…

I have to get out of this room.

I swig back my gin, emptying the glass, then say, 'Why don't we go and see Carlotta?'

'What?'

I know it sounds like the worst idea in the world, but at this point I would suggest anything that would get us both out of this office and away from that fucking desk.

'If there's a new blood bar in town,' I say, 'the Seekers should know about it. I should check the place out. And we can talk there,' I add, though I have no intention of talking to Drake about what happened between us, not today or any other day.

Drake knocks back his whisky, then says, 'I should warn you, she'll probably proposition you again.'

The first time I met Carlotta Arden, she suggested a threesome with Drake. Even though she was, until lately, the most desirable Silver bachelorette in the world, I turned her down. Mostly because of Tabitha. Slightly because of Drake. It was possibly my stupidest decision ever and, from Drake's dark tone, it sounds like he has no intention of letting me rectify that error.

Shame. Messing around with his girlfriend would feel a tiny bit like payback. After all, he messed with mine first.

'Poor pampered Drake,' I say. 'It must be awful to to spend your time holidaying around Europe with a rich, beautiful, sexually adventurous film star. I can't imagine how you cope.'

'We all do what we must to survive,' he says. His tone should be flippant, but he doesn't quite pull it off.

'Come on,' I say, not wanting to linger on his strange mood and accidentally invite any details of his private life. I don't need to hear them. 'Let's go see your other half.'

He gives me a look, fixing me with his bottomless eyes, and says, 'Are you serious about this?'

'Yes. Deadly.' The more he protests, the more determined I become.

Then, unexpectedly, he gives in. Drake never gives in, especially not to me, but I'm not going to question it. I'll just call it serendipity and be grateful. While he summons a car, I send another message.

The coast is clear.

Mission accomplished. Now I just have to survive an evening out with Drake.

I'm not sure what Drake thinks about Carlotta setting up a new open blood bar, but personally I find it more than a little suspicious. Only a few months ago, before she and Drake briefly broke up before quickly reconciling, she was not only staying at Sir Percival Wanker's country house, but she was also one of the ringleaders of the pro-revelation vote. Since Sir Percy was the stakeholder behind Oxford's first failed open blood bar, since it was a publicity stunt for the pro-reveal faction, and since it was established using money stolen from murdered humans, it's hard not to see this new bar as a successor to Crimson's legacy. That makes me wonder who exactly is fronting the money for it, and why.

'Baron, darling!' Carlotta greets him with a kiss as we walk into the bar.

It's weird that she still calls him by his title, but not quite as weird seeing the two of them together. Not that I've haven't seen them out as a couple in the past, it's just that it was before... Well, it was before a lot of things. Before Drake and I indulged in The Night That Is To Be Regretted, before either of us knew about Carlotta's affiliations, and before they broke up as a result. If Drake hadn't silvered for her, then I can't imagine that the two of them would be together now, and that's just terrifying. For someone as controlled as Drake, to have the course of your existence altered so dramatically by something that is essentially biochemical magic must feel like a nightmare.

I suppose I can understand how he feels, if only a little. At the end of the day, we're all controlled by our emotions, driven to do stupid things for the people we love.

Stupid things like this.

'And chère Jacquéline,' Carlotta says, kissing me on both cheeks. 'So lovely to see you again after so long away. Perhaps now that you're single again…?'

'We talked about this, Carlotta,' Drake says quietly.

She ignores him and looks only at me, letting the question hang. Whatever else her relationship with Drake is, it's clear that it's very, very open.

Of course she looks incredible, as always. Her skin is a shade darker than usual and her chestnut hair is pinned at the nape of her neck so it cascades over one bare shoulder. She's dressed in a strapless, midriff-baring top despite the freezing cold, paired with loose trousers that sit low on her hips and are tailored to perfection. I've had a crush on Carlotta for decades, ever since I was turned Silver, but what I've learned about her this year has changed her in my eyes. I can't think of her as the gorgeous pin-up anymore; instead, she's a conspirator in Windsor's kill-humans-quick scheme, complicit in who knows how many deaths.

I might joke about it, but even with her sun-bronzed skin and her sensuous curves, there's nothing in the world that would persuade me into her bed now. The sad thing is that I know Drake once felt the same, if only briefly. Whatever the bond to Carlotta has given him, it's taken just as much away.

'I appreciate the offer,' I say, 'but I'm still unavailable.'

Drake gives me a look, but I just shrug back. Let him wonder.

'Ah, well,' Carlotta says with a coy smile. 'I didn't imagine you'd stay on the market long. So, what do you think of our little place?'

'It's not so little,' I reply.

The place is like a warehouse. The ceilings stretch up to double height, with mezzanine floors hanging liberally around the walls. As Carlotta takes us on the full tour, it becomes clear that the bar isn't just a bar, it's a full clubhouse with different rooms for different vibes. In addition to the huge main floor, there's a VIP bar, a Silver-only bar, a Silver VIP-only bar, and a heated roof terrace with panoramic views across the city. There's even a hot tub in one corner, as though the designer became confused and momentarily believed they were making over a beachside resort in the Greek islands instead of a rooftop bar in the centre of Oxford city. It's outrageous and decadent, and – unlike Crimson – it's going to bring the Silver running from every corner of the country. Maybe the world.

Carlotta settles down with us in the Silver-only bar; apparently I've not cleared the hurdle to be considered a VIP. It's still plush enough, filled with quirky furniture and raw wood, and surprisingly comfortable for all its hipster charms. We're at the table furthest from the bar, tucked around a curtained corner next to the window that looks out onto the High Street.

'Mirrored glass,' she says, deliberately tapping a jewelled ring against the smoky pane. 'We can see them, but no one can see us.' As she speaks, her eyes twinkle almost as much as the diamond on her finger.

I'm still working out how to reply when a waiter brings some drinks to the table – champagne, to celebrate, I suppose – along with a whispered message for Carlotta.

'*Désole*, darlings,' she says. 'The VIPs need me upstairs. Make yourselves at home.'

Then she's gone, leaving Drake and I alone facing each other across the table in our nest, all high-backed bench seating, privacy drapes and one-way glass. The silence stretches. It is not comfortable.

'Well,' I say eventually. 'You'd think that giving her an engagement ring the size of your eye would entitle you to VIP status, wouldn't you?'

'I was—'

'You must have mortgaged your mansion for that rock. I'm not one for shiny stones myself, but Christ, her hand must be tired.'

'I was going to tell you,' he says.

'Why? It's none of my business.'

'Valentine—'

'Don't call me that.'

It was his name for me at another time, in another place, before Carlotta was wearing his ring on her finger and he was wearing her silver in his eyes. We aren't those people anymore. I'm not sure we ever really were.

Drake looks down at his hands as though he's trying to contain himself, and when he looks back up at me there's something like despair in his eyes.

'Jack,' he says, 'I know you don't want to talk about this
—'

'So let's not.'

'*I* want to talk about it.'

I groan. 'Why? It was one night, Drake. We agreed that. It didn't mean anything. Why do you have to make such a big deal of it?'

'If it meant nothing, then why did you run?' he asks.

'Why did *you* run?' I reply.

'You know why!' he says, exasperated, then he lowers his voice and leans towards me across the table. 'You know why,' he whispers.

The truth is that I don't, not one hundred percent, not certainly enough for the intensity he's bringing to this conversation. My guess is that the bond sent him running after Carlotta, but the way he's looking at me makes me wonder whether there's some other reason he left. I'd like to be certain. I think I'd like to hear the words from his own mouth, but even the idea of him confessing his undying love for Carlotta turns my stomach.

In any case, I can't show him that I'm anything less than sure. I can't let him in my head, not again, so instead of asking him to explain I just say, 'Yeah. I know,' as if I know everything that's in his.

He leans back in his seat and lets out a long breath.

'Right,' he says after a moment's angry silence. 'So that's it?'

'Why are you getting pissy with me?' I say. 'I'm not the one who wanted to talk about this.'

'Fine, then I won't bring it up again.'

'Perfect. I never wanted to talk about it in the first place.'

'Fine.'

'Fine.'

'Fine.'

My phone buzzes in my pocket before we can prolong this scintillating conversation any further.

She's out, the message reads. *We'll be home in ten.*

'Well,' I say, getting to my feet, 'delightful though this reunion has been, I've got work to do. Some of us can't take a three-month holiday on zero notice without anyone caring.'

'Oh, you cared, Jack.'

'You'd be amazed by how wrong you are. You've been gone a long time, Drake. Things have changed.'

I move towards the exit, but unfortunately that takes me straight past the banquette where Drake is sitting. He grabs my wrist before I reach the curtain and pulls me down beside him before I realise what's happening. His eyes are locked on mine, so close that I can feel his breath on my cheek, close enough that I could count his eyelashes. I've been ignoring it since the moment I first saw him tonight, but now that we are this close I can no longer keep the scent of him from flooding onto my tongue: copper, spice and something darker.

Even with all the time and distance he put between us, my reaction to his scent is instant.

'Admit it,' he whispers. 'You missed me.'

'No, I didn't.'

'You can't lie to me.' He raises his hand to my cheek, pushing the loose tendrils of hair away from my face, and just like that the pheromones are swirling in the air, proving him right. Stupid Silver super senses.

'It doesn't matter how my body reacts to you,' I say. 'I liked it better when you were gone.'

His hand stills on my skin, his eyes narrowing in question, so I explain myself in a way he can't misunderstand.

'I don't like who I am when I'm around you,' I whisper, unwilling to speak the truth too loudly. 'You make me feel raw, like I have to lash out, to hurt you before you hurt me.'

'If you only knew…'

He leans in closer, as though he's making to kiss my pain away, but he stops abruptly before his lips touch my skin.

'Whose scent is that on you?' he says. It's just transference, not a possessive scent mark, so he's had to get this close to pick up on it. It's one of the many reasons I was hoping he would keep his distance. 'I can't place it.'

'I told you,' I say, finally pushing him away. 'I'm off the market.'

'You were serious about that?'

I am going to smack him around the head.

'Yes, I was serious!' I whisper-yell. 'And, unless you've forgotten, we are sitting in the club owned by your—' Ugh. '—fiancée.'

'We're not exclusive,' he says, as though that lump of diamond Carlotta's parading around is nothing at all.

'Amazingly,' I say, 'I'd worked that out for myself. But I *am* in an exclusive relationship, and even if I weren't, what happened between us was, as I keep reminding you, just a one-night thing. It's not going to happen again.'

He sits back, breaking contact, composing himself. It's clear that the idea I might have found someone new has blown his tiny little mind. It's more than a little insulting.

'Well,' he says eventually. 'Are you going to tell me about them? Who are they? It's someone I've met before; I know that much from the scent.'

'That is absolutely none of your business,' I reply.

'Why? We're still friends, aren't we?'

That's a laugh. I treat his comment with the scorn and derision it deserves. 'We've never been friends, Drake. We never will be.'

'Come on, Jack. With everything that's going on with the Invicti, the Primus… We can still work together. We're still allies, at least.'

'No,' I say, getting to my feet. 'Actually, we're not.'

I'm not on his team anymore. I have a team all of my own, and they're waiting for me.

'Storming off again?' he asks, with something that sounds like hope. He wants things to be the same as they used to be between us, but that time has passed. Nothing will ever be the same again.

'I'm not storming. I'm just leaving,' I say. 'Bye, Drake.'

As I'm walking away, I hear the whispered reply.

'Goodbye, Valentine.'

It's only when I've left him behind that I realise what was missing: contrary to all expectations, he wasn't wearing Carlotta's scent mark.

15

IT'S DARK BY the time I get my meagre possessions packed into one of the Seekers' cars and drive them up to Jericho. Parallel parking is not my forte, but I manage to get the thing within a foot of the pavement without leaving any noticeable dents in the cars either side of mine, which I count as a victory. Even more of a victory is the fact that I have achieved emancipation. After twenty years of inertia, I have finally left the shadow of Solomon College.

I dump my suitcase down on my gorgeous new hardwood floor, kick off my shoes and breathe in the air of my freedom. It's only then that I realise I'm not alone.

'Did you miss me?'

She's sitting on the sofa, waiting in the dark. Her outfit is casual, just jeans and a T-shirt, but somehow she still exudes the sense of power that I remember from the night I first met her. She owns not just the space she occupies, but the space around her too. The air is filled with the scent of warm sugar, the scent of her skin.

I feel it creeping over me, flooding around me in a way that makes me panic. She's so strong, so present, so imposing that it's intimidating.

Then I smile.

'I always miss you,' I say. 'I did for twenty years.'

She takes my hand and pulls me down onto the sofa beside her. Now that we're alone, finally, away from the Seekers, I can do what I've been aching to do for days.

I take her face in my hands and kiss her.

It started with a kiss like this, two decades ago. A small cut on Winta's lip was all it took, one drop of blood in my mouth before she bit me, and my life was changed forever.

It's possible that, while telling you this story, I might have missed a few things out. Just a few. Nothing important, really. Well, maybe a little bit important. Okay, *very* important, but here I am, repenting of my sins and ready to confess them, one by one.

When I told Cam that I couldn't remember anything that happened in the week I was missing? Yeah, that wasn't strictly the truth. Except during the two brief periods when I was knocked out by Tabitha's drugs, I remember every second.

Let me explain.

16

IT STARTED A week ago with Winta's scent surrounding me as I woke in an unfamiliar place with a thumping head and an ache in my neck. One minute I'd been on the High Street, sheltering from the rain, and the next I was somewhere else entirely.

I've seen enough TV shows to know how you're supposed to act when you wake up during an abduction: play dead while you gather information, then spring into action and take your captors by surprise. Unfortunately, there were several factors working against me on this occasion. Firstly, whatever was in the Solis Invicti's knock-out formula was strong as fuck, and my battered body wouldn't let me sit up, let alone spring. Every inch of me hurt. Secondly, since my abductors were likely Silver, they'd have noted the change in my respiration the moment I'd roused. Thirdly, and perhaps most importantly, I'd jerked myself awake with a snort. It would have been hard to sell the sleeping beauty act after that.

Quite apart from all of these exceedingly good reasons, the possibility of subterfuge never even occurred to me until later. You try being kidnapped sometime. It's not as easy as it looks.

'Hello, Jack,' a familiar voice said. 'I heard you'd been looking for me.'

'Winta?'

That explained the scent. It hadn't been long since I'd last smelled it – in my rooms at the college, and on the skin of Yolande Leclercq as we boxed her in Drake's crypt. I'd been expecting Winta to come for me. Hoping, really, that she would. I still wasn't ready to find myself alone with her in a small bedroom, her dark skin shining in the moonlight that poured in from the window behind me. I blinked a few times to clear my vision, then hauled myself into a seated position in the single bed. She was sitting by my feet, so close that I could have reached out and touched her. I didn't though, not yet. My hands itched to reach for her, but instead I reached up to push the hair away from my face, and I discovered that it had escaped from its hairband and knotted into a mess at the nape of my neck. I must have looked a state.

Despite the intervening years, Winta looked much the same. Her hair was short and natural now, rather than braided as it had been back then, but otherwise she was exactly as I remembered her.

I had no breath. I was seventeen again, drunk in the grungy back alley of an Oxford pub, insecure and feckless, watching the world turn upside down at Winta's whim. For a purposeless teenager like me, there had been nothing more attractive than someone self-possessed enough to know what they wanted, and for some bizarre reason, for that night only, Winta had wanted me. I couldn't have resisted even if I'd tried.

Twenty years later, her presence had exactly the same effect.

I had to blink a few more times to be sure I wasn't hallucinating. Even after that, I wasn't entirely convinced that this was real life rather than some very weird dream.

'You shot me with a tranquilliser dart,' I slurred. Apparently the drug was still working its way out of my system.

'Not to hurt you,' she said. 'Just to have a chance for the two of us to talk.'

I was barely coherent, but as I struggled back to alertness I was starting to feel rowdy. I'd been drugged and kidnapped and it hadn't left me in a good mood, even if it had delivered me to the woman I'd been missing for two decades.

'That was you back in May, wasn't it?' I said. The words were less slurry, at least. It was definite progress. 'You're the one who shot Drake with the dart.'

'The baron was an accident, actually,' she said, 'though I can't pretend it wasn't satisfying to watch him squirm after everything he did to me.'

'He nearly died.'

She shrugged, as though his life was nothing at all.

'That would have been a bonus,' she said, 'but it wasn't my objective. Turns out you need a bit more practice with tranquilliser guns than I anticipated, and my aim was off. I was trying to hit you.'

My mouth went dry and my skin got cold.

'You were trying to kill me?' I whispered.

'No, you idiot,' she said. 'I was trying to kidnap you. But then the Invicti got in the way, and everything started to get messy. Yolande and I had to get out of town until things cooled off.'

'You two were working together?'

'She's a friend,' Winta said cryptically, and refused to elaborate under my gentle questioning. Leclerq seemed to be a subject that was off limits.'Did you like your Christmas present?' she asked.

'My… what?' My mind was racing, trying to push

through the confusion and disorientation to put the pieces of the puzzle in place. I'd started off angry, but now she'd spun me around and I was just feeling confused.

'I know it's a bit early,' she went on, 'but since I've missed a few Christmases and birthdays, I thought I'd better make up for it with something good.'

'Like?'

'It might have been a while,' she smiled, all sharp teeth and mischief, 'but I've been keeping track of you. It wasn't hard to find the perfect gift to wrap up with a note and send to you, special delivery.'

Oh. *Oh.*

I can only blame the tranquilliser hangover for how long it took me to make the connection.

'You killed Matthew Felton?'

She didn't respond directly, but the look on her face was clear enough. She'd killed Felton, all right.

For Jack, with love.

With love.

After twenty years of absence: with love.

Maybe that shouldn't have hit me so hard. *With love.* From Winta, my first love. *With love.* Why couldn't I get those words out of my head?

'There are some things we need to talk about,' she said.

'Um, yeah,' I said, feeling dazed. I suppose I should have been scared. After all, she'd just confessed to murdering one Silver and she'd obviously abducted me, for a purpose I couldn't begin to guess at. Still, despite her imposing presence, I didn't feel any threat from her.

'You probably have questions,' she said.

'Some,' I said, which was an understatement. They were filling my head so quickly that I was having trouble organising my thoughts, but one in particular kept rising to the surface.

Why did you run?

It wasn't the most relevant, and it certainly wasn't the most urgent, but it was the one I most wanted answered. Of course, it wasn't the information Winta chose to lead with.

'Just so you know,' she said, 'you're not a prisoner. You can leave whenever you like. I just want to talk without you and your Seeker friends taking me into custody. Okay?'

'Okay,' I said, pulling myself together. 'What do you want to talk about?'

I'd thought that it'd be about how she'd killed Felton, or how she'd turned me Silver, or why Yolande Leclercq was wearing her scent mark as I'd locked her in the box, or why she'd kidnapped me, or what had happened in Tabitha's house, but she wasn't interested in talking about any of that.

She said: 'We need to talk about Baron Drake.'

Because of course she did. Finally, after twenty years of searching, I was reunited with the first love of my life, and she wanted to talk about Killian fucking Drake.

I could feel my eyes narrowing. 'No,' I said. 'He is the very last fucking thing we need to talk about.'

'You're involved with him.'

'No,' I said, loudly. 'Drake and I are definitely not involved. I don't even know where he is, in fact. Probably eating gelato in Rome with his girlfriend.'

'But you're sleeping with him.'

Jesus Christ, did the whole world know about the most shameful night of my life?

'*No,*' I insisted. 'It happened one time. *One time*. And that was months ago. It was nothing.'

'We were only one time,' she said, 'and that was decades ago. Was that nothing too?'

Was I imagining the vulnerability in her eyes as she spoke? Was it possible, even slightly, that for all these years she'd been nurturing the memory of our brief liaison just as fondly as I had? I wasn't sure I could allow myself to believe it.

'I guess I need to explain why I ran,' she said.

I blinked. Maybe she had read my mind.

'I know you think I went on a murderous scab rampage,' she said. That was exactly what I'd always thought, because that's why the Seekers had been chasing her back then, and ever since. 'But it's not true.'

'You confessed it to me,' I said. 'Back when you were in that cell, you said you'd tried to live outside the laws of the Silver. I saw the blood in your flat. You were killing, Winta.'

Her name felt like velvet on my lips. I'd been holding it quiet in my heart for so long that saying it out loud was almost sacrilege.

'Most of that blood wasn't human,' she said.

'Silver?'

'Yes.'

It wasn't immediately clear to me how that made the situation any better.

'Don't be thick, Jack. There was a fight,' she said. 'With the Seekers and the Invicti. I took a chunk out of one of their guys and escaped, but eventually I got too close and they locked me up in the baron's basement.'

'The Seekers were there?'

'One of them, at least. A guy called Cameron.'

'Cam?' I said. 'My Cam?'

'He never told you?'

I'd asked him about his history with Winta, but he'd treated it just like any other case. I'd asked him a hundred times in that first year while we searched the globe for her, tracking her across Europe, through Asia to Australasia, before finally losing her somewhere in the Pacific. I'd known why *I* was chasing her so hard, but he'd never let slip that it was personal for him too.

'Oh, Jack.' Winta smiled at me. 'You haven't changed, have you? Twenty years Silver and you still trust every single person who shows you the slightest bit of love. And that's not a criticism, because it's a beautiful thing to be that trusting, but not everyone is worthy of it.'

'And I suppose you are?'

She laughed. 'Of course not. But for what it's worth, I swear that what I've told you is the truth.'

But I couldn't believe it.

'Drake told me the blood belonged to your landlord,' I said. 'That you killed him.'

'No.' Her face clouded over. 'That was the Invicti. From what I've worked out since, they got him to let them into my place, then killed him while they lay in wait for me.'

Through my still-groggy brain, I was struggling to fit all the pieces together.

This is what I knew: in the summer of 1999, I'd met a beautiful girl, had an intense one-night stand, and had fallen immediately and irrevocably in love. It's stupid, I know, but cut me a break; I'm sure you did some stupid shit when you were seventeen too.

Then the nightmare had started. We'd arranged to meet the following night for a drink and, to start with, everything had been going well. We'd gone to the vampire place on Holywell Street with the grumpy bouncers, and somehow Winta managed to get me through the door, even though I'd been human and underage at the time. We'd been sitting out on the terrace, flirting up a storm, only to be interrupted by one of the aforesaid grumpy bouncers. He'd said something about "Killian", then something else I hadn't been able to hear, and then Winta was gone, promising to come right back.

I'd waited, long beyond the point at which I'd outstayed my welcome at the club, but she'd never returned. I hadn't seen her again until that night in Drake's basement a few months later when, after some serious sleuthing, I'd managed to track his name to his Summertown mansion.

After that, I wasn't sure exactly what I remembered. I knew the basics: I broke in to free her, but she ended up biting me and freeing herself. What I could no longer remember were the details. After such a long time, I didn't know for sure how many of my memories of those crucial moments were real, and how many I had fabricated in dreams and nightmares since.

Had she really looked at me with longing in her eyes, telling me she remembered the taste of my lips, just moments before she kissed me again?

Or was the other memory real, the one where she hadn't even remembered my name?

'You left me at the club,' I said. 'You just up and left. You said you'd be right back.'

'I got word that the baron knew where I was, and that he was willing to talk. I believed him. That was my mistake. All he really wanted was to throw me in a cage and leave me there. When I realised that, I ran.'

'But they found you eventually,' I said. 'I was trying, you know. All those months, I was trying to track you down. You could have come to me. You could have—'

'I could have what, Jack? You were human. I was in the middle of a fucking war with the Invicti. I wasn't going to drag you into that, not when I wasn't done fighting yet. And, for the record, they didn't track me down. I got caught trying to sneak into the baron's place.'

'What? Why?'

She pressed her lips together for a moment, and I could see her determination in the gesture. 'I'll tell you,' she said, 'but not yet. There are other things I need to explain first – a *lot* of things I need to explain. That one can wait. You must be tired.'

'You have no fucking idea,' I muttered.

After just a short while sitting up in bed, my head was pounding and it felt like the room was spinning. That tranquilliser was the least fun I'd ever had with pharmaceuticals. Add to that the fact that Winta's story was making me reexamine everything I thought I knew about her history and my own current alliances, and I was in a right state.

I closed my eyes against the pain while we sat quietly for a moment. When I opened them again, I thought she might go back to talking about ancient history, but as it turned out it was more recent events that were playing on her mind.

'I've been watching you over the past few months,' she said.

'I know. You left your scent behind in my rooms.'

'I wasn't sure you'd still recognise it.'

I looked away for a moment, self-conscious despite the darkness in the room. 'You're my sire, Winta. I'm not likely to forget it.'

'I suppose not.' Was I imagining it, or did she sound just a little pleased about that? 'Look, I know you've had your fair share of trouble with the Invicti. You know they have only one purpose: to protect the Primus and his interests.'

'They don't even seem to be doing that lately.'

'Maybe they're not doing exactly what he says anymore, but my point is that they're not trying to save people, or see that justice is done, or anything like that. They're in it for themselves, which means there are the same problems with the Invicti as there are with the Seekers: there's no morality with either.' I felt a flare of defensiveness, but I couldn't pretend that I didn't have my own issues with the way the Seekers worked. I tingled with a sense of communion. It was like she was voicing my own thoughts. 'When they came after me, they didn't do it because I'd done anything wrong. They did it because I was trying to expose them for their own wrongdoing.'

'What do you mean?'

She took a deep breath, as though she was about to launch into a long explanation, then interrupted herself, saying, 'Can we leave it until tomorrow? It's a long story, and I think we both need to rest.'

'Okay.' Perhaps I should have said no and demanded to return to Solomon College, but I was exhausted and there was nothing waiting there for me except a squabbling squad, a suite of rooms with no floor, and a whole heap of questions. Here, in the darkness with the first woman I ever loved, I felt strangely at peace.

She left the room for a moment, returning with a couple of bottles of water and a couple of bottles of blood. Living off the radar as she was, I wondered where she'd sourced the blood, but at that moment I didn't care enough to push through my exhaustion and ask. She perched on the edge of the bed as we both drank, so I could see every detail of her features picked out in the moonlight. It made the whole experience more surreal, seeing every swallow in her throat, every blink of her lashes fluttering in greyscale as we sat side by side and drank the blood we both needed to survive.

She was exactly the same, and yet entirely different. She had the same electrifying presence, but she used to have a contained rage about her too. That had now transformed into quiet determination. Whatever reason she had for bringing me here, it was bigger than wanting a chance to explain her past to me, bigger than setting the record straight and stating her innocence. After twenty years, why would she care what I thought? She'd brought me here for a reason and, intrigued though I was, now that I'd refuelled on blood my body was trying to shut down and repair itself. I was so sleepy that I barely managed to put my empty bottle safely on the floor beside the bed before my eyelids were closing.

'I hope you don't mind me sharing,' Winta said as she kicked off her shoes and shuffled onto the bed with me. 'I haven't furnished the rest of the house yet.'

That woke me up.

'No,' I said. 'That's fine.' The words came out strangled and squeaky, but I relaxed again as she settled down beside me, leaving more than enough space between us for modesty.

Which is how I ended up sleeping next to the first love of my life, shortly after she'd shot me with a dart and kidnapped me. It had been twenty years since we'd last shared a bed, and yet it felt as though no time had passed. I could feel the pull of her, but now that I was Silver, her magnetism was even stronger. Despite her absence, despite all the questions I still had, the urge to move into her arms was almost irresistible. Irrationally, irritatingly irresistible.

But resist I did. All night.

She was still beside me the next morning, smiling sleepily as we lay on the bed, bathed by the sun. That was when she told me that she needed my help. I should have asked for details. I should have thought more carefully before I committed. I should have done anything other than what I did, which was say yes.

Not that careful thought would have stopped me. It was Winta.

When she asked, as usual, I was dying to help.

17

'WE'RE GOING TO kill the Primus.'

Those were the first words Winta said to me the next morning. Not *how did you sleep*, or *do you want some breakfast*, or even *sorry for drugging and kidnapping you*. Just, *we're going to kill the Primus*.

'We're what?' I replied.

I was feeling a bit foggy in the head the morning after, so I didn't quite believe my ears. I say *after,* but nothing had happened, still, despite the tension that was hanging in the air between us.

'We're going to kill the Primus,' she repeated, shuffling off the end of the bed as though she'd not just asked me to do the impossible. Instead of asking the more obvious questions, like why on earth I'd want to do that, I grasped for practicalities.

'How?'

'Come and eat,' she said from the doorway. She was already on her way downstairs. 'I'll explain everything over breakfast.'

And she did, sort of, though the fogginess in my brain persisted. It was difficult to tell whether that was related to the drugs, or her proximity, or a combination of the two. After so long apart, being near her was intoxicating enough on its own. I kept blinking, expecting to wake up at any second, but she never disappeared. She just smiled at me over her toast and made me wish I'd been brave enough to make a move the night before. Instead of touching, we held eye contact just a little too long for comfort. Instead of kissing, we smiled smiles that might have looked genuine but for the desperation in our eyes. Instead of ripping each other's clothes off and just getting on with it, we suppressed the need and sedately passed each other the milk over a couple of cardboard boxes that served as our breakfast table. I longed to touch her, but first we needed to get the talking out of the way.

'He has to die,' she said.

'What did he do to you?'

'Look, I'm not going to deny that I have personal reasons to despise him for what he and his attack dogs have done,' she said, 'and we'll get to that soon enough. But let's start with the big picture.'

'Which is?'

'He's evil,' she said simply.

'I'm going to need more than that.'

'Are you?' she said. 'He's the one who shaped our society. Hell, as far as we know, he's the progenitor of our entire race. And how does he use that power? Not to strive towards any kind of utopia, but to deploy the Invicti to keep us in line, and the Seekers to cover up the mistakes of his friends and root out those who object. You do realise you're a tool of a fascist dictatorship, right?'

'I'm not sure I'd go that far,' I said.

'Maybe you should,' she said, pointing her toast at me. 'What the Primus says goes. It always has, and it always will, however much he tries to give the rest of us the illusion of free will. Don't fool yourself. He's behind every single decision that affects us: who lives, who dies, who's allowed to do what they like, and who gets punished.'

Thanks to the recent voting fiasco, I knew that we were living in a Silver aristocracy. I knew that we were not equal, and that the rules that applied to the rest of us never bothered the conscience of the powerful few. But if even the views of the powerful few were ignored by the guy at the top, who manipulated the results at his whim, what did that make our society?

'Maybe you're right,' I conceded.

'Of course I'm right. The question is, what are you going to do about it?'

'But killing him?'

'It's the only way. Either we remove him, or he continues to control everything, forever. How many innocent people will die then?'

She was talking sense. After months of having my conspiracy theories dismissed by my team and my friends, someone was finally talking sense about the ways in which our world was rotten.

'I know it seems drastic,' she said, 'but just hear me out. Okay?'

'Okay.'

I let her talk.

She told me about her own experience of Silver society over the past eighty years, and the decline she described was one I recognised. Once upon a time, the Invicti had just been the Primus's bodyguard, and the Seekers had done the job of protecting humans from Silver who meant them harm. Now, the Seekers were controlled by the Invicti, who only gave a shit about the interests of the Primus. Protecting humans went out of the window in favour of doing whatever would keep the big man happy. Even the Invicti were starting to rebel – hence the pro-reveal move – but they hadn't dared push too far. Even they were scared of their master, and it would be hard for them to give up the trickle-down privilege they got from his power. Everyone had a piece of the pie: the Invicti, the barons, even some of the Seekers. As long as they toed the line, they got to do what they wanted, and as long as he was pleased with them, they'd probably get bumped up the ladder.

I knew this. I knew it all, though I'd never been able to express it as clearly as Winta expressed it to me. Still, knowing all this, I was not prepared for what she told me about His Lordship, Baron Killian Drake.

'Did you never wonder how he became so powerful?' she asked.

'Failing upwards?' I suggested. 'Overpromotion?'

'Brutality,' Winta said.

'Drake's not so bad.'

'He works for the Primus. He's as bad as the rest. Worse.'

'He's a dick, I grant you, but—'

'You said you'd hear me out,' she said, interrupting me before I could defend Drake. The fact that I'd had the impulse at all had been a bit of a shock. 'I told you before about the night the baron caught me,' she goes on, 'the night you found me in that cage. I'd been trying to sneak into his mansion.'

Between the aftereffects of the drugs and the shock of seeing Winta, the things she'd told me the previous night were all something of a muddle, but the disillusionment I'd felt persisted. It was following me around still, this sense of the world turning upside down, because everything I'd thought had been true about Winta's capture was in question. All these years, all these decades, I'd thought Winta had been just another scab killer. I'd been looking for her not just for myself, but for the Seekers too, because I'd thought she deserved to be boxed. But now, I didn't know what to think.

'Have you ever heard of a woman named Elise Santiago?' Winta said.

'No,' I said, but then the name tickled some distant recollection in the back of my brain. 'Wait, you mean Elise who used to go out with Drake?'

'That's her.'

Cam had told me the story only a couple of days ago.

'She went scab, right?' I said.

'Who told you that?'

'Cam.'

Winta laughs. 'And you believed him?'

'Yes,' I said simply. 'Cam's a good guy, and my best friend. He was there. He wouldn't lie about that.'

'Well,' Winta said, rowing back her derision, 'whatever she did or didn't do, she ended up in a box, but she didn't stay there.'

'He let her out?'

'No.' Winta's expression darkened.

'What are you saying?' I asked.

'She's dead, Jack. He killed her.'

'What? How?'

This made no sense to me. You don't just kill the Silver, even when you are one yourself. There are ways, sure, and I'd seen a few of them myself over the years, but they're messy, protracted and hard work. To kill one of the Silver, you have to be prepared to mess around with acid, explosives, or both, all whilst holding down an opponent who is struggling to stay alive as much as you're struggling to kill them. It's not for the faint-hearted, and it's not easy.

But then, I had seen one Silver killed recently with relative ease: Matthew Felton.

'Here's another name for you,' she said. 'Have you ever heard of Dr Jahan Khalyed?'

Back then, the name was unfamiliar. 'No.'

'It's a long story,' she warned me.

'I've got time.' I poured myself a second cup of coffee and took a third croissant. Shocking revelations make me snacky.

'All right then,' she said, pouring another cup for herself. 'If you're sure.'

That was the first time I heard the story of Dr Jahan Khalyed and the serum he'd made. The story I had from Winta was pretty much the same one that Ed told me a few days later, with one crucial difference: Ed never mentioned that the first man Dr Jay had bitten – the one who lived, but never fully recovered – was Dr Kayode Ladipo, Winta's father.

'Mum was a Seeker back then,' Winta said. 'They worked together, him in the lab and Mum in the field. But after the bite, Dad couldn't do anything. He was sick all the time, needing constant blood transfusions. The Seekers promised they'd find a cure. They promised they were working on it, and that it wouldn't be long before Dad would be back on the job, but it never happened. As time went on, we realised they'd never intended to cure him. They wanted him to end up the same way as Dr Jay, in the ground where he couldn't cause any more harm.'

My instinct was to argue with her. She had to be talking about Ed – he was the only person in the Seekers with the expertise to engineer a cure like that – and I couldn't imagine that he would abandon a friend to a slow, painful death.

Or would he?

Sure, Ed was generally a good guy. He worked hard, and mostly got us the answers we needed, eventually, with minimal damage to himself and the building. But Ed wasn't like Cam. His business wasn't people, but figures and formulae. Although I couldn't imagine Ed refusing to investigate a cure just because it was dangerous, I could imagine him weighing the cost of Dr Kay's life against the potential loss of life that might result from a failed cure and further proliferation of the deadly serum. I'd seen how he'd treated Cam over the years and during their break up. I knew that emotion didn't loom large in his calculations. I could see him making a cold, hard decision like the one Winta was suggesting.

She must have seen that I wasn't quite convinced, because she reached over the cardboard-box table to take my hand.

'I know these are your people,' she said. 'I know I'm telling you things that you don't want to believe, but I'm not asking you to do anything other than hear me out, then you can make up your own mind. Okay?'

I nodded tersely, trying to moderate my defensiveness. 'Go on.'

'Mum didn't like doing things by the book, not when the book was full of rules that made no sense. You remind me of her, actually.' She smiled at me – a quick, tender smile that made my insides warm. There was something seductive about her attention when it focused on me like that, as though she was proud of what I had become. Approval isn't something that comes my way often and, until that moment, it had been something I thought I didn't need. But when it came from her... I wanted so badly to make her proud. 'She asked the baron to give her access to Dr Jay,' she continued, 'so she could take samples of his blood to do her own research. When that didn't work, she tried taking samples from the lab at Solomon College, but Dr Castell caught her every time, and wouldn't give them up, saying they were too dangerous to release from the lab. In the end, she couldn't stay with the Seekers, so she left. Then she tried taking the samples for herself from the baron's basement, but the baron's guards chased her off before she could even get in the building. So, without either of them knowing, I decided I'd try it.'

'That's how Drake caught you,' I said, filling in the gaps for myself. 'You came back to Oxford to get Khalyed's blood, and they caught you in the basement. That's how you ended up in the cage.'

'Where you found me and set me free,' she said with a small smile. 'Where you were made.'

Drake's basement wasn't a very apt setting for such a life-changing event, but she managed to make it sound almost romantic. Before, every time I'd remembered that night I'd felt a wild tumble of negative emotions: shame that I'd let myself be tricked, hurt that she'd betrayed me, and horror at the memory of the pain. But that day, hearing her talk about it in such soft words, for the first time I reminisced on my making with a kind of peace.

'You left,' I said.

'I had to leave,' she replied. 'I'm sorry, so sorry, but my father needed me. You understand that, don't you?'

'So did you save him?'

'No. By the time I got out, lost the Seekers who were trailing me and made my way back home, it was all over. My parents were gone. It didn't end well. The Seekers…'

'Tell me,' I said.

'Are you sure you want to hear it?'

'Maybe I need to.'

She took a big gulp of coffee, as though steeling herself for what was to come.

'They called in the Invicti,' she said. 'They came for her at home, and Dad too. One minute they were all sitting around the table together – my brother and our parents – eating dinner, and the next minute the door smashed to the floor. They started hauling our parents away. Mum fought them, and so did my brother, but Dad was already so weak that he couldn't do anything. They carried him out, and Mum chased after him, and then they were all just… gone. That was it. That was the end. We never saw our parents again.'

'But what happened to them?'

'I don't know, but I think the Invicti have them.'

We sat quietly for a moment, Winta lost in her memories and me trying to digest everything she had told me and puzzle it into my existing view of the world. It wouldn't fit. There was no way that I could believe all that she'd told me – and I did – at the same time as maintaining my opinion of Ed, of Cam, of the Seekers as a whole. I'd known the Invicti were rotten to the core, and I'd seen evidence with my own eyes that that Primus was no different, but the Seekers? The people who'd taken me in after Winta had left and who'd given me something to live for? That was a harder pill to swallow.

'I need to tell you the rest,' she said. 'I need to tell you what I saw in that basement before I was caught.'

'You actually got into the basement?' I asked. 'You found Khalyed?'

'Yes. I knew what I was looking for, and I've always been a good tracker. The thing is, I knew Dr Jay quite well. I was always in and out of the lab, going to visit Dad, and he was always there. The two of them were like a comedy double act. I mean, they really loved each other. They called each other their *work husbands*, you know? So when I finally got into the basement, I knew his scent well enough to track it to the box where the baron had buried him. Even in the short time that had passed since he'd been boxed, I expected to find his door cobwebbed and dusty, being that far down, but instead there were worn marks in the dirt floor, as though someone was regularly coming to visit him. It wasn't until I busted the door and looked inside that I understood why.'

I was leaning forward by now, hanging on her words, but

she seemed to be so stuck in the horror of her memory that she had forgotten I was there at all.

'After only a few months in the box, he shouldn't have looked like that,' she said. 'It looked as though he'd been there for years, decades even, and there were holes in his skin. All over his skin. You know when they've been in there for years, and the skin goes kind of hard and leathery?' I'd seen it before. It was never pleasant. 'Well,' she went on, 'it showed all the pinpricks, tracing the lines of his veins along his arms, up his throat. When he finally opened his eyes and saw that it was me, he explained in a whisper what had been done to him. Day by day, vial by vial, the baron had been stealing his blood.'

'What?' I said. 'Why?'

'To kill the boxed Silver, the ones he decided should never see the light of day again.'

My instinct was to disbelieve her. I could only think that if Winta was right, and there had been as many needle marks in Khalyed's skin as that, then that was a hell of a lot of deadly blood. For all his faults, for everything he'd done, I couldn't imagine Drake as a mass murderer.

'You don't believe me,' she said.

'No,' I said. 'I mean, I don't know. Yes?'

'Okay, but consider this: there are a lot of Silver who went into the baron's basement and never came out again. Elise was given a year in the box, but after that year was up, she didn't emerge. The baron said she'd been released, but she was just nowhere, and she wasn't the only one. After a while, a few of us began to suspect that he was keeping the ones he didn't want to let free. But even with the basement as big as it is, he can't keep everyone locked up forever. He'd run out of room. So he had to come up with another solution to deal with the people he thought couldn't be redeemed.'

'And you think Elise was one of those people?' I asked.

'I'm certain of it. Every time the baron wanted someone to disappear, he just injected them with Dr Jay's blood and then *poof*, they were gone.'

It was neat. It was efficient. It was cost-effective. It was a solution that sounded very much like the kind of thing Drake would do. He'd always told me he wasn't a good man. I just hadn't realised quite how bad he'd been.

'I can't believe it,' I said, but my tone told her that I did. 'How many has he killed?'

'I don't know,' she said sombrely. 'Tens. Dozens. A hundred? We'd need to open every door in his basement to check.'

'Then we should call him out,' I said. 'Tell everyone what he's done.'

'With what evidence? The absence of Silver scabs? That's hardly going to sway anyone, not against someone as powerful as the baron. He'll just say he released them. It's the elegance of his chosen murder weapon: all it leaves behind is dust.'

My mind flashed me an image: a plastic bag filled with ash.

'It's what you used to kill Matthew Felton,' I said.

She looked away. 'Not quite. That was something slightly different.'

'Oh?'

'Yes.'

'But it's what you want to use to kill the Primus. What exactly are you planning?'

She smiles and says, 'I think we've covered quite enough for one meal. Don't you?'

In truth, I was exhausted. I was feeling the aftereffects of the dart like the worst Massacre hangover in history and, even though it was only mid-morning, my eyes were already starting to feel gritty and tired.

But before I went back to my bed, I had to get something off my chest.

'I was one of the Seekers who trailed you back then,' I confessed, because I thought this was an honest space and I felt I owed her some truth for all that she had given to me. 'I chased you. For years.'

'I know.'

'I didn't know about your parents, though. I didn't know I was keeping you away from them.'

'It's not your fault,' she said. 'I'm the reason you ended up where you are now. If it wasn't for me, you never would have wound up with the Seekers. If I'd taken you with me, you wouldn't have been indoctrinated by the corruption of the Seekers, the Solis Invicti, the Primus. You'd be able to see it all as clearly as I do. It was my responsibility to get you out.'

'The Seekers are my family, Winta,' I said quietly.

'No, I'm your family. I'm your sire. And they've kept me away from you for far too long.'

'They kept us apart?'

I thought back to those first days with the Seekers and all I remembered was loneliness. Most people had been kind enough, but I'd had to cut myself off from my human family, from everything I'd ever known, and it had been hard. On top of that, I'd been abandoned by the person who'd dragged me into this life in the first place, the woman I'd convinced myself I loved.

This woman.

'They kept me running and they kept you penned,' she said. 'I would have come sooner if I could, but I wasn't strong enough then.'

'And now?'

She smiled. 'Now I have everything I need to take them down, get my parents back, and get my revenge. And you're going to help.'

18

THERE'S MORE TO tell you about the week I spent with Winta, but that'll do for now. Important shit is happening and I can't spend all my time reminiscing, you know.

Back in the present, I'm sitting on the sofa in the house that is now mine and Winta's to share, greeting her with kisses. But I can't concentrate on Winta because there's a perfume in the air that doesn't belong: dry paper, a library smell, the scent that belongs to a platinum-haired woman who looks and moves like a ghost.

'They bought it, then?' Winta asks me. 'Tabitha's in her box?'

'Worked perfectly.'

'No one suspected anything?'

I give her a teasing look. 'Are you questioning my acting skills?'

'Just as long as you got away clean.' She doesn't tease me back. 'You didn't stick to the plan, though, did you?'

'It all worked out fine, so what does it matter?'

'It only worked out because you were lucky,' she says. She's irritated with me now. 'I asked you to do things the way I did for a reason. Did you forget what you were supposed to do, or did you just decide to ignore what I told you?'

'I didn't—'

'You could have fucked everything up,' she says. 'If you pull that shit next time—'

'I won't,' I promise. 'I'm sorry.'

I try to take her hand, hoping to gentle myself back into her favour, but it's too late. She shakes me off and walks into the kitchen to fetch a bottle of blood from the fridge. She doesn't fetch one for me.

I should have stuck to the fucking plan.

'The plan is *what*?' I said.

Yes, I know I said I was done reminiscing, but it turns out that I do need to give you one more flashback. Just a little one. Teeny tiny, really.

'It's the only way,' Winta said. We were sitting on the new sofa in the living room of her Jericho house. She'd been laying out the details of how I was going to help her take down the Silver hierarchy, and we'd reached the planning stage of Phase One: get Khalyed's blood.

'You'll have to deal with Kulika first,' she said. 'Do you think you could get her out of there?'

'Unlikely,' I said. 'I could give it a go, but I doubt I'd get anywhere with it. She's too loyal to Drake. But she's overworked enough that she probably won't notice someone moving around in the basement.'

'But she'll notice if you're gone too long. That's why you need Yolande,' she said. 'It's a maze down there, and we have no idea where they're keeping him. You need to be able to go in and out, just like you normally would when dropping off a scab, without any unreasonable delay. You can't do that if you have to go searching through all the boxes to find the right one, then waste more time breaking the door down and extracting his blood. We have a Trojan horse already in there, just waiting to be activated, so use her. To pull this off, we're going to need Yolande.'

That was Winta's plan. To get Khalyed's blood out, we needed a reason to go in, and boxing Tabitha was the perfect excuse. Because of course, Tabitha didn't kill Felton, and she was never intending to take out the Primus. Winta framed her. Once her capture had given us a reason to go to the boxes, I was supposed to take Tabitha into the basement, stop by Leclerq's box just long enough to pass her some blood so she could free herself, and a syringe so she could extract some of Khalyed's blood, then I was supposed to leave and wait for Leclerq to do the rest.

It was a stupid fucking plan.

Maybe it made sense to use Leclerq. Winta trusted her, and she was perfectly placed to help us out, but still. I didn't want to involve her, and if I was honest with myself, it was because of the scent mark.

'I don't like it,' I said.

'Your dislike is noted.'

'But you want me to do it anyway.'

'Yes. To the letter.'

I was sceptical, and I didn't bother to hide it.

'Come on, Jacky,' she said. I wasn't sure about the new nickname, if I'm honest, but coming from Winta it felt like a gift I couldn't refuse. 'I've been doing this a long time. I know the Invicti, I know the Seekers, and I know the baron. You have to trust me.'

I thought I knew Drake pretty well myself, but it seemed unwise to start in on that argument, particularly now that she was leaning in towards me. The sweet scent of her skin was impossible to ignore. I'd missed her. I'd missed her so much, and the past couple of days had been filled with nothing but words and tortured yearning. I wanted to touch her. I wanted to be back in her arms again, finally, where I belonged.

'I do trust you,' I said.

'Then trust that I know what I'm doing.' Her expression softened into something more suggestive. 'Why don't you let me prove it to you?'

So I did.

When she looked at my eyes, then my lips, and leaned in further with the unmistakable intention of kissing me, I almost couldn't believe it. When our lips finally touched, I felt drunk with triumph. Then she was kissing me. Her lips were moving on mine, and mine were moving on hers, and yet for some reason I wasn't feeling the pull of it in my chest like I expected. It was as though I was outside the moment looking in. I was getting in my own way.

Her hands were at my waist now, pushing me gently backwards until I was lying down with my head on the arm of the sofa. For a moment, her hands felt foreign, as though they should belong to someone else, but then her scent hit my nostrils again and I knew exactly who she was. She was the woman who'd found me outside a club in Oxford when I'd been just a stupid teenager, but had seen enough of something in me to pick me out of the crowd. She was the woman who, even after spending some time with the mess that was teenaged me, had still thought enough of me to turn me Silver. At least, that's what I needed to believe.

I brought down my barriers and I let her in.

After years of putting Winta on a pedestal, I let myself believe that it was me she wanted. I let her fingers and her lips convince me that I was wrong about how much of a disaster I was. I began to imagine that she didn't notice any of the things I hated about myself or that, more incredible still, she liked them. From the way she was kissing me, as though she seriously intended to see me naked on this sofa, it was difficult not to be swept up in that belief.

Then she said, 'I love you, Jacky,' and kissed me again.

I'm not sure I can put the feeling of catharsis into words. I felt like crying. When I realised that there was a tear trailing down my cheek, I wriggled onto my side on the sofa, moving Winta with me, so the cushions would absorb the teardrop before she could notice.

It was all I'd ever wanted. No, needed. After everything that didn't happen with Drake, I needed Winta to love me. But it was more than that. I needed the act that gave me this weird, magically-extended life to be rooted in something beyond her desire to escape. Now, finally understanding why she'd done what she'd done, and being reunited with her at last, I was at peace.

It didn't take long for us to divest each other of our clothes. She was just as beautiful as I remembered, and her attention just as focused. I was so nervous I couldn't really get into it properly, and I didn't want to start adjusting her technique to my preferences when we'd only just found each other again, so it took a while before we were both finished. But really, it was enough to be beside each other again.

Afterwards, the tension between us was gone.

'What happened to your eyebrows?' Winta said, stroking my hair away from my forehead.

'You did.' I smiled. 'I was too close to Felton when he went up.'

'Oh, right.' She smiled back. 'Sorry about that.'

'Best Christmas present I ever got,' I said, but really my gift was her. She was back in my life, back in my arms, here to stay. In the space of one basic fumble on the sofa, my abandonment issues were cured.

And that was that.

Over the next few days, Winta showed me how the entire plan fitted together. She showed me how we fitted together, too: two minds, two hearts, two bodies aligned in purpose.

With her by my side, I felt truly powerful for the first time in my life. We had knowledge, we had intent, we had honesty and we had each other.

We were united.

Except…

Except.

I couldn't ask about the scent mark on Leclerq. She was locked away in a box, out of reach, so I convinced myself that it didn't matter. I didn't want to know.

Until now.

I'm still not wearing Winta's scent mark. We've been avoiding kisses since I returned to the Seekers, just in case, because we didn't want anyone to find out that we're together. But apparently all that caution was for nothing, because even now that we've started kissing again, she's not marking me. She's never marked me. She says she's holding back, that she's controlling it, but I've done enough of my own marking to know that if you feel it, *really* feel it, then there's no holding back.

I can't tell her that, of course, because the last thing I want is to have our sexual histories hanging between us, so I worry in silence about what it means that Leclerq was wearing Winta's scent mark the day I locked her away in the basement, and I am not.

I worry that, now that Leclerq is free, I will have to share.

And I don't share.

'Yolande got out fine,' Winta says, returning from the kitchen.

I suppress a wave of irritation and paste on a smile. 'Great.'

And it is great. It was part of the plan, and it went perfectly, except I was super efficient and not only discovered where Khalyed was days ago, but I also managed to get what we needed from him all on my own. Leclerq was entirely useless.

'Where's the syringe?' Winta asks.

My smile is real this time as I pull the tool wallet from my back pocket and unzip it. The syringe is glass, because the serum in Khalyed's blood would destroy plastic, but it's full and intact.

I'm feeling unsettled, though. Winta told me she'd seen the evidence that Drake had been stealing blood from Khalyed over the decades, that his skin was riddled with needle marks and his body was unnaturally decayed. I'd seen none of that.

'Dr Khalyed…' I say to her, not sure how to ask the questions that are plaguing me.

'What about him?'

'There were no other needle marks in him.'

'Yeah, well,' she says dismissively. 'It was a long time ago that I saw him, and the baron's been away. Maybe Dr Jay healed.'

'In a box? And anyway, when Ed asked Khalyed if anyone had been taking his blood, he said no.'

'You think he'd dob in the baron?' she scoffs, then her eyes narrow as she looks at me. 'Are you doubting me, Jacky?'

'No,' I say quickly. 'It's just that—'

'Good. Let's hear no more about it, then. You did well.'

'Um, thanks.'

I want to ask her again, to push for the whole truth, but she's got her attention on the syringe now and it's clear the subject is closed.

'No problems getting it out unseen, then?' she says absently.

'Other than bloody Drake? No. I could have done without having to make nice with him, though.'

'I'm sure you managed,' Winta says. I don't like the insinuation in her tone.

'Do you think I actually enjoyed spending time with him?' I say. 'After everything you've told me about what he's done?'

'I don't know,' she shrugs a little, looking away. 'You don't seem to believe it's true.'

Maybe I don't, not entirely, but that doesn't change the fact that I've chosen my side. There's no going back.

'Winta,' I say, walking over to take her face in my hands, 'you know I'm with you.'

'He's going to ruin everything,' she says, pulling my hands away. 'He's going to get in your head and mess you around, and you're going to end up standing next to him instead of next to me.'

'Why would you think that?'

'I've heard things, Jacky. Word gets around.'

'What kind of *word*?'

'About the Baron of Oxford and the Seeker whose heart he broke.'

'He did *not*—'

'It's what everyone's saying.'

'Then everyone can go to hell,' I say, putting my hand on her cheek again so I can turn her face to mine. 'You made me, Winta. You understand me. We're on the same side of this, and whatever Drake says won't change that. I'm yours. You know that, don't you?'

She smiles a little then, but she doesn't seem convinced. That's been the story of our relationship since her reappearance: a new doubt to dispel every day, one test after another that I have to pass to show her that I'm serious. I don't blame her for that. After all, she's been on the run for two decades. When you've been watching your back for so long, you'd be stupid to trust anyone, let alone someone who's been working for the enemy. I get it. But still, I wish she'd let me in.

I can feel there's more she isn't telling me, and I want to know it all. If framing Tabitha, betraying the Seekers, lying to Drake, freeing Leclerq, and stealing Khalyed's blood isn't enough, then how am I ever going to prove to her that I'm on her side?

There's a thump from upstairs, and it's coming from the master bedroom. Leclerq has fully invaded our home.

'What's she doing in our room?' I ask.

'Oh,' Winta says, 'I told her she could sleep in there.'

'What? Why?'

'She's spent months in a box. The least we can do is give her the double bed.'

'Then where are we going to sleep?'

'We'll work something out,' she promises. I want to pin her down on specifics. I want her to reassure me that we'll be together tonight, as we were every night of my so-called abduction, and that Leclerq being here won't change that. But she doesn't volunteer that reassurance and I can't push for it, not when things between us are so new and fragile. I don't want to risk chasing her away.

'We didn't even need her help in the end,' I say, because I can never resist prodding an open wound. 'I did it all without Yolande.' I let the silent accusation hang in the air: since we didn't need her help, why did we have to release her at all?

'Would you rather we'd left her in the box to be murdered?' Winta asks, suddenly furious.

'No, I didn't—'

'Because that's what would have happened. She'd have ended up like Elise. We're just lucky he went on holiday so we had a chance to get to her before he did.'

'I'm sorry.'

She shakes her head and walks over to the dining table in

the corner where we've spread out a bunch of scribbled maps we've been using to plan Phase Two. She moves them around a bit, but it's clear that she's doing it as a way to vent her frustration rather than because she's particularly interested in the drawings at the bottom of the pile. 'I just don't understand you sometimes, Jacky.'

'I'm sorry. I didn't even consider that Yolande would be a target.'

'Why not?' Winta says, turning to face me. 'Yolande got ten years. Elise was only supposed to be boxed for a year, and the baron didn't hesitate to kill her.'

'I'm sorry,' I say again. 'I should have thought.'

The truth is that I hadn't thought much about Leclerq at all since she'd been boxed, and I'd been trying to avoid thinking about her since Winta and I had got back together. But whatever the history between the two of them, Winta obviously cares about Leclerq and she must have been going out of her mind with worry. I can see for myself that she's pained by the pain Leclerq has suffered on her account. Maybe I should've been thinking about that instead of trying to turn this into a competition between me and a woman who – however much I dislike her – deserves some consideration after spending months in Drake's basement.

Can I be magnanimous enough for that? I resolve to try.

'Besides,' Winta says, more to herself than to me. 'There's no way we'll be able to pull off the next part of the plan without Yolande.'

'What can I do?' I ask, coming over to join her at the table.

'I'm working on it.'

'I can help,' I say. 'I know the building. I've been there before. And I know the people, too. Let me help you plan.'

'I don't need help with the plan,' she says, sitting up and pushing her fingers into her hair as she stretches. She looks exhausted, and no wonder. It's been days of this for her: poring over the details, going through every possible permutation, trying to eliminate any flaw from her design. 'What I need is an opportunity,' she says, 'and that's just a matter of chance and time.'

I move around the table to stand behind her, trailing my fingers up her arm until I hit the bare skin where the collar of her loose T-shirt gapes. 'Then maybe I can help like this,' I say, settling my hands onto the taut muscles of her shoulders. She groans and tips her head back as I rub the tension out of her body. Her skin is warm and soft beneath my fingertips. I want to feel it against my lips.

'You must be tired, Jacky,' she says after a while. 'It's been a big day.'

This is what she usually says when she's got some intimacy in mind, so I take it as a cue.

'Yeah,' I say with a forced yawn. 'I might turn in.'

I'm anticipating an early night filled with something more than kisses, so I'm disappointed when Winta says, 'Okay. I'll be up later.'

'Um. Okay. Night, then.'

'Night.' She doesn't even look up from her papers.

She's preoccupied, I tell myself as I walk upstairs and into the single bedroom where I woke up from the tranquilliser. With Phase One now complete, she's concentrating hard on Phase Two. It's hardly surprising that she's a bit distracted.

I can tell myself whatever I like, but I still feel insecure. With all these emotions rushing around, and with Leclerq peacefully snoozing in *our* bed next door, I'm not expecting to sleep myself, but it really has been a big day – finding and boxing Tabitha, stealing Khalyed's blood, dealing with Drake – and to my surprise, rest comes easily.

I don't stir at all until Winta finally joins me in the single bed at who knows what hour of the morning. She brings with her the scent of old paper and betrayal.

19

I HEAD BACK to Solomon College early the next day. I don't know what to say to Winta, or how to deal with Leclerq, so I employ the classic la-la-la-I'm-not-listening strategy of running away before either of them is awake.

The Seekers common room should be empty at this time of the morning, providing the perfect place for me to grab a quick nap before the day begins properly, but someone else has beaten me to it.

'Naia?' I say.

'What?' she says sleepily, pushing off her blanket. 'Nothing, I mean, I just lost a pen down the back of the sofa, and I was looking for it, and—'

'Why are you sleeping in the common room?' I say, asking the question she's already trying to answer with a lie.

'Oh,' she says. 'It's just you.'

'Why, who did you think it was? Budge up.' She swivels her legs off the cushions to give me space to flop down next to her. I tip back my head, closing my eyes. It is far too early for me to be conscious.

'I didn't want Cam to see me and think I was coming back for good,' she says. 'Because I'm not.'

'But?' I say, opening one eye.

'Everything's gone from bad to worse in the house,' she says. 'It's only been two days – two days! Can't everyone just… chill out?'

With that, I give up on any hope of a nap.

'I guess there's always going to be a, you know, adjustment period, or whatever?' I say, trying to find something helpful to offer. This is not my area of expertise. 'When new people move in together, maybe they're always going to rub up against each other a bit.'

Naia smirks and says, 'Oh, really?' Even in the depths of despair, she still can't let an innuendo pass her by.

'*I mean*,' I say, 'that it'll take a while for everyone to get used to everyone else, right? Everyone needs time to work out how they're going to compromise in order to get along.'

Yes, it has not escaped my notice that this advice applies equally to my new living situation with Winta and Leclerq. Part of me feels that if I can convince Naia to give it another try with her housemates, then maybe I can muster up the tolerance to get along with Leclerq, whatever she and Winta might be up to while I'm sleeping.

'They always used to get along,' she says.

'Maybe polyamory's just tricky,' I suggest.

'Oh, come off it, Jack. It's too early for you to be coming at me with your bullshit prejudices.'

'I don't mean it's bad, it's just that… Well, it seems kind of hard. How do you do it? How do you balance the needs and feelings of all those people and come up with a solution that works? I find it difficult enough with just two in the mix.'

'It's always a work in progress,' she says. 'But then that's every relationship. People change, and they change the things they need and want, so I guess you've just got to be willing to shift things more when there are more of you. And also, not get pissed off with people because their needs and wants change. It's kind of basic, really.'

I think about that for a minute.

'So what's changed with your housemates?' I ask.

'It's all change, isn't it?' she says. 'But mostly, I think the problem is that Rajni and Chris used to live together on their own, and now they're joining the rest of us, which makes Rajni worry that their relationship will suffer.'

'Is that what Cam thinks the problem is?' I say, remembering their numerous chats on Christmas Day.

She laughs. 'You think I worked all that out on my own? Yeah, it's what Cam thinks.'

'Then maybe you should be talking to Rajni,' I suggest.

'That's what Cam said, too.' She sighs out a breath.

'So why are you talking to me?' I say. 'Oh, you're avoiding it. Which is why you're sleeping in the common room.'

'Yep.'

I'm not going to judge Naia for her avoidance tactics. After all, I can relate.

'Well, if you want somewhere to stay in the meantime,' I offer, 'then I have a place you could use.'

'What, your shitty rooms with no floor?' she scoffs. 'Thanks, but no thanks.'

'No, I have my own place, actually.' Fuck it, I'm never using it again so there's no harm in telling her. 'As it turns out, Tabitha bought me a flat in the city centre. It's in my name, so, yeah. It's mine.'

'Wow. She bought you a flat and you locked her in a box. I've said it before and I'll say it again, Jack: you have relationship issues.'

'I'm aware. Do you want to stay at my place or not?'

She looks as though she's considering it.

'I thought you didn't want to live with me?' she says.

'I absolutely do not, which is why I have somewhere else to stay. You'd be staying in the flat on your own.'

'All right, moneybags. How much are you asking for rent?'

'Just keep it clean and tidy for the next little while, and you can stay there for free. I'm sure you won't be there long. You'll work things out with the others eventually.'

'Maybe. I hope so.' She pauses, and I can see the cogs turning. I know she's going to ask the question before she even opens her mouth. 'I don't suppose you've changed your mind about the room?' she says hopefully.

'I do not want to live with you, Naia. Besides, I still don't think I could do the polyamory thing. I'm not sure how anyone does.'

'Well,' says Naia, 'most people don't have your weird issues.'

'My what?'

'You know, the whole thing with the baron.'

'There is no thing with Drake,' I say. 'We have no thing.'

'Oh, right,' she says, rolling her eyes. 'I forgot. I guess you don't think you're possessive, either, or that you like to hold a grudge.'

'Jesus, you're cranky in the mornings.'

'Nope, I'm just a frank realist, always,' she says. 'I mean, look at the way you are with Cam.'

'What are you talking about?'

'Well, he's always *your* partner, *your* best friend. It's juvenile, Jack. And that thing with Dr Ross? The minute she put one foot out of line, she was basically dead to you.'

'That's not fair.'

'Isn't it? You put her in a box, Jack.'

'Because she killed a person!'

'No, she killed Matthew rat-weasel Felton, and we both nearly did that ourselves, so who are we to judge?'

'Seriously, Naia? She spied on us for the Invicti, she's been working with the pro-revelation rebels, and if you really need another excuse to hate her, she was going to kill the Primus.'

Naia shrugs. 'She had her reasons, I'm sure. Plus, she bought you a flat. And I know she tried to talk to you after the vote, but you wouldn't hear it, would you? You were in full-on Grudge Mode, so you didn't leave her much choice but to try and get your attention another way.'

'Are you saying this is *my* fault?'

'No, it's still hers. I'm just saying I can see why you're set on serial monogamy. Maybe it's best you don't move in with us, after all.'

'I didn't want to in the first place!'

'No, you're right,' she says, kicking me off the couch and settling back under her blanket. 'If you tried polyamory, I think your brain would explode. Now I'm going back to sleep. Wake me if something important happens.'

Apparently that's all Naia has to say on the matter. I traipse out of the common room and into Boyd's still-wrecked office, picking through the boxes of salvaged detritus while I sulk.

She's so annoying, like the sister I never asked for. And she's wrong, anyway. I don't have to be possessive. I might not want to share any part of Winta, whether it's her time, her attention or her love. But if having Leclerq in the mix is the only way I get to have Winta at all, wouldn't I be able to compromise?

At this point, I don't feel like I have much of a choice.

Cam doesn't find Naia in the common room, so at least he's doesn't have the opportunity to be disappointed by her yo-yoing, but he stumbles across something worse instead.

'You're here,' he says, finding me in the canteen a little

later that morning. 'I went by your rooms – the temporary ones – and you weren't there. The door was open and your stuff was gone.'

'Cam—'

'And then I went back to your old rooms,' he says, looking at me with a hurt expression, 'but they still don't have a floor, so I went to the lodge to see which rooms you were staying in and they told me you'd moved out.'

'Cam, I—'

'You didn't tell me,' he says. 'You could've told me, any time this week, but I had to hear it from the porter.'

'Cam,' I say again, standing up to take his hands in mine and guide him down into the chair opposite mine. 'I'm sorry. I know I should have told you, but I didn't know how. I didn't want to upset you.'

'You didn't want to upset me? So you didn't talk to me about this monumental change in your life, at all, not through all the time you must have been planning it.'

'It happened so quickly, and we've been so busy…'

'Too busy for you to house hunt, I'd think,' he grumbles, crossing his arms over his chest and looking away. I feel awful, but also he's adorable when he pouts.

'I'm sorry,' I say. 'I suck. You deserve better.'

'Unless,' he says, turning to me with sudden interest, 'you've moved into the flat? You know, the one you don't want to admit that Tabitha—'

'No, actually. Somewhere else. I'll have a housewarming party when I've properly moved in,' I promise, hoping to head off further questions.

'Which will be in about a decade's time, if ever. You'll have stuff in boxes for years.'

'I only had one suitcase to take with me.'

'Still.'

'Your lack of faith is almost hurtful.'

'It's not that I don't believe in you,' he says, leaning back in his chair. 'I just know you, Jack, and you suck at unpacking. And cleaning. And tidying.'

'All right.'

'Seriously, what are you going to do without the college scouts to clean your room?'

This is a very good point and not one I've considered before. I bet Winta's not planning to do any cleaning, and I wouldn't know where to start. My mother did not raise me right. In reality, I guess we won't be in Oxford long enough for it to matter. We'll probably never be in one place long enough to need to clean it. Once we've done what we're planning to do, we'll be running for the rest of our lives. That might seem like a tough life, but if I'm doing it with Winta at my side, it might be the most exciting thing I'll ever do.

'Um, I guess I'll hire a cleaner?' I suggest to placate Cam.

'With all that money you have lying around? You can barely afford food. Speaking of which, you'd better make the most of college meals while you can. If you're not eating three meals a day here then you'll probably starve to death, because you absolutely and totally suck at cooking.'

'Not pulling the punches this morning, are you?'

'You're a tiny, helpless little bird who's not ready to leave the nest,' he says, trying to manipulate me with his big puppy dog eyes. 'At least try to learn to fly before you hurl yourself into the great unknown.'

'I'm still moving out, Cam,' I say gently. 'Or rather, I have already moved out, and I'm not coming back.'

He slumps in his chair. 'First Naia, now you. Is Boyd going to leave me too?'

'Probably, now that he has Mildred. And would that actually be a bad thing? Do you even want to socialise with him at the moment? Plus, we're still all going to work here.

We'll see you every waking hour. Nothing's going to change.'

'I won't be able to come over for ice cream sleepovers anymore,' he says, deploying his big brown eyes once again. 'I'll miss hearing you come home rolling drunk in the early hours of the morning.'

'If anything, that seems like a bonus.'

'And I won't be able to carry you home from the bar when you have a bad day and trash yourself senseless on Massacres. I bet you didn't think of that, did you?'

I hadn't, but there won't be any more days like those. My life is about to change. The *world* is about to change.

And Cam is oblivious.

I know that lying to him is a shitty thing to do, but what other options do I have? He might be my best friend, but he works for the Seekers and he worships the Solis Invicti. If I tell him a single thing about my and Winta's plans, he's going to try to talk me out of them and, when that fails, he'll probably report me to Captain Boyd. I can't have that. It isn't that I don't love Cam, or that I don't trust him with my life, it's just that I can't trust him with this particular thing.

Not yet.

Maybe not ever.

I can feel the weight of the unspoken things between us. It's not just that I'm lying by omission about every important thing in my life, it's that there are things I want to ask him – things I think he's omitted to tell me – that are pulling me down.

I want to ask him about that night in Winta's flat. I know I was new to the Seekers back then, and I was just a stranger to Cam, so I can well believe that he might have been involved in the failed takedown with the Invicti and failed to inform me. What I can't quite believe is that, after all these years of friendship and intimacy, he didn't tell me about it later, after we'd become close. He knows what Winta means to me, and what she's always meant to me. However hard it might have felt to divulge a secret he'd been keeping from me for so many years, he should have done it. I want to ask him why he chose to keep me in the dark.

For obvious reasons, that's a bad idea. He'd know that the only person who could have told me Winta's side of the story is Winta herself. With Cam's sense of smell being as powerful as it is, the last thing I want is for him to pick up on a residual scent and work out why I might suddenly be asking about my long-escaped ex. It's too much of a risk.

But I still wish I could ask.

'I'll miss you,' he says, letting the sombre mood sweep over him.

'I'll miss you too.' I really, really will.

'So,' he says, instantly brightening up like the optimistic Labrador that he is. 'Where's the new place? You're not moving into the baron's bedroom, are you?'

'Christ, no,' I say. 'He's brought Carlotta back with him, joined at the hip as always. Did you know she's the proprietor of a new open blood bar in town?'

'What? No!'

So I tell him all about it, sharing every detail of the new bar and most of the details of my encounter with Drake, the ones that don't involve the residual sexual tension that I'm sure will dissipate over time. Please, god, let it dissipate in time.

But there is so much about my recent days that I leave unsaid.

With that knowledge weighing heavily on my mind, there's no way I can say no when Cam repeats his suggestion that I submit myself to hypnosis. It'll be easy as pie, and it won't take much time at all, in fact by pure chance there's a hypnotherapist due to arrive at the college later today, isn't that a stroke of luck?

'It'll only take ten minutes,' Cam says. 'Half an hour, perhaps. An hour, tops.'

'Cam…'

I fully intend to keep arguing, but we're interrupted before I can get him to call the whole thing off.

'We've got a call,' Naia says, shouting from the doorway across the canteen. 'Grab your shit. I'll find Raul and meet you out front.'

We duly grab our shit, which means I fetch the blood capsules and Cam fetches Ed. We're going to need both.

20

GOING BACK TO work like this is… weird. I know I'm only here to keep up appearances while Winta puts together the rest of our plan, but it's funny how easy it is to slip right back into my usual role. I know I'm not staying with the squad, and I know that none of them will understand my motives for doing what we're planning to do, but I still believe in the work the Seekers do. I may not give a shit about the death of a Silver rat like Matthew Felton, but I will always care about the humans who unwittingly get caught up in our world.

Naia briefs us from the front seat while Cam drives the van across the city to a tiny two-bedroom house on Osney Island.

'One of the local Silver was walking his dog along the canal,' she says.

My nose wrinkles involuntarily, and I can see Cam grimacing even from the back seat. I'm horrified at how many Silver choose to share their lives with dogs; our noses are so sensitive that the reek of them is overpowering.

'Yeah, yeah,' Naia says before I can go off on one. 'I know, but this particular Silver has no sense of smell.'

'Huh,' I say. 'I didn't know that was possible.'

'Actually, it's increasingly common,' says Ed. He likes to ride along with us these days, which he says is to ensure that evidence is collected correctly, but really I think he's just lonely now he's the only one in the lab. 'Modern pollutants,' he continues, 'plus the use of drugs that interfere with regeneration... There are any number of factors that can render a Silver anosmic.'

'Well, there you go,' Naia says. 'Anyway, he saw someone moving at Silver speed in broad daylight and got a little suspicious, so he walked over to the front door and saw a smear of blood on the jamb. Then he called us, and here we are at Osney Island. That's all I know.'

'All right,' says Cam, parking on the road. 'Let's take a look.'

If Osney Island sounds awfully grand, then allow me to disillusion you. Osney's only an island in the most technical sense. It doesn't feel any different from the rest of the city, except it's soggier. The hallowed moniker is attached to a collection of terraced Victorian streets off Oxford's Botley Road, surrounded by various river tributaries that are never more than a few metres wide, all of which are bridged by the main roads anyway. If you ask me, the name's just an attempt to make the residents feel better about living on a flood plain. If what you're looking for is a house with a leaky basement, then you couldn't choose a better spot.

When we get into the basement of this particular house, the scent of Silver violence is hanging in the air. It's strong, despite the pervasive odour of damp and mould, so whatever happened here must have only just stopped happening.

I'm already handing out the blood capsules when Naia looks at me and Cam and says, 'Go scout.'

We run. I mean, we *run*. Cam's the tracker, because my nose is comparatively useless, but I'm fast enough to keep pace with him as he speeds out of the house, down the street and along the towpath, following the canal out of the city, past the college boathouses, through the locks and past the point where the river parts company with the city and strikes out on its own across the countryside.

Which is where the trail ends. Cam stops in the long grass beside the towpath and looks down at the rushing water.

'They went into the river?' I ask.

'They did,' he says, and he looks troubled.

'What?'

'It's weird.'

'Is it?' Passing through water is one of the only effective ways to lose a scent trail, so it doesn't surprise me that our scab has had the idea. 'I've seen it enough on the television.'

'But not in real life,' Cam insists. 'In real life, I've only seen it once before.'

'When?'

'Elise Santiago.'

Which makes no sense at all because, as far as I know, Elise is dead.

By the time we get back to the house and down to the basement, Raul and Naia have learned pretty much all we're going to from the scene.

'We lost him,' I say.

'How?' asks Naia.

'He went in the river,' says Cam. 'Way out in the countryside, halfway to Radley. He could have doubled back or carried on going for who knows how many miles, but either way, the trail's gone.'

'Fuck,' she says. 'We haven't got much here either, I'm afraid.'

The victim's a young guy, maybe a student going by his age, dressed in pyjama bottoms and nothing else. He's got shoulder-length blond hair and a face I can imagine might have been pretty while he was still alive. There's a huge chunk bitten out of his throat, leaving the traces of toothmarks behind, which are easy to spot because there's no blood at all. I can see every layer of his neck's anatomy revealed, and I really wish I couldn't.

'He's been drained,' Raul says.

'No shit,' I reply.

Raul's carrying a sealed evidence bag with a few strands of dark hair inside. His hands are shaking so hard that it's rustling incessantly.

'Why don't you take that back to the van?' I suggest. 'We'll be up in a minute.'

He nods mutely and shuffles out of the basement, tripping a little on the stairs on his way out.

'Bad memories,' I say to the others when he's gone.

It's not surprising that a human with a catastrophic neck injury gives Raul flashbacks to the incident that got him boxed earlier in the year, but he's going to have to get over it if he wants to keep his job. They're the commonest cause of death we see.

'You think this was an accident?' Cam asks.

'I don't know,' says Naia. 'It looks too clean for that, doesn't it? For someone to drain the body that completely, either they had help or they've been camping out here a while, keeping him alive, taking it bit by bit. That doesn't sound anything like an accident to me.'

'Is there anything in the rest of the house to suggest there's been an unwanted houseguest?' I ask.

'Ed's looking now.'

The man himself appears at the top of the basement stairs as if summoned. 'This place is a tip,' he says. 'Student rental. Dirty plates on every surface in the kitchen, unwashed sheets, wet towels in the bathroom, exactly what you'd expect. Even if there is any useful evidence up there, we're never going to find it.'

'What about the housemates?' Naia asks.

'There must be two,' Ed says, 'because the sitting room's been converted into a bedroom, but those areas look relatively clean. I'd guess they've gone home for the Christmas holidays.'

'Leaving one housemate home alone,' I say, 'and easy to target.'

'An opportunistic killing, then?' Naia says.

'It makes sense,' says Cam.

'You'll want to have a poke around in his room yourselves,' says Ed. 'Up the stairs at the front of the house. I thought I'd better wait for you before going through it. Give me a shout if there's anything worth collecting.'

Cam and I leave Ed and Naia in the dank little basement and go to look at the rest of the house for ourselves, but it's much as Ed described it. The whole place smells of week-old Chinese food and unwashed teenaged boys, and the front bedroom is the worst of all. There are half-drunk cups of coffee on the desk, dirty clothes strewn around on the floor – or maybe they're clean, who knows? – and more books than I expected. Apparently these students actually do study.

'It looks a lot like your rooms used to,' Cam says, earning himself a thump on the arm, though he's not wrong.

'Here's our guy,' I say, pulling a photo from a bunch that are stacked on the desk. They're all the kind of print outs you get from the novelty photo booths they have at parties. This one looks like it was taken at a student ball, because everyone's in evening dress and they're all too young to hold as much booze as they've tried to.

'The blond guy?' Cam asks.

'I think so.'

He's holding a champagne flute and smiling at the camera,

pink-cheeked and shiny with sweat. He looks like the kind of lad you'd trust to feed your cat while you're away on holiday, all soft eyes and sincerity.

'He looks nice,' Cam says sadly. 'And so young.'

'They all are, to you.'

'I suppose.'

I look through the rest of the photos, then pull the drawers out of the desk and rifle through the detritus they contain. There's everything I'm expecting to find – cigarette papers, pens, paperclips, condoms, lighters, empty chocolate wrappers – and one thing I'm not.

'Look at this,' I say to Cam, passing the item to him.

'A matchbook? I didn't think they made these anymore.'

It's one of the old-school variety where the matches are made of cardboard so you can tear them away from the book. I remember seeing them everywhere when I was first turned, because every bar, hotel and restaurant had them printed with their logos on, but since the smoking ban was brought in they've been few and far between. Now that no one's allowed to smoke inside, the smoking crowd have become undesirable patrons. No one would invest in that kind of marketing these days, except those fusty old landlords who've fallen seriously behind the times. Landlords like Sir Percival Wanker.

It's a matchbook for Crimson.

'That thing must be a collectible, right?' I say. 'The place was barely open a week.'

'Maybe that's why he kept it.'

'Maybe,' I agree, but it doesn't sit quite right. There's a match missing from the book, and it's just been tossed in a drawer. That doesn't seem like the way you'd treat something you cherished.

'Either way,' Cam says, 'we know he had contact with the Silver. Maybe he met someone at the bar. Maybe they even started seeing each other.'

'You think he had a Silver fuckbuddy?'

'I think he might have been in a *relationship* with a Silver,' he gently corrects me.

'Then are you going to look at the sheets, or do I have to?'

In the end, we compromise and agree to look together. We've left our latex gloves in the kit downstairs, so we peel the covers back gingerly with pincered fingers and hope to god we're not touching anything that's contagious.

Student bedsheets are… not nice. It's not just that they're made of the kind of synthetic material that crackles when it rubs together, it's that they're covered in stains I'd rather not categorise. Fortunately, that's not my job.

'Ed!' we both yell at the same time.

We've found blood. The sheet is pockmarked with it, thousands of tiny dried specks of it, so finely distributed that it looks to me like arterial spray.

Ed brings his sample kit with him and gets to work.

'Oh, hello,' he says, squinting through his glasses as he works methodically to swab a few areas and tweeze a few hairs into specimen bags. Once that's done, he gets out his big bags to bundle away the whole lot: sheet, duvet, pillows and all.

'Did you look at the hairs?' he says, handing me a specimen bag. 'They're different.'

He's collected a few. They're too long to be the victim's and too blond to match the ones that Ed found on the body.

'A girlfriend?' Cam suggests.

'Maybe,' I say.

I grab the stack of photos again and flick through them, trying to find hairs that match. There's one girl that could be a candidate: her hair's bleached blonde, unusually long, and draped all over the victim's shoulder in one of the snaps.

'I'll run some tests when we get back,' says Ed. 'It

shouldn't take long to determine whether the hairs are human or Silver, though it'll take longer to get a precise profile.'

'Sure,' I say, 'but concentrate on the hairs you found on his body first. These could have been left here any time in the past month or more. I don't think our victim did much laundry.'

'Roger that,' Ed says. He gives us a dorky salute he probably thinks looks cool, then he takes his evidence haul downstairs and leaves Cam and me to finish up.

'What are you thinking?' Cam asks once we're alone.

'It started here,' I say.

'It probably ended here too if he had an artery cut and no one did anything to stop it bleeding.'

'But that would have been a quick death. The guy was stone cold, Cam. Don't forget there was a scent trail for us to follow to the river, so they hadn't been gone long when we got here. If they'd drained him up here then just chucked the body in the basement when they were done, he still would have been warm when we arrived.'

'I can't make those facts fit together,' Cam says, pushing his hair away from his face and grabbing a handful of it as he thinks. 'The violence done to the victim must have been recent, or the scent mark wouldn't still have been so strong, but a body that cold must have been dead a while. The two facts contradict each other.'

I shrug. I've got nothing.

To keep my hands occupied while I think, I take another look around the room. We should try to put a name to the poor kid at least.

'Conrad Sommer,' I say, reading from a passport I've found in the desk. 'German national. He must have been here on a student visa.'

'Bag it with the photos,' Cam says, handing me one of the

evidence bags Ed left behind.

'And get the matchbook too,' I say.

Nothing else jumps out at us, so we leave the rest behind and follow Ed back down to the basement with the last bits of evidence.

'Did you see this?' Ed asks when we enter. He's kneeling down next to the body now, closer than the rest of us want to get, and his attention is fixed on the horrible mess that was once the boy's neck. 'Right here.' He's pointing.

I don't want to look, but Naia gets up close.

'It's a puncture mark,' she says.

'Oh no.' I say. 'No, no. Not more mystery serums.'

After all of Felton and Tabitha's various concoctions, I'm not sure I can cope with another round of Name That Poison.

'No,' says Cam, sniffing the air as he gets closer. 'It's nothing like that. I'd be able to scent it if it was, but there's nothing except blood.'

'Maybe he was drained through a needle, then bitten to cover the mark,' Naia suggests.

'Or maybe it's just a scratch. Jack's right,' Ed says, voicing words I'm not sure I've ever heard, 'we've had too many poisoning cases recently and I'm seeing needle marks everywhere. It's probably just part of the bite, and it's too chewed up for me to be certain anyway.'

Cam and I exchange a look. Given the conundrum of the cold body with a strong scent mark, I'm not so sure Naia's wrong. If someone came back here to cover up their work after Sommer was dead, that could explain the anomaly.

'Can we get a proper post mortem?' Cam asks.

'Not without calling the police,' says Ed. 'The Mortuary Service isn't working with us anymore.'

'Then is there any reason not to call the police? We've seen all there is to see here, right?'

'Right. Raul's got the hairs we found on the body?'

'Yes,' I say. 'He's waiting in the van.'

'Then I'll take a look at them and the other bits back at the lab.'

'I'll call the police,' says Naia.

'Anonymous tip?' I ask.

'Sweet old lady walking past,' Naia says in a creaky little voice. 'Mrs Doris Anderson. She'll say she's going to wait for them at the scene, but mysteriously do a runner before they show up. We should probably do the same.'

We do exactly that, and hope this case is a one-off, because we all know it's unlikely we're going to solve it. Sure, we're superhuman, but so are the people we're chasing. The uncomfortable truth is that sometimes the bad guys get away.

There's a man I don't like the look of waiting for us in the lodge when we get back to the college.

'Dr Haine?' Cam asks.

Oh god, no. Please no. I would run away, far far away, but I'm fairly certain Cam would catch me and haul me back, so I'm stuck with this... person.

Haine resembles nothing so much as a wet rat dipped in hair gel. He has dyed hair, rubbery pink lips and, despite being well into his forties, he's wearing a leather jacket. Perhaps it's a bit rich for me to judge him for that last one, but in my defence I would point out that I look awesome in my trademark accessory – at least I did until it was sacrificed to Leclerq's improvised explosives – whereas he looks like a creep.

'Mr Sawyer?' the man says. 'Ms Valentine?' His voice is nasal and irritating, so irritating that I'm not sure how he makes a living from lulling people into the gentle, restful state of semi-consciousness that hypnotism requires. 'I'm Dr Adrian Haine.'

'Cam,' I whisper. 'He's human.'

'Yes,' he whispers back. 'They all were, so I picked the one with the best credentials.'

'And this guy is what you were left with? Is he even qualified, or did he get his doctorate by sending off box coupons from his Sugar Puffs?'

'Is everything all right?' the quack asks, giving us the smarmiest smile I've ever seen. It makes his lips look like ham wrapped tightly in clingfilm. I feel a little sick.

'Yes, Dr Haine,' Cam says, rushing forwards to shake his hand. I restrain myself, assuming that it'll be as much of a sensory horror as his face. 'Everything's just fine. Jack's just a little nervous, never having been hypnotised before—'

'Oh, my dear,' the quack says, turning his smarm on me before I have a chance to escape. 'There's absolutely nothing for you to be worried about. I shall be right there beside you every step of the way.'

I do not find this reassuring.

'Excellent,' Cam says, ignoring my discomfort. 'Would you please come this way?'

I know I'm a traitor, but right now I'm inclined to believe that Cam has me beat in that department.

21

'LET'S START WITH a nice, deep breath, shall we?' says Dr Haine.

I already want to throttle him.

We're settled in Cam's tiny sitting room, or as settled as we're going to get, anyway. I suggested using one of the interrogation rooms, but apparently the atmosphere was too brutal, or some such shit, so here we are crammed onto Cam's sofa, all three of us, side by side like we're waiting for a fucking bus.

I feel like an idiot and I'm pretty sure Cam does too.

'So, Jacqueline,' says the loathsome alleged-doctor. 'May I call you Jacqueline?'

'I'd rather you didn't,' I say.

'Jack,' Cam says, his tone a reminder that I'm supposed to be playing nice. Which is all very well and good, and I did promise, but he's brought me a human snake-oil salesman who looks like he's wearing a rubber mask, so I feel like that changes things a little.

'Well,' Haine says with a breathy little laugh, trying to make a joke of it, 'I can't very well call you Ms Valentine all the way through the process, can I? That's not very

219

conducive to a relaxed state of mind.'

'I'd find it perfectly relaxing,' I argue. More relaxing than this guy getting any more familiar with me than he absolutely has to be, anyway.

'All right,' Haine concedes, with surprisingly good grace. 'We'll give it a try. Now, Mr Sawyer has told me a little over the telephone, but what exactly is it that we're hoping to achieve today, hmm?'

Well, that's a loaded question. I'm not sure how to answer it, since Cam and I want very different things from this, but he jumps in to save me the trouble.

'Something weird happened to Jack,' Cam says. 'She disappeared for a week, and when she came back, she couldn't remember anything that happened during that week.'

'Are you sure you want to explore that?' Haine says, looking between the two of us. 'There could be very good reasons for Ms Valentine to be repressing the things she can no longer remember.'

What do you know? A genuine insight from Dr Fraud.

'That's a good point,' I say, looking at Cam. 'Maybe it's for the best that I can't remember.'

'But what if you remember something that could save the Primus? Um,' Cam says, turning to Haine, 'that's what we call the college president. There have been some threats to have him, um, fired. We're wondering whether we should take them seriously, and whether Jack's disappearance might be linked.'

I turn to Cam with horror. He's building a house of cards here, and there's absolutely no guarantee that I'll be able to keep his story straight if a miracle occurs and Haine actually manages to put me under. Cam just nods back at me encouragingly. The boy has lost his mind. He's so caught up in his desire to protect the Primus that he's risking exposing us all. Perhaps he thinks it's worth it to put his best foot forward with the Invicti.

Suck up.

'Is that right?' Haine asks.

'Maybe,' I say.

'Well, that's very noble of you, Ms Valentine, to do this for the sake of your president's career.'

'It is, isn't it?' Cam says.

Which leaves me with very little choice but to agree to the whole rigmarole.

'What's the last thing you remember, Ms Valentine?' Haine asks.

I sigh and resign myself to the process. 'I was going into town to go shopping, then I went into an alley, then nothing.'

'And the next thing you remember?'

'Waking up in the college sick bay a week later.'

'We found her in a car on Iffley Road,' Cam adds.

'How very strange,' Haine says.

'Not really,' Cam says. 'We have a friend who lives out that way, and Jack was in her car, so we think she was probably visiting.'

'And have you talked to the friend?'

Uh oh.

'No,' Cam says. I wonder how he's going to explain his way out of this one. 'She's out of contact at the moment. Uh, on sabbatical. You know. Academics. Always in the library, impossible to track down unless they're teaching. Never answer their phones.'

'I see,' says Haine, clearly suspicious now.

'She's my ex-girlfriend,' I say, stepping in to rescue Cam. 'She probably isn't that keen to take our calls right now.'

'Ah. I understand. Then I shall do what I can to help.' He makes it sound like he's doing us a favour out of the goodness of his heart, rather than providing a service in return for the no doubt extortionate fee he's extracting from Cam. 'Are there any questions in particular that you'd like answered?'

I look to Cam. It feels safer to let him set the parameters of this fishing expedition, so I can work out in advance how I'm going to get around them.

'We'd like to know who Jack was with,' Cam says carefully. 'And we'd like details of anything that was discussed that relates to the Primus. Right?' Cam says to me.

'Right.'

It sounds safe enough, as long as I can stay in control.

'We'll have to see where the session goes,' Haine says, 'but if I can, I'll try to move things in that direction.'

'What are the chances that we'll get the answers?' I ask.

'As long as you're open to it,' he says, 'chances are good.'

Bugger.

'Of course,' he continues, 'these things rarely happen instantly. It might take ten, even twenty sessions to pull out the memories you've repressed in your trauma, and we may need to conduct a series of psychotherapeutic interventions alongside hypnotherapy in order to deal with the reason that you've created the block in the first place. What we often see in these kinds of cases is that there's a protective barrier erected around the source of the trauma, and the physic dissonance between that barrier and the memory itself causes a feedback loop that can only be dismantled by the application of intensive regressive therapy. Does that make sense?'

It makes no sense at all, but since he's talking to me in the slow, condescending voice you'd use to calm a skittish pony, I pretend that it does and say, 'Of course.'

'Good, good,' he murmurs. 'Then let's get started. Perhaps you could swap seats with Mr Sawyer?' he suggests to me.

I am not keen on this idea. I deliberately put Cam in the

middle seat so I'd have a buffer between me and the doctor, and I do not want to get any closer.

'I'm comfortable where I am, thanks,' I say, but Cam's already on his feet, shooing me sideways.

'Come on, Jack,' he whispers as he shoves me along. 'It's just for an hour, and it's not going to work if you don't let your defences down. Don't you care about saving the Primus at all?'

I don't, of course, which is part of the reason I'd rather not have this guy rootling around in my brain.

'Don't you care about keeping the Silver secret at all?' I whisper back. 'This guy is *human*. I'd report you to the Seekers, but you bloody are one.'

'I can feel there's a lot of tension in the room,' Haine says as we settle into our seats. He's got his eyes closed, and his hands stretched out in front of him – palms down, elbows bent – while he moves them up and down as though he's feeling how bouncy the air is. He looks ridiculous. Well, more ridiculous. 'Let's breathe that out of our bodies and breathe the positive energy in. Ready? Deep breath in. And out. In. And out, taking all that worry and anxiety with it.'

I cast a sceptical glance in Cam's direction, but he's got his eyes closed. His hands are resting palm-up on his knees, mimicking Haine's posture, and he's breathing in time. I consider breathing in when I should breathe out and vice versa, just to be obtuse, but Cam would notice and it would only end up pissing him off, so I close my eyes and fall in line. Under internal protest.

After a few minutes' of this, I'm irritated to discover that I do feel better, and then the next breath takes even that irritation away, leaving me feeling pleasantly chilled. Very chilled. In fact, I feel as though I'm almost floating, half-conscious and so relaxed that I'm not sure I could—

No... Too relaxed.

I struggle to pull myself back out of the fog, because there are secrets in here with me that I can't let out.

'Don't resist it,' Haine's voice says. 'Just let go.'

But I'm resisting for all I'm worth. I can't possibly let this strange, wax-lipped human into my brain.

'How do you feel?' he asks after a few more breaths.

'Relaxed,' I lie. At least, I think I'm lying. Given my generally recalcitrant nature, I expected to be a natural at resisting hypnosis, but it turns out I'm more suggestible than I anticipated.

'Good,' he says. 'I want you to go to the place you're happiest. Think back through the past weeks, the past months, the past year, until your brain latches onto a moment that makes you joyful. Can you see it?'

My minds scrolls as directed.

Ice cream with Cam on my sofa at the college, before my rooms fell through the ceiling.

Rolling around in my single bed with Tabitha, before she betrayed me.

Going to a party with Drake, his hand on my bare back, his fingers in my hair, his lips on mine, his hands slipping over my velvet dress as he presses me up against the—

Nope. Not that memory.

'Now let yourself fall into that moment,' Haine says. 'Wrap yourself in the sights, sounds, sensations and smells of your memory.'

I'm surrounded by the scent of copper and spice, the feeling of breath on my skin, of fingertips teasing that spot at the back of my neck the way I like best, and the sound of moaning.

Shit, no, the moaning isn't a memory. It's me, right now.

'Ummm…' I hear Cam say.

Haine clears his throat. 'Yes, er, yes. Good. Now that you're feeling relaxed, let's take you back to the day you disappeared. You're in central Oxford, about to do some shopping. Look around you and describe what you see, as you see it. Your mind can free-associate if you prefer. Just let the words flow through you.'

And, weirdly, I do feel like I'm back on the High Street that day before Christmas when everything changed.

'It's Oxford,' I say. 'There are too many people.'

'You're pushing through the crowds,' Haine improvises. 'And you don't like the crush. You wish you could escape them all. So you turn into an alley for a little peace.'

This is so clearly not what happened, and his version of events is delivered in such an irritating, know-it-all, semi-soothsaying fashion, that it pulls me a bit further towards consciousness. Thank fuck.

'What happens next?' he asks.

'I fall over. Everything goes away.'

'Just that?'

'I hit my head.'

'Ah. That would explain it,' he murmurs to Cam. 'Perhaps this is a physical rather than a psychic issue?'

'Unlikely,' Cam murmurs back.

Because of course, if it were, then my body would have healed it by now. Psychological issues, however, are a little harder for the Silver body to shake. It's like Drake said to me once: some versions of ourselves embed like bullets then fragment until they're too small to pull back out again. That was the night of the party, the night he stroked my velvet dress and—

Jesus Christ, I wish he'd get out of my head. I guess it's a relief that Winta's not showing up in here yet – good job, Subconscious – but the things I'm finding instead are more than a little disturbing.

'You're opening your eyes now,' Haine says softly, 'for the first time since you fell. What do you see?'

'It's Winta,' I say. Then I hear my own words and try to modify them. 'I mean, it's cold. There's a lot of very heavy rain.'

I hear Haine murmur to Cam, 'When did her disappearance occur?'

'A few weeks ago,' he replies. 'During a rainstorm.'

'Good, then we're on the right track.' Then Haine speaks a little louder, addressing me this time, saying, 'And what else do you see?'

My mind is scrolling through memories of the single bed in our new home, Winta sitting by my feet, bringing me blood, crawling into bed with me, and with all that crowd of imagery in my befuddled head I can't come up with a compelling lie. Instead, I keep my mouth shut.

'Hmm,' Haine says quietly. 'There's a blockage there. Let's try this.' Then, in a louder voice, he says, 'Try to think yourself back to that missing week. Imagine your memory is like a window hiding behind a curtain, and draw it back. Who's there with you?'

'Tabitha,' I say, the name slipping unwillingly from my lips. I don't want to go back to the cellar where Winta kept her captive, but I can't seem to resist the draw of whatever shit Haine is pulling. I'm starting to think he might not be such a fraud after all.

'The ex-girlfriend,' Cam whispers.

'And what is Tabitha doing?' Haine asks. 'Can you see?'

'Just sitting,' I say. I try to stop myself there, but my mouth is running off without me. 'There's something awful on the floor in front of her.'

She's sitting on one side of the bars, I'm standing on the other, and on the floor at my feet is...

'What is it?' Haine asks.

'I don't want to look.'

'Why don't you want to look?'

'It's a piece of me,' I say, and I can hear the panic in my voice. 'There's a piece of me lying on the floor.'

'Your tattoo?' Cam asks, and his voice jerks me a little further awake.

'I need you to stay quiet for this part, Mr Sawyer,' says Haine.

'Sorry.'

'Take a deep breath, Ms Valentine,' Haine says. 'You're safe here. Whatever happened to you is over now, but I want you to go back to the moment you were just watching and watch it again for me, as though you're watching a film. You're not in the film, it's just an actress who looks like you. You can watch it in a detached way and know that nothing that happens in it will affect you. All right?'

'All right,' I hear myself reply.

'Now, what do you see?'

'A cellar room,' I say, and the words come rushing out, out of control. 'There are notes scattered all over the workbenches because Tabitha's been working on the serum. There's a cage, and she's on the other side of the bars. There are flasks and machines too, and fridges where she keeps the vials. On the wall there's a whiteboard with every colour. I don't understand any of it, drawings and maths and stuff. And on the floor there's a trail of blood, and then there's a piece of me… a piece of me on the floor, the piece of me that was cut out of my hip and it burned so badly and there's a piece of me— a piece of me—'

'All right,' Haine says calmly, 'you're safe here. The film's finished now. It's over, and you're watching the credits roll, and everything's fine. Now take a deep breath in, and out. In, and out.'

Where moments beforehand I was struggling not to suffocate under the weight of memories I was trying not to relive, now the breaths come easily, as refreshing as a cool breeze over my skin.

'Let's go back to a relaxed place. Find a happy memory, a *calm* happy memory,' Haine emphasises. 'The image of a moment that relaxes you, making you feel pleasantly sleepy, as though you're in a cocoon of drowsy happiness.'

I feel like I'm waking up from the best sleep of my life.

Drake's bedsheets are made of soft cotton. When I wake the morning after the night I don't remember right now, I can feel their high thread count against every inch of my skin. It's pure luxury. Even better is the warmth behind me, spicy and metallic. It's like being surrounded by chocolate and desire. It has me remembering the previous night and every wonderful-awful thing we did together. Killian Drake naked is a fucking treat. His backside is so biteable that even though right now it's just a memory, I feel like I might expire from pure, concentrated lust.

There's that moaning again.

Somewhere so far off in the background that I almost can't hear it, someone is snickering.

'Er,' another voice says. 'Does Ms Valentine have any, er, *problems* I should be aware of? Is she particularly inclined towards the, er, you know?'

'Sex?' the first voice says.

'Yes,' replies the second.

'No. But there are definitely some feelings she's been repressing about a previous lover. Denial, you know.'

'Ah. And is that something Ms Valentine is interested in working through at all?'

'I doubt it, and anyway, we don't have time.'

'I'm happy to make this a regular session if that would help?'

'No amount of time is going to help her with that problem. Shall we just concentrate on…'

'Yes. Of course. Let's try something else. Ms Valentine,

imagine that you're on a beach.'

I can't remember the last time that happened, so it takes me a moment to grasp the concept.

'Or somewhere more familiar,' the voice continues. 'Imagine you're lying on the lawn in the college gardens. The sun is above you, the grass is beneath you, and it's pleasantly warm. You're safe and comfortable and happy, and there's nothing you're supposed to be doing. You're enjoying simply existing.'

I'm not usually a fan of the sunshine, but this is nice. I think I'll probably have a nap right here on the lawn.

'Your mind is wandering, thinking about nothing in particular, and the image of the Primus creeps into your mind.'

I can feel my body stiffening as every muscle prepares for action. I'm ready for this. I know what I have to do, I have everything I need in my pocket and all that remains is to find the moment I can——

'You're relaxed,' the voice insists. 'You're breathing easily. In, and out. In, and out. You're not worried about the threats against the Primus at all, because it's all over now. It's been dealt with. But you're thinking back on the memory of what you learned in the week you were missing, safe in the knowledge that it's all been resolved. Sink into those memories more deeply. What do you hear?'

You're talking about anarchy.

Yeah, I am. Isn't that better than the corruption we have right now? At least it's real, true. I'd rather that than live a lie. Sometimes you have to burn everything to the ground and start again.

What about all the people who'll suffer in the process? Don't pretend this is anything other than a personal vendetta.

I'm not pretending. There's nothing but personal.

Everything that anyone ever does is for themselves, in the long run. Sometimes what you want aligns with what other people need, and you can try to make a virtue of that if you like, but at the end of the day you do things for your own benefit.

'Who's speaking, Ms Valentine?' the voice asks.

'Her and me.'

'Tabitha?'

'Yes. She doesn't want me to go. She wants to keep me in the cellar and make me forget about everything else. She wants it to be just me and her, without...' I close my lips around the name before it can come out of my mouth. Winta's my secret, and I'm not going to give her away.

'Without who?' another voice asks. 'Are there other people involved?'

'I can hear her moving around upstairs. We've been talking down in the cellar too long and she's getting impatient. I'm scared—' Wait, that's not right. I'm not scared of Winta. I *love* Winta. '—of what might happen if she has to come down here. I'm afraid of what she might do.'

'To you?' says the first voice.

'To both of us,' I whisper.

It's not true, though. My subconscious must be pulling this from somewhere that's not my memory, because I wasn't afraid. I'm not afraid. People shouldn't be afraid of the people they love.

'Who's upstairs, Ms Valentine? Who are you afraid of?'

I can feel my lips parting. I don't want them to. I think I'm fighting it, but another part of me wants to open my mouth wide and shout her name, so this can be over and I can be done with it all.

Is it possible to love someone so much and still betray them?

There's a knock at the door and I startle. I wouldn't say

that I wake up, because it doesn't feel like I was exactly asleep. It's more as though I was preoccupied by a very important task and someone's just interrupted me.

Just in time, thank god.

'Here you are,' says Boyd. 'The baron wants to see you, Jacqueline.' He looks extremely pissed off about the fact that he is, once again, playing messenger.

'About what?' I ask, shaking away the cobwebs.

'How should I know? He just said to send you up there, so here I am, sending you up there. All right?'

'Yes, fine, all right. I'll go now, then, shall I?'

'Yes,' Boyd says, exasperated. 'Was I unclear?'

'Sorry, Dr Haine,' I say insincerely. 'I guess we'll have to cut the session short. Thanks for trying and all that, but I guess some mysteries are just never meant to be solved, right? Cam'll see you out.'

Then I'm gone, following Boyd out before Cam can say a word.

It's only when I've escaped the room that my enthusiasm starts to wane. I might have avoided creepy Dr Haine, but only at the cost of seeing Killian fucking Drake.

Out of the frying pan, into the much hotter frying pan.

I mean—

Jesus, I did not mean that like it sounded.

22

I WALK UP to Summertown as slowly as I can, because despite my initial enthusiasm to escape Dr Smarm, I'm dreading seeing Drake again. He sees so much that I'm worried he'll see straight through me. For that reason, amongst many others, I'm planning to make this quick.

When I get there, I'm surprised to find Cam getting out of his car in the driveway.

'What's going on?' I ask him. 'I thought you were dealing with the quack.'

'He didn't hang around. Something about the way you ran out of the door made him feel like another session wouldn't be welcome.'

He's grouchy with me because I ran off, but that's not really why he's unhappy. He's desperate to know where I was during the missing week, and he was putting all his hopes on hypnosis. Now it's failed, he's sulking.

I could give him the answers he wants. Maybe I should, but instead I go on the defensive.

'I tried, Cam,' I say. 'It's not my fault it didn't work.'

'I wouldn't say it didn't work, exactly,' Cam says. 'Don't you remember?'

'Not really.' It's gone all fuzzy in my memory, which is worrying. I left the college feeling like I'd kept my secrets nicely under wraps, but now I'm panicking that I might have given Winta away, or said something about our plans, but if that were true, wouldn't Cam have called me on it already? 'What happened?'

'You were pretty relaxed at the beginning there,' he says, and he's smirking. Why is he smirking?

'What?' I say.

'Nothing.' He continues to smirk.

'Cameron Sawyer, if you don't tell me what I said right now—'

'You moaned,' he says.

'I *moaned*? Like, a relaxed moan?'

'No.' He's smirking again. 'Not that kind of moan. Not that kind of moan at all.'

'Oh, god. What did I say?'

'Nothing in the moaning bits. The rest wasn't much that we didn't already know. You were with Tabitha in a cellar. She did… Well, it sounded like she cut out your tattoo. And there was someone else in the building above you.'

'Who?' I say, panicking a little. I didn't realise I'd said anything at all, and the possibility that I might have let slip —

'You didn't say.' His face falls so quickly that it almost makes me miss the smirk. 'That's the problem.'

'Oh, well,' I say cheerfully. 'We tried.'

'You weren't exactly keen going in though, were you?' he says. 'Maybe if you'd been a bit more receptive—'

'And maybe if hypnosis weren't a huge pile of—'

'Hello, you two,' says Kulika, exiting the mansion to greet us. She's back on door duty, I guess because she likes it rather than because she's been assigned there. It's a little below her pay grade, and her aptitude.

'Hey, Kulika,' I say. 'Do you know what this is all about?'

'Remember that guy from the Invicti, Adewale Ladipo? He's here to see you.'

'He came here?' This is not good news. Why did Winta have to have a brother in the Solis Invicti? Either he wants to talk to me about his parents, which would put us on dangerous ground, or his sister, which would put us on *extremely* dangerous ground, all right under Drake's nose. 'I thought he was going to get in touch with me at the college.'

'Evidently you weren't there. They said you've moved out.'

'Oh.'

'Right,' Cam says with a sideways glance at me. '*Oh*. Maybe leave a forwarding address next time, Jack.'

'Yes, yes, all right,' I say to him before turning back to Kulika. 'Where is he?'

'He's waiting in the first floor conference room, but the baron wants to see you in his office first,' Kulika says to me.

'Er,' Cam says, 'I think I'll wait down here.'

'Coward,' I say.

'No,' he replies. 'I just have a well-developed sense of self-preservation. See ya.'

Cam peels off to the kitchen to dig in the fridge while I stomp my way reluctantly upstairs to Drake's office. I should have worn my boots; they stomp so much more satisfyingly than trainers can.

I find Drake with his head in a bunch of letters, handwritten. Some of the Silver have stayed old school, and I guess his penpals are amongst them.

'What do you want?' I ask him.

'Hello to you, too,' he says, then he looks up and sees my face. 'Are you sleeping all right? You look awful.'

'Well, fuck you too.'

'I don't mean—'

'What do you want, Drake?'

'I want you to tell me what's going on. You're hiding something and I want to know what it is.'

'Because you have to know every little detail of my life?' I say, hyping up my outrage in an attempt to throw him off. 'Jesus, you're such a control freak.'

'Apparently I have to be. Kulika told me about the new guest in my cellar.'

He was bound to find out sooner or later. When a doctor who used to work for the Invicti gets boxed for killing a coworker and kidnapping her Seeker ex-girlfriend, the news gets around.

I laugh. 'Merry Christmas, I guess.'

'You call that a gift?' he says. 'Your ex is in my basement.'

'And your ex is back in your bed.' I shouldn't have said it. The moment the words slip out of my mouth, I realise that they're more than idle repartee.

'You're right,' Drake replies. 'We should talk about Carlotta.'

'I don't think that's necessary, do you?'

'The two of us have… an arrangement,' he says, ignoring my protest.

'Oh, I know,' I say. 'A very open arrangement.'

'No, I'm not talking about that. What I mean is that me and Carlotta, it isn't what it looks like.'

'So you're not banging each other's brains out on the regular?'

'No,' he says. 'Well, yes. Fairly regularly, but that's just Carlotta. She's…'

'Insatiable?'

'Let's just say she's undiscriminating. My point is that the ring isn't what it looks like.'

'Then what is it?'

'A gift,' he says. 'A *proper* gift. Or maybe a bribe. She likes shiny things, and the prestige that comes with being my fiancée. I needed her help so we made a deal.'

'Help with what?'

'We've been working together, going around Europe and taking soundings from the other Silver.'

This is a surprise. After the debacle at the vote, and their break-up soon afterwards, the last thing I expected was that Drake would team up with Carlotta for reasons beyond the carnal.

'Soundings about?' I ask. Getting information out of Drake is like pulling teeth sometimes, I swear.

'The Primus. The possibility of revealing ourselves to humanity. How we should structure our society. All of it.'

'But I thought you were anti-revelation?'

'No, I'm anti-war, remember? Whatever happens, I just want it to happen with the minimum of death and chaos. Although Carlotta is pro-reveal, she understands that. She doesn't want to see a repeat of the events of voting night any more than I do.'

'Okay. So what was the result of your little European excursion?'

'The same as the night of the vote, whatever the official count reported,' he says darkly. It sounds like he's worked out what I already know: the Primus rigged the vote. And if Drake has worked it out, how many of the pro-reveal rebels will have done the same? 'One way or another,' he goes on, 'we're heading for a change. Either the Primus is going to get behind it, or he's going to be pushed out, but right now he's standing in the way of the majority.'

I might have a solution for that problem. Of course, I'm not going to tell Drake about what Winta and I are planning, but I can't be hiding my thoughts very well because he gives me an odd look.

'What have you got yourself involved in, Jack?' he asks.

'I don't know what you're talking about.'

'You're up to something,' he says. 'Why is Tabitha in a box?'

'When someone gives you a gift, the polite thing to do is say thank you.'

'If putting your ex in a box is a gift at all – which, as I think I have made clear, I would argue against – then I think it's a gift to yourself rather than to me, and if we're doing gifts for you, then…' He gets up from his desk and goes over to a cupboard in the corner to extract a paper carrier bag. 'Here,' he says, passing it to me.

'What is it?' I ask suspiciously.

'Call it a late Christmas present.'

That's enough to put me on my guard. Drake's never got me a gift before. I've never got him one, nor would I. As previously established, we aren't friends, and even if we were, we'd be more the steal-each-other's-shit kind than the give-each-other-gifts kind.

'Is it dangerous?' I ask, squinting at the bag.

He sighs impatiently. 'Just open it.'

It's one of those fancily-wrapped things that you get from high-end shops where they smother everything you buy in tissue paper, so it takes me a while to get inside.

'I found it in Italy,' he says while I struggle my way to the bottom of the bag. 'I thought that since your last jacket met its demise in the service of the Seekers, the least I could do was replace it.'

Holy fuck.

It's a black leather jacket, but that description doesn't do it justice. It's not a leather jacket like my old one, all pale wrinkles and wet-dog smell, it's a leather jacket that's just fallen off the catwalk in Milan. It's genuinely stylish, and it's going to make me look like the absolute shit.

Maybe it's weird that people keep buying me clothes, but I'm just grateful I don't have to shop for myself. I suck at it.

'Try it on,' he suggests.

I throw the bag aside and make to shrug into the jacket, but before I can do so Drake is holding it out for me in invitation. My arms slide down the sleeves like silk. I wouldn't be surprised to find that's what the lining is made from; it's dark purple and gorgeous. When I zip the front together, it fits like it's made to measure.

I don't know what to say.

Drake looks like he's struggling for words too.

For a long moment, we just stare at each other in silence. I break it by saying, 'Thank you.'

They're words I never thought I'd say to him, but what else can I say? The weight of the beautiful garment on my shoulders is almost nothing, but it feels like the whole world. He thought of me. He might have been touring Europe with gorgeous Carlotta, but despite everything that's happened between us, despite all the ways in which we've hurt each other, he thought of me enough to buy me the perfect gift. And all the while, I'm standing here betraying him.

The backs of his fingers slide along my neck as he frees my hair from the collar, and I feel like I'm back where we started, at Windsor's terrible party with Drake's fingertips dancing at the nape of my neck.

I should be past this. I have Winta. I have our mission. I know what Drake truly is.

And yet.

'I know that scent,' he says, his breath warm on my neck, and I freeze. Behind me, Drake does the same. 'When did she come back?' His voice is flat.

'I don't know who you're talking about,' I say, shrugging out of the jacket. It suddenly feels too warm.

'Fuck.' He walks away, heading back to the safety of his

desk, then he picks up a crystal paperweight and hurls it at the bar. It detonates in a shower of shards that takes out several bottles of whisky, spilling their contents to the floor. 'Fuck!'

Kulika is through the door within a second, doubtless expecting to find her master in some kind of jeopardy. She looks first at Drake, then at me, then at the ruined bar.

'Sorry,' she says. 'I didn't mean to interrupt... whatever this is.'

'You're not interrupting,' I say. 'I think we're done here.'

'Well, if you're ready,' says Kulika, 'then Adewale Ladipo's waiting downstairs.'

I'm halfway to the door when Drake says, 'That's why he wants to speak to you, isn't it? Because of her.'

'How should I know?' I reply.

'I'll just, er... wait downstairs too,' Kulika says, sensibly excusing herself before Drake and I start shouting at each other.

'It's all because of her, though, isn't it?' he says when we're alone again. 'Matthew Felton was her doing, I suppose, and your kidnapping. And Dr Ross too?'

I don't reply. I'm not sure what to say.

'So she attacked Dr Ross, drugged you, then had you put Dr Ross in a box, and you didn't question it? Jack,' he says, incredulously. 'She makes you so blind.'

'No, Drake, she opened my eyes.'

He laughs, and the sound is sharp and bitter. 'Have you forgotten what happened the last time you trusted her?'

'She made me immortal.'

'She meant to kill you.'

'You don't know that.'

'I do, actually,' he says. 'She's a killer. She always has been and she always will be.'

'And you wouldn't know anything about killing, would

you, Drake?'

He blinks at the change of subject. 'What are you talking about?'

'You judge me for putting Tabby in a box, but where's Elise?' I ask. 'What happened to her? How many Silver have gone into your basement, and how many will never come out?'

Until this moment, I wasn't sure whether I believed Winta's accusations against Drake. I thought maybe, particularly now we'd found a scab with Elise's M.O., she might have been freed. Now, as I watch his face pale, I can't believe I ever doubted her.

'It's true, isn't it?' I whisper. 'You murdered them.'

Drake slumps into the chair behind his desk. He can't even meet my eye.

'What do you want me to say?' he asks.

'I want you to tell me it isn't true.'

Now he looks at me. 'You want me to lie to you, Jack?' he whispers. 'You've said it yourself: heroism doesn't suit me. So I do what has to be done.'

'Murder?'

'Yes, murder. What would you do with people like Charles Legrange?' he asks.

Legrange is a scab who killed three humans in exhibitionist fashion back in May, displaying their deaths at public events. He's in Drake's basement now. At least, I think he is.

'Silver like that not only have no respect for human life,' he continues, 'but they actively enjoy destroying it. All they want is the feeling of power they get from turning each death into a personal vanity project.'

'And you think that justifies bumping off everyone who ends up in a box? Not every Silver who kills a human is a psychopath like Legrange.'

'You say that as though psychopathy is as set in stone as someone's height, or the colour of their eyes.' He looks up at me, running a hand back through his hair as he grasps for an explanation that will placate me. He's unlikely to find one. 'The truth is that any of us can become that twisted, given the right conditions and sufficient time, and the Silver have all the time in the world. But once you've crossed that line, even once, there's no coming back. It changes you.' He says this like it's supposed to be a warning, which is rich given what I know about his own kill list.

'It must have changed you,' I say. 'Two decades, and so many dead Silver.'

'And how would you know if it had?' he asks. 'You didn't know me back then, before. How can you look at me now and judge me for what my actions have turned me into, when they've made me the man you've always known? You liked him well enough to let him take you to his bed, if only once,' he says. He's stood up from his chair and now he's leaning towards me, his hands splayed on the guilty desk. 'You like me the way I am, Valentine. Don't pretend that the danger I carry with me doesn't excite you as much as it horrifies you.'

I hate him for bringing it up. I hate him for using my weakness against me, as though I have any control over what my body wants. But I don't have to listen to it. I can see him as he is now, arrogant and unrepentant behind his stupid megalithic desk, and however much his scent calls to me I can remember how he made me feel in this moment and deny him for the rest of time.

'You have no power over me, Drake,' I say. 'You're just as much of a psychopath as they are.'

'But not as much as your old-new girlfriend, I think,' he says. 'Have you never wondered why you seek out people who mean you harm?'

'Are you talking about yourself? Because I'm actually

trying to get away from you.'

'I've never harmed you, and I never would. I've upset you, maybe.'

'I've never cared enough about you for you to be capable of upsetting me,' I say.

'You're a bad liar.'

'And you're a cold-blooded killer.'

'Perhaps,' he says. 'Perhaps I need to be in order to keep the others in line. Did you think of that? We're a species designed to feed on humans, and the parameters within which we can coexist with them peacefully are vanishingly small. I'm just policing the edges.'

'By what right?'

He shrugs. 'Someone has to.'

He makes it sound so reasonable. It makes sense, almost, until you insert real people into the equation, at which point it all falls apart. Because what if he's wrong? What if they'd caught Winta all those years ago and boxed her, thinking she'd killed her landlord, and Drake had murdered her before hearing her explanation? And what if the Invicti put people in Drake's basement under false pretences, and Drake ended them too? Or what if the pretences were Drake's all along, and he's simply using the boxing process to get his rivals out of the way?

It's too much power for one man, especially a man like Killian Drake.

'No,' I say. 'It still doesn't make it right.'

'What's the alternative?' he says, still acting the politician. 'Either I box them forever or I let them free to kill again. What would you prefer?'

'You can't kill them all just because it's easier,' I say.

'But you would if it were you, wouldn't you? You think I'm a villain, but you condone what was done to Matthew Felton. Can't you see the hypocrisy in that?'

'Matthew Felton was a rat.'

'A rat who – until a few months ago – had never taken a life. A rat who, despite the terrible things he did, had left not a mark in his wake up to that point. He didn't terrorise, traumatise or manipulate. For all that he treated his victims like things he could use for his personal enjoyment, he left them – as far as they knew – unscathed. You're telling me you think he deserved his death, but that I'm a monster for putting down the Silver who have repeatedly delighted, and will always delight, in torture?'

'You're telling me you *wouldn't* have killed Felton?' I ask.

'No.'

'So you would have just left him to escalate his behaviour further, to kill more people?'

'No, I would have left him in a box where he belonged.'

'He's better off dead,' I say, with all the vitriol I can muster.

'If that's what you really think, then you shouldn't be judging me.' He fixes me in his gaze. 'You should be offering to hold the syringe.'

'You think I trust your judgement? You killed your ex-girlfriend for one lousy mistake.'

'Were you hoping I'd kill yours for the same? Is that why Dr Ross is in my basement?'

'If you like,' I shrug. 'I don't really care either way.'

'Don't lie to me, Jack.'

He looks towards the wrecked bar for a moment before dragging a bottle of whisky out of his desk drawer. He takes a slug straight from the neck. It's not like him to slum it. Hell, it's not like him to lose control, smash up his own bar and start yelling expletives. Obviously I've struck a nerve.

'I'd offer you some,' he says, 'but I know how you feel about whisky.'

I make no secret of the fact that I think it tastes like mud.

Drake never forgets it, the same way he always remembers my favourite drink, and my favourite brand. He is nothing if not attentive to details.

After another hit from the bottle, he asks, 'What did she tell you about Elise?'

'The truth.'

He laughs. 'The whole truth, I bet. Did she tell you that they were friends back then?'

'Of course.'

'And that they used to go out drinking together?'

'She told me everything, Drake.'

'Drinking blood from the vein, Jack. Before Elise committed the crime I boxed her for—'

'You mean executed her for,' I interrupt, but he keeps talking.

'—the two of them had killed not just one or two, but *twenty-three* humans together, and buried their bodies in the boxes beneath this house.'

That shuts me up.

'I've never pretended to be a good man,' he goes on. 'In fact, I believe I've told you more than once that I'm not. But I do have my own moral code, of sorts, and it doesn't include killing people who've done nothing to deserve it. It does, however, mandate that I take action to neutralise those Silver who are governed by no morals at all. Elise was one of those people, and your maker is another. So my question is this: what are you becoming?'

He's leaning over the desk towards me again, but this time there's nothing inviting about his posture. I read it as a challenge.

'Is that a threat?' I ask.

'No,' he says. 'I couldn't be less of a threat to you.'

It's my turn to laugh then, because he has done nothing but threaten me since the moment he came into my life: by his presence, by his interference, by the way his shark-black eyes fasten onto mine.

'Don't let her twist you up,' he whispers. 'Whatever else you let her do to you, don't let her turn you into what she is.'

'Don't tell me what to do,' I say, affronted. 'You don't know anything about her.'

'No, *you* don't know anything about her. I've known her for decades, and I know what she wanted to take out of the crypt last time she was here,' he says. My stomach turns. 'If I went down to the very bottom of this house right now, would I find that you've stolen it for her?'

'I don't think you're in any position to judge me,' I say, 'given that you've been stealing it for years.'

'Stealing?' Drake says. 'He was begging me, Jack, every second of every day, hoping that taking it away might lessen his pain, screaming for my help. Was I wrong to oblige him?'

'What you did with it afterwards was wrong.'

'But you think justice is on your side? I can guess what she's planning to do with what you took,' he says. 'I wish you'd let her do it alone.'

'Are you going to stand in our way?'

'In hers, if I can. In yours…' He trails off without giving any indication of what he means to do. Perhaps he doesn't know yet. That might be enough.

'I've got an appointment with the Invicti,' I remind him.

'Don't do this,' he says.

'I've got to go,' I say, walking towards the door.

'Please, Jack. Don't do this.'

His words follow me out of his office, but I'm not listening to them. Drake can think he knows what we're planning if he likes. He can imagine that he's one step ahead of us, if it gives him any satisfaction. He's not going to do anything about it, though. Even if he were strong enough to stand against me, Winta and Leclerq, he's too much of a coward to come out against us. All this time, through the whole revelation debate, he's been on the fence, pretending his failure to align himself with one side or another is a valid choice rather than a time-wasting strategy. Instead, I think he's just waiting to see which side wins so he can pretend that it was the one he supported all along.

The truth is, he's not just an arrogant, high-handed, murderous scumbag. He's a coward, too.

23

AFTER THAT ENCOUNTER, I'm more than a little pissed off by the time I make it downstairs to speak with Adewale Ladlpo. My mood is not improved when I see that the fucking Secundus has come with him. He's talking to Cam quietly in the corner, because apparently his only job these days is to hang around and try to steal my partner. I was wondering earlier why Cam followed me here from the college; here's my answer.

'Shouldn't you be with the Primus?' I ask the Secundus, interrupting their cosy tête-a-tête. 'What with the recent death threat? Or are you trying to make it easy for the people who want him dead?'

The Secundus's face becomes distinctly stormy. Cam looks at me like I've just pissed in his cereal. I guess it's possible that I might have crossed a line with that last insinuation.

'Ms Valentine,' the Secundus says, getting to his feet. 'Do you like your job?'

I shrug.

'Do you want to keep it?' he asks, the threat clear in his tone. He's starting to sound a lot like his buddy Benedict.

247

'Less and less every day,' I say, deciding to be frank. I figure I might as well carry on the way I've started. 'The way things are going, it seems like the Seekers might be less than useless pretty soon.'

'I wouldn't be so sure of that,' he replies.

'Oh? Then we're not anticipating more pro-reveal attacks any day now? And the Silver don't overwhelmingly agree that the secrecy pact is outdated anyway? I must have been misinformed.'

'Apparently so,' the Secundus replies in a low growl that discourages further chit-chat. Unfortunately, I'm still riled up after my set-to with Drake and I'm ready to cause havoc.

'Funny thing about that vote, huh?' I say. 'Funny how I was actually there, in the room, seeing all the votes cast, and I'd swear that even by a rough count—'

'Yes, all right, Ms Valentine,' the Secundus says. 'You've made your point.'

Which confirms that he knew the Primus rigged the vote, but gives me no information at all about what that means to him, except that he wants it kept quiet. Is he working with the pro-reveal group to redress that injustice? Or is he helping the Primus to cover it up?

I wish I could work it out, because then at least I'd have some information to take home to Winta, but I'm not given the chance to probe any further.

'Let's chat in the other room, Mr Sawyer,' the Secundus says. 'Adewale, I'll meet you there when you're done.'

'Thank you, sir,' Adewale says. 'This won't take long.'

He looks nervous and dangerous, as though he's trying to keep something wild trapped beneath his skin. Suddenly I'm not so sure that I want the Secundus and Cam to leave, but it's too late. The door's already closed behind them.

'You've seen her,' he says, getting to his feet. 'Haven't you?'

He carries with him that sense of an animal caged as he approaches me across the room. Now that I know the relationship between him and Winta, I can see the resemblance. Even though they're only half-siblings, they both have the same imposing presence, the irresistible charisma and the confidence in the way they carry themselves. That, more than any physical resemblance, is what betrays their common ancestry.

'I don't know what you're talking about,' I say.

'Yes, you do,' he says. 'I've been looking for my sister for years. Decades. Ever since the night she made you. And I know she came for you, Jack Valentine.'

'I don't know why you'd think that.'

'Because right now she needs disciples, so she's collecting you, the little dolls she's made, and she'll make more before this is over. You and the French woman are just the start.'

'I'm not sure who you mean.'

But of course I know exactly who he means.

Leclerq. I didn't know that Winta was her sire too, but now he's said it, I don't know why I never suspected before. Leclerq is bound to Winta the same way I am, by blood and by love. It's a combination that's hard to resist.

'I can help you,' he says. 'I love my sister, Ms Valentine. I really do. But sometimes she lets herself get carried away. I suppose she's told you how she tried to save my father by stealing from Baron Drake's basement?'

I cross my arms over my chest instead of answering.

'I'll take that as a yes,' he says. 'Did she tell you what happened next?'

I can't answer him honestly, because if I do then I'll be admitting that I've seen Winta, but I'd be lying if I said I didn't want to hear his side of the story.

'Why don't you just tell me?' I say.

'If that's the way you want to play it. Then here it is: when

Winta escaped from the Seekers, they called in the Solis Invicti to find her. After she'd turned you Silver and tried to steal Dr Jay's blood – yes, I know about that – they had no choice but to run her to ground. They couldn't risk her attempting to steal it again. That's how deadly the formula is. Dad told us, again and again. He warned us to leave it, and promised that Mum and Dr Castell would find a cure eventually, but Winta wouldn't do as she was told. She's never been good at drawing a line under things and moving on. So when the Invicti came for our parents, it had to be the end. Do you understand?'

'No,' I say, not following at all.

Adewale sighs. In that moment, he looks like nothing other than an exhausted brother dealing with an errant little sister.

'Dad was the reason she tried to steal the blood,' he says. 'So to stop her from trying again, the Invicti had to remove the reason behind her attempt.'

'What are you saying?'

'They killed him, Ms Valentine. The Invicti killed my father, and my mother when she fought them, using the very blood my parents needed to create a cure.'

My skin goes cold. I remember Cam telling me that Adinde and Kayode Ladipo had died, back when I was scouting out where Khalyed was buried, but I hadn't believed him. After all, the Invicti aren't exactly reliable when it comes to the location of their captives, and I couldn't imagine them just killing two Silver who could be useful to them. Apparently I'd given them too much credit.

'Are you sure?' I ask.

'I'm one of the Solis Invicti now, Ms Valentine. I've seen the records. I know exactly what happened to my parents, and where they are buried. I'd like to be able to tell Winta too.'

It's tempting. It sounds so innocuous, to give a man the means to recount his parents' fates to his estranged sister. It doesn't sound like it could cause any harm, and yet I hesitate, because there's something in his story that I don't quite believe.

'And this is why you went to the trouble of joining the Solis Invicti?' I ask him. 'You just wanted to know what happened to your parents?'

'Yes. Exactly so.'

'Then why are you still working for the Invicti? Why aren't you angry with them for what they did? Doesn't it seem unjust to you, that your parents were nothing but collateral damage?'

He smiles. 'I'm not a vindictive man, Ms Valentine. Unlike my sister, I see no purpose in seeking revenge. I understand why the Invicti did what they did, and perhaps I would have done the same myself in their shoes. All I want is reconciliation and resolution.'

'Pretty words,' I say.

'They're more than just that.'

'Would Winta think so, I wonder?'

'I know my sister, and I know how impulsive she can be. I need to protect her from herself, like I always have. I don't want her to do something she can't undo, because it won't do any good now. Our parents are gone. There's no purpose in fighting for them any longer. You see that, don't you?'

I don't reply, because he's assuming an awful lot of knowledge that I haven't copped to.

'I know you must feel strongly for her, Ms Valentine,' he goes on, giving me a smile that in other circumstances I might find irresistibly charming. There's that family resemblance again. 'If you didn't, she would never have been able to turn you Silver, after all.'

That pulls me up. 'Excuse me?'

'It's in the old lore,' he says lightly, as though this is common knowledge. 'For someone to be turned Silver, they have to have a strong connection to their sire. Usually, there has to be love involved. Our scientists have been researching it recently, and there are some very…'

He carries on for a while, but I'm no longer listening. I got caught up on the bit about love, and my chest feels like it's going to burst. Winta *does* love me. She's said it of course, but to have the proof… She *loves* me. She must, because otherwise she would never have been able to turn me Silver. That's basically what he said.

When I zone back in again, he's brought the subject back to the meeting he wants me to arrange.

'…that it's really in her best interests for you to put me in touch with her. I'm her brother, after all, and I love her too.'

She loves me.

'Sorry,' I say. 'I can't help you.'

'Tell me where she is, Ms Valentine,' he says.

If I need to stand between Winta and her brother to keep her and our plan safe, then that's exactly what I'll do.

'No,' I say.

In that moment, the Adewale I met at Solis Invicti HQ back in September is gone. He's not relaxed. He's not easy. He's not laughing. And neither am I.

He moves quickly. I should have expected it – after all, he's been training with the Solis Invicti, hell, he *is* one of the Solis Invicti – but it's enough of a surprise that he has my upper arms locked in his grip before I can react.

'Do you think I can't smell her on your skin?' he asks, his face so close to mine that I can smell the blood on his breath. He prepared for this meeting, and he's not going to leave without the answers he wants. 'I know her scent better than I know my own. She made me too, you know, and her blood calls to mine. Now tell me where she is.'

I feel a thump, and everything changes.

One minute Adewale is up in my face, squeezing my arms so tightly that I can feel my hands going numb, and the next he's gone, the pressure is released, and Drake is holding my face in his hands.

'Are you okay?' he whispers, his eyes searching me for injuries.

Behind him, Adewale is getting to his feet. Drake follows my gaze and turns to face his opponent, blocking me with his body. I'd be irritated at his archaic chivalry if I wasn't so grateful for it.

'I just want to talk,' Adewale says, holding up a hand. 'I got… carried away. That's all.'

'Then talk,' Drake says. He steps to the side a little, but he doesn't move entirely out of the way.

'I need to see my sister,' he says to me, and now his eyes are pleading. 'I don't know exactly what she's planning, but I know it won't be good. If she does what I think she might, she could endanger us all. If you won't help me for Winta's sake, Ms Valentine, then maybe you'll help me for your own. You can't let this happen. Please.'

He turns to Drake then and says it again: 'Please.'

'You've said your piece,' Drake replies. 'She's heard it. It's time for you to leave.'

'But, Baron Drake—'

'I'll remind you that you're on probation, Mr Ladipo. With one word to the Secundus, I could have you thrown out of the Solis Invicti. Bear that in mind.'

'My apologies, Baron.'

'Don't apologise to me,' Drake says, stone-faced. 'Apologise to Ms Valentine.'

So he does. It's intensely awkward and I wish Drake hadn't made him do it. He might as well have put a target on my back.

After Adewale has left, I turn to Drake and punch him in the arm. 'You're such a dick.'

'What?' he says, rubbing at the spot as though that could possibly have hurt him. 'Unless you didn't notice, I just rescued you like the dashing hero you're always accusing me of not being. And I brought you your jacket, which you left upstairs,' he says, handing it to me.

I shove my arms into the sleeves, keeping far enough away that Drake can't help this time. 'You didn't need to make him grovel,' I mutter.

'He put his hands on you,' Drake says. His playful tone is gone, replaced in an instant with a version of him so dark that I recognise myself in it.

'You don't need to protect me, Drake.'

'With what you're planning, I'm the only one who can.' He looks into my eyes for a long moment and time hangs between us. It feels like the prelude to a kiss, but then he says, 'Are you sure you know what you're doing?'

'Are you sure you do?' I shoot back. 'You're trying to play both sides, as usual, but now you've aligned yourself with Carlotta, and she's never been shy about her views. Have you forgotten that she was staying with Percy Windsor? Have you forgotten what he and Benedict did to all those humans who wanted to turn Silver? You're setting yourself against the Primus.'

'And what are you doing, exactly?' he asks.

Well, he's got me there.

'Then I guess we're both resolved on our courses,' I say.

'You could reconsider,' he suggests. Desperation hushes his tone. 'You're feeling powerless and you want to spread a little chaos. I know how that feels.' I scoff; as though the great Killian Drake has ever felt powerless in his whole life. 'But you have to pick your battles, and who you trust. You don't have to follow blindly.'

I'd like to tell him about the irony in those words; it was exactly when I failed to follow Winta's plan that all the trouble with Leclerq started. But that's none of Drake's business, so I keep it to myself.

'I can do without your condescension,' I say. 'If I wanted good advice, I'd hardly come to you.'

'Well, you're getting it anyway. Don't make the same mistake again, Valentine: don't start something you can't finish.'

He's staring into my eyes and I know he's not talking about me and Winta anymore. Somehow, the distance between us has narrowed and I'm standing too close for comfort, or not close enough. I can't decide which. Thankfully, I'm still making up my mind when the door slams open.

'Baron, darling!' Carlotta trills. 'And chère Jacqueline. Here you both are.' She trots over to Drake and kisses him on the mouth, then turns back to me. 'You could stay?' she suggests. 'He'll deny it, but it would make him happy, I think.'

'Carlotta—'

'Got to go,' I say. 'Busy. You know. Seekers stuff.' In reality, my non-existent desk is as clear as it's ever been, but I've got to make an exit before I do something I'll regret, so I practically run for the door.

When I turn to close the door behind me, they're kissing again. Carlotta has her beautiful back turned towards the door, but Drake isn't paying it any attention. Instead, in a way that is disturbingly sensual, his lips are locked on Carlotta's while his eyes are locked on mine.

I know that look. I remember the hunger in it, and it calls to me with a ferocity I can't explain. What is it about this man? Despite the fact that I'm now with Winta, which is all I've wanted for my entire Silver lifetime, I can't stop the power that draws me to him. Worse, I'm not sure I want it to stop, because the thrill I get just from looking in his eyes at this moment and knowing that he wants me is enough to spark a hunger of my own.

I could change my mind. I could walk back into the room and let him peel the leather jacket right back off me, followed by the rest of my clothes. After days without being touched by anyone at all, I think I could stand to be touched by him.

But it's not just Drake in the room, and it wouldn't be just a one-night deal. With us, whatever we say to each other, there is no such thing as no strings attached.

I step back, then close the door behind me to spoil his view as I walk away.

In the car on the way back to the college, Cam drops the bomb.

'I'm leaving,' he says.

I feel like I'm going to be sick.

'Don't,' I say.

'I have to. You've said it yourself more than once, Jack: if the Silver are coming out sooner or later, then what is even the point of us anymore? Our whole purpose for existing is to keep the secrecy pact in place, but when that falls apart, there's no reason for the Seekers to exist at all.'

'Someone's got to be a check on the Invicti,' I insist. 'Someone has to pull them back into line when they overstep.'

'And how's that going so far?' he says. 'They outrank us, and they can overpower us. We haven't changed their behaviour one bit, and we never will. The only way we can make any kind of positive change is from the inside.'

'So if you can't beat them, join them. Is that it? Jesus, Cam.'

'There are good people in the Invicti. I want to be one of them.'

'Jesus,' I say again, looking out of the window because I can't cope with looking at Cam's face right now. He's telling me this in the car deliberately because he knows I won't try to thump some sense into him while he's driving.

Well, probably not.

Honestly, I'm having to hold myself back.

I know he's always wanted to be one of them, but why did it have to be now? I don't want to be on the opposite side from Cam in this fight. He's always had my back, but now we're going to be facing each other across the divide, and there's nothing I can do about it.

'When?' I ask eventually.

'At New Year.'

'*New Year?* But that's only two days away.'

'They want to move quickly,' he says.

I wonder what that means for the Seekers. I suppose we're already falling apart – not just our team, but our network, our funding and our fucking building. This last little push might be a mercy.

'I'm sorry, Jack,' he whispers. 'I wanted you to be the first person I told.'

'Hmph.'

'There'll be a ceremony, and a party,' he says, as though that'll make it all better. 'Everyone's invited. Drinks, socialising, all that.'

'Socialising with the Invicti? No thanks.' I'm sulking, and I'm not going to pretend otherwise.

'It'll be at Solis Invicti HQ,' he says, trying to entice me out of my mood. 'They've got this cool bar area up top, blood on tap, and everyone will be there.'

That gives me pause.

'Everyone?' I ask.

'Everyone,' he promises. 'All the Invicti, the Primus, and the Seekers. So what do you think?'

'All right,' I say. 'You've convinced me. I'll be there.'

'Awesome!' He smiles so widely that I feel a little guilty about my ulterior motives.

Finally, some useful news. With this bit of information in my back pocket, I might be able to buy myself back into Winta's favour for good.

24

THERE'S SOMETHING STRANGE about first love. It gets under your skin and into your blood, quite literally in my case. Being with Winta again those first few days was like recapturing my lost youth, along with the innocence I'd had before her disappearance dragged me into the world of the Silver. Maybe that explains why I did what I did, and why I let her do the things she did. Maybe nothing can explain it. Maybe I was a fool to pledge myself to her, or maybe I'm worrying about nothing and my trust will pay off in the end, just like she says.

I guess we'll see.

But I'm starting to feel bad about Tabitha. More than bad. Awful, really. Not only have I locked her away in a box, I've locked her in the basement of a man who's known to kill boxed Silver.

If it had been up to me, I wouldn't have involved her in this at all. Yes, she's the only one who could have made the imitation serum that killed Felton, but was that really worth the trouble, given how easy it was to swipe Khalyed's stuff with the real thing in it? If it had been up to me, I would have left Tabitha to whatever exciting post-Invicti future she had planned.

But of course it wasn't up to me. Nothing seems to be these days.

That sounds bitter, but despite my grousing, I do understand why Winta needs to keep control of everything right now. It's a tense time, and she needs her pieces to line up right. She loves me and she needs me and I should be supporting her without question. It's just…

There are things I haven't told you.

Back in my missing week, before Drake and Leclerq turned up and started complicating things, Winta and I had the house in Jericho to ourselves.

It took a few days before I noticed the noises coming from the basement. I know that sounds ridiculous coming from a Silver, but all I can say in my defence is that the Solis Invicti's tranquilliser is fucking strong, and I was more than a little distracted by having Winta suddenly reappear, professing her love and enticing me into a plot to murder the Primus. I'd been busy, okay?

We were poring over the plans one night when the rhythmic thumping finally irritated me into attention.

'What *is* that?' I asked Winta. 'It's driving me crazy.'

She laughed, and a twinkle came into her eye.

'I'm sorry,' she said. 'That's just funny. You'd understand if… Well, it's time I told you anyway.'

'Told me what?'

'It's Tabitha Ross,' she said. 'I've got her caged in the cellar.'

'You've…'

'It was the baron's place that gave me the idea,' she said. 'First thing I did when I moved into this place. I thought, hey, that'd be a useful addition to any townhouse. Right?'

I was so busy processing this information that I didn't

immediately know how to respond. I knew there were unanswered questions about Tabitha, but I'd sort of convinced myself that she was off holidaying at one of her other exotic homes, and that Winta had just broken into Tabitha's house and staged the abduction scene in order to draw me there so she could kidnap me. I should have asked earlier. I should have made myself focus on the gaps in the story that Winta was weaving for me, but I hadn't, and so I'd been living in the same house as Tabitha for days without even realising it.

Some detective I am.

'Why is my ex-girlfriend caged up in your cellar?' I asked eventually.

'I was using her to create the formula,' Winta said. 'You know, the one I used to torch Felton. It turns out that she can't refine it enough for our purposes though, so she's outlived her usefulness. I guess we can get rid of her now.'

'*Get rid* of her?'

'Yes, get rid of her.'

'As in, released into the wild, or…?'

'As in, I have some of the formula left over and she should go up like a Roman candle. You can do it if you like.'

The casual way she suggested this should have given me pause, but inside my only thought was: *not me*. I should have been bargaining for her life, but my only thought was that I didn't want to be the one to take it.

'I can't kill Tabby,' I said.

'Tabby? So that's what the crappy cat tattoo is about?'

I cringed. I was hoping she hadn't noticed it in the course of our nighttime activities, what with the low lighting and the distractions, but of course she had. She's Silver, and she's only stayed free this long by being observant. She was hardly going to miss the tabby cat tattoo on my hip.

'Well,' she said. 'We'll have to do something about that.'

We went back to the plans then, as though we'd never discussed Tabitha at all. I thought she'd forgotten it entirely until, later that same day, she led me to the bathroom.

'Pull down your trousers and underwear,' she said, all business. 'I want to get a good look at this tattoo of yours.'

I unbuttoned my jeans and bared my hip.

'No,' she said. 'I mean, all the way.'

'Why?'

She gave me a look that said she was running out of patience. 'Because otherwise you'll get blood all over them. I have few enough clothes that fit you already, Jacky. Don't make me trash them.'

Then I noticed the knife in her hand.

'Oh.'

What was I going to say? I couldn't tell her I wanted to keep the tattoo – which would have been a lie anyway – and I didn't want to be squeamish about removing it because our plan involved much worse than this. If I balked now, she'd start thinking I couldn't do what needed to be done when the time came. There was only one way I could go.

I took everything off, leaving me naked from the waist down in the freezing bathroom. The radiator was broken and apparently there was no fixing it. It made my skin pimple into goosebumps, making the already-sensitive skin more sensitive still.

While I stripped, Winta held a jet lighter under the blade of the knife until I could smell the heat in the air.

I realised then that this was a test.

She wasn't going to use any painkillers. She wasn't going to mark me to take away the pain, because that seemed to be something that she and I simply didn't do. She was going to make me stand here half-naked and hold still while she came at me with a hot blade and cut out every inked layer of—

* * *

Look, this is about to get a bit grim. I don't think you need to hear the gory details, do you? Even if you want them, I'm not keen to relive it.

I've been injured frequently in my years as a Seeker. It goes with the territory: chase baddies, get into fights, lick your wounds after. One little tattoo removal shouldn't be a big deal, and it certainly wasn't the most painful wound I've ever taken, but there's something particularly traumatic about watching pain come towards you. You have time to anticipate and imagine it, and your sense of impending agony – however inaccurate – magnifies every moment. I haven't been in that situation often, and I certainly didn't expect it at the hands of someone I loved.

Let's just say it was bad and move on, yeah?

Winta handed me a bottle of blood after. I drained it, and by the time I'd swallowed the final drop I was already healed up.

'There,' she said. 'That wasn't so bad, was it?'

'No,' I lied.

It had been so much messier than I'd expected. The wound might have healed, but the blood it had produced was still dripping down my hip. It was hard not to look at the knife, or at the piece of me she'd cut away. She wasn't being discreet with either, almost as if she wanted me to see. I wondered whether there was intention behind that, but then she wiped the blood away from my skin with a damp towel and kissed the spot where my tattoo had once been.

'Much better,' she breathed, tickling the skin and raising sensations of pleasure where so recently there had been only pain.

It was fucked up. I knew that, but still my body was responding. It made me feel a tiny bit sick, but I couldn't tell Winta that, so instead I asked a question that I knew was guaranteed to derail things.

'What are you planning to do with Tabitha?'

At least, I thought it was guaranteed.

'Forget Tabitha,' she said. Then she kissed her way down my hip to the top of my thigh and beyond, and made me forget absolutely everything.

Temporarily.

We'd ended up in the bed, wrapped in a tangle of limbs and sheets, with the electric heater blasting so much warmth it made us sweat. In the artificial heat of our bedroom, the smell of Winta's skin was amplified so much that I could almost believe she'd marked me, filling the air with a sweetness I wanted to bathe in. I wished it were real.

'What?' she said sleepily, stroking a lazy finger along my healed hip. 'I see that thoughtful look on your face.'

'It's nothing.'

'Jacky.'

'Really, it's just I was smelling your scent in the air and, you know.'

It's a conversation we'd had before, practically every time we'd hit the sheets, which had been frequently. Those days, we'd plan and we'd have sex, and that was pretty much it.

'I've told you,' she said softly, pressing little kisses into my shoulder. 'It's voluntary. I can choose to mark you or not, and right now, for both our sakes, I'm choosing not. It'll come, Jacky. When it's time.'

'I know,' I said. 'It's just... not been like that for me.'

'You mean with her?'

'Yeah,' I said, because I definitely didn't want the spectre of Killian Drake turning up in bed with us when Tabitha was already downstairs. 'I didn't control it. It just... happened.'

'You're young,' she said. 'You'll learn. But people can only be marked if they invite it. The fact that you're not marking me is because I'm resisting, but I won't resist forever.' She kissed me on the lips, long and slow. 'I promise.'

The way she said it, I believed her.

'Do you want to see her?' she asked.

'Tabitha?'

'Yes.'

'No. Yes. Maybe.'

'You can, you know,' Winta said. 'If you want. I don't mind. I don't want her getting out and running straight to the Invicti, but as long as you keep her controlled, you can decide what we should do with her. We don't have to kill her.'

It was a weird kind of gift, but it felt like one nonetheless. After what she'd just taken from me, she was giving something back. Or was this just another test?

I was juggling five feelings at once. That was the thing with Winta; she always had me second-, third- and fourth-guessing myself. I hated Tabitha for the way she'd betrayed me to the Invicti, and I wanted to prove to Winta that I was on her team, but I had also loved Tabitha once, and hurting people who aren't absolute scum isn't in my nature. For all that she'd done to me, I knew Tabitha believed she'd done it for the best. That had to count for something.

Didn't it?

'I'll go see her,' I said.

'Great,' Winta replied, too brightly. She swung her legs off the bed, pulling out of my arms, and started looking for her clothes.

'I don't have to if you don't want me to.'

'No, go ahead.' She wasn't looking at me. She'd turned her back the moment I'd first declared my intentions and she was keeping it turned as she got dressed.

I scrambled across the bed and came to stand in front of her, holding her face between my hands. She still wasn't looking in my eyes. 'I won't if you don't want me to,' I said. 'But Tabitha is my problem. Why don't you let me deal with her, so you can concentrate on the plan?'

She smiled a little at that, and finally met my eyes. I knew the plan had been bothering her. Now that I was fully in the mix, she'd had to rejig things a bit, and she was worried she hadn't had time to fill all the gaps. She didn't need to be distracted by Tabitha, or me, for that matter.

'Okay,' she said. She kissed me quickly on the cheek. 'Thank you.'

'I might have a suggestion about how we could use her, though.'

'Oh?' Her smile widened. 'Then tell me.'

So I did.

Which is why it's my fault, and my fault only, that Tabitha got boxed.

We spent a lot of that day working on my part of the plan for Phase One, so it wasn't until later that I finally got downstairs. It wasn't that I didn't want to go. Well, part of me was definitely reluctant, but when you know your ex is locked up in the cellar beneath your feet, it's difficult not to find that thought intruding into everything you do until you make yourself go and look. It was a necessary thing, and my desire to placate Winta had kept me away too long.

Still, I waited until Winta went out before I went down to the cellar, which was just as well. When I saw Tabitha behind the bars, hair released from its pencils and chopsticks, teal tights laddered and white lab coat dirtied, I couldn't help the catch in my breath. I'd expected to feel nothing. After everything Tabitha had done, after all the ways she'd invaded and infected every aspect of my life, it should have felt good to see her brought low. Instead, she looked so awful that I felt as though my stomach had been hollowed out.

Then I saw it.

There was something awful on the floor outside the bars, just beyond Tabitha's reach.

It was my tabby tattoo.

I swallowed a couple of times in rapid succession. I felt like I was going to be sick.

'Jack, hen,' Tabitha croaked, pushing herself up onto unsteady feet. 'Thank god you're okay. I saw that—' She nodded at the tattoo on the floor. '—and I thought the bitch had—'

'Careful, Tabitha,' I said.

She stopped and looked at me on the other side of the bars, healthy and unharmed, and her attitude changed.

'You're not a prisoner here, are you?' she said.

'No.'

'You're working with her.'

'Yes.'

'Oh, hen,' she said, and her face fell. 'You're sleeping with her, aren't you?'

'That's none of your business,' I said, not enjoying her tone.

She sobbed and I felt it like a blade in my gut.

'Don't you judge me, Tabitha. Don't you dare judge me.'

She'd moved to the front of the cage and was standing with her hands wrapped around the bars, looking even shorter than usual since she didn't have her shoes. I wasn't sure why Winta had bothered to take them away; Tabitha had been so drained of blood that she was barely managing to hold herself up.

'Hen—' she said.

'Don't call me that. After everything you did to me—'

'I never cut pieces of your *skin* off. What the fuck is that about, Jack?'

'It was a piece I didn't want anymore,' I said, kicking it into the grime that had collected at the corner of the room. I didn't want to look at it. I didn't want to feel the way it gave beneath the sole of my boot. I wanted it to be invisible, rolled in the dust until I could no longer make out the blood. 'You spied on me. You manipulated me. You hurt me.'

'And she isn't doing exactly that?'

'She loves me.'

'*I* loved you.'

'If you'd loved me, you wouldn't have sold me out to the Invicti,' I said.

'Loyalties change,' she said desperately. 'Mine did. I was leaving them, Jack. I did leave them.'

'I know.' The Secundus had told me as much when we'd met at the house in Henley.

'For you,' she said, and her voice was almost a whisper. 'I left them for you.' She was pleading with me now, her eyes big and wide and her cheeks so bloodless that it made me wonder exactly how far Winta had pushed her. Sure, she had to be drained to make sure she couldn't break out of the cell, but it looked as though there was no blood left in Tabitha at all.

'You didn't tell me,' I said.

'I wasn't ready. There were things I needed to do first. Mistakes I needed to correct.'

'Khalyed's blood?'

She nodded. 'I was trying to find a cure. I'd promised I would, a long time ago, and I was close.' She gave me a long, rueful look. 'Close enough to make you wait.'

'We went looking for you,' I said, trying to avoid her eyes. I couldn't cope with her guilt, not when I was standing here on the other side of the bars. 'They gave us a list of your addresses. We went to the flat, me and Cam.'

'You found it, then? It was supposed to be a...' She

coughed a little, then tried to clear her throat, which just made her cough more. By the time I'd rushed up to the kitchen and returned with a bottle of water, she was doubled over.

'Here,' I said, reaching through the bars to hold the bottle to her lips. She drank half of it, then held onto my wrist to upend the bottle so she could drink the rest.

It was only then that it occurred to me what an idiot I'd been to reach inside. You'd think I would have learned by now not to reach into a drained vampire's cage, particularly when the vampire in question was my ex-girlfriend. This was how Winta had broken free all those years ago: I'd trusted her enough to reach through the bars, then she'd bitten me and bought her freedom with my blood. Now here I was again, twenty years later, making exactly the same fucking mistake.

But Tabitha didn't take my wrist and bite it. Instead, she squeezed it gently, almost tenderly, then took the nearly-empty bottle and let me go. I snatched my hand back before she could change her mind.

'Thank you,' she said. 'For the drink.'

'Thank you for the flat. Don't worry, I won't keep it.'

'You can if you like,' she said quietly. 'I bought it for you.'

'I don't think I'll be sticking around in Oxford long after… After things change.'

I wasn't sure it was possible, given how little blood was left in her body, but she paled even further. 'What exactly is going to change?' she asked.

'Not all change is bad,' I said. 'You wanted change. That's why you were working to expose the Silver, right?'

'What's going to change, Jack?' she repeated.

There was no way to sugarcoat it, so I just came out with it. 'We're taking down the Solis Invicti. And we're killing the Primus.'

There was a moment of utter silence.

'What?' I said. 'You should be happy. You wanted a change in governance, and that's what you're going to get.'

'I went about it the wrong way,' she said. 'But I did what I thought was right, not what I *knew* was wrong. This is wrong, Jack. You must see that, don't you?'

'So you didn't think it was wrong to spy on me? To pretend that you loved me? To sell me out to the Tertius for whatever ridiculous price the Invicti paid you? Don't lie to yourself.'

'Everything I did was for the good of the Silver. What you're doing… I don't know what this is.'

'It's the end of the world as we know it,' I said. 'It's coming sooner or later anyway. We're just speeding things up a little.'

'You're talking about anarchy.'

'Maybe.'

She stared at me for a moment, searching my face for something she couldn't find. 'I know our world isn't perfect,' she said, 'but wouldn't you rather build on what we have and try to fix it from within than burn it all to the ground? It's not clean. It's messy and it's hard, but it's the better choice.'

'No,' I said. 'I think I'd rather watch it burn.'

There are tears on her cheeks now. They're running down her throat.

'This isn't you, Jack,' she says.

'You don't have the slightest idea who I am.'

'I know you well enough to know you wouldn't be doing this without a good reason.'

'I have plenty of reasons,' I said. 'Do you know what the last year has been like for me? Ever since I joined the Seekers, ever since I was turned Silver, I thought I was doing good. Catch the bad guys, protect the humans, keep the

Silver secret. It felt like I was benefitting everyone and it made *sense*. Then I find out that actually, not only is there one rule for us and another for the Silver powerful enough to do what they like, but that the Solis Invicti, and the fucking *Primus*, regularly go around killing people for fun or money or whatever venal purpose they have in mind.'

'That doesn't mean you should join in.'

'Someone has to hold them accountable. You have to take drastic action if you want drastic results.'

'And what results are the two of you aiming for?'

'Restitution. Revenge,' I said. 'Maybe we just want to stir up a little trouble and see what rises to the surface. After the stunt you pulled at the vote, I guess you know a little something about that.'

'It was a bad idea,' she said urgently. 'If I had my time again, I would do things differently. It was a mistake, Jack. I made a mistake.'

'You didn't think, though, did you?' I said. 'You never do. You just come up with an idea you can solve with science, and you never stop to think about what's going to happen when it falls into the wrong hands. And it's not just the stuff you made to reveal the silver in our eyes. Remember the tranquilliser serum in the darts, the stuff that nearly killed Drake? Remember the stuff Felton made when he was trying to copy your formula, the stuff that killed Raul's friend and nearly killed Mildred Chen too? Remember the way you poisoned *me* with your own blood? You never think about the consequences, do you?'

'I wasn't the one who drugged Drake, or Raul, or—'

'You didn't have to be!' I yelled. I was pacing back and forth now, kicking up brick dust in my agitation. 'That's exactly my point! You make these weapons and they fall into the wrong hands. They always will. You have to take some responsibility for being the one who put them out into the world in the first place.'

'I do,' she said. 'I do, Jack. I've made so many mistakes. I trusted the wrong people, I can see that. But just because a thing exists, that doesn't mean you have to use it. You don't have to do whatever it is she's planning to do with the stuff I made.'

I wandered over to the workbenches and fridges against the far wall. I guessed Winta had let Tabitha out of the cage to work on the formulae, supervised her during, then locked her away again afterwards. She hadn't done that once since she'd brought me here because everything was finished now, and Tabitha had served her purpose.

'You were working in Felton's basement,' I said. 'In his lab. After everything he did—'

'I know what you're going to say.' She winced. 'But he had the facilities, and he was helping with the cure.'

'It was a necessary evil? Is that really what you're going with?'

'Yes,' she said. 'I made a promise to find a cure, and I intended to do exactly that.'

'But you chose to do it with Felton. You could have chosen anyone else, but you chose him.'

'There wasn't much of a choice,' she said, exasperated. 'It's specialised work, Jack, and there are only a few people in the country who can do it.'

'Like Ed? Why not him?'

'Dr Castell?' She shook her head. 'It was better to go with a known quantity. I'd worked with Matthew before.'

'So it's *Matthew* now? All that time we were dating, and you never even let on that you knew him. I told you I'd set him on fire and you laughed, Tabby. You *laughed*.'

She shrugged, like it was nothing at all. 'I knew what he was,' she said. 'I've always known what he was, so I won't pretend he didn't deserve it. But at least he doesn't work for the Invicti anymore. We were in the same boat. Working with Matthew made more sense than showing up at Solomon College and expecting Dr Castell to work with your ex-girlfriend, particularly since Dr Castell's own affiliations are in question, wouldn't you say, hen?'

'They are?'

This was news to me. I thought he was firmly on the Seekers' team.

'He and Cam might not be together anymore,' she said, 'but they still come as a pair. I can't be the only one who's heard rumours that the Invicti are interested in recruiting your partner.'

'It'll never happen,' I said. I was in denial, I realise now, but at the time I never thought Cam would actually leave us, despite all his Invicti fanboying. 'Just like your cure never happened.'

'We're nearly there,' she said. 'If I ever get out of this place then – with Matthew's help – I can do it. The cure is worth the price of working with a scumbag like him.'

'Felton died,' I said.

'He's dead?'

'He went up in flames. Your formula, apparently.'

'Oh god.' She slid down to the floor, holding the bars all the way. 'I was just trying to find a cure, I swear, but she made me replicate the serum. I didn't expect it to work. I hoped it wouldn't.'

'You're good at what you do, Tabitha. That's why you're here.'

'And you're okay with that, are you?' she said, but it was less a question and more a statement. If I wasn't, she'd already be free.

I shrugged. 'You can't kick a dog then complain when it turns around and bites you.'

'Revenge,' she said. 'Is that all this is? What are you

really doing here, Jack? What's in it for you?'

'Love makes us do crazy things,' I said. 'You know that as well as I do.'

'And just how crazy are you for this girl?'

'She's my sire,' I said, like it was all the answer Tabitha needed.

She looked at me for a long moment and then, very deliberately, looked away. It was the only answer she'd give in return.

I heard the front door open and close above our heads, then steps moved across the floorboards to the kitchen. Winta was home.

I stepped in close to the bars again and crouched in front of Tabitha, hoping I could trust her not to do something stupid and screw us both over.

'She's not going to let you go,' I whispered, low enough that I hoped only she would hear.

She laughed, a hollow sound that was little more than a breath. 'I knew I was dead from the moment she put me in this cage. She's sent you to do her dirty work, then, has she?'

'I'm not going to kill you,' I whispered, holding onto the bars as I leaned closer. 'I'm going to put you to sleep.'

Her eyes brightened as she realised what I was suggesting, and what it meant. 'How?'

'The tranquilliser formula. Can you adapt it, or at least pretend you have? I need you to be out for a couple of days so I can get you somewhere safe. Can you do that?'

She nodded.

'Tell me you're not going to go through with the rest of this mad plan,' she whispered, putting her hand over mine. 'Please.'

'I'm going to do what I have to do.'

'You don't have to do *anything* you don't want to. It's not too late to change your mind. You can make a different choice.'

'No, I can't,' I said.

Then the door at the top of the cellar steps opened and Winta called downstairs for me.

'Coming,' I called back.

With one final look at Tabitha, I left her behind in her cage.

Now I can only hope that Drake's the kind of man he makes himself out to be, and that Tabitha will still be alive in his basement when I come to release her.

25

'YOU WERE RIGHT about Drake,' I say to Winta when I get home. 'He killed Elise.'

'I know,' she says, looking up from a bulky device that she's tinkering with on the table. 'I thought you believed me.'

'I did, but there's believing you, and then there's seeing his smug face fall when I told him what I knew.'

'You *told* him?' she says, and she's not happy. 'What else did you tell him?'

'Nothing,' I lie, because I don't want to make her any more angry than she already is. 'I didn't tell him anything.'

'Stop talking to him, Jacky,' she says, returning to the device. 'Nothing good's going to come of it.'

She's in concentration mode now, which for Winta is pretty intense. There's not much that can grab her attention when she's already fully focused on a task, but I know she'll be upset if I let any more time pass without telling her the rest. I take a seat next to her and try to work out how to broach the subject.

'I saw your brother today,' I say.

'You saw Ad?'

'He asked to see me. He came to Drake's mansion, which is why I had to talk to Drake,' I say, belatedly trying to excuse myself a little. It has no impact on Winta; she's too interested in the other thing.

'Did he find Mum and Dad?'

'No.'

I have to tell her, I really do, but I have no idea how to say the words. When I'm silent for a moment, she puts down her tiny screwdriver and turns to look at me.

'He told you they're dead, didn't he?' she says, which is a surprise and a relief, because god knows I didn't want to be the one to break the news.

'You already knew?'

'You believed him?'

I blink. 'Why would he lie about something like that?'

She looks between me and the device for a moment, as though she's trying to decide which is in greater need of her attention, then she gets up from her chair and wanders into the kitchen to fetch some blood from the fridge. She gets two bottles, opening both before offering one to me. I wonder how she gets her hands on the stuff. It looks just like the bottles we have at the college, so either she's stealing it or she has a contact inside who steals it for her.

Given my precarious position, that's an unsettling thought.

'It's time we talked about this, I guess,' she says, taking a long drink as she reclaims her seat. 'Ad and I, we're not exactly on good terms.'

I take a sip from the bottle and feel it sink into my bones. It's a weird sensation, but you get used to it. This feels weirder than normal, but that's probably just the shock I got from the confrontation with Winta's brother. The fight or flight response burns through a lot of your reserves.

'When did you last see him?' I ask.

'A while ago. Too long, I guess, since he's joined up with

the Invicti while I've been doing other things. He's been trying to track me down for some time, but I've managed to keep ahead of him until now.'

'You don't want to see him?'

'I might, if he cared more about seeing me than he did about making sure I don't show him up. All our lives, I swear, he's been trying to hold me back, even when he was human. I turned him, you know,' she says, like it's an incidental fact and not at all pivotal to their relationship dynamic.

'You seem to do that a lot,' I say.

'Three times in eighty years is not a lot,' she says.

'Compared with most Silver, it is.'

Which is true. Turning people Silver isn't just a matter of biting them and going *ta-da!* From what I hear, most of the time it doesn't work at all, and even when it does work, sometimes it goes sideways and you wish it hadn't. That's just what I've heard, but it makes sense, because if we were so easy to make then we'd probably outnumber humans by now, which would be no good for anyone. Which all goes to say that three successful turnings in less than a century is an impressive tally.

'My point is that we used to be close,' she says. 'We used to have fun together, but then Mum joined the Seekers and Dad started working with them, and Ad jumped on the moral rectitude bandwagon. I'd hoped that he'd change his tune when they were taken by the Invicti, but then he got the idea into his head that our parents somehow brought everything on themselves by meddling with the formula in the first place. He thought if only he could join up with the Invicti, he could fix everything. He's always trying to fix everything, and everyone.'

'He said he wanted to see you so he could tell you what happened to them and where they're buried,' I say.

She laughs. 'Oh, I know that already, Jacky. They're buried in the Solis Invicti's basement – yes, they have a boxing facility of their own – and they've been there ever since they were taken. The Invicti'll keep them there until they think they can be useful, and in the meantime they'll leave them to rot. But I don't intend to let that happen. Adewale might be happy to leave them there, but I'm going to bust them out before the Invicti get some bright idea about using my parents in some sick experiment or whatever.'

'You didn't tell me they were at Solis Invicti HQ,' I say, in a voice that sounds small and hurt.

'It's new information,' Winta replies, and I know from the way she returns to her tinkering that she doesn't intend to elaborate.

'From where?' I ask.

'Yolande.'

'And you're just... trusting that she's right?' I say incredulously.

'I knew you'd react this way,' Winta says, putting her screwdriver down again. I've gone and pissed her off now. 'This is why I didn't say anything. I don't want you to start second-guessing the plan and trying to back out just because the source of my information isn't one you personally trust.'

'I'm not backing out,' I say.

'Even if Yolande's wrong – and I don't believe she is – we still need to do this. The Invicti still abducted my parents. They still fucked you over. The Primus and the Invicti still dictate our lives in ways that serve only themselves. You've seen it from the inside, Jacky. You know how twisted they've become. You know someone has to show them they can't just do whatever they want and get away with it. We're the rebels, remember? We're the only ones with the courage to stand up to them, so we have to do this.'

'You don't have to persuade me,' I say, before she

launches into her whole speech. I've heard it so many times that I remember all the words. 'You know I'm with you. I'm sorry. Just tell me what you need and I'll do it.'

'Right now, I need you to give Yolande a chance. Promise me.'

Ugh. I wish she'd asked anything else, but she's right. I shouldn't be bitter. I'm with Winta, whatever's going on with her and Leclerq, and does it really matter anyway? If it's not happening in front of me, maybe I can accept it, for the time being. In a couple of days, everything's going to change.

'I promise,' I say, at which point Leclerq ghosts her way down the stairs looking like a fae goddess, and I regret it immediately.

'I felt my ears burning,' she says, which is code for *I overheard everything you just said and I will be acting accordingly.* 'Are we talking about the extraction?'

'We are,' says Winta.

'Where does your information come from?' I ask Leclerq, because it seems less bitchy to be honest about my misgivings.

'Matthew Felton,' she says. 'He's seen the Ladipos at Solis Invicti HQ.'

'I forgot you two were friends,' I say. I'm trying to be nice, so I keep the snark out of my voice.

'Not friends, exactly. Colleagues.'

'But you were living with him, weren't you?' It was where we finally ran her to ground in September: in Felton's spare room.

'I did what I had to do. It's a small world when you're Silver,' she says, as though I'm not exactly as Silver as she is. Hell, more Silver, because – if what Adewale said was true – I've been this way longer than she has. 'Sometimes it's necessary to use less-than-savoury associates in order to get the job done.'

The way she looks at me makes it perfectly clear that she considers me to be one such associate. I know I said I'd give her a chance, but she's already on thin ice.

'You're sure they're in the sub-basement?' Winta says to Leclerq. She's turned away from the device and is looking at the building plans again. Her obsession with them makes more sense now that I finally have the whole picture.

'I'm sure,' says Leclerq. 'This lot are all garages—' She points to the plans. '—and it's easy to get turned around, but they're boxed in sub-basement seven. He saw the box labels himself, and he gave me precise directions.'

'You're sure they're correct?' says Winta.

'He wouldn't have dared lie to me.'

'We should run through the plan again, just to make sure.'

'Stop agonising,' Leclerq says. 'We get in, we take out the Primus, then we get your parents out. Done.'

'This matters, Yolande,' Winta says. I'm quietly pleased that Leclerq's flippancy is irritating her. 'We have to get it right.'

'We will. We have everything we need to make it easy.'

Then Winta's irritation just seems to melt away, like it never does for me. She smiles at Leclerq. 'Bottles, bombs, blood.'

'Right.' Leclerq smiles back with unveiled intimacy. It makes me think they've discussed this before, in different circumstances. 'Bottles, bombs, blood.'

They've got their own fucking catchphrase.

'I've got the bottles,' Winta says, holding up the new vials she had Tabitha make before we boxed her. 'Jacky's got the blood.'

Actually, Winta has the syringe in the wallet on the table in front of her, controlling it like she's controlling everything else in this plan, but I don't point that out.

'And I've got the bombs,' Leclerq says, holding up some

stuff with wires attached to it that I'd really rather she didn't wave around like that. This is, apparently, her speciality. Well, she has to be good for something.

'Now all we need is the opportunity,' Winta says. 'And that's going to be the problem.'

'I can make an opportunity,' Leclerq offers, waggling the bombs again.

'I wish you'd stop doing that,' I say.

'What?' She looks at me like I've just slapped her around the face.

'That,' I say, gesturing at the bombs.

'It's not as though they're primed. Do you think I'm some kind of an amateur?'

'Yes. No one's paying you to build those things, are they?'

'Not in cash,' Leclerq says, then she looks at Winta.

Nope.

I've tried, I really have, but I can't deal with this. I'm a one-woman woman, and if Winta wants to be something other than that, then I'm out.

'Put them away, Yolande,' Winta says before I have a chance to say something I'll regret. 'And stop bickering. We need to keep it together, just for a little longer.'

I want to ask her what happens after that, when all of this is over. Do she and I ride off into the sunset together, or are we going to need a third horse? But she's clearly not in the mood to be argued with, so I shut my mouth and hope I'm wrong.

'And how long are we going to have to wait?' says Leclerq. 'I'm not intending to spend the next few months locked up in this pokey little house waiting for an opportunity that might never come. I've just got out of one box; I don't want to go straight into another, thanks very much.'

'It won't be long,' Winta says, with more gentleness in her

tone than she would use with me if I asked a similar question. 'If there's nothing by the end of the month, we'll make our own, okay?'

'Actually,' I say, 'I don't think we'll have to wait as long as that.'

'Oh?' Winta turns to me with an arch look on her face. 'Why is that?'

I tell her about the party they're having for Cam's admission to the Solis Invicti. 'They'll all be there, and the rest of the building will be practically unguarded, or unguarded enough for you anyway,' I say to Leclerq. I might hate her a bit, but I have to admit that she moves like a ghost. With her skills, she could be in and out without anyone noticing, even when the Solis Invicti are the ones on guard. 'In the meantime, we can do what needs doing.'

When I finish speaking, there's nothing but silence. I wasn't expecting applause, not exactly, but I was hoping for some acknowledgement of my excellent contribution to the plan.

No such luck.

'This should have been the first thing you said when you walked in the door,' Winta says. She's angry. This isn't how I expected this to go at all. 'You're so fixated on the bloody baron that you bury the fucking lede in bullshit.'

'I thought the thing about your brother might be more important,' I say quietly.

'Nothing,' she yells, '*nothing* is more important than Phase Two. What do you think we're doing here? Is this all a game to you?'

'No, I—'

'Then stop playing, Jacky.' Then she turns to Leclerq and says, 'Can you believe this?'

Leclerq just shakes her head. I feel like mine is about to explode.

Why is it always them against me? They treat me like a child and act like I just have to suck it up and do better, but I'm starting to believe that it doesn't matter what I do. I'm proving myself to Winta again and again, and what I get in return is nothing at all.

'I told you, Jacky: stop talking to the baron. He's a fucking distraction.'

'Did he tell you about your friend Gabriella?' Leclerq chimes in. I want her to shut up, but her tone has a smug edge that suggests I'm not going to like what she's about to say, and I can't just leave it hanging there.

'Gabriella?' It takes me a moment to place the name. 'Gabriella De Palma? What about her?'

'Do you know where she is?'

'Yes,' I say, too defensively. 'She's in a box, but she'll be out in May.'

Leclerq raises an eyebrow at me. 'Will she?'

I realise then what she's suggesting.

'No,' I say. 'Drake wouldn't kill her.'

Not Gabriella. Not just because she killed David Grant, a sub-human predator who preyed on young women who didn't deserve his less-than-tender ministrations. He earned his end even more than Matthew Felton earned his.

'Ask him,' Leclerq says. 'Or better yet, go and see for yourself.'

But I don't need to. I remember that busy night in the basement when I boxed Tabitha, freed Leclerq and stole Khalyed's blood. I was too distracted at the time to pay it much mind, but I passed right by Gabriella's box on my way through the labyrinth, and it was silent. There was no sound at all from inside, not even the painfully slow beat of beat of Gabriella's blood-deprived heart, or the gentle settling of her empty veins. There should have been something. Not much, but something.

'Enough bickering,' Winta says while I'm still reeling. 'If Jacky's right about this, then it might be the best chance we'll get.'

'But it's the day after tomorrow,' says Leclerq.

'All the more reason to shut up and get on with it, then,' Winta says, exasperated. 'You see to your bombs. I'll get the vials ready and plan our route. Jacky, go sleep. I need you to go and speak to Carlotta Arden early tomorrow morning, after the club shuts.'

'What?' I say. I wasn't even aware that Winta knew Carlotta, so this is coming out of nowhere. 'Why?'

'Because she's working with us?' says Leclerq in her most irritating tone. 'Catch up, Jacky.'

She'll be lucky if she lasts the night.

'Yolande…' Winta says.

'Since when?' I ask.

'Since the vote,' says Leclerq. 'She's on our side.'

'I thought we didn't have a side?' I say. 'I know she's pro-reveal, but I thought the whole point was that we weren't—'

'She's a contact,' Winta interrupts, getting impatient now. 'Nothing more.' But I have the feeling there's something she's not telling me. 'I need you to get a message to her. Okay?'

'Why me?' I say, buying time because I really, really don't want to go and talk to Drake's girlfriend.

'You want me or Winta to go waltzing into Oxford's newest blood bar when we're both wanted fugitives?' Leclerq says. 'Get a clue, will you?'

'Does Drake know about this?' I ask.

'Carlotta knows how to keep a secret,' says Winta.

'Unlike some people,' Leclerq adds, so I guess Winta's told her about my slip up with Drake earlier today.

I hate that. I hate the feeling that they're talking about me behind my back, bitching about what a liability *Jacky* is, and laughing at my expense.

'Finish your drink,' Winta says to me, picking up her own empty bottle and motioning for me to take mine. I've barely touched it, but I down the rest of the bottle and pass her the empty. 'Now go to bed. I'll get the message ready and bring it up in a bit.'

'I'm not tired,' I argue, but it's a lie. I feel suddenly exhausted.

I look at the empty bottle in my hand and can't help but wonder. She wouldn't drug me, would she? Not again.

No. That's ridiculous. I'm just tired, that's all.

'You need your sleep,' Winta says, and she's not wrong, but I wish she hadn't said it as though I were a five-year-old trying to stay up beyond my bedtime.

Leclerq smirks.

'I'll be up in a bit,' Winta insists.

I get up with bad grace and turn in for another early night, leaving them together to do things I'd rather not think about. I consider stomping my feet on the way upstairs, but that probably wouldn't help me prove how grown up I am.

Winta doesn't make me wait long before she arrives in the bedroom with a sealed envelope in her hands.

'Don't open it,' she says gruffly, then she kisses me with a tenderness that I don't understand. 'I know this thing with Yolande is hard, but for the moment, we need her. The day after tomorrow,' she whispers. 'This will all be over, okay? And we'll be together. I need you to trust me, remember?'

'Okay,' I whisper back, then she's gone before I can ask her to stay.

It's probably for the best. I'm not sure my heart could take another rejection.

26

'CHÈRE JACQUÉLINE,' CARLOTTA says cheerfully when I join her on the roof terrace at the top of the club. I didn't bother with the front door, which is likely locked anyway, but that's one advantage of being Silver: you don't need stairs to climb a few storeys.

I guess Carlotta's had a long night of schmoozing because she's propped up her Louboutin-clad feet on a nearby stool and she doesn't get up to greet me.

'I'd offer you a drink,' she says, 'but I'm afraid you've come too late. We're closed.'

'That's all right. I'm not here for the drinks.'

'Oh?' she says, more surprised than I'd like. Do people really think I spend my whole life in a Massacre-induced haze? That hardly seems fair, given that I haven't had a proper drink for weeks.

'No,' I say. 'I came to see you.' Then I take a seat next to her on the padded bench without waiting for an invitation. Winta never came to bed last night, so I'm not really in the mood for civility.

At this time of the morning, the view is spectacular. In the middle of winter, the sun is only now starting to rise above

Oxford's dreaming spires, painting them in tones of pink and purple that warn of bad weather heading our way later on. Right now, the sky is clear and the patio heaters are doing their magic, so there's nothing to stop us from sitting together and enjoying the city's colourful panorama. I never take the time to appreciate it, but we really do live in a beautiful place.

I'll be sad to leave it behind.

'Would you like a dip in the hot tub?' Carlotta asks. 'It's heated.'

'I didn't bring my swimsuit.'

'Neither did I.'

She smiles at me, and if I were in any way a morning person, despite our circumstances I might feel the urge to tear off my clothes and dive in. As it is, I'm still tasting toothpaste and craving caffeine. A frolic in the hot tub is the last thing on my mind.

'I'm here on business,' I say instead. 'We have some mutual friends.'

'*Le baron, oui*?'

'Yes. Him. But also others. One with another French friend, is the one I'm particularly thinking of.'

'Oh,' she says, then she sits up straighter, puts her feet on the floor and says, 'Oh,' again.

I pass her a folded piece of paper, the one with the message from Winta.

Yes, I opened the envelope. Of course I opened the envelope. Do you blame me for needing a little reassurance? There's deciding to trust people, and then there's being a credulous idiot. I'm trying very hard to walk the line between the two.

'You've read it,' says Carlotta.

'Yes.'

'No one's supposed to read it except me.' She's pouting in

a way that is idiosyncratically French.

'We're all doing a lot of things we're not supposed to. I don't think anyone's in a position to judge.'

'But we have to trust each other, Jacquéline,' she says, waving the letter at me. 'We have to have an understanding between ourselves, or we lose everything.'

'Sure,' I say dismissively. 'I think we understand each other well enough, Carlotta. Just tell me your answer, will you?'

She pouts again and starts tapping the letter against her lips, making me wait.

'All right,' she says eventually. 'Tell her I'll do it.'

'Thank you.'

Winta's asked Carlotta to arrange somewhere in Argentina for us to stay, along with transport, early in the morning of the first of January. As soon as we've done this, we're running, and Carlotta has the connections to give us an escape route.

Two tickets. Just two. When this is over, Winta and I will be alone together.

Finally.

'Well, if that was all…' Carlotta starts shifting in her seat, gathering her things as though she's about to leave. Belatedly, I realise she's signalling that she wants me to get lost.

'There was one more thing, actually,' I say.

'You should talk about it with him, not me,' she says, which catches me off guard.

'What?'

'I can't help you with the baron. We have an arrangement,' she says, flashing her massive diamond ring at me. 'You need to speak to him. I keep trying to get you two to talk to each other—'

'No, you keep trying to get us to sleep with each other.'

'Pffft, whichever. One leads to another, I often find. The point is, he doesn't know about this, does he?' she asks, waving the letter at me again.

'No.'

'He should.'

'Should he?' I ask incredulously.

'You were intending to leave without saying anything at all?'

'Why not? He did.'

'Now you're just being puerile, Jacquéline,' she says with a moue of distaste. 'He cares for you. And you care for him, too.'

I snort. It's a less graceful sound than I'd like to be making in front of the perfectly-poised Carlotta Arden, but it's the only appropriate response.

'Still puerile,' she says with a smile. 'And rude.' She leans towards me, placing one perfectly-manicured hand on my knee in a suggestive manner. 'But I can see the attraction.'

'Knock it off,' I say, pushing her hand away. 'It's too early for me. Also, you smell of him,' I say. I don't mean to, but the words tumble out before I can catch them.

She smiles. 'You recognise him, chérie? He recognises you, you know. He'll know we were together this morning, the same way you can tell he was here last night. What should I tell him?'

'Tell him I came in for a drink.' Since everyone seems to think I'm an addict, I might as well lean into my bad reputation.

'Or I could tell him you're in over your head. Because you are, you know. These new friends of yours aren't playing.'

'What makes you think I am?'

'You'd do better to involve him than keep fighting against him,' she says with a tip of the head that invites me to consider this as a serious suggestion. Fat chance.

I imagine trying to sell that to Winta. *Hey, you know how Drake tried to lock you up and murdered your old bestie, then handed you over to the Seekers, then boxed your... whatever Leclerq is? Yeah, we should bring him in on this plan to rescue your parents, overthrow the Invicti and kill the Primus. It'll be awesome. We won't end up locked away in his basement at all, I promise.*

'He could be useful,' Carlotta insists. 'You should consider it.'

'No. I don't think so.'

'He might surprise you,' she says.

I think of Gabriella De Palma and I laugh, though what I really want to do is cry. I'd half fooled myself into thinking Drake might be better than he is, but now I'm worrying for every person I've ever left in the cold care of his basement. If he considers even Gabriella to be fair game, then who's off limits? Will Tabitha be safe, or have I made a terrible mistake?

'Can I ask you a favour?' I say.

'You can ask.' She pulls a cigarette from the packet on the table in front of her and lights up, then uses the flame to burn Winta's letter to ash.

'When this is over,' I say, watching the smoke curl up as the paper disintegrates, 'do you think you could get Drake to release Tabitha Ross?'

She takes a drag of her cigarette and taps the ash off onto the ground to join the remains of the letter. The smell reminds me of the first time I met Winta, outside a club not far from here, while I was getting a quick nicotine hit. That was the last cigarette I ever smoked; Winta doesn't like the taste.

'Why not ask him yourself?' she asks.

'I won't be here,' I say.

'And you can't ask him now because...?'

'I don't think that would be good for any of us.'

Carlotta shakes her beautiful head and murmurs, 'So stubborn,' but she's smiling with an affection I feel I haven't earned.

'I'm not,' I say, which probably doesn't help my point.

'You are. Even when you want to bend, you'd rather break just so no one will think you weak. Maybe it's your age. So young, so uncompromising, so fierce.' She crosses one leg over the other and leans towards me, examining me as though I'm a fascinating conundrum rather than an under-slept, caffeine-deficient vampire with rumpled clothes and messy hair. 'I bet you're just as fierce a lover as you are a fighter,' she says in that seductive drawl she does so well. 'Are you sure about the hot tub?'

'Yes, thanks,' I say, getting to my feet before I can change my mind. 'But thank you for the offer and the… you know,' I say, gesturing to the ash on the floor. 'And Tabitha. It's important to me.'

'I won't forget,' she promises.

She walks me to the edge of the roof. I'm expecting a brisk goodbye, but instead she surprises me by pulling me into her arms and holding me close.

She really does smell of Drake. It's faint, a simple transference rather than a scent mark, but it's impossible to ignore. Funny that I'm picking up on it, because I've never been particularly sensitive to scent, not for a Silver. It's the sort of thing Cam would notice, but would normally escape me entirely. Perhaps that should worry me, but instead I just enjoy being soothed by the scent without having Drake nearby to complicate things. If only Carlotta didn't smell quite so strongly of cigarettes, it would be a perfect hug.

'I wish you the best, Jacquéline,' she says, kissing me on both cheeks. 'I really do.'

'Um, thanks.'

'Take care,' she says as I step off the edge of the building and plunge into the darkness of the alley below. As gravity takes me, I'm almost certain she says something else too, but the distance and the motion must distort it, because it doesn't make sense.

I thought I heard her say, 'Take care of him, too.'

When I get to the college that morning, everyone's sitting around in the common room, moping. I guess Cam's told them his news. He is conspicuously absent, but most of the others are here: Quentin, Naia, Ellie, Raul, even Boyd.

I flop down on the sofa next to Naia and, wordlessly, she passes me a piece of white card. It's an invitation, a fancy one, with gold leaf detailing, raised text and crimped edges. I hope they used a discreet printer.

'You are invited to the Fidelis ceremony of Cameron Sawyer,' I read aloud. 'Eleven thirty p.m., thirty-first of January, Solis Invicti HQ, London. RSVP. They make it sound like a fucking birthday party.'

'You knew?' Naia says. Her tone isn't friendly.

'He told me yesterday,' I admit.

'What the fuck, Jack?'

'Late yesterday. Too late to tell you.'

'Whatever. It's not like you ever come into work anymore anyway.'

'Did you want the keys to my flat,' I say, dangling them in front of her, 'or are you just going to carry on being a dick?'

As she goes to take them from me, I lift them out of her reach. She narrows her eyes at me.

'I'm sorry, Jack,' I say, doing my best Naia impersonation. 'I'd love to stay in your flat *for free*. I didn't mean to be a dick. I apologise.'

'Yeah, sure,' she says, swiping the keys before I can move them again. 'All that. Now what are we going to do about

Cam?'

'What can we do?' Quentin asks. 'He's leaving. Maybe we should think about doing the same.'

'Don't you dare,' says Boyd. 'We're short-handed as it is.'

'And whose fault is that, Mr Cut-Costs-At-Any-Cost?' says Naia.

Boyd presses his lips together, tight. I can see the indecision on his face, but then he breaks. 'We haven't got any more money,' he says. 'The Primus cut our funding. I'm doing the best I can, but there's only so much we can earn from leasing out bits of the building and doing odd security jobs, and that's only going to get worse now that...'

He closes his mouth.

'Now that what?' Naia says.

Boyd says nothing.

'Now that *what?*' she repeats, louder this time.

'They've asked us to vacate the college,' Boyd says.

'*What?*'

That's done it. There'll be no calming Naia down now. Boyd cowers back a little in his seat before correcting himself and sitting up straight again, trying to play the formidable captain he's supposed to be. I can't blame him for his reaction; Naia's on her feet, and although she's not a particularly tall woman, right now she seems it.

'Apparently the issue with the ceiling collapse gave them the impression that we're poor stewards of this historic building,' he says. 'If some of us could learn to control our tempers a little better—'

'You're blaming this on *me?*'

'If we're out, then who's taking over?' Ellie says, diplomatically interrupting the Boyd/Naia situation before it can escalate further.

'The researchers,' Boyd says. 'Dr Castell, and a new team from London. The college will continue, but the Seekers are out.'

'What the Seekers are is *finished*,' I say. 'If we can't afford another base and, let's face it, most of us can't even afford places to live, then we're done. As soon as they kick us out, the Seekers are extinct.'

'And when is that, exactly?' Ellie asks Boyd.

'Hmm?' he says, as though he hasn't heard. That might work on sweet and polite Ellie, but it's no use on Naia.

'Boyd,' she says. 'Spill it. Now.'

'At the end of the year,' he says quietly.

'Which is tomorrow,' I say, feeling the bottom fall out of the world.

'*Tomorrow?*' Naia yells, and then all hell breaks loose. Everyone's standing up and yelling at everyone else. Quentin looks like he's hyperventilating, Raul's in tears, and I'm just sitting on the sofa staring at the floor.

Tomorrow.

I knew the Seekers wouldn't last much longer. With all that's happened over the past year, our eventual demise was inevitable. And I know I'm leaving them anyway, so this should be irrelevant, but it isn't. There's a big difference between leaving your home because it's something you choose, and leaving your home knowing it's no longer there for you to return to. There is no safety net for me.

Once I leave this place tomorrow, there's no coming back.

'But why?' says Ellie. 'Why would the Primus pull the rug out from under us like that? I don't understand.'

'We're not needed anymore,' I say, opening up about the things I've been keeping in my head for months. 'Most of the Silver are pro-reveal. Sooner or later – sooner, I guess – we're coming out.'

'But the vote,' says Quentin. 'The Primus won by a landslide.'

'Um, no,' I say. 'No, he didn't.'

'What?' Boyd says.

'He rigged the ballot,' I say. 'He switched out the voting urn to make sure he'd win, but I saw the votes as they were cast. He lost. By a landslide.'

They're all looking at me open-mouthed. I'm expecting them to start arguing with me, to tell me I can't possibly have seen what I saw and that I must be mistaken, but that's not what happens. Instead, Boyd just looks shocked and hurt – they all do – and I realise then that I've made a mistake.

I should have told him. Six months ago, before Boyd became captain and started throwing his weight around, I probably would have done. I should have told them all, but I remembered the way they'd reacted when I told them about the conspiracy at Windsor's parties, and I decided to keep it all to myself. None of them had wanted to doubt the Invicti. The idea that they might have believed the Primus was compromised too, when upholding his edict was the whole point of our jobs… I was scared they'd accuse me of being a conspiracy theorist again. Crazy Jack, off on one of her vendettas.

I should have given them more credit. They're my team. Or they were. For two decades, they've had my back and I've had theirs. They deserved my trust, but I've given it to someone else now, and it's too late to change my allegiance.

Fuck.

'I didn't think you'd believe me,' I murmur, before anyone can ask why I kept it to myself.

'You idiot,' Naia says, not without love. 'You should have told us.'

'I know.'

'So it's all over?' Quentin says. 'The Seekers are disbanding?'

'That's about the size of it,' says Boyd. 'I've spoken to the other teams already, and they've agreed to keep working for as long as there's money in the pot.'

'And how long will that be?' Ellie asks.

'A month? Maybe a bit longer, if we're careful.'

'Shit,' Naia says.

'Can't we just move into one of the regional bases?' Ellie asks.

The Seekers have bases all around the country, and although we'd have to split up because none of them is very central, at least we'd have somewhere to work from. It's a good solution for us.

I say *us* as though I'm going to be sticking around, but it's *them* now.

'The Invicti are taking those over too,' says Boyd with a sigh. 'Safe houses, apparently.'

'Fuck, they're really trying to screw us, aren't they?' says Naia.

'It's difficult not to come to that conclusion,' says Boyd. 'I'll admit that at first I was taking their reticence personally. I thought maybe they didn't want to work with me in particular, but over the past weeks it's become clear that they're shutting all of us out.'

'And they still expect us to go to their stupid party?' Naia says.

'Yes,' Boyd says. 'And you're all going to go and present your best selves to the Invicti, because maybe then they'll hire you as well as Mr Sawyer.'

Who chooses that moment to appear at the door, looking so sheepish that I'm sure he's been listening from outside.

'Is it safe to come in?' he asks.

The silence that greets him suggests that maybe it isn't. I sigh and get to my feet, tugging him into a hug.

'It's okay, Cam,' I say. 'We still love you.'

'Speak for yourself,' grumbles Naia.

'I know this is bad timing,' Cam says. 'And I'm sorry. But

the captain's right – I think they'd be keen to take all of us on.' He looks around the room, and I see his gaze stutter a bit as it reaches Quentin and his hair, which is turquoise and spiky this week. 'Most of us, at least,' he adds.

The others look like they're thinking about this carefully, but it strikes me as wishful thinking, and it's not just Quentin. There's Raul, who's far too green to join up with the Invicti, and Ellie, who's so gentle that they'd just crush the joy right out of her. But change is coming, one way or another, and we're all going to have to adapt to survive.

Right now, there are no good choices for any of us.

'What about you, Captain?' Raul asks. 'Would you join the Invicti?'

'No, I'm done,' he says. 'It's over for me. All I ever wanted was to be captain of the Seekers and… Well, look how that turned out.'

What a hollow victory. It's hard not to feel sympathy for him, despite the stupid rota, and the open plan office, and the multiple firings, which make sense now given this new context. He's been doing all this to try to cut costs in a desperate attempt to keep us afloat, and we've just bitched and moaned the whole way.

Some team we've been.

'But we're going to go out with a bang, all right?' he says, looking around at each of us. 'Let's show the Invicti just how slick we can be. One final outing for the Seekers in their glad rags. Okay?'

I've never thought of Boyd as a motivational speaker, but the squad's reaction makes me reassess that. They whoop, smile and laugh. Apparently this is going to be our last hurrah, and they mean to make it count.

'That means you, Jacqueline,' Boyd says, pointing at me. 'Glad rags. Yes?'

'Yes, fine,' I say, running through the options in my head.

'Okay.'

My velvet dress from May was a casualty of the ceiling collapse. I can't wear the leather dress from Christmas; it's too tight and I need to be unrestricted for the fight tomorrow night. It'll have to be something floaty, because I'm getting the distinct impression that jeans will be unacceptable for this shindig, which leads me to a miserable yet inescapable conclusion.

Bugger.

I'm going to have to go shopping. *Again.*

Boyd's phone is ringing. When he answers it, his expression becomes even grimmer that it was already. The call is as brisk as his manner when he tells us the news.

'We've got another call,' he says. 'Headington this time. Cam, I want your team on it.'

'I have to go buy a dress,' I say. 'Can't Ellie go in my place?'

'No,' Boyd says in a tone that discourages argument. 'It sounds as if it's the same scab as the Osney killing. I need you all there.'

'Shit,' Naia mutters.

The Seekers are disbanding in thirty-six hours, and it looks like we have a serial killer on our hands.

27

HEADINGTON'S A BUSY suburb on the road to London, full of families and parks and student halls for Oxford's second university, the one you've probably never heard of. It's about a forty-five minute walk from the city centre, and much the same if you're driving, because Oxford's traffic-calming measures have successfully calmed traffic to a standstill. Today, on the fringes of rush hour, it would have been quicker to walk.

I'm driving the van and wishing I wasn't. We've left Ed behind this time – he's working hard on what we collected from the Sommer house – but the rest of the team is along for the ride. Cam's talking to Faizan on speakerphone in the seat beside me, while the other two listen in from the back.

'It's a weird one,' Faiz says. 'Frankly, I think they'd rather not deal with it.' He means the police; one of his former colleagues has called him about a house in one of the terraced streets off Headington's main drag. Despite no longer working for the Seekers, Faiz is helping us anyway. He's that kind of person. 'They sent someone over to take a look, but by the time they arrived the blood smear on the door was gone, so it's been recorded as a prank.'

'A blood smear?' Naia says from the back seat. 'On the front door?'

'Yes,' says Faiz. 'I heard about the Osney case and thought you'd want to know.'

'That's all we have?' Cam says.

'There's one more thing,' Faiz says, but then he stops talking. There's silence on the other end of the phone.

'Faiz?' I say. 'Are you still there?'

'Yeah, I'm here,' he says. 'But look, it might be nothing.'

'Spill,' I say.

'The guy I spoke to, he knows I'm into bite marks,' Faiz says. 'That's why he called me. Turns out, there have been three more of these since Christmas. All students, all bitten, all bloody, all dead.'

'And no one thought to call us?' Naia says.

'You've forgotten,' says Cam. 'They don't do that anymore.'

'Well, apparently this guy felt bad enough about it to do something,' says Faiz from the other end of the phone. 'I'll try to get the files for you, but no promises.'

'Thanks, Faiz,' says Cam. 'Anything else you can tell us?'

'Nope. For now, that's all I've got.'

'Someone should be paying you,' says Naia.

'Tell me about it. Maybe you can take it up with the captain.'

'Yeah,' Naia says with a derisive snort. 'No promises there, either.'

Cam thanks Faiz again and hangs up, leaving the rest of us to wonder what's going on in the city we used to look after.

I'm concentrating on the road. When the shark hoves into view, I know we're close.

That's the other thing I should tell you about Headington: it's host to the weirdest house in the city. Right at the top of New High Street, so close that you can get a clear view of it from the main road, there's an otherwise normal terraced house with a twenty-five foot fibreglass shark sticking out of the roof.

Seriously. Google it if you don't believe me.

The house we're heading to is so close to the shark that when we park up and disembark from the van, I can still see the tip of its tail from the front garden.

'I don't see any blood,' Raul says.

'I don't *smell* any blood,' says Cam, which means either the police were right and it's just a prank, or someone's used a serious detergent on the stain.

Naia knocks.

We wait.

She knocks again.

When there's no response, she casually pulls her keys from her pocket, as though she has every right to be here, and pretends to insert one in the door lock. That doesn't open the door, of course. What opens the door is her shoulder slamming into it and splintering the frame.

'That was loud,' Raul says.

'Shut up and get inside,' says Naia, ushering us all in then trying ineffectually to close the door behind us. She's managed to bust one of the hinges, so it's a lost cause.

'We'd better do this quickly,' Cam says.

Which isn't a problem. We're used to working fast.

'I smell unwashed students,' I say.

There's a bedroom immediately to the left of the door in what I guess was once the house's sitting room, and the reek of month-old bedsheets is wafting out towards us. There's another scent besides, coming from the bathroom at the very back of the house, and it's even less pleasant.

'How long ago did Faiz say the blood smear was first reported?' Naia asks.

'He didn't,' Cam says.

Naia groans. 'You go first. I just ate.'

'You've never lost a meal in your life. Keep walking,' I say, then I prod her in the back to make sure she'll go on ahead of me. I recognise that smell and I'm about as keen as she is.

Raul, apparently in a world of his own, is wandering along happily after Cam and doesn't clock the unmistakable odour of decomposition until he's already in the bathroom. The moment he does, his face turns green and he rushes past us at Silver speed, back out of the door and into the front garden. I can hear him retching. It doesn't help.

The body's in the bathtub.

We don't usually have to deal with this kind of shit. Normally, we'd either get a tip from a Silver the moment a body drops, or one of our Silver moles in the police would call us for help with a suspicious death where a violence mark has been scented or a bite is involved. Generally, that means we get to the scene while everything's still nice and fresh. This kind of gooey situation only comes along once in a blue moon and, while I'm not complaining about the infrequency, it does mean we're ill-prepared to handle it.

'Fuck,' Naia says, looking down into the tub while she holds her hand over her nose and mouth. 'What do we do now?'

'Not much,' I say.

It looks like the bath was full of water when the body was put in it, fully-clothed, so everything's liquefied into a gruesome slurry that I'm not going to be touching anytime soon. If there's evidence still on the body, then it's staying there for the time being.

'Are we thinking this is a… guy?' Naia asks, squinting at the head sticking out of the mess.

The hair's short, that much is clear. It's also a bright, fiery red, which might help with the identification. The thing we can't see at all is the one thing we really need to see: the neck. If the killer left toothmarks in this body the same way they did with the first, we'll never know about it. Any imprints that might have been left in the soft tissue are gone, dissipated into the water with the rest of the flesh.

'Search the house, then?' Cam suggests.

'Good plan,' I say.

'Quickly,' Naia reminds us. 'With Raul making a scene outside—' We can still hear him vomiting into the flowerbeds. '—I reckon we've got maybe ten minutes before the plods show up.'

Our sweep is quick and efficient, and it ends with all three of us crammed into the box room at the top of the stairs. It looks like this was the victim's bedroom.

'Gareth Naismith,' Cam reads from a driving licence he's found in a wallet on the windowsill. 'Flaming red hair. Twenty years old.'

'Fuck,' I say. 'Student?'

'Yep.' Cam pulls out a student card and flashes it at me. 'He's got a Bod card, so probably one of the Oxford colleges.'

Mindful of the evidence we found at the Sommer house, we check the sheets carefully for blood and hairs, but they're clean. So clean that I might have to readjust my student stereotyping and concede that this student, at least, occasionally did his laundry. And, judging by the state of the floor, his hoovering as well.

'There's nothing here,' I say.

'It'd be difficult to miss it if there was,' says Naia.

She's not wrong. The room is as neat as a pin and absolutely tiny, only large enough for a single bed and a small desk, and not much else. Naismith's clothes are hanging neatly from a bare rail in the corner of the room, and his books are stacked on a shelf that's supported on precarious brackets above the bed. It takes us less than a minute to search the entire space, and that includes the time it takes to flip through the books to look for stray papers.

'Look,' says Cam.

He's been feeling his way along the clothes rail, checking pockets, and he's found a flyer. All three of us crowd around to look at it. We look some more. We look at each other, then we look back at the flyer.

'Any ideas?' Naia asks.

The paper is glossy black with a single word printed in white across the top: *Welcome*.

'Welcome to what?' I say.

Cam flips the paper over, but the other side is just plain black. At least, it looks that way, until the gloss catches the light and I swear I can see the vague sheen of lettering dancing across the page.

'Bring it,' I say. 'We need to get gone.'

We bag the flyer, collect Raul and skedaddle, just in time. The first police car pulls up as we're driving away. They're going to get a surprise when they reach the bathroom.

Here's the unexpected silver lining of being cold-shouldered by our police contacts: if someone has to wade through that muck, better them than us.

When we get back to the college, we gather everyone together in the common room. It's become our default rallying point, because no one wants to work in the open-plan monstrosity, nor be reminded of the impending collapse it represents.

Raul's looking a little less green now, but I'd be lying if I said he looked well. There's something weird about his eyes, as though they're each focussing on slightly different points. It's unsettling.

I should probably check in with him and make sure he's

okay, but I'm a little distracted. While I was sort-of concentrating on the road on the drive back, I had an idea.

'Hand me that flyer,' I say to Cam.

He pulls it out of his bag while I extract a black light from my pocket, a gadget I picked up from the lab on my way back from parking the van. I shine it on the piece of glossy black paper, and the words appear.

Dress to the nines, for nine til late.

Free drinks and acts to captivate.

Silver members welcome too; there's plenty catered just for you.

Then the address is listed on the reverse, an address I know.

'It's Carlotta's new open blood bar,' I say.

'This is getting weird,' says Cam. 'First the Crimson matchbook in Sommer's room, now a flyer for… What's the new place called?'

'If it has a name, I don't know it,' I say. 'It's the kind of pretentious joint that wouldn't bother.'

'Well,' he says, 'now a flyer for there turns up in Naismith's room. Do you think someone's picking off students who go to Silver clubs?'

'You're sure we're looking at a rogue Silver?' Naia says. 'We only found one scent mark, and that was at the Sommer scene.'

'Only because Naismith had been dead a while,' I say. 'A long while.'

'And then there are the other murders, the ones we didn't get called to,' says Cam. 'There may well have been scent marks there, we just never got the chance to check.'

Boyd joins us then, venturing out from wherever he does his work these days, so we fill him in on the Naismith scene and everything Faizan told us over the phone.

'We have a scab serial killer,' Boyd says.

'It looks that way,' says Cam.

Boyd checks his watch. 'Barely twenty-four hours before we're evicted from the college.'

'The timing sucks,' says Naia.

'At least you've already moved out,' says Raul. 'I've still got to pack. And find somewhere to live.'

'You can move into my flat,' I offer.

'No, he can't,' says Naia. 'I'm staying there.'

'There's more than enough room for the two of you.'

Naia makes a discontented hmph, but Boyd interrupts her before she can argue further.

'If we could digress from your living arrangements for the time being and get back to the case?' he says. 'We're on a rather urgent deadline.'

'And there could be more murders,' Cam says. 'There could be a lot more, either already committed or coming soon. If the scab's targeting students who are staying behind to study over the holidays, I wouldn't be surprised if no one notices they're missing until their housemates come back in January and find them.'

'As if five wasn't enough,' says Boyd.

'For what, though?' Raul asks. 'Who needs that much blood?'

'Someone who enjoys taking it,' I say. 'Or several someones.'

'That seems more likely to me,' says Cam. 'With the number of deaths and the volume of blood, this has to be a sizeable crew.'

'Are you thinking cuckoos?' I ask, remembering a series of cases we'd had years ago.

It works like this: a gang of Silver gather together in the house of a human, draining them of blood and cash and squatting in their place until there's nothing left for them to take, then they move on to their next victim. It's an efficient and ruthless way to live cost-free and under the radar.

'If it is cuckoos,' Cam says, 'then they're moving from house to house pretty quickly. And students would be a bad choice if what they want is money.'

'But if they just want blood and shelter?' I say.

'Maybe,' Cam concedes, but he doesn't look convinced. 'I didn't pick up on a load of Silver scents, though, not at either scene. There's a kind of overload factor I get when there are lots of us in the same place. I didn't feel it.'

'Did you pick up any scents at all?' Boyd asks.

'Not clearly enough that I could recognise one and pin it to both scenes, but then the odour of the Naismith house was… overwhelming. If there was a common Silver scent there, I wouldn't be able to tell you.'

'What's next?' Boyd asks, turning to Naia as though she's in charge of the team, which is a little insulting to Cam if you ask me.

'Ed has some hair and blood samples from the Sommer case,' she says. 'He's analysing them now.'

'And the other cases?'

'Nothing useful from the Naismith case,' says Cam. 'But maybe the police'll find something on the body.'

'In the meantime,' I say, 'Faiz said he'd try to get the files for the other three.'

'Speaking of which,' says Cam, responding to a ping on his phone, 'here they are now.'

'What have we got?' Boyd asks.

Cam passes his phone to me and I scan the files quickly. Taking in information at speed is my speciality.

'All three victims were students,' I say. 'All three were the only ones staying in their student houses over the holidays. All three died within the past week from wounds to the neck and exsanguination, but there was little or no blood left behind at any of the scenes.'

'So far, so familiar,' says Naia.

'Some weirdnesses,' I continue. 'One of them – what looks to be the first one, if estimated times of death are accurate – had defensive wounds on her hands that looked like they were caused by a knife. The other two, like Sommer, didn't have a mark on them.'

'So maybe the killer's learning as he goes,' says Raul.

'Which would make sense, because the more recent ones all had ligature marks on their wrists,' I say. 'One of them was even found suspended from a beam by a strap wrapped around his ankles.'

'To make it easier to drink?' asks Raul.

'I guess.'

'But there was nothing like that with Sommer,' says Naia.

'Maybe he was drunk,' Cam suggests. 'They might turn that up in the post mortem.'

'Or maybe he was willing,' I say.

They all look at me as though I've suggested he enjoyed licking alley walls.

'Seriously,' I say. 'Some people like that kind of thing.'

'Are you speaking from personal experience?' Naia asks. 'Do you go around biting humans for fun on the weekends, Jack?'

'No!'

'Just wondering. I do know someone, actually.' Of course she does. 'It's a subculture thing. I could ask them about it.'

'Do that,' says Boyd. 'Anything else?'

'Not until the lab results come back,' I say. 'Right now, Naia's kinky friend is the only lead we have.'

It's not looking good, and we all know it. If you want to secure an endless blood supply in Oxford without anyone noticing what you're doing, you couldn't do much better than targeting students during the holidays. There are even two universities to choose from, if you like a bit of variety in your meals. With the Seekers on their way out – which I'm sure is an open secret by now – this scab's going to get away with murder. Repeatedly.

'We can't solve this in time, can we?' Cam says.

'Probably not,' says Boyd.

'Sorry, Cam,' I say. 'Looks like you're not going out in a blaze of glory.'

'I'd settle for not leaving a bloody mess in my wake.'

'That doesn't look very likely, either,' I say. 'How about a drink instead?'

'I've got to pack,' he says miserably.

'And whose fault is that?' Naia asks. 'You can't mope when you're the one who's chosen to desert us.'

'I didn't think this would be the end, though,' Cam says. 'If I'd known—'

'Then you wouldn't have been able to change a thing,' says Boyd, 'so there's no point agonising over it. We'll work these cases until the Invicti kick us out tomorrow, then we'll carry on working until we either get a solve or the Primus stops us.'

'Do we still have to go to the stupid party?' Naia asks.

'Naia,' Cam moans. 'I want you there.'

'Yes, we're all going to the ceremony,' Boyd says. 'In the meantime, everyone get some sleep. There's nothing we can do until the lab results come in, and we could all do with some rest.'

It's not until he says this that I notice the creases around his eyes, deeper and more pronounced than usual. I like to think of Boyd as a robotic kind of Silver, immune to emotion, but he's taking this hard.

'No one wants to come for a drink, then?' I ask.

'Go to bed, Jack,' Cam says. 'You need to look pretty tomorrow.'

'No, I don't,' I say. 'You're the one who has a date with

the Invicti.'

'Then I'll need my beauty sleep,' he says, blowing me a kiss as he leaves the room.

The rest of the squad aren't far behind.

'No one?' I say querulously. 'Seriously?'

'Go to bed,' Naia yells at me.

'Yes, Jacqueline,' says Boyd. 'Go to bed.'

'Fine,' I say. 'Spoilsports.'

But with the tension running high back at my place, I have absolutely no intention of doing what I'm told.

28

DESPITE THE RETICENCE of the rest of my team, tonight feels like a good night to drown my sorrows.

Well, it's probably the worst possible night actually, given what we're planning for tomorrow and given how much I'm having to keep in my head at the moment, but as soon as the thought occurs to me it's pretty inevitable that I'm going to end up with bottles of gin and blood in my hands and a knife at my wrist. I shouldn't, I know. If I'm drinking at all right now, I should be sticking to the straight stuff, but I feel like I need things to be bendy, so back to the Massacres I go.

I do take some precautions, at least. I'm not drinking in the college bar, or at the Holywell Street club, or at Carlotta's new open blood bar, so there are no other Silver around for me to go spilling secrets to. And I'm not drinking at home either, where Winta or, god forbid, Leclerq might see me and judge. No, like the classy wench I am, I take my bottles down to the canal and find a quiet railway bridge to sit under in peace. In this freezing weather, I'm not expecting any company.

I just need a moment to myself, in my own head, to work everything out. I get exactly that – a moment – before I'm

312

joined by the most unwelcome person possible.

'What are you doing here?' I ask, taking a slug from my messy Massacre. My wrist's already healed, but I spilled some of the human stuff down the side of the bottle when I was mixing the drink, and there's a fair amount of my own blood on my new leather jacket too.

Whatever. It needed a little weathering.

'I was about to ask you the same question,' Drake says, joining me under the bridge like a stoner looking to bum a hit.

'I'm drinking,' I say, raising my bottle. 'Ideally, alone.'

'Idealism always ends in disappointment.' He sits down next to me, dirtying the trousers of his fancy suit in the frozen soot and fag ends and god knows what else that's collected in this rank corner of the city. Apparently the cold isn't going to put him off. I can barely feel it myself, since I'm now wearing a very comfortable booze jacket.

'Haven't you seen enough of me recently?' I ask. 'How did you even know I was here?'

'I have my ways.'

'Are you stalking me again? Because that didn't end so well for you last time.'

'No,' he says softly. 'Just trying to keep you out of trouble.'

I laugh bitterly. 'Good luck.'

'You have something of a talent for getting into it.'

'And I can get myself right back out again, thanks very much. Piss off, Drake.' I go to take another drink, but he intercepts the bottle on the way to my mouth and takes one for himself instead.

'This isn't a sharing circle,' I say, snatching the bottle back. 'If you wanted a drink, you should have brought your own.'

He extracts a hip flask from his pocket, because of course

he has a hip flask, the pretentious bastard. I share some of my human blood with him so he can mix his own Massacre – never let it be said that I am wholly ungenerous to fellow drinkers in need – but he can contribute his own blood to the mix if he wants Silver blood too. I'm not wasting mine on whisky.

He raises his wrist to his mouth and, looking me dead in the eye, he bites until it bleeds. Something flips in my stomach. Holy fuck, that should not be sexy, but I have a feeling the image will be seared into my brain for the rest of time. It doesn't help that the air is full of the scent of him, taking me right back to that night in his office when we bit each other, and did everything else besides. His blood is calling to me, and that's just… weird. So enticing I can barely resist it, but also weird.

'You know,' he says as he guides the gentle flow of his blood into his flask, 'you're a little fucked up.'

'No shit.'

He leans back against the bridge piling and turns to face me. 'I like that about you,' he says, his voice low. 'We had fun together, didn't we, Jack?'

I really do not want to talk about this. I came here for a bit of self-destructive peace and quiet and now *he's* here bringing back memories of all the things I want to forget. This man isn't my life. He isn't my future. My future is in a little house in Jericho, plotting the demise of the Silver with her maybe-ex-girlfriend. I shouldn't be thinking about Drake. I should be working out how to move forward with Winta.

'If I asked really nicely,' I say, 'would you go away and leave me alone?'

'Unlikely,' he says, taking another shot from his flask.

'How about if I asked less nicely?'

'You could try it,' he says, 'but you're probably stuck with me for the time being, so we might as well talk.'

I sigh a world-weary sigh. If he's determined to stay, then I guess there are words we need to have.

'I heard you have a serial killer on your hands,' he says.

'Did you hear about our funding cut too?'

'I did.'

'Then you know how likely it is that we're going to catch whoever's doing this.' I take a long drink. 'It's not like the Invicti are going to care.'

'I can keep you funded if you like,' he offers.

'Why bother? The Primus will only make you stop.'

'Probably.'

'And you'd do what he says.'

'He'd probably make me eventually,' Drake says, taking his own drink. 'But you might get time enough to find and box the killer, at least.'

I'm struck by the irony of it – one serial killer offering to help me catch another – and I can't restrain a bitter laugh.

'Takes one to catch one, right?' I say. 'Where's Gabriella, Drake?'

He looks surprised. 'What are you talking about?'

'Gabriella De Palma. Where is she?'

'She's in a box in my basement. You should know, since you're the one who put her there.'

'Only she's not,' I say. 'The box is empty. I passed by it when I boxed Tabitha, and it was silent. So let me ask you again: where is she?'

He breaks eye contact with me, like the coward he is, and I lose it.

'You bastard,' I yell, hurling a handful of rubbish at him from the ground beside me. 'You absolute *bastard*.'

'It's not what you think,' he says, deflecting the detritus I'm pelting at him with more ease than I'd like. Why does he have to make everything look so effortless? 'She's fine. I let her go.'

'Really?' I say, with a heavy dose of incredulity.

'Yes,' he insists. 'Back in June. She's living in Italy with her new husband.'

'I don't believe you.'

I've got the knife out of my pocket and I fully intend to stick him with it.

'*Wait*,' he says, holding up his hands. 'Jack, wait.'

'You have thirty seconds.'

Drake pulls his phone out of his pocket – the latest model, of course, because he's that kind of wanker – and makes a call on speaker. It rings for five seconds, ten seconds, and then he starts to get antsy. Apparently I have succeeded in discombobulating the unflappable Killian Drake.

'Pick up,' he whispers. 'Pick up the fucking— Gabriella!'

'Baron, darling!' comes the voice from the phone. 'What can I do for you? Are you and Carlotta back in Italy?'

'No,' he cringes. 'No, Gabriella. But I have Jack Valentine here with me – you remember her? – and she was worried I might have murdered you in your sleep. I'd be obliged if you could please reassure her that you're well.'

Gabriella's laugh tinkles down the phone. 'Perfectly well, Valentina,' she says, deploying the nickname that only she has ever used for me. Despite the tension of the situation, I can see that Drake is making a mental note of it.

'How do I know that's not just a recording?' I say to Drake.

'One second, Gabriella,' he says into the phone, then he converts the audio into a video call. 'There,' he says, showing me the screen. 'Gabriella, in the flesh.'

Gabriella waves at the camera. She's resplendent in a navy suit that's paired with one of those fancy patterned scarves you see on well-dressed Parisian ladies. She's smiling, fully made-up, with her golden hair so perfectly tamed that it looks like a painting.

'It could be a deepfake,' I suggest, but my tone betrays too much uncertainty. Drake has already relaxed, and I've lost my advantage.

'I promise you, Valentina,' Gabriella says from the phone. 'The baron has been very good to me.'

'He put you in a box,' I say.

'And he got me back out again, for the same reasons you were reluctant to put me in. You're the same, the two of you. After what happened with your Tabby cat, you'd do well to stop fighting the inevitable, *cara*.'

'I don't know what you mean,' I say.

'Yes, you do.'

'Give up, Gabriella,' Drake says. 'She has a new girlfriend. Or an old one, depending on how you look at it.'

I glare at Drake. 'And he's engaged to Carlotta Arden,' I say to Gabriella. 'Did she show you the ring during their European tour?'

'Well,' Gabriella says with a laugh, 'it sounds like the two of you have a lot to talk about, and I have a boat to catch. Come and visit the next time you're in the area, won't you both?'

'Thank you, Gabriella,' Drake says.

'*Ciao, bello.*'

He cuts the connection and gives me a look.

'Fine,' I say. 'Maybe she's not dead, but you're not any less of a bastard. I'm still deciding whether or not to let you live.'

'Have another drink while you decide,' he suggests. 'Then at least maybe I'll get away with just a flesh wound.'

'Bastard,' I say, but I take another swig anyway. I came here to drink and I'm not going to let him distract me from my purpose.

'I know you're not going to believe this,' Drake says, 'but

I'm going to tell you anyway: you can trust me.'

'Yeah, right,' I scoff.

'You've got a bad track record,' he says. 'I'll give you that. I know things with Dr Ross didn't end well, and I dread to think what might be going on with you right now, but have I ever lied to you? Ever betrayed you? I'm on your side.'

'You're on your own side.'

'They're the same side,' he says, exasperated. 'That's what I'm trying to get you to understand.'

'You don't mean that.'

'I do,' he says, ducking his head to make me meet his eye. 'I mean it, Jack. Whatever happens. Whatever ridiculous thing you're planning with your crazy ex—'

'Watch your mouth, Drake.'

'She's got that hold over you, hasn't she? Why else would you being doing this?'

'I just happen to agree with her,' I say, too quickly, too adamantly. I'm protesting too much.

'It's the thrill, isn't it?' he says, and there's a hopelessness to his words, as though he knows that nothing he can say will change my course. 'You want what you had when you first met her, but you can't seem to recapture it now, so you just chase her and chase her and chase her, hoping that one day there'll be a click and suddenly you'll feel now the way you did when you first fell in love.'

I wish his words didn't resonate so hard. I want to tell him that he's wrong, and that what Winta and I have now is just as good as – no, better than – what we had that night twenty years ago when we touched and set each other alight. But it's too big a lie.

'You can't freeze a moment in time and go right back to it as though nothing between you has changed while you've been apart,' he says. 'It doesn't work like that.'

I look at him carefully for the first time this evening, tracing the sadness in his eyes and wondering why he cares enough to sit beside me in the freezing mud.

'It works like that for us, though,' I say. 'Doesn't it? May, September, December, whenever I see you, whatever we do to each other, however long you're gone, however much I try to stop it, we end up falling back together the same way.'

'You're strangely insightful this evening,' he says. 'Do you know how irritating it is that you're admitting this *now*?'

'I'm not admitting anything,' I say, more out of habit than anything else. 'And I'm drunk.'

'I should have tried that sooner. Maybe if I'd brought you a Massacre back from Italy instead of that leather jacket you're ruining—'

'I'm wearing it in. It needed a little softening up.' I fiddle with the cuff, wiping the blood off onto my shirt. 'Thank you, though. I love it, and it means a lot that you… You know.'

Neither of us knows what to say to that, so we both take another drink. The bottles are nearly empty now, and it's a time of dangerous confidences. I should have stopped drinking the moment he sat down, but since we seem to be diving headfirst into the lake of stuff-we-don't-normally-talk-about, and since I can blame anything I say on my inebriation if he dares to bring it up in future, I decide to go for it.

'So why is it like this with you,' I say, 'and not with her?'

'We're different,' he says, as though that explains everything.

'But why?' I insist. 'What makes us different?'

'I can't answer that. We just are.'

'But *why*?'

He drains his flask, then says, 'What do you think *this* is?'

'This,' I say, gesturing between the two of us with my

empty bottle. Somehow, although we started off this discussion with a yard between our bodies, his thigh is now brushing up against mine. 'It's easy. We argue, but it's almost – sometimes, just a little bit – fun.'

He smiles.

'And if I don't concentrate very hard on resisting it,' I say, whispering the confession, 'then your scent just wraps around me and I sort of... fall into you, like it's the most natural thing in the world.'

'You could let yourself, you know,' he says, stroking his fingers through my hair. I don't remember putting it there, but my head is resting on his shoulder and I'm breathing in the irresistible perfume of his skin.

'No,' I say. 'I can't do that.'

'It's like you said.' His fingers are brushing through my hair, pulling it back over my shoulder so he can reach the spot at the back of my neck that he knows makes my toes curl. 'It's easy. It's always easy with us, if you let it be.'

'I'm spoken for,' I say, but I'm not moving away. I should be moving away and I hate myself for lingering. How would Winta feel if she knew I was sitting here with my head on Drake's shoulder, contemplating the things I'm contemplating? It's the worst kind of betrayal, but I can't make myself reject his touch when it's the only thing I've felt over the past week that's brought me any real pleasure.

'You're not a child anymore, Jack,' he whispers. 'You've outgrown her.'

My own denial is what moves me off his shoulder once and for all. 'That's not true,' I say. 'We're just finding our feet again.'

'She's just using you, making you do her dirty work. You can see that, can't you?'

'She just needs to know she can trust me,' I say, dismissively. 'That's all.'

'I think it's gone a little beyond that. You let her cut out your tattoo, for fuck's sake,' he says, and my blood runs cold.

'You spoke to Tabitha, didn't you?' It's the only way he could have heard about the tattoo; Cam still hasn't worked it all out. 'Is she okay? Tell me you didn't hurt her.' Sure, I screwed Tabitha over, but I made sure she never felt any pain, and despite all she did, I certainly never wanted her dead. To my surprise, I can feel tears welling in my eyes. I must be drunker than I realised.

'I thought Dr Ross kidnapped you and was planning to kill the Primus,' Drake says, in a tone that makes it clear he believes not a word of it. 'Isn't she just the kind of psychopathic Silver I should be putting out of their misery? That's what you said, isn't it?'

'Are you really that petty?' I'm yelling now. 'She didn't deserve that! *She did nothing wrong!* If you've hurt her, I swear—'

'She's safe with me,' he promises, trying to calm me down. 'Tabitha's safe. Put the knife away.' I didn't even know I'd pulled it out again, but it's there in my hand. 'I wouldn't do that to you, or to her,' he says once I've sheathed the blade. 'I know she doesn't deserve to die, but she didn't deserve to be boxed either. You do realise that?'

I nod, wiping away the tears. I can't seem to find words just at this moment.

'Then why did you do it?' he asks me softly, like I'm a child who's been caught in a lie. 'Just because she asked you to? Does she really have that kind of power over you?'

'She's my sire,' I whisper back. 'I love her.'

'Do you? Or are you chasing the memory of something you lost?'

'Isn't that what you're doing?' I ask, because I tend to lash out when I'm upset, angry and drunk.

'I haven't lost you, Valentine,' he says. 'Not yet, at least. But if you stay with her much longer, even you might lose yourself.'

'That's a very dramatic way of saying that you're jealous.'

'Have you ever killed someone?' he asks, which I take as the deflection it definitely is.

'I haven't racked up your kind of death toll,' I say, taking a long drink.

'I don't think you've killed anyone at all,' he says.

'I almost killed Matthew Felton.'

'Almost doesn't count. Lighting a Silver's house on fire and walking away is very different from looking in their eyes as you end their life.'

'If you're trying to convince me that you're not a psychopath, you not doing a very good job of it.'

'I'm trying to explain to you that killing people in the full consciousness of what you're doing isn't an easy thing. It shouldn't be. It should be hard to watch someone die, knowing that you're the one making the decision to end them. The moment it starts being easy, you've already changed yourself beyond redemption.'

'Like you have?'

'I don't carry those deaths easily. Each one is a rock at the pit of my stomach. I can list them for you, every single name, in order, with dates and times. I keep all the ghosts in here.' He taps the side of his head. 'There's no way to exorcize them, because they're part of me. But every one of those deaths was a decision, not a mistake. I don't regret them, much as I might wish they hadn't been necessary.'

'What are you telling me?'

'I don't want you to make a mistake. Murder is hard. Murdering the Silver is harder. But choosing the Primus for your very first murder…'

I want to hush him, terrified that he's dared to say the

words aloud. Here we are, under a bridge in the middle of nowhere in the freezing heart of winter, and I'm still worried that someone will overhear us.

'Carlotta told me that you're planning to run,' he says.

What the fuck?

After the lecture she gave me about keeping trust with your conspirators, I'm genuinely outraged, but I pretend his words mean nothing to me.

'I haven't seen Carlotta in days,' I say.

'Liar. She came back from work this morning with your scent on her skin.'

Bugger. I forgot about that. I've definitely had too much to drink.

'You'll never be able to run far enough,' he says. 'If this goes wrong, they'll never stop coming for you.'

'I don't know what you're talking about.' He's about to interrupt me, so I cut him off. 'But, just supposing I did, they'd never find me.'

'You could never hide well enough either, but it's irrelevant, because I'd find you first.'

'And turn me in?'

He looks away for a moment, and I know from the flexing and clenching of his fist that he's composing himself. I like being able to piss him off like this; there's a kind of power in it.

'No,' he says after a moment. 'Not to turn you in, you idiot.' He mutters something under his breath, so quiet that even I can't hear, then says, 'I told Carlotta the truth yesterday. It was time.'

I blink a few times to clear my head, because he's just made a conversational leap that I can't follow.

'What are you talking about? What truth? I thought you guys were already into the transparency thing, what with all the propositioning.' I was starting to regret refusing this morning's hot tub invitation. I deserve a little fun before I probably die.

'She didn't know I'd silvered,' he says.

'Oh. You told her?'

'Yes.'

'Then where is she?' I ask, because this makes no sense. Surely she should be glued to Drake's side. She's just found out that the most eligible bachelor in the Silver world has not only proposed to her, but is also magically and irrevocably bound to her for the rest of their lives. It's a pretty big deal. Even with her open approach to relationships, I'd expect her to care.

But the look on Drake's face tells me there's something here I've missed.

'She's at the club,' he says, looking as bewildered by my question as I am by his words. 'You don't get it, do you?'

'Look, Drake, it's been a long day. Make that a long week. Fuck it, a long year. Can you just cut to the chase?'

'Fine.' He takes a deep breath, as though he's steadying himself. 'You asked me why I ran.'

'Huh?' This conversation is going all over the place, and I can barely keep up.

'To Europe,' he says. 'You asked me why I ran. Remember?'

There's something in the fuzzy haze of the past few days that rings a bell, and I've definitely been asking the question in my head. Repeatedly. For months. But this is not the time.

I make a non-committal noise in response. It's supposed to encourage him away from this topic, because there's an intensity in his eyes right now that I don't like, but instead he takes my hands in his and turns me to face him.

'Now ask me again,' he says softly.

'Ask you what?'

'Ask me why I ran.'

I don't want to. I can feel him drawing me along with him through this conversation as surely as he's drawing my hands into his, and that really pisses me off, but at the same time I'm warm and fuzzy from the drinks and I have to know.

I've been waiting for him to voice the answer to this question for three months and several long days.

I have to hear him say it.

'Why?' I say.

'You know why.'

I am going to hit him, I swear.

But before I can, he flashes his silver, showing me the glinting metallic threads through the darkness of his irises.

'Because this is for you,' he says.

'No,' I say. It's a reflex response.

'Yes,' he replies. 'Come on, Valentine. You already know. You knew it without me ever needing to tell you.'

But it can't be true. It just can't, because if it is, then what am I supposed to do now?

'It was always you,' he goes on. 'But I ran because it freaked you out. Because it hurt. Because it was easier to run than to be around you and know that you didn't want this. But I'm not running anymore. It…' He swallows and bites his lip, as though he's trying to bite back the words he hasn't yet said. 'It hurts to be far from you.'

I should be laughing at him, because it sounds a little pathetic. If anyone else said those words to me, I probably would. But somehow, when he says them, they don't sound so funny. His breath hangs in the air between us, condensing in the cold.

'I don't know what you expect me to say.'

I don't want to say anything at all. My feet want to run and my head just feels dizzy, though to be fair that might be the Massacres.

'This thing we have between us? It's different,' he says.

'You feel that as much as I do, however much you choose to ignore it.'

He has to be wrong. I know he's got the bond doing weird stuff to his emotions, but mine aren't affected. What I feel for him is nothing. It's a passing fling. Given a fraction of the time with Winta that I've had with him, I'm sure she and I will be more than Drake and I ever were. He'll pale into insignificance and become exactly what I've always wished he could be: nothing but a bad memory.

I can comfort myself that by keeping this secret, he's only hurt himself. It wouldn't have changed anything if I'd known sooner. I would have done everything exactly the same way, because he's nothing to me, just a guy I sometimes want to fuck. That's all.

It sucks for him, but I can walk away. I have to walk away.

'Why didn't you just tell me?' I ask. 'We could have dealt with this months ago.'

'You *knew*,' he says, frustrated now. 'I was hoping you'd come to this on your own – I've been dropping enough hints – but if you're intent on getting yourself killed or running away tomorrow, it looks like I'm out of time to declare myself.'

'And what exactly are you declaring?'

'Are you really going to make me say it?'

'No,' I say hastily. 'I don't think either of us wants that.'

'*Really*? Sometimes I think you're going to keep fighting me forever.'

'No, Drake. Not forever. Only until tomorrow night, when I'll be out of your life for good.'

'Then you're still going to go through with this?' he says. There's a hollowness to his voice. 'You're telling me this changes nothing. You're still going to carry out whatever ludicrous plan she has you mixed up in, and if by some miracle you survive, you're going to run.'

'Yes,' I say, standing up and brushing the bridge crud from my trousers. 'So I guess this is goodbye.'

'Don't,' he says, and I swear there's a crack in his voice. 'For once, please, don't run away from me.'

He's on his knees at my feet.

Isn't this what I've always wanted? Killian bastard Drake, humbled at last. I should be crowing my victory but instead I want to take his hand and pull him up beside me. If I'm being honest, I want to do much more than that, but there's no stopping the train I'm on. Tomorrow's going to happen, one way or another, and I can't leave Winta now.

I'm hers, and maybe after this is over, she'll be mine. *That's* what I've always wanted.

'Don't make me choose between the two of you,' I say, 'because that's a fight you can't win. I'll pick her, every time.'

Then I do exactly what he asked me not to do.

I run.

29

I HATE YOLANDE Leclerq.

When I finally crawl home in the early hours of the morning after falling asleep in a nice warm attic – people really should lock their roof windows – she's already awake doing yoga or pilates or some such bollocks on the bare floorboards of the front room.

'You reek,' she says, not even bothering to open her eyes. 'You do know what you're supposed to be doing this evening, don't you?'

'Yes, thank you very much,' I say, walking past her on my way upstairs.

'Don't wake Winta. She's still asleep in our room.'

Their room?

'She's not,' says Winta, coming down the stairs. 'She's up. Where have you been all night, Jacky? Those are the same clothes you were wearing yesterday. Walk of shame?'

'Just blowing off steam,' I say. 'You know, so I'd be ready for tonight.'

Even I can admit this is a generous interpretation of my evening, so I'm not surprised when Winta doesn't buy it either. She meets me at the bottom of the stairs, her expression changing as she gets closer.

'You've been with someone else,' she says. 'Who was it?'

I consider lying. I didn't think she'd be sensitive enough to pick up the scent of another Silver on my skin after so many hours, and it's some small mercy that she doesn't recognise it. But I can't lie to her, and definitely not about this.

'I saw Drake,' I concede.

'Are you serious?'

'I didn't want to,' I say. 'I mean, he came and found me. I was having a quiet night of reflection on my own—' Yes, I know, but allow me a little latitude for bullshitting. '—and he just turned up.'

'So, what? The two of you blew off steam together, is that what you're telling me?'

Oh, she's angry. She's very angry, which is rich given that *our* bedroom has suddenly become *their* bedroom, but I have the feeling that it's not going to do me any good to point that out.

'Nothing happened,' I say. 'We had a drink. We talked. He annoyed me. I left.'

'I told you to stop talking to him.'

'She did, you know,' says Leclerq, coming to stand next to Winta.

Normally, I'd snap back with some witty retort, but Winta and Leclerq are standing shoulder to shoulder with their arms crossed over their chests and honestly I'm intimidated. They're each imposing women in their own rights, but together they are a force to be reckoned with. Even I can see that the two of them fit together in a way that Winta and I don't. They make me feel like a child in a room full of grown ups, as though I'm just playing at being Silver, and playing at being a rebel, even though I seem to be the one doing all the damn work.

'I tried,' I say in a small voice. 'I really did.'

Winta looks away for a moment, and when she looks back at me it feels like she's seeing me for the first time since Leclerq barged her way into our lives. 'It worries me that you have to try so hard,' she says.

'One more day,' I say, looking only at her, 'and I'll never have to see him again.'

'I'm not sure you can walk away that easily.'

'Of course I can. I will. Whatever happens,' I say. 'One more day.'

'And then we'll all be out of here,' Leclerq says, barging her way back into the conversation. 'Just don't fuck it up, Jacky.'

'I'm not going to fuck it up.' I can hear my teeth grinding. I can't bloody wait to leave her behind us.

'Are you all set?' Winta asks.

'I need an outfit,' I say. 'The Seekers are dressing fancy. Plus a matching bag, I guess, for the… you know.'

'I'd offer you something of mine,' Leclerq says. She looks me up and down. 'But I doubt it'd fit.'

'I doubt it'd be good enough anyway,' I snap back. 'This is a classy party, not a trashy club opening.'

'You—'

'Here,' Winta says, pulling out some cash and handing it to me before the bickering can escalate further. 'Get whatever you want. But right now: breakfast, blood, final checks. All right?'

I fetch and carry the drinks, bottles and plates while Winta and Leclerq get down to details. It's become an unpleasant routine over the past few days: compliant little Jack scurrying back and forth like Cinderella. I'm not sure why I put up with it, but for some reason I feel like I've been cast as the junior and it's my job to skivvy.

'And you know what you're doing, Jacky?' Winta asks.

'Yes.'

We've been through it enough times.

I'm not sure about this plan. I'm not sure at all, but I can't say anything to Winta, not after last time. She wants me to follow it to the letter, whatever my personal opinion of its pitfalls, so that's what I'll do.

If it gets us all killed, at least I won't be the one to blame.

'Right then,' Winta says, packing the last items away in their bags as she gets to her feet. 'We're off to get set up.'

She hands one of the bags to me. It's lighter than it should be, given the weight of what it contains.

'Don't fuck it up,' Leclerq says, pointing a finger at me.

'I'm not going to fuck it up,' I reply, biting out the words.

'Good. Bye, then.'

I was hoping Leclerq would piss off out of the door so Winta and I could have a moment alone to say goodbye, but instead she just waits.

'Bye, Jacky,' Winta says to me. 'I'll see you tonight, when it's all over.'

I want to kiss her. It might be the last chance we have. If everything goes to shit tonight, as I suspect it might, then this might be goodbye for good. I decide to go for it despite Leclerq's hovering presence, but Winta moves away just as I start to lean in, and then she's following Leclerq out of the door and away.

'Bye,' I say.

'Make sure you shower that scent off yourself before you go,' she calls back to me.

'I will,' I promise.

But, in the jumble of emotions that follow her departure, I forget entirely.

Shopping in Oxford is… Well, it's not shopping in Milan. Let's just leave it at that, shall we?

I'm shit at it. I've always been shit at it, and however often I have to do it, I don't seem to get any better at it. This is why I like it so much when people buy me clothes – it means they have to choose them for me.

'Help,' I say to the assistant in the first shop I enter. I've learned my lesson well enough to know that I need to throw myself on the mercy of people who know better. 'I need a dress.'

'Okay, ma'am,' she says, looking me up and down sceptically, just to make it clear that I look nothing like the kind of person she should be addressing as *ma'am*. 'Were you after a cocktail dress, an evening dress, a summer dress, a body con dress, a party dress—'

'I need a dress,' I repeat, helplessly. 'For a fancy party. And shoes and a bag. About yea big.' I box out a small rectangle with my hands.

'Okay,' the assistant says. She takes a deep breath as though she's reassessing the situation, then she adjusts her approach. 'Sparkly, slinky or slutty?'

'Slinky,' I say, because it's the only option that doesn't give me the horrors.

'All right, then. Let's make some magic.'

And she does. The woman is a godsend. I'm starting to think I've been wrong about shop assistants all this time, because I've not met one in the past year who wasn't some kind of outfit wizard.

'And there's a bag to match,' she says, handing it to me. 'Shoes comfortable enough?'

'They'll do,' I say. I won't be wearing them long.

'Perfect. Then I'll let you get changed and meet you at the till to ring you up.'

The total makes my eyes water, but Winta's paying, and she's given me more than I need. There's even enough to buy a shiny thing for my hair.

I'm just handing over the notes when my phone vibrates in my pocket.

'Hey, Cam,' I say. 'Cold feet about tonight?'

'No,' he says. His tone is worryingly serious. 'We've got a call.'

Of course we have. Sod's law that it happens today, on the very last day of the Seekers' existence, when I still have to shower and get ready and travel to fucking London for tonight.

'What kind of call?' I ask.

'The kind you want to be here for.'

He gives me the address. I pack up my purchases and run all the way there.

I know that while I'm telling you about Winta now, with our weird living situation and the constant fucking annoyance that is Yolande Leclerq, you might be wondering why I'm willing to kill for her. It seems like a stretch, I'm sure, and sometimes it's felt that way to me too, but then I remember my lost week when it was just the two of us, and it all feels worthwhile.

It was dreamlike. There was a lot of sex, a lot of laughter, and a lot of reminiscing. More reminiscing than should be possible when we had such a short acquaintance to look back on. Short but intense, she said, and our secret week together proved to be the same.

Granted, I wouldn't have chosen to have my ex chained up in the basement for the duration, so that was a little strange, but the times above ground were better. There was a lot of planning. There were some realities I was trying not to see too clearly – for us to have our happy ending, I'd have to take a life and bring our civilisation to its knees – but it was easier to avoid thinking about those things when I hadn't actually done anything yet. I hadn't lied to my team, I hadn't stolen Khalyed's blood, I hadn't boxed Tabitha, I'd just taken a little holiday without telling anyone, and sometimes it felt like exactly that: a holiday.

After a week living together with Winta in what felt like a life outside my own, I didn't want to leave her.

'You have to, Jacky,' she said. 'I need you to get this done for me. For us. If you're not back with the Seekers, how are we going to get Yolande out? And if we don't get Yolande out—'

'I know,' I said. 'The rest of the plan falls apart.'

'Yes, it does.'

'I still don't want to go.'

'You'll be back soon,' she said, then she kissed me in a way that was designed to make sure I'd come home. I kissed her back just as hard.

'We could just go upstairs,' I suggested, whispering the words against her lips. 'One last time before we hit the road?'

She laughed. 'We're already running a day behind.'

'We've got time.'

'No, Jacky,' she said ruefully, running a fingertip down my neck. 'We don't. They're looking for you, and we can't wait forever.'

I pressed my forehead against hers and closed my eyes, breathing in the sugary scent of her one final time. 'I wish the rest of the world would just go away and leave us alone.'

'Misanthrope.' She kissed me on both cheeks, and once more on the mouth – briefly – before finally pulling away. 'Come on. We've got to get you in the car.'

'Fine,' I groaned. Of course it had to end. I'd always known it would have to end, and like this, and that I'd see her again soon enough, but it wasn't just the anticipation of her absence that made me hesitate.

From the moment I woke up, I knew that I'd be lying to

the people I loved. Cam, Naia, Raul… hell, I even loved Boyd a little bit, though I'd never tell him so. It was worth it, I was telling myself. It would all be worth it, and it needed to happen, but the next couple of weeks were going to be hard and I wasn't in a hurry for them to start.

'Are you sure?' I said. 'Do we have to—'

'You know we have to. And you know why, too.'

'Yeah. I know.'

'Look, Jacky,' she said, putting her hands on my shoulders. 'Whatever happens next, I need you to trust me. Until this is over, whatever I do, whatever I say, I need you to remember that I love you. Can you do that?'

'I trust you.'

'No, really.' She pins me with her gaze and looks so deeply into my eyes that I feel like she's trying to watch herself in the reflection of my pupils. 'This is going to be hard. I'm going to do and say some things you don't like. So promise me: whatever happens, you'll trust me.'

I don't even think about it, I just promise, 'I'll trust you,' without asking what she means, or what she's planning to do.

Which, in retrospect, was really fucking stupid.

Standing in the sitting room of what was, until recently, our house, my faith is shaken. No, it's worse than that. My faith is hanging by a thread. All I have to hold onto are those few words she gave me, so long ago now that it feels like years: *trust me*.

'The body's in the bedroom,' Naia says. She's standing by the front door, where Winta was standing with Leclerq only this morning as we said our goodbyes.

'Do we know who it is?' I ask. I'm feeling so numb that it's the first thing I've said since we arrived five minutes ago. Cam's already checking out the area for scents while Ed takes samples from the victim. I should be springing into action to scout the scene, but I can't make myself walk upstairs and see the bedroom that used to be mine and Winta's covered in…

'Not sure yet,' Naia says.

Everyone's buzzing around in a frenzy, up and down the stairs, fingerprinting doors and swabbing taps. I know why I'm so anxious to solve this case, but I'm not sure why they are.

'And, um… Do we know anything about this place?' I say, looking around nonchalantly.

I have no idea how to play this, but my palms are sweating and it won't be long before Naia notices that I'm more nervous than I should be. My stuff's all upstairs in the single bedroom. My scent is hanging in the air. I'd be seriously surprised if Cam hasn't picked it up already, probably before he even made the call. Someone's going to put two and two together, which means I have to decide quickly whether I'm going to get ahead of this thing by confessing my connection to the house now, or whether I'm going to try and brazen it out by acting the innocent.

'There's nothing in the house to suggest it's occupied, and the victim doesn't even have a bag with her,' Naia says. 'The place is empty.'

What?

Then where's all my shit? Did Winta come back and clear it out after I left? Is this all part of the plan, a part she chose to keep to herself? It wouldn't be the first time she's deliberately kept me in the dark.

She warned me. She said, *whatever happens*, like she knew this was coming.

Trust me.

So I do, against my better judgement, almost certain I'll regret this tomorrow.

'Who called it in?' I ask.

'Don't know,' Naia says absently, looking towards the stairs. 'Anonymous tip. Female voice. No recording; they called the lodge and left a message with the porter instead of ringing through to our direct line.'

'Almost like they knew,' I say, with a sinking feeling in my stomach.

'I guess. It's a weird one, no doubt.'

'Make way,' says a voice from up top.

Raul's coming down the stairs towards us carrying an evidence bag filled with the kind of thin tubing you see running from IV bags. It's stained red in places, and I can smell the blood before he's halfway down. I don't recognise the scent of the person it belongs to.

'Where did you find that?' Naia asks.

'Under the body,' he says, looking up at us. The distraction makes him miss a step and he tumbles the rest of the way, which is a fucking weird thing for a Silver to do. By the time he comes to a stop at the bottom of the stairs, he's bleeding in three places and one of his teeth is missing. That's a big deal. Sometimes, those fuckers don't grow back.

'Holy shit,' I say, finally shaken into action. I'm by his side in a blink without thinking about it, so I must have moved at Silver speed. All that Massacre blood has to be good for something. 'Are you okay?'

'I'm fine,' he says, but there's blood pouring from his mouth and his tooth's on the floor. It's a canine, which isn't as essential to us as the old vampire stories would have you believe – our teeth aren't weird sucking straws or anything – but it's still serious. 'I just slipped.'

'You slipped?'

'Missed my footing.' As he speaks, he's spraying blood on the floor, which doesn't make sense. Even if it's been a while since he last refuelled, he should be healing already.

Something's wrong.

'The victim's human,' Ed says from the top of the stairs. 'There's a phone, so maybe you can crack it and find who the number's registered to…' He trails off as he sees what's going on. 'What's going on?'

'I slipped,' Raul says. His eyes are welling up a little, and I know him well enough to know he doesn't want to be the centre of attention right now, so I take his arm and help him up, leading him to the postage-stamp garden at the back of the house.

It helps. In the middle of my own crisis, I'd rather focus on him than try to work out what the fuck is going on with the body upstairs. I have to keep busy and try not to look suspicious, and the best way to do that is to concentrate on something other than the shit-show that's going on in my house. Besides, the guilt is hitting hard. Raul was supposed to be my responsibility, to train and to protect, but I've clearly dropped the ball because this isn't normal. As I think back over the past month to all the little things that have been off about him – the mood swings, the mania, the way his eyes glaze over sometimes like he's not even in the room – I realise I've missed something obvious.

'You're back on the Starblood, aren't you?' I say.

'No,' he says, but his denial comes too quickly.

'Raul.'

'No, I promise, I'm off it,' he insists in a hushed tone. Then there's a pause during which his gaze roams over my shoulder to the door back into the house. 'At least,' he adds, 'I am now.'

'For fuck's sake. Since when?'

'Yesterday.'

'Raul, I swear to god—'

'I know,' he says. 'I'm sorry. I tried, I really did, and I managed for a while, but being a Seeker is no joke. I needed it sometimes, just a little bit, to help me keep up.'

'I vouched for you,' I say, feeling less betrayed than my tone suggests. This is my fault too, because I've hardly been giving him the support he needs. I've done him dirty as much as he has me.

'I'm sorry,' he says, and he looks it. He's such a softie that when he deflates like this I can't muster up anything except sympathy. After everything with Rachael... He's had a rough road. This scene must be bringing back a whole host of bad memories.

'It's okay, mate,' I say, pulling him into my arms. 'Though I can't work out why you thought this would be a good time to go into withdrawal.'

He wraps his arms around me and hugs me tight. Raul has always given the world's best hugs. He presses his face into my shoulder and says, 'The Invicti wouldn't take an addict.'

'Oh, fuck the Invicti. You're too good for them anyway.'

'I've got nowhere else to go.'

'You'll find somewhere. You don't need them.'

Now I feel guilty for leaving him behind. I feel guilty for leaving them all behind, knowing what kind of chaos we're going to leave in our wake.

When Winta laid out the plan in the first place, when it was all theoretical, she made it seem like we had no option but to take the Primus down. But now the time has come, it's hard to ignore how the consequences of our actions will hit everyone around me. The legacy I'm leaving them is just poisonous, however righteous our rebellion might be. I'll have to live with the fact that I'm trading their present for a future we might never see.

When people talk about this in a year's time, I can't imagine they'll remember me kindly. But it's like Drake says: someone has to do it. Someone has to hold them accountable.

'Jack,' Naia calls from the front of the house. 'We need you in here.'

'Will you be okay?' I ask Raul.

'Sure,' he says, feeling his gums tentatively. 'I think it's healing up now.'

'Take these,' I say, handing him a pack of blood capsules. 'Then go back to the college and rest up. We'll finish off here.'

'No.' He swallows a handful of capsules dry, then straightens his back like a soldier on parade. 'If this is our last case, then I'm going to see it through.'

I give him a long look, but he's obviously determined to do this. I guess it makes sense that Raul, and the others, are keen to wrap this last one up before the Seekers go out.

'Okay, then,' I say. 'Let's go.'

30

THE VICTIM IS a twenty-two-year-old woman called Holly. I forget her surname the minute Naia tells it to me, because I don't recognise it at all. I'm desperately trying to find a connection that doesn't exist.

'What do we know about her?' Boyd asks. Since this is our last case, he's condescended to join us at the scene. Given the circumstances, I wish he hadn't. There are already too many people here.

'Not much,' says Naia. 'She's a DPhil student at the university.'

'So this is her place?'

'No, she had college accommodation. No one lives here. It's a rental property, but it's been off the market for three months for refurbishment. I spoke to the letting agent, and she says the new tenants don't move in until next week.'

This is news to me. I didn't realise we'd been squatting. I'm not sure what the new tenants are going to do with the cage in the cellar, but as it turns out I don't need to worry about that, because the place is empty now, the bars and all trace of them completely removed. The rest of the house is the same: as clean as a show home, with only a few bare items of furniture left behind. When I finally bring myself to go upstairs and look at the scene, the only thing in the room is a bloody mattress on the floor.

Cam comes up beside me, lounging in the doorframe at my side as I look down at the horrific stain. Everyone else is downstairs gathering the evidence for transport, all except Naia, who's on the way to the hospital with Holly's body.

'This is your house, isn't it?' he says quietly. 'This is where you've been living.'

Fuck.

If anyone was going to detect my scent in this place, it was going to be Cam. It was stupid of me to think I could blag my way through.

'You know I had nothing to do with this,' I whisper back urgently. 'You have to know that I would never—'

'Why do you think I removed your suitcase from the scene and put it in the car?' he asks. 'You're just lucky I'm the one who got here first.'

'You found my stuff?'

'Before anyone else did, thank god.'

'Thank you. Really, Cam, thank you. I'm sorry to put you in this position, but—'

He waves my words away, handing me my leather jacket. I left it here this morning.

'I put the papers in your jacket pocket,' he says.

He must mean the purchase paperwork for the flat, which I grabbed from the fridge when I went to get the keys for Naia. When I press the outside of my jacket with my palm, I can hear the paper crinkling.

'Thank you, Cam,' I whisper back. 'Really.'

'We're going to have words later.'

'I know.'

'They'd better be good,' he says. 'And I mean really, really good.'

We have to cut the conversation short because Ed, Boyd and Raul are coming up behind us now, gathering for the traditional team confab. Normally we'd wait until we're back at the college for this, but we've got about twelve hours left to solve this case and time is ticking.

'What do we know?' Boyd says, looking to Ed for the starter.

'She's only been dead for about an hour, going by body temperature,' Ed says. 'The Silver violence mark was fresh, so that's a pretty clear indicator too.'

'Plus the next door neighbours heard screaming and called the police,' says Raul. 'That was about an hour ago.'

'Where are the police, anyway?' I asks.

'They've been and gone,' Cam says. 'They pulled up just before I did, checked the house, saw it was locked up tight, and left.'

'Bloody plods,' I say.

'Good for us, though,' says Boyd. 'They didn't see anything, so we can investigate this without interference.'

'The neighbours didn't see anything either,' Raul adds. 'No one coming or going.'

'You interviewed them?' Boyd asks.

Raul rubs his arm self-consciously, right in the spot where he was recently bleeding, then says, 'Naia did.' Raul's in no state to be interviewing potential witnesses, but the others don't seem to have noticed. Yet.

'What else?' Boyd asks.

'There was a bite mark on her throat,' Cam says, giving me a pointed look, 'and she lost a lot of blood.'

'We probably don't need to wait for the post mortem to determine cause of death,' says Ed. 'It's a pretty straightforward case.'

'Except we have no suspects,' says Boyd.

I'm pretty sure I could name two, but I'm not going to

correct him.

'The tubing is weird,' says Ed. 'I'll take it back to the lab for testing, but my best guess is maybe it was used to siphon some of the victim's blood off to save for later.'

Cam looks around at us, then says, 'These cases are still connected, right? We're all feeling that? It's not just me?'

'This one's messier than the others,' says Raul.

'Maybe they were in a rush,' says Ed. 'That would explain why they left the tubing behind, and didn't collect all the blood.'

'You think they were saving it for later?' Cam asks, and he just can't seem to stop giving me that look. If he doesn't cut it out, he's going to give me away.

'I'd say so,' says Ed. 'It looks like someone's sourcing a personal blood supply. I won't know for sure until I've tested the tubing, but there's no guarantee I'll get the results before tomorrow, and by then—'

'It'll be too late,' Boyd finishes for him.

'There was one more thing,' Raul says quietly. Now he's giving me that look too, and I have the feeling I'm not going to like what he's about to say. 'I found this in the corner of the cellar.'

He holds out his hand, palm up, and uses the other hand to lay the thing out flat on it. I don't want to see it, but I can't help myself. It's a dry little curl of awfulness, discoloured and dirty, but the picture on it is clear enough.

Not many people would know what it is. Naia probably would, but she's not here. Cam certainly does, but he's keeping his mouth shut. If I can just control my reaction until I can get out of this room—

'Isn't that your tattoo?' Ed says, giving me a horrified look.

Son of a *bitch*.

* * *

I'm feeling sick as a dog, so Cam takes me back to the college while the others pack up what's left. I didn't want to stay in that house any longer than necessary, and Cam seemed as keen as I was to get the hell out of there. As soon as we hit the road, I realise why. This isn't a lift; it's an interrogation.

'Start at the beginning,' he says, as though spilling my guts to him is the easiest thing in the world. It's not an unreasonable assumption, because usually, it would be.

'I can't do that, Cam,' I say quietly. 'I'm sorry.'

'I know you don't remember the week you lost,' he says, giving me far more credit than I deserve, 'but can you at least tell me how you came to be living in that house? Is it another one of Tabitha's secret purchases? Is she the new tenant?'

I don't answer. I'm not sure what I can say that wouldn't catch me in a lie, so I choose to say nothing at all.

'That basement would have made a good laboratory,' he goes on. 'I could smell the chemicals in the air. And your blood.'

'Can we please not talk about that?' I ask, suppressing another wave of nausea.

'Okay,' he says. 'But if you won't talk to me, then I need to take your blood.'

'What? Why?'

'For Ed to compare to the victim, and the other five. Just to rule you out. I won't tell him it's yours.'

'But I didn't kill her, Cam. I didn't kill anyone.'

'You've been living in that house. You can't pretend you haven't. I don't even want to think about what your tattooed skin was doing in the basement—'

'Me neither.'

'So for the moment I'm going to pretend that you kept it as a sick souvenir, then got tired of it and threw it on the basement floor, and that you definitely weren't holed up in that house with Tabitha for the week while you were missing. Because you'd tell me if that was true, wouldn't you?'

Again, I keep my mouth shut.

'I don't know what to do with you,' he says. 'If you were anyone else, I'd be hauling you up in front of the baron about now, you do know that?'

'Let's leave him out of this,' I say quickly.

'Jack, this is serious!' He's losing his patience.

'I know that,' I say softly. 'I do.'

'Six students are dead, and right now you're the only Silver we can tie to any of the scenes.'

'You know I wouldn't have killed those kids,' I say.

'I know, but this case is going to get handed off to the Invicti if we don't solve it by the end of the day, and I want to be able to *prove* you had nothing to do with it.'

I'm shaking my head, because I remember the tubing under Holly's body. Then I remember the blood bottles Winta's been feeding me, and the twenty-three humans she allegedly killed with Elise – whose escape M.O. was the same one used to flee the scene of the Osney murder – and I'm not entirely sure that my blood's going to come up clean.

Is Winta trying to set me up?

Trust me, she said, but just how far am I supposed to make my trust stretch?

'Please, Jack,' Cam says. 'One little sample and you'll be cleared by the end of tomorrow.'

By which point I'll be on my way to Argentina with Winta anyway, so should I risk it for the sake of keeping Cam sweet? It might be the only way I'll be able to do what needs doing tonight.

'Okay,' I say.

'Thank you.' His relief is palpable.

He continues driving in silence for a few minutes. I'm hoping it'll last all the way back to the college, but no such luck.

'Ed got the results back on the hairs from the Sommer house,' he says.

'Oh?'

'Both had multiple DNA profiles, so the donors were Silver,' he says. 'One with textured black hair, the other long and platinum.'

Shit.

Shit.

I know which two Silver match those hairs.

'It might mean nothing,' I say. 'They could just be people Sommer met at Crimson and brought home.'

'I wouldn't be so quick to dismiss the hairs if I were you,' Cam says. 'Right now, they're the only other evidence we have, and – if they were left behind by Sommer's killers – they exonerate you.'

'Right.'

Cam glances over at me briefly.

'You should be happier,' he says.

'About what? About the fact that we have a bunch of scab murders, about the fact that I'm caught up in the middle of them – through no fault of my own, I might add – or about the fact that you're leaving me for the Invicti this evening?'

'I'm going to London, not Mars. We'll still see each other.'

No, I want to tell him. *We won't.*

'I still can't believe you're going over to the other side,' I say instead.

'The Invicti aren't our enemies.'

'Maybe not *yours*.'

'Will you please try to be nice this evening?' he asks. 'For me? I know they're not your favourite people, and I know you've got history with them, but it would mean a lot if you could get along with them. Just for one night.'

I sigh. 'Fine.'

'And the baron too,' he adds, as if it's an afterthought.

I have a flash of memory from his confession last night and my stomach rolls.

'Cam…'

'Please?'

'If I'm busy being pleasant to the Invicti, I won't have any civility left for Drake.'

'I'll make you a deal,' he says. 'I'll get you off on the six scab murder charges, and you'll be charming at literally everyone for the night. You only have to be nice to their faces. You can be as vicious as you like behind their backs.'

'Fine,' I say.

'And no Massacres,' he adds quickly.

'Do you not want me to have any fun at all?'

'Promise me.'

'I promise,' I say, hoping that the behind-their-backs loophole will cover me for what I'm planning tonight.

'Great! Did you get a dress?'

'Yes. Well, at least half a dress.'

'Jack…'

'It's fine, it's just a bit sexy. I'm trying to be charming, remember?'

'I was expecting this from Naia,' says Cam, 'but I didn't realise I needed to have the keep-it-in-your-pants conversation with you too. Maybe I should be having the don't-murder-anyone conversation too,' he adds darkly, which is frankly getting a bit too close for comfort.

'Thanks for getting my suitcase out,' I say.

'What are best friends for? Though just to be clear, if I thought you'd killed anyone I'd be shopping you to Boyd right now.'

'I know.'

Which is why I've told him nothing about what's going to happen later. Cam is too innocent for this world, and definitely too innocent for his new job. As much as he's playing the narc right now, I'm pretty sure he'd be at least conflicted about turning me in. In fact, I'm fairly certain that he'd stand by me, and I can't put him in that position. It'll be bad enough for him to be on the other side of all this, standing with the Invicti. I can't put him in the middle.

When we arrive back at the college, he hauls my suitcase out of the boot. God knows what I'm going to do with it now.

I look it over, checking for bloodstains.

'It's clean,' Cam says. 'There was no blood in the bathroom.'

'The bathroom? What are you talking about?'

He looks at me for a moment, confused. It's clear there's a misunderstanding somewhere, because I left my suitcase in the little bedroom, along with all my clothes, which were strewn across the floor. I was going to get around to packing eventually. Honest.

'What are *you* talking about?' he says.

'Where and how did you find it?' I ask, going back to basics.

'In the main bathroom at the top of the stairs, packed and zipped.'

'Oh, right,' I say, as though I've just forgotten how I left it. 'Well, thanks again.'

'Don't make me regret it,' he says, then he jabs me in the arm with a needle, steals a sample of my blood and goes off to park the car.

I'm already regretting it myself.

I have no idea what any of this means. Well, actually I do, though I'm trying to stop myself from reaching inevitable conclusions.

The two hairs in Sommer's bed mean that Leclerq and Winta have been murdering students together. The tubing found under Holly's body means that the blood Winta has been giving me to drink likely came from the victims and, if I'm right, that means the DNA of at least one of the murdered students is rushing around in my veins right now.

It's so horrific, yet fits so perfectly, that I'd rather not think about it too hard.

But there's one thing that doesn't fit: someone packed my suitcase, then left it in the house with Holly's dead body. If they wanted to implicate me, why bother packing it at all? And if they didn't, then still why would they bother? I just can't come up with a reason for someone to pack for me, unless it was a passive-aggressive hint from Leclerq that she wants me out. But we're all about to go on the run, and she doesn't know we won't be taking her with us to Argentina.

I don't know what to make of it. I just don't know.

Which is a problem.

I'm about to go into the fight of my life, for the love of my life, and I think she might have just set me up as the fall guy.

31

BECAUSE THE SOLIS Invicti love a dramatic moment, they hold the Fidelis ceremony at ten o'clock on New Year's Eve. With the gravitas of the late-night appointment and the Latin ritual and all that bollocks, I'm surprised to find that the ceremony itself is in the gym on the top floor of Solis Invicti HQ. Granted, they've cleared out all the gym kit, but the room is still lit by fluorescents, the floor is still marked out with colourful outlines for various ball courts, and we're still sitting on shitty little wooden benches. I feel like I'm back in school assembly.

Given the recent friction between the Seekers and the Invicti, I was worried we wouldn't be welcome here today, but this is ancient ceremonial bullshit and we're all invited, or rather mandated, to attend. When the Invicti say jump, we're supposed to say *And which of your enemies would you like us to jump on, sir?*

So here we are: Boyd, Naia, Raul and I, with all the other Seekers too, arrayed along the back row like a bunch of naughty schoolchildren.

'I can't believe you're wearing that,' Naia whispers to me.

'What? You don't like it?'

'You're wearing less clothing than I am.'

Which is saying something. True to man-eating form, Naia's gone with a barely-there minidress that shows off the killer muscles in her arms and thighs to equally good effect. It also shows a fair amount of her arse when she bends over, but so far no one's complaining.

'Shh,' Boyd says, pointing at the stage, by which I mean the bit of sports hall at the front of the room, underneath the basketball hoop. 'It's about to start.'

The ceremony itself is worse than school prize giving. It goes on too long, it involves congratulating a load of people I don't give a fuck about, and only one I do, and frankly the whole thing could have been done via email.

I won't bore you with the details. There was Latin and blood. It sucked. The end.

When it's all over, Cam's beaming from ear to ear.

Afterwards, there's a drinks reception on the roof terrace upstairs. I didn't see this part of the building when I was last here, and assumed the gym was the best use the Invicti could make of the amazing panoramic views of London that you get at this height, but it turns out they do know how to have some fun after all. There's a garden full of hardy plants that don't mind the wind, plus a bar area with clusters of seating warmed by patio heaters. There's barely a breeze in the air, but there's ice on the ground, so we need them tonight.

I'm regretting my outfit choice already. My back is bare, the long skirt's slit up to my hip, and the flimsy material the dress is cut from does nothing to warm the meagre areas of my body it does cover. I've got my new leather jacket with me, draped over my arm, but I can't put it on yet. If I'm going to get the Primus's attention then I have to make him look, and that means skin. The obvious problem, which you've probably spotted by now, is that playing the femme fatale isn't comfortable for me. At all. And if that wasn't bad enough, on top of my emotional discomfort, and the freezing cold, I have to deal with the fact that my strappy gold heels are rubbing in three separate places and I've already got them stuck in the paving slabs twice before I've even reached the bar.

'Gin,' I say to the woman guarding the drinks. 'Straight. Lots of it.'

I gulp down one glass and motion for her to fill it up again. By the time I'm halfway down the second, my hands have stopped shaking and I'm starting to feel more in control.

Focus.

Just one more hour. I have to push away my doubts about... everything, because if I let them invade my mind now it's all over. I've chosen my side. There's no turning back now. I know exactly what I have to do, and how I'm going to do it. If I follow the plan to the letter, everything will be fine. I'll be fine, Winta will be fine, we'll be in Argentina, and everything will be just fine.

I take another big mouthful of gin.

Fine.

'Good evening, Ms Valentine.' The Primus is standing next to me at the bar. I wasn't supposed to make contact this early. It's already going wrong. 'No blood drinks for you tonight? I heard they're your speciality.'

'I promised Cam I wouldn't,' I say, because my mind is racing too fast to let me think straight and it just... comes out.

'Ah yes, Cameron Sawyer. A friend of yours, I take it?'

The Primus orders himself a whisky, then leans back against the bar and smiles at me as the starstruck bar person scrambles to pour it for him. I don't blame her for being flustered; the Primus has a presence that feels overwhelming. He's got wavy blond hair and bright blue eyes, but there's a weird aloofness to the way he carries himself that makes you wonder whether or not he's real. He looks like he's been airbrushed or filtered, but in real life, twenty-four seven. It's difficult not to find that equal parts attractive and intimidating.

'Cam's my best friend,' I say.

'And you're irritated that we're taking him away from you?' the Primus asks, picking up on my tone.

'A little.'

'We'll take good care of him.'

'Like you did the rest of us?' I'm supposed to be seducing him, not antagonising him. This isn't the plan at all, but I can't help myself. I did try to tell Winta that I wasn't the seductive type. 'I've been a Seeker for twenty years,' I hear myself saying. 'Almost everyone else has served longer, enforcing your secrecy pact just as you asked, protecting humanity from the Silver who go out of bounds, and you're disbanding us, for what? To calm down the rebels? To quash them? Or just on a whim?'

'Ms Valentine—' he says, but I'm not done.

'It's a crap job, you know that?' I go on, determined to say my piece. 'The pay's shit, the working conditions are laughable and the victim at yesterday's crime scene was so far gone that I swear I can still smell decomposition every time I breathe in, but we did the job, we did it well, and we never complained.'

The Primus raises an eyebrow.

'Much,' I add.

'Are you done?' he asks.

'No. Yes. I don't know,' I say helplessly. 'I just want to know why, that's all.'

He smiles at me, but the expression is the tolerant, avuncular smile given by a long-suffering grandfather to his errant grandchild, not the kind of smile that says he finds my stubborn insolence strangely alluring and wildly seductive. I knew this wasn't going to work.

'Later,' he says. 'Let me have a drink and a few discussions, then there'll be time for your questions. I might have more answers for you by then, too. For all of you.'

It's good, but it's not enough. I need to get him on his own. This is the best opening I'm going to get, so I set about widening it.

'I don't know if anyone's told you,' I say casually, 'but I'm notoriously impatient. Bad at keeping secrets, too. Which reminds me, I haven't seen you since… Well, since the vote. And everything that happened after,' I add ominously. 'You know, with the voting urns.'

'What is it you want, Ms Valentine?' His tone has changed dramatically, so I guess he's got the message.

'Perhaps we could speak more privately?' I suggest. 'Just before midnight, over there maybe,' I say, pointing to a roof terrace on an adjoining building. It's smaller than the Invicti's, but there's more foliage to screen us from view.

'Very well,' he says, though he doesn't seem happy about it. It doesn't matter. I don't have to keep him sweet, I just have to get him there.

'Great, see you then.' I grab another drink then give him a little finger wave. 'Toodles.'

The tolerant smile is back again while I walk away, as though I'm just a rascally young scamp rather than a killing machine who means to turn her wrath on him. He's about to learn a hard lesson about underestimating me, though it won't do him much good since the rest of his life will be so very short.

'Jack!' Cam yells at me from across the terrace, where he's standing with Naia and Ellie. He waves me over, all wide smiles and pink cheeks, but when I arrive he looks me up and down and says, 'Where's the rest of your dress?'

'Hush,' I say. 'And congratulations. Well done for not tripping and falling on your face.'

'Thanks.'

His grin is so wide that I'm worried he might hurt himself. I'm momentarily irritated that leaving us for the Invicti has him so overjoyed, but then I remember what's coming next and decide it's better that he enjoys it while he can. Things are only going to go downhill from here.

'Cameron!' says a voice from behind me. It's Adewale, with his fellow recruit Alistair, coming to welcome Cam into the fold. 'And Ms Valentine,' he adds, his mouth twitching out of his smile as he says my name.

I take that as my cue to go and mingle, except all my friends are standing with Cam and I don't know anyone else here.

'Good evening, Valentine.' The voice is a promise, a breath on the back of my neck in the dark.

Except him, of course.

'I was hoping you'd give tonight a miss,' I say.

Given how thoroughly I rejected him last night, I wouldn't have blamed him for skipping this one. But of course it makes sense that he's here, being the baron of Cam's home turf. There's probably some ridiculous rule of etiquette about not recruiting Seekers without Drake's approval. Who knows, with the Silver. Either way, it sucks, because it means I have to deal with him tonight, of all nights, when I really should be concentrating on the job at hand. Him hanging around, spinning me out and distracting me from my purpose, is close to being the last thing I need.

The actual last thing I need is the scent of spice and copper that he draws with him as he circles me, like a shark. It does things to me that it shouldn't, still.

'I was a little late,' he says. 'I had to deal with something at home before I left.'

'Oh?' I reply, telling myself I don't care, that I'm just being polite, making conversation, you know.

'Carlotta's going back to France,' he says. 'On her own, this time.'

'Oh.'

No wonder Carlotta had wanted me to talk to him. When I met her at the club yesterday morning, she already knew about the… the thing I'm trying not to think about.

'Look,' he says, 'last night went—'

I interrupt him before he can say something we'll both regret. 'Let's not talk about last night.'

'There's no escaping it.' He offers me his hand. When I look at it sceptically, he says, 'Indulge me. Please.'

Cam catches my eye from over Drake's shoulder and tips his head, encouraging me to make nice. I roll my eyes, but it's Cam's night, and I did promise. Since I'm about to ruin everything for him, how can I refuse?

Drake takes my hand gently and leads me around to the other side of the building, where the C-shape of the access staircase has created a tiny secluded garden that no one else has found yet. It's walled on three sides with brick and on the fourth by jasmine hanging from an arched trellis. Drake pulls me through the curtain of foliage, and then we're in a world of our own. If it wasn't for the sound of the party outside the arch, I might believe we were entirely alone.

'Are you trying to kill me with this dress?' he says.

'No, not you.'

'That's not funny.'

'It wasn't a joke.'

'Then it's happening tonight?' he asks.

My silence is response enough.

'I could make you forget all about it,' he says, trailing a fingertip down my bare spine.

I believe him.

'I remember the last time you wore a dress like this to a party,' he whispers, then he leans in to me so I have no choice but to back up into the dark. He follows every step of the way until my back is pressed up against the wall and, somehow, my hands are fisted in his shirt. 'You rumpled my clothes then too, if I recall.'

I make my fists relax and smooth out his shirt, but then I realise I'm just caressing his chest, which is worse, if anything. I snatch my hands away but he catches them by the wrist, holding me close.

'You can't run from this,' he says. 'I know you don't want to acknowledge it, but there's something between us, and I'm not the only one feeling it. You said as much last night.'

'I was drunk last night.'

'You often are.' Why does everyone think that about me? I swear I'm not. 'But what you said was still true,' he adds.

I look away. I really don't want to get into this now, and if I keep looking into his eyes it's all going to go wrong because yes, fine, I do have some feelings for the bastard – very small and extremely conflicted feelings – but I'm hardly going to tell him that, especially not now.

'Look at me,' he says.

'I've got things I have to do, Drake.'

'No, you don't have to do anything.'

'I do actually, and then I'll be out of your life and you can stop following me around like a lost puppy, okay?'

'No,' he says. 'I'd search the world for you. You can run wherever you like, but I'll find you. I'll always find you.'

'Is that a threat?'

'Why do you always think I'm threatening you?' he says, exasperated, letting go of my wrists. 'No, it's not a threat. Tell me not to come after you, and I won't.'

I look him in the eye and say, 'Don't come after me.'

'Don't ask me to let you go.'

'Drake—'

'Don't ask. Don't leave. And don't do this.' He's up close again now, holding my face in his hands. 'If you cross this line, there's no coming back.'

'I have to do this.'

'Why? For her?'

'Yes, but also because it needs doing. Someone needs to keep them in line. Isn't that what you do with the boxed Silver you kill?'

'That's different.'

'Because you think the Primus doesn't deserve it?'

'Because a Silver in a box can't fight back. You're going to get yourself hurt.'

'I'll heal,' I say, with more nonchalance than I feel.

'And even supposing this goes the way you intend it to, which it won't, what happens afterwards? Have you thought about that at all?'

'You think we don't have a plan? Give us some credit, will you?'

'And what about you? What about the way this is going to break *you*?'

'If I get hurt, I'll heal,' I insist.

'That's not how it works,' he says, stepping away in frustration. 'We're still creatures of entropy. We can fix our outsides, but on the inside we break and break and don't come back together again.'

'And you don't want your toys broken. Is that it?'

He gives me a look I can't mistake and says, 'There's no way you can break yourself that will make me want you any less. You remember the lightning bolt?'

I remember. It was months ago, but it feels like years have passed since then. We'd been talking about Winta, ironically enough, and about the thrill of first love, the way it hits you like a rush.

'I feel it,' he says. He puts his fist to his sternum, just like he did that night, then he takes a step forward until we're toe to toe once more. He moves his fist until it presses against my ribs, over my heart. 'Don't you? Like a lightning bolt,' he whispers. 'Right here.'

His knuckles are resting against my bare skin, raising goosebumps that I tell myself are more a reaction to the freezing temperature than they are to him.

'Say something, Valentine.'

I'm shaking my head, but the words come anyway.

'It can't be you,' I whisper. 'There's Winta. There's… things you don't know.'

'I know you're in deep. I don't know exactly what you're planning, but I'll tell you now that I don't care what it is, or whether it's right or wrong. I'm on your side. Whatever you do, however mind-numbingly stupid, I'll be there beside you.'

They're pretty words, but I can't trust him, not really. Even now, I'm not sure I believe what he says about the bond. I've been betrayed by a lot of people who say they love me lately, and I'm not about to fall for another line.

But.

For all that he's my nemesis, the one thing I'll say for Killian Drake is that he's never let me down. Even before The Night That Is To Be Regretted, he has always been on – or adjacent to – my side. Maybe that counts for something. Or maybe it means nothing at all.

Maybe I should tell my brain to shut up and let the rest of me do the thinking for a while.

'This is big,' I say, feeling my feelings. 'It's too big, too much, too soon.'

'It doesn't have to be,' he says. 'However much you want, it's enough.' He trails his knuckles over my collarbone and up my throat, like an invitation. When his hand comes to rest, it's at the nape of my neck, playing with the hair at the base of my skull and driving me absolutely insane. He knows what that spot does to me and he's not playing fair.

'I'll be whatever you want me to be,' he says, 'I don't care.' Then he leans in to press his lips lightly against my neck. It's a reminder of everything we've done before, and a promise of more to come.

I let out a little moan. I don't mean to, really, but you try having an incredibly sexy – and, yes, deeply annoying – man throw himself at you and see how you react.

'Even if you only want me in the dark,' he whispers, 'it's enough.'

It would be so easy to give in. My body remembers him: the smell of his skin, the pressure of his fingers, the shape of his embrace. But I know it would all be over the moment I touch my lips to his. We'd mark each other, instantly, just like we always have, and then what would I tell Winta?

It would all be over.

Whatever she's done, she doesn't deserve that from me. And anyway, I'm not ready to say goodbye to her.

'I don't know what we are to each other, Drake,' I say, forcing the words out. 'But we're not… that.'

Then I extricate myself from his clever fingers before I lose myself in his scent and do something I'll regret.

'Valentine—'

'Just don't watch the fireworks, okay?'

'The fireworks? What have the—'

'Just don't. Please.'

I don't look at his face.

I don't even pause.

I can't.

I leave him alone in the dark and walk away to do what I came here to do.

32

THE WOMAN BEHIND the bar is still looking
shellshocked when I go back for more gin. She's working at
about half the speed of the guy who's joined her there. He's
whizzing around on the other side of the bar, filling orders
with a smile and a wink, while the woman looks like she's
been frozen in time.

'I've never seen the Primus in person before,' she says as
she hands over my drink. Her eyes are watching him over
my shoulder instead of watching what she's doing, so more
than a little of my booze ends up on the bar top.

'Maybe you should have a drink too,' I suggest.

'Oh no,' she says. 'Not while I'm working.'

'Not even a teeny, tiny one? Not even a bit of straight
blood?'

She looks tempted. 'I'd be lying if I said I wasn't curious
to try it,' she says, looking at the tap on the bar marked
Warmblood.

'What is it?' I ask, pretending I don't already know.

'It's this new thing,' she says. 'One of the Invicti came up
with it, I think. It's just pure blood, but there's this pump
attached to the reservoir that keeps the blood moving around,

so it never congeals, and it warms it at the same time.'

'Really?' I say, acting as though this is the most interesting thing I've ever heard. 'Would you mind if I took a quick peek? I'm sort of into gadgets,' I add, lying my arse off.

'I don't know…' She looks over at her colleague, but he's got her back to us and is about to ferry a huge tray of drinks over to the Primus's table, so he's paying zero attention to us.

'Go on,' I say with a smile, resting my elbows together on the bar so one strap of my dress slides down my arm. It's almost as though I planned it. 'We can try some together.'

Apparently my seduction attempts work better on her than they did on the Primus, because suddenly she's only got eyes for me and there's a warmth in them that wasn't there a moment ago.

'Really quickly,' she says, ushering me behind the bar with a smile that tells me this might be the most wicked thing she's ever done.

She has no idea.

I crouch down out of sight under the Warmblood tap and take stock of the moving parts beneath it.

'Clever, right?' she says, crouching down next to me.

'Very clever,' I say.

The basic structure is a large tank, but there's a load of extra nonsense going on up top that's making a weird chugging sound every couple of seconds. I guess that's the pump circulating the blood; I can see a few wide tubes looped over the top of the tank that have blood running through them, and another going up to the tap on the bar. The bit I'm most interested in, though, is the refill port on the top of the tank, which is sealed shut with a screw top lid a few inches across.

'You just pour the blood in here?' I ask her.

'That's right. I just fill it up, and the machine does the rest. Imagine having one of these at home. Warm blood on tap, twenty-four seven. Do you want to try some?'

'Definitely.'

She draws us a couple of short glasses of the stuff, but then the bar gets busy and, with her colleague out serving drinks from his tray, she has to do her job.

'Sneak out while they're not looking,' she whispers to me, then she leaves me at this end of the bar on my own.

Time for Part One of Phase Two.

While she's distracted, I move at Silver speed to extract the vials from my clutch, unscrew the refill port and empty the serum inside the blood reservoir. It only takes a second to get that done and tidy up afterwards, so I'm back on the other side of the bar before my new friend has even finished taking the first order.

This sounds bad, I know, but it's not like I'm poisoning the well. Really. This isn't the Khalyed serum, or the one that makes people's silver show in their eyes, or the Invicti's tranquilliser, or any of the other ridiculous concoctions we've had to deal with over the past year. This is just a little leveller, a slow-down formula that makes the Silver respond more quickly to alcohol. With any luck, it'll have the Invicti pissed as newts and thoroughly hamstrung in short order.

'Cheers,' I say, raising my glass of unadulterated blood in a toast to the woman behind the bar.

When she's finished serving, she comes back to join me and tries her own drink. 'Ooo,' she says, licking her lips. 'That's not bad.'

'Has anyone else tried it yet?' I ask.

'I don't think so. It's only just come up to temperature.'

'Well, that's a shame. Grab a couple of trays,' I say, reaching over the bar to fetch a load of shot glasses. 'Let's get this party started, shall we?'

This next bit isn't technically part of the plan, but I've got some time to kill and – as I believe I've said before – I am nothing if not dedicated to insobriety. I'm going to get the Invicti properly drunk if it's the last thing I do. Finally, a task that leans into my personal forté.

'Can I offer you a Bloody Mary shot?' I ask the Secundus, offering him a drink from my tray. My new friend is circulating the party in the other direction, making sure we don't miss anyone, and helping me to avoid Drake.

'Not while I'm on duty,' he says.

'Come on, it's barely even alcoholic. And it's a party.'

With a little cajoling from me, and a lot of cajoling from his fellow Invicti, he finally relents. Once his underlings see him indulging, there's nothing to stop the rest of them from doing the same, and now it looks like we really do have a party on our hands.

Unfortunately, I see from across the terrace that Raul has also been persuaded to take a glass. He's having a hard enough time kicking the Starblood. The last thing he needs is more pharmaceutical interference.

'Ah-ah-ah,' I say, rushing over to intervene before the glass reaches his lips. 'Not for you.'

'What? Why?' he asks.

'Jack,' says Cam, appearing at Raul's side to give me a serious look. 'What have you done?'

'They're Bloody Marys,' says the woman from the bar, whose name I really should have asked. 'A bit of blood, a bit of vodka, a bit of tomato, and a lot—'

'And she means a *lot*,' I chip in.

'—of tabasco.'

Which I know for a fact Raul hates.

'Ah,' he says, returning his glass to the woman's tray. 'I guess I'll stick to wine.'

'Good plan,' I say, patting him on the shoulder before

continuing my circuit. I can already see a few eyes streaming, but that's not putting people off. A lot of them come back for a second round, and a third.

By ten to midnight, the alcohol and laughter is flowing, and I'm pretty sure the Drunky Serum is doing its work. It is very raucous out here, raucous enough that no one notices the figure on top of the building across the road from us. The building's a bank, so it's enormous, easily twenty storeys taller than Solis Invicti HQ, which puts it bang in the Invicti's eyeline for the fireworks that are just about to begin.

I don't have much time.

As fast as I can – which is pretty fast with the amount of blood capsules I've taken – I rush over to the secret garden to get ready for Part Two of Phase Two. I pull the syringe out of its case in my clutch bag, then take out the disassembled dart gun pieces from the same place and put them together. That done, I shrug into my leather jacket and hide the whole mechanism up my sleeve.

The time for seduction is over. Now it's time for action.

It's going to go quickly, so try to keep up.

Everyone knows what happens at midnight on New Year's Eve. It's so universal that the Invicti haven't even bothered to announce that fireworks are going to be part of the evening's entertainment, because everyone simply assumes – correctly – that New Year's Eve equals fireworks. By midnight, everyone's already looking upwards, anticipating the display that's about to begin. They are not disappointed.

I'm standing by the edge of the roof, outside the crowd, as the first few go up.

Winta lets them have a minute or so to enjoy the pretty lights, but the pyrotechnics are barely beginning when an alarm goes off on my watch.

I cover my eyes.

Phase Two: Part Two.

I know when it's safe to open them again, because the screaming and shouting is loud enough to drown out the sound of the fireworks. The scene that greets me is like something out of a horror film: glasses are smashed on the floor, there's blood everywhere and everyone's shuffling around with arms outstretched, trying to work out where they are now that their retinas have been burned into blindness.

Remember that device Winta was tinkering with the other day? Well, that was it. I'm not sure where she picked it up, but it was designed to send out a cluster of intense laser beams in a blast of light that would be impossible for anyone watching the fireworks from the roof to avoid. I hope there are no humans nearby, because there goes their vision. The Silver will heal, with help, but in the meantime, that laser eye damage is no joke.

This is the beauty of the Drunky Serum: when the Invicti rush to drink the Warmblood at the bar, hoping to repair the damage to their retinas in double-time, the extra Drunky Serum they consume gets to work on the alcohol they've already got in their systems, magnifying the effect. The more blood they drink in an attempt to sober up, the drunker they get, until they're all staggering around like seriously cheap dates.

I've got to hand it to Tabitha: she is good at what she does.

I don't intend to hang around to watch the carnage. I've got a date.

But then there's a muffled pop from the building below us, and the terrace rocks.

'What was that?' Cam asks from across the terrace, looking around. He's one of the few people who seem to have escaped the lasers. Then he sees me. 'Jack,' he says, looking panicked now. 'What have you done?'

'I haven't done anything,' I say.

He must see the truth in my eyes, because he doesn't hang around.

I didn't exactly lie to him, but I do know what the noise was.

Phase Two: Part Three.

The problem is, it's happening about a minute too early and I'm not in position.

By the time the second pop happens, Cam's joined his new Invicti friends – who are all decidedly worse for wear – and when the third pop turns into a *whoosh* that sends flames rocketing out of the stairwell to engulf the foliage nearest the door, they've already started evacuating people to the street below.

This is why I was worried.

I didn't know exactly what Winta was planning to do with the bombs, but I knew it was going to be big. She's trying to distract the Invicti with a threat to their HQ, but the Secundus starts looking for the Primus from the moment the first charge blows. He hasn't found him yet, but it won't be long, despite the effects of the Drunky Serum.

It makes my part that much harder.

Moving at Silver speed, I rush to the top of the building next to Solis Invicti HQ. Not the one I promised I'd be at just before midnight, though. I go to the building on the other side of it, which has a slightly higher elevation and is therefore a perfect vantage point for sniping. I'm no sharpshooter, but my dart gun has a scope calibrated for idiots so it's not like I need to be.

I set myself up and look down the scope. The Primus is exactly where he's supposed to be and, for the moment at least, he's alone.

So far, so smooth.

Phase Two: Part Four.

Finally.

I line up the scope. I twiddle the dial that automatically adjusts for wind speed. I rest my finger alongside the trigger. I centre the Primus in my sights. And then…

In the final moment, I hesitate.

Just long enough to see him look in my direction, right down the scope of the dart gun, and then he's gone.

'Ms Valentine,' he says, appearing behind me. 'I do believe you've stood me up.'

He reaches over my shoulder and takes the gun out of my hands, snapping the barrel in half. The syringe falls out of the mechanism and I catch it before it can hit the ground, but not so quickly that he doesn't see me doing it. If he was watching the fireworks at all, the lasers obviously had no effect on him, because he's not having any trouble with his eyes.

'I can smell your fear,' he says, leaning over my shoulder to whisper the words into my ear. 'What an interesting life you lead. Saving me from the rebels' poison one day and trying to kill me the next. It's harder than you think, you know.'

I believe him.

'If I were you,' he says softly, running a hand down to my wrist to take the syringe from my hand, 'I would perhaps rethink my affiliations. Quickly.'

There's a huge roar of sound from the direction of Solis Invicti HQ. It's not only deafening, it also comes with a wave of heat so intense I swear I feel the hairs on my arms singe.

Without wasting time assessing the situation, I take the interruption as the gift it is and slip out of the Primus's grasp, snatch back the syringe and run. I don't even think about making another attempt on his life; I'd like to survive tonight and I have the distinct impression that, whatever I tried, he would be faster.

I run.

He doesn't try to follow. When I've put several buildings between us, I turn back to try to work out what's happened. Smoke is pluming into the sky. The Primus is still standing where I left him, looking back at the wreckage that was once the centre of his empire, shattered to rubble and burning into ash.

Holy shit.

We just blew up Solis Invicti HQ.

33

THE BUILDING'S STILL going up in flames when I reach the rendezvous point on a nearby helipad. Winta and Leclerq are already there.

'What the fuck happened?' I ask.

'The building blew up,' Leclerq says. 'What do you think happened?'

'Did you *plan* to blow up the building?'

'No. Did *you* plan to come back here with a full syringe of blood?'

'Jacky,' Winta says, looking in horror at the syringe I'm still holding in my hand. 'Tell me you didn't fail.'

I don't intend to say anything, because I have a feeling that saying anything at all will make this a hundred times worse, but I can't help but notice something we're missing.

'Where are your parents?' I ask.

'They weren't there,' says Leclerq.

'Ever?' I ask, but no one replies.

Maybe Adewale was right after all. Maybe they're both already dead.

'I don't believe this,' Winta says under her breath before turning back to me. 'Did you at least manage to put the drug in the blood?'

'Yes.'

'How many of them were still mobile when you left?'

'I'm not sure. I was a bit busy at the time.'

'Doing what exactly?' asks Leclerq.

'Um. Running away from the Primus,' I say, looking back towards the burning building. There's movement on the roof next to it, close to the place where it all went wrong, so I can't imagine we're going to be safe here for long. 'And I'd really like to carry on doing that,' I add.

'Fuck!' Winta passes a handful of blood capsules to Leclerq and yells, 'Go.'

The other woman hesitates for a moment, but then Winta kisses her full on the mouth, hard, and their intermingled scents of dry paper and sweet sugar are swirling through the air. My mouth drops open. After all this, after every time Winta's sworn to me that she loves me, and after everything I've done for her, Winta and Leclerq have just marked each other, right in front of me.

'Yolande, go,' Winta says again, more softly this time, and she passes something to Leclerq. I have to double take because at first I can't believe what I'm seeing, but it's true: Winta has just handed over the tickets to Argentina.

With one last, wistful look back, Leclerq disappears into the night, taking our escape route with her.

'We have to move,' Winta says to me, as though I didn't see what I just saw.

'What the actual fuck,' I say.

Behind us, the building next to the remains of Solis Invicti HQ is a hive of activity. Even with my relatively new ears, I can hear them mobilising. It'll be seconds or less before they're on their way.

'Move!' Winta yells at me.

I want to stay put just to spite her, or to go running off in a different direction and leave her behind to face the music on her own, but despite all this I obey. Despite everything, I still do what she tells me. Maybe it's something about the fact that she's my sire, or my first love, or maybe I'm just a sucker, but even now I can't seem to break free.

We race the rooftops, side by side, running through the night as we jump from building to building across the lights of the traffic below. We only stop when there are miles between us, the Invicti, and our failure.

I bend over double on the church roof where we've paused and try to catch my breath. I might be Silver, but I've just sprinted for my life and I feel like I'm about to cough up my own lungs. When the wheezing's mostly subsided, I say, 'They're not following.'

'So far,' says Winta. 'What the fuck happened in there?'

'He was quicker than me.' I can't explain to her what went wrong. The set up had been perfect, the distraction had been adequate, but… I think I hesitated. There's no way I can tell her that. 'I guess there's a reason he's the Primus,' I say instead.

'Fuck!' Winta kicks a roof tile and sends it skimming down into the street below, then paces the rooftop. She's so agitated that her fists are clenching and unclenching in a rhythm fast enough to make me worry what she's planning to do next.

I'm just thinking that things can't get any worse when I spot a blur of movement heading our way.

'Winta,' I warn her, but it's too late.

They've caught up with us.

Except the person who comes to rest on the edge of the roof isn't the Primus, or even one of the Invicti. It's Killian fucking Drake.

'What the fuck is he doing here?' Winta yells at me, as though it's my fault he's followed us.

'How should I know?' I yell back.

'Well, now we're going to have to kill him or he'll just go running back to the Primus.'

'I'm not going to do that,' Drake says, taking a step towards us.

'Why aren't you feeling wobbly?' I ask.

'Come on,' he says with an incongruous smile. 'Do you think I was made yesterday? I know better than to drink what the Invicti serve me, especially at a party where you're hanging around the bar. You forget, I've had your cocktails before.'

'Fuck,' Winta mutters.

'Stay where you are,' I warn him. I'm still holding the syringe that was supposed to end up in the Primus, using it to ward Drake off. 'Seriously. Don't move.'

'What exactly are you planning to do with that, Jack?' he asks, his voice soft, as though he's soothing a wild cat. He takes another slow step forward.

'Take someone down,' I say, and I mean it.

'Kill him, Jacky,' Winta demands. 'We've got to go. The others won't be far behind.'

But Drake's looking at me with his bottomless eyes and I'm falling into them, like I always do.

'I'm not afraid to use this,' I say, wielding the syringe. 'I mean it, Killian.' My voice is supposed to be strong, but it cracks under the stress, and my last word comes out as a whisper.

Something flickers in his eyes when I say his name. He holds my gaze for a moment.

'She's not wearing your mark,' he says to Winta. 'She's never been wearing your mark.'

'Is that what it'll take for you to understand what she is to me?' Then she turns to me, tenderly. 'Is this what you need to end this, once and for all?'

'I don't think this is the time for—' I start to say, but I'm interrupted when Winta wraps one arm around me and pulls me close, so close, like she's trying to crawl inside my bones.

Then she whispers, 'I've always loved you, Jacky. Just like I said,' and kisses me.

At first, there's nothing, just the play of her mouth on mine, but then it's everywhere: sugar and chocolate and the richness that my own scent brings to the mix, a mingled cocktail of me and Winta in a perfume so sublime I want to cry. Ever since the day she left me in Drake's basement, I've been waiting for this. All that time, I've been searching for the one thing that would make me whole and here it is, surrounding us both on a rooftop in the night.

She was telling me the truth all along: she can control it. She loves me, she wants me, and I want her right back.

It could be perfect.

Even if I have to share her, it might be enough.

But.

The way she's made me feel. The people she's killed. The way she wants to change the world.

The things she'd have me do to *him*.

I know Winta. I know her grit, her determination, and the quiet persistence that's had her chasing this goal for twenty long years. She will never, ever stop.

I slam the syringe into her chest as hard as I can, so hard that the needle breaks on impact as it grazes against her ribs on its way to her heart. It doesn't matter, though: the syringe has already emptied its contents into her body.

'Jacky,' she whispers, falling out of my arms and onto her knees. 'What did you do?'

'I'm sorry.'

'For him?' she says, looking at Drake.

'No.'

Whatever her denials, she still tried to frame me for this and run off with Leclerq. Whatever promises she's made, she'll break. Whatever abuses she's dealt out, she'll double, and she'll make me do worse. Whatever love she gives me, she'll deny me more.

'No,' I say again, needing her to understand this in her final moments. 'For me. For everything you took from me, and everything you made me into. You have too much power over me.'

She smiles, and a trickle of something black leaks from the corner of her mouth. It leaves an ashy residue in its wake.

'You're lying to yourself if you believe that,' she says. 'It was me or him, and you made your choice.'

The ash on her lip is burning, but the heat isn't coming from the ash. It's coming from beneath Winta's skin, cracking her face into lines of white and red like glowing coal. It starts slowly, as a light from within her, but pretty soon her clothes are ripping away in strips of flame and her whole body is so hot that I have to take a step back. When the flames finally take her, they burn white hot for just a few seconds, and then she's only dust.

She blows away on the breeze, as though her memory weighs nothing at all.

When the dust settles, Drake is still there.

'Was she right?' he asks.

'She betrayed me,' I say, which isn't exactly an answer, but I'm not sure I have a simple one to offer him. I feel like someone's reached into my chest and crushed my heart, as if losing Winta is something that was done to me rather than something I chose.

No, I didn't lose her. I just murdered her.

I think I'm going to be sick.

'Valentine?' Drake is by my side, one arm around my

shoulders to prop me up.

'How did you find us?' I ask.

'The bond.' He flashes his silver at me, showing me the evidence of what he told me last night. 'Remember?'

'I don't feel very well,' I say.

He goes to take the syringe from me, then says, 'Your hand,' as the colour drains from his face.

My head feels wobbly. Looking down, I see what he sees: the syringe is still clasped tightly in my fingers, clenched there from the urgency of my assault on Winta, but my grip was stronger than I realised. The glass has cracked in my fist, splintering fragments into my skin, along with the remnants of the blood it once held. It's in my own blood now, threading burning trails through the veins of my forearm. It won't be long before the fire reaches my heart.

I've just used Khalyed's blood to murder my first love, and now it's going to kill me too.

Poetic justice is a bitch.

Drake meets my eyes, and he looks like his world is ending.

Then the realisation hits me.

'You're going to die, aren't you?' I say. 'You're going to die when I do because of the stupid fucking bond.'

'I guess so,' he says dismissively, as though that's the least of his worries.

'Can't you just… reverse the silvering or something?' I ask. I'm panicking now, because I can feel the heat in my shoulder already and I'm not sure how much time we have left.

'It doesn't work like that,' he says. 'And even if it did, I'm not sure I'd want to.'

'You don't mean that.'

'I think I do, actually.'

I know the poison's reached my heart then because my

legs go out from under me in a rush as the blood gets pumped out to the rest of my body. I might be imagining it, but it's as though I can feel the fire spreading out cell by cell, filtering through each capillary and leaving a trail of sparks along the way. It won't be long before they turn to ash.

Drake catches me before I can hit the ground.

'At least when I die I'll have you in my arms,' he says. 'Finally.'

'Yes, great, that's all very touching and tragic and whatever,' I say, the words coming more slowly than I'd like, 'but we're not Romeo and bloody Juliet, and it's not helping. Can't you do anything?'

'I don't think either of us can.'

He's cradling me close, staring right into my eyes with what looks like peaceful resignation. I'm freaking out as my body twitches and shudders in a vain attempt to save my miserable little life and Drake is an ocean of calmness that surrounds me. It's really fucking irritating, but at the same time he's drawing me in the same way that he always does, his scent and his gaze and his essential Drakeness worming their way under my skin and settling into my bones with a finality that grounds me and stops the tremors. I can feel his breath on my skin, his fingertips pressing into my upper arm, his thighs beneath my back. I know this is going to hurt like a bastard, but I feel better for having him here with me.

That irritates me too.

'I hate you sometimes, you know that?' I say, my voice little more than a whisper as the fire reaches my throat.

'I love you sometimes,' he says. 'All the time, actually. And I think you love me sometimes too.'

'I'm not admitting to that,' I whisper.

'Not even now, at the end of it all?'

He isn't bothering to hide his silver anymore, and I can see it shining in the black of his irises. It's beautiful, the way it creates constellations in the night sky of his eyes. *He's beautiful. I feel like I'm seeing him for the first time.*

And he's mine.

'Maybe a little,' I confess eventually, surprised to find that it's true. 'But a very, very little.'

He smiles.

'Don't get smug about it,' I whisper. 'It's only sometimes.'

'Just shut up and kiss me, Valentine.'

He has to lower his face to mine, because I can't seem to move anymore, but when our lips meet that changes. Everything changes.

I've been kissed before. Obviously. I've kissed a number of people, and I've kissed a lot if we're talking about total number of individual kisses. And of course Drake and I have kissed before, more than once, but it wasn't like this. This is… a revelation. In a fraction of a second, Winta's mark on me is erased by his, leaving behind only a memory of that mingled scent I'd been chasing for so long. I can't remember now why I thought it was worth the pain she put me through, because this blend of Killian and Valentine is so much better.

I don't know whether it's the bad blood in my veins, the silver in Drake's eyes or the fact that we're both about to die, but I have never shared a kiss like this. My body is on fire, but it doesn't feel like the serum. The serum burned, but whatever this is feels like it's warming me, breathing life back into my limbs and urging me to pull Drake closer, to drink in the taste of him.

He sits back, but I follow his mouth and sit up with him. When he moves his lips away from mine, he can't go far because somehow I've raised my hand and my fingers are twisted into his hair, holding our faces close together.

I feel… better.

'I wish you didn't have so many clothes on,' he whispers. I'm wishing the same thing about him, but although I'm preoccupied with thoughts of Drake naked, it's still not the most urgent thing on my mind.

'Aren't we supposed to be dead?' I ask.

'Are you disappointed?'

Despite my urge to pull him close, I unravel my fingers and let him go. 'No,' I say, 'but—'

'Valentine.' Drake is staring at me with an expression I've never seen on his face before. It looks like horror but, belatedly, I realise it's something more like awe. 'Your lips weren't silver before, were they?'

'What?' I rub at my lips, but there's nothing there except the memory of Drake's kiss. 'No. You know I don't wear lipstick.'

'Your lips are silver,' he insists.

I pull my bottom lip out, going cross-eyed in my attempt to see it for myself.

He's right. In the ambient glow of the spotlights that illuminate the church from below, I can see a shimmering silver that won't come off.

'What the fuck is going on?' I ask, getting to my feet without any assistance from Drake, though it's not that he isn't trying to help.

'Well, you seem to be feeling better,' he says.

'It's the bond, isn't it?'

'It's the bond,' he confirms.

'You just healed me and turned my lips silver.'

'Apparently. I've read that it can leave behind marks.'

'Well, that's weird.'

'Hmmm.'

And now things are awkward. When someone's all set to die beside you because their love for you is that strong, and you've literally murdered your ex to save them, and you both say tragic and romantic things, but then you miraculously survive because of some magical healing ability that goes along with the love bond thing… Well, maybe it's not that relatable a situation, but my point is that it's anticlimactic and it's awkward as hell. Things have been said that can't be unsaid now that we're no longer taking them to our graves.

He told me he loves me. And I sort of told him I love him a bit too, maybe.

My feet are feeling itchy.

'You're going to run again, aren't you?' he says.

I don't have to reply, because he can see it in my face.

'Fuck,' he says, crouching down with his head in his hands. 'Of course you are.'

'Drake—'

'Killian,' he says, looking up at me with despair in his eyes. 'To you, it's Killian.'

When we hear a noise coming from across the city, at first I'm relieved; if I can look away to see what the noise is, then I don't have to look at Drake's pain. But then I realise what direction the sound is coming from.

'It's the Invicti,' Drake says, standing quickly and moving to the edge of the roof.

'Shit. I didn't expect them to be so persistent.'

'You tried to kill the Primus.'

'Well, yes,' I admit. 'But I didn't do it very well.'

'Do you think that makes it *better*? Jesus, Valentine. He doesn't know it was you, though, right? He never saw your face, so—'

'No,' I say hopelessly. 'He saw me well enough.'

'*Fuck.*'

They're already dangerously close. We have only seconds to make a move.

'What do we do now?' I ask.

'I'll stay here,' Drake says urgently. 'I'll spin them a story, or draw them off. Something.'

'And me?'

'You should run,' he says, and the fear in his eyes terrifies me. 'Right now, Valentine. *Run.*'

34

ON A ROOFTOP far away, in a city I won't name for my own safety, my supply of blood capsules finally gives out and I have to stop running.

I'm alone.

I think.

The sun's already on its way, so it must be getting close to morning, which means the night is at its absolute coldest. Now that I'm no longer moving, the cold is catching up with me and my outfit – flimsy dress, bare feet, leather jacket – is not doing much to keep me warm. I huddle into my jacket and hope the dawn will illuminate a conveniently open window in a toasty snug house.

Which is when I hear the crinkle.

I'd forgotten about the papers Cam put in my pocket. The deeds to the Oxford flat aren't much good to me now, but maybe I can use them to start a fire or something, if I get really desperate. I pull them out, but they're not the shape I'm expecting. Instead of a few sheets of A4, what I have in my hand is an envelope I've never seen before with a small sheet of notepaper inside, along with some thin, glossy card in shapes I don't recognise.

I have to wait for the sun to rise before I can read any of it.

Jacky ~

I've packed your suitcase. Make sure you get it out of the house and somewhere safe before you leave today, because shit's going down and I don't want you to get caught in the aftermath.

Sorry about the cloak and dagger stuff. Long story short, Yolande's the fall guy for tonight, amongst other things. I didn't want to tell you before because I thought you might not like it, but it's already done so please don't be angry. It'll be like she never came out of the box in the first place, so where's the harm?

Don't forget to bring the plane tickets tonight. I'd have kept them myself but I didn't want to risk Yolande finding them. I hope you don't mind that we're not going to Argentina, but you'll like Vancouver, I promise. I've got us a house on the coast, just for us this time.

Just the two of us, from now until forever.

W

I was supposed to shower before I left. I would have gone into the bathroom and seen the suitcase, and this note. She made me promise to shower before I left the house this morning and I said I would, but then…

Fuck.

If you enjoyed *Winta's Day*, why not read *Valentine's Day*? It's the fourth book in the *Seekers* series, and it carries on right where *Winta's Day* left off.

***

Join my Readers' Club and receive a FREE short story

www.josiejaffrey.com/subscribe

***

Please leave a review!

If you enjoyed *Winta's Day*, I'd be so grateful if you would please review it. Book reviews can make a huge difference to the success of a novel, particularly those of self-published authors like me. If you have time to leave a review, even if it's just a sentence or two, then I'd really appreciate it.

***

Explore the rest of the Silverse…

This book is just one small part of the Silverse, a whole world of vampires that's waiting for you to explore. There are more novels, short stories, serialised story episodes, and even audio drama podcasts. They're all interrelated, although each series stands alone.

Find out more on my website at www.josiejaffrey.com

Acknowledgements

Thanks to Asha for proof-reading and beta-reading everything, and for all the time she spends holding my hand through every tiny author decision.

Thanks to Vicky for beta-reading, even after I ruined our holiday and turned it into a never-ending hell loop of disaster.

Thanks to Jen for hand-selling the Seekers series to all her friends, and thus accounting for the majority of my sales this year.

Thanks to the Silverse Squad for all their support, and for bearing with me while I delayed this book again and again. Look, it's finally here!

And thanks always to my husband for everything, and to my wonderful son for sleeping like a trick baby so I have time to write.

CONTENT WARNINGS

General warning for violence/murder.

General warning for blood/gore, including blood drinking, description of injuries, dead and decayed bodies, forensic investigation, detailed autopsy.

General warning for sexual content (consensual).

Some swearing (up to and including 'fuck').

Use of drugs and poisons, including depiction of long-term addict relapsing.

Arson, including burning of living people.

Pressure to undergo hypnotherapy, including character not remembering what they did while hypnotised.

Depictions of emotionally abusive/toxic relationships.

Kidnapping/imprisonment.

Skin flaying/removal.